For Marian,
A kind soul & lovely
lady, a treasure to
have in my life!

Diane

MEETING JACK

Diane Charko

Order this book online at www.trafford.com
or email orders@trafford.com

Most Trafford titles are also available at major online book retailers.

Printed in the United States of America.

ISBN: 978-1-4269-0361-8 (sc)
ISBN: 978-1-4269-0362-5 (hc)

Trafford rev. 04/19/2012

 www.trafford.com

North America & international
toll-free: 1 888 232 4444 (USA & Canada)
phone: 250 383 6864 ♦ fax: 812 355 4082

ACKNOWLEDGMENTS

Many thanks
to those who gave their time and energy
by reading various drafts and providing feedback.

Special acknowledgment
is due to the following people for their valuable
editorial and research information:

Dr. Angela Price
who cheerfully educated me during her busy neurology residency.

Dr. Marianne McKinley
for reining in the realism of defibrillation.

Mike Kaufmann, my lifelong friend
whose editorial skills were the creative turning point in the project.

Jeff Crerie, for his brilliant insights and kind support.

Brenda Wilson and her paramedic colleagues
for their on-site advice.

An anonymous Calgary Police Officer
a very patient advisor and friend of many years.

Two anonymous family physicians
who deserve much more recognition than I could ever properly convey.

For Steven Douglas McKinley
whose love and support
made this possible.

For Steven Nels Madson
whose short life and sharp wit
will always be remembered.

PROLOGUE

If ever time marked a pivotal moment, it was when they first met. An unwitting seed to desire and heartache took root that day. Only much later did the timing overlap and settle into place.

That introduction transpired during grade twelve, when possibilities beckoned to a teenage mind. For Donna Carlin, it sparked her most cherished connections and extinguished the easy choices of youth.

She knew they were easy too. Adults kept telling her, especially the one inside that warned her of an impending future, when real life would propel her into a world of responsibility. High school was just a lumbering train, crawling steadily through the rocky terrain of adolescence. Other than a prerequisite to university, it served no other purpose, not even nostalgically. In fact, meeting Jack was the only school event to color her memories.

And color them, he did.

From then on, time offered glimpses of the past and future, blended together. Always unconsciously registered, she could never put her finger on the lure of the moment, but the breathtaking significance must have haunted some deep part of her. Intellect suspended, the soul took command to turn her inside out for a split-second of wonder.

Of course, hindsight removes life's veil. Jack's importance wasn't truly understood until Donna squarely faced death. Paralyzed with fear as the concrete wall flew straight at her, a thousand compressed memories unfolded instantly. Time froze while each one revealed itself—so many, brilliant and pulsating—crossing over into multiple layers, but somehow remaining distinct with utter clarity.

Immersed in that terrifying moment, even physical sensations were relived as though they had never ended: toddler's tears streaming down her cheeks, the jarring transfer of force when a baseball bat connected with its target, as powerful as a first kiss, his hands on her, just bare skin on skin. No ring. He'd lost it before its rough indentations could add to the delicious friction, ever-so-slight, of his hand gliding up her thigh and curving inward. Her mind wonderfully suspended, she became unable to speak or even kiss him back, while his lips dragged passionately across her throat, and the prelude became a concert overpowering all senses: sight and sound, taste and smell. And touch. His touch ... It enfolded her with tender power.

That transition into helplessness, so smooth and encompassing, answered years of yearning. All those nights crying herself to sleep, clinging to one instant of mind-boggling passion.

Until Jack's entrance, she hadn't even envisioned that kind of wanting. Her life had moved at its own monotonous pace. Go to school, do assignments, present another glowing report card year after year.

In a way, it was comforting. The death of a parent has a way of forcing kids to focus, to separate important matters from unimportant and conquer the most severe, and Donna was no different. Her mother's struggling breaths impressed upon her the reality of the unexpected. From this, Donna learned discretion in playing life's cards. She could see where she wanted to be, who she wanted to be, and quietly kept her ambitions to herself. Predictable routine became necessary, a false security to camouflage the self-doubts, which at seventeen were numerous.

Perhaps a large family, like Jen's, could have sparked her creative side, but there were no siblings to bring her out of her shell, only her father who was dealing with his own worries: his job, the mortgage, maybe a social life on the side. Donna didn't even want to think about that last one. Raymond Carlin had been the center of her monotony and she couldn't fathom it any other way, but even that changed when Jack came on the scene. Everything changed.

Maybe it was due to the sense of renewal, lingering just under her skin. Suddenly, scenes were shaded with a familiarity invisible before his arrival. Everyone had remarked at one time or another, "I've seen this before! It's déjà vu."

Déjà vu? Sounded like a big rationalization. People simply weren't paying attention, believing they were reliving an event, when elements had just conspired with similar memories to fake intimacy. That's all it was, scientifically explainable. One of her professors called it Cognitive Justification. Her dad countered with a more colloquial description—Brain Bull.

But those feelings ...

(Have we met before?)

Yes, if she had to pin it down to one spot in time, it would be the first day of grade twelve. Things had just angled off in a different direction after that, and she slid through her choices with a dangerously mistaken sense of control. Did those choices even make a difference? Or did one moment, fleeting as it was, and yet so influential in the suffering to follow, infallibly lead her to where she was right now?

Here ... enveloped in this black abyss.

Things were happening within arm's reach, but she couldn't resist the sinking pull of darkness. It swirled around her menacingly, much like his arms had surrounded her and dragged every feeling to the surface. Except now her mind was curiously numb.

Small distractions kept her tuned in: the sensation of being lifted, bright lights flashing rhythmically against her eyelids, and the voices with their clipped military tones. They spoke commandingly while hands impersonally touched her, the way she had assessed so many patients in her residency. The enveloping sensations kept her mind's eye poised for danger, but it all seemed unreal or simply far away, displaced by violent vertigo, flipping her uncontrollably over and over and over. ...

***

The woman in the lab coat rubbed her neck as another yawn escaped. At least the nurses were sympathetic, since they were often subjected to her supervisor, Dr. Capri. "Too many patients on the board," he'd say, and toss another clipboard at the nearest resident. They'd learned to run for cover at the sight of him.

This was a particularly grueling rotation of shifts. Every third day, Dr. Wendy Moyer—five years and that title still felt new—was scheduled for twenty-four hours straight, but it usually stretched to thirty. Stay until the work's done, that's the rule. It was hard on the residents, though patients benefited by having one doctor straight through.

Spotting Capri's profile three curtains away, she quickly scooped up a stack of papers. Just staff schedules, but at this distance, he wouldn't know. Turning away, she heard muffled footsteps approaching and clutched the papers closer.

"Doctor?"

Whew, just the triage nurse. Julie had a way of appearing out of nowhere. In another life, she would have made a good spy.

"Uh-huh," Wendy mumbled, searching among the clipboards, "Where's my case?"

"Which one? MVA or GSW?"

"Think Julie, what would a neurologist be doing with a gunshot wound?" This morning Wendy almost felt like one herself.

"Come to think of it, nothing. He wasn't shot in the head. I don't think he made it anyway. Poor cop ... You know it happened just down the road from your case? Same time too. Paramedics were scrambling." Julie smilingly lifted a clipboard off the top of the pile and handed it to her. "You either need glasses or caffeine. Dr. Capri wants to know if you've charted her results yet."

"That's why I want it. Tell him to take a pill. Better yet, Demerol in the coffee. He should be on his fourth pot by now. I don't think the man sleeps."

"I'll get right on that. What did the CT show?"

"Epidural hemorrhage. I think we got it drained in time, but she's still unconscious and with the bilateral pain response, it's fifty-fifty. Have you had a break?"

"The breakfast special was stellar."

"Message received—I'll wait for lunch. I'd like you as the primary in the ICU. Name's Carlin. See if John and Cathy can split your load. Ask them to keep an eye on the aphasia in curtain five."

"What was that, another car accident?"

"Bar fight."

"You need anything else?"

"Girl, what I need you don't have."

For a few blessed minutes, Wendy was left alone to catch up on charting as Julie prepped the other nurses to take over. Some of being a doctor, especially neurology, was just plain tedious. Check and recheck progress, document details often to no avail.

There were two kinds of head traumas: Reversible and No Hope. Reversibles were coherent but couldn't hold a thought longer than a second or two. "Who are you? Why am I here? ... Who are you?" The staff could save a lot of time and effort by simply installing voicemail. "To find out who you are, press *one*. To find out where you are, press *two*. To find out why you hurt, press *three*. ..." Julie had thought that one up.

No hope cases were a lot simpler. And sadder. This one might go that way. Just wait and see, do the tests, and chart everything as usual until a family member could find the strength to give consent.

Coming from nowhere, Julie touched her elbow and caused a line of ink to skirt across the chart.

"Quit sneaking up on me!"

"Sorry doctor," Julie answered, not sounding sorry at all, "The patient Carlin? Her father's in Waiting."

"OK, thanks." Wendy tucked the pen into her breast pocket and hurried out to break the news.

***

Shortly before 6:00 a.m., a distraught man raced into the emergency ward. The desk nurse directed him to a row of chairs while she sent for the doctor. Running his fingers through his thinning hair, Raymond looked nervously at the people scattered throughout the waiting area. Most were staring up hypnotically at a TV in one corner of the ceiling. Those were the fighters.

Picking up a magazine always marked a moment of resignation. He believed nothing reeked of "hospital" more than a stack of conservative Canadian magazines, and to flip through one meant sad acceptance of the mortality, pain, and disease that ensnare all who enter. No, forget the reading material. He couldn't even take a chair.

When Raymond received the call twenty minutes ago, he was barely awake to comprehend the situation, but in a matter of seconds, adrenaline obliterated all fatigue. Now it just felt as though the wind were knocked out of him.

For years to come, he would never forget that drive, which took mere minutes and seemed like hours. With the Calgary streets almost bare, early morning crispness filled the air with false promises for the day ahead. Every minute of the trip exuded a surreal quality, almost dizzying; a horrible morning deceptively cloaked in the arcing rays of timid dawn beauty.

He stayed in the waiting room for an eternity, until a young woman in a lab coat called out, "Mr. Carlin?" and Raymond sprang to his feet.

They hurried past bed after bed with Raymond scanning each one for the face he knew so well. The doctor led him through a maze of corridors, speaking rapidly. Raymond had never been so alert for information in all his life.

"… near the university. There were no witnesses, but police determined that she must have been driving at a high speed without a seat belt. Her car rolled several times. No other vehicles were at the scene, but they haven't ruled out a hit and run. She's been moved to Intensive Care. She sustained several fractures and an epidural hematoma—"

The doctor tapped the side of her head.

"—internal bleeding from the trauma was causing intracranial pressure, but we did a procedure to relieve that. Right now, she's not conscious and requires the aid of a ventilator to breathe. The hope is that

xiii

she regains consciousness soon, so we're monitoring her responses. The next forty-eight hours will tell us more. ..."

As Raymond soaked up every word, his mind hungrily sorted the details into layman's terms: Donna was still alive, her brain had been bleeding but they fixed that, broken bones, not awake, trouble breathing, it could go either way. ... It all meant nothing if the summary didn't end with, "But she'll be fine." So he grabbed onto scraps of hope. What had the doctor said? Something about movement ... Oh, right, that had only been her hands responding to pain. But maybe, just maybe, it was the kindling of a full recovery.

There was also something about landing on grass, how it was *lucky*, and Raymond blinked at the stethoscope hanging limply around the doctor's neck, trying to connect the concept of grass with this sterile environment. It made no sense. The whole thing made no sense. Donna was the one who fixed people up. She wasn't supposed to be getting poked and prodded to see if her brain still worked.

"Should we try to reach anyone for you?"

Through a choking feeling, he forced an answer, "No," and the word cut jaggedly along his throat.

(Her mother should be here.)

Donna had always resembled her mother, but since darkening her hair, the resemblance was striking. His mind flashed back to his dying wife in a hospital bed and his twelve-year-old daughter, an innocent blonde version, unprepared for loss. Denial had kept him as unprepared then as he was now.

He stubbornly focused on what this woman had described earlier, something about grass. Long cool blades reaching up out of the dark earth to wrap around his daughter's broken body. He remembered mowing the lawn, Donna chasing him with her own toy mower. She ran with a spring to her step, following the path her father cut while her bare feet skipped along, stained green from the freshly cut clippings. There was a sharp slope at the front of the lawn and Donna suddenly dove onto it. Rolling like a pencil off a table in perfect stiff little circles, peals of laughter rang out as she spun over and over. ...

They stepped under a hanging sign, "ICU" and through two large swinging doors. Another sharp left, into a smaller room, and there she was.

Despite the warnings about her battered state, Raymond's eyes went wide. Donna looked nothing like the pretty young woman who had graced his life for thirty years. He didn't notice the nurse who quietly positioned herself beside him. She had learned where to be in case shock overwhelmed people.

"Oh, God ... God ..." He stared at the bed, his face crumpling at the sight of her. "Can I talk to her? I mean, will she hear me?"

"She probably won't respond to your voice," explained the doctor, "but stay with her as long as you like. ... I know this is rough."

For a long second, Raymond just stared sadly at the woman. Of all the doctors in this place, the one they sent to announce his daughter's demise was one who cut the exact image of Donna's best qualities and suddenly, he could see her standing before him in her crisp lab coat, clutching her diploma, the stethoscope dangling awkwardly around her neck. He'd whispered, "Way to go, Pattycake!" She hated that nickname. Those graduation gifts, so appropriate at the time, were miniscule compared to what he would give now, could time be reversed only a few hours.

The doctor gestured to the nurse. "This is Julie. Please let her know if you need anything or you can have me paged. I'll be back soon."

Then, the doctor left and Raymond had no idea what to do.

Early morning sunlight slid across the horizon to gently fill this hospital room. Not bright yet, but it shined with a raw quality, a freshness that holds an array of promises for the day ahead, and the surrealism enveloped him again. A room at this height was designed to distract its visitors with a brilliant show of landscape, but Raymond only saw the little girl lying on the grass clippings, laughing away. Her childlike voice echoed so loudly in his head, it almost reverberated through this room. A faint origin of a memory a million miles away and yet, right beside him all along. Never truly forgotten, only placed aside.

The nurse made note of Donna's vitals, all conveniently displayed on a small machine by the bed. At first, Raymond followed her every move, as though pushing a button would reverse this nightmare; she turned the machine to better view the numbers, marked them down on a chart, brushed hair out of her eyes, slid the machine toward the wall, shifted a small table. ... Everything was on wheels here. Then he realized she was making room for him.

A chair sat near the window and Raymond pulled it over. It protested being dragged across the tiles with a sudden scraping sound. No, not everything was on wheels. Lifting it instead, he carefully placed it beside the bed. Nothing should disturb her.

It was so quiet here, the kind of quiet that's humbling in its enormity, the kind that fills a room until there's no air left. His eyes darted to the ventilator supplying her oxygen, which was simultaneously comforting and disturbing. Invasively protruding from her mouth with a measure of robotic defiance, it refused to let her die. A rasping noise escaped the machine: air going in, air going out, again and again. It was hard to think with that sound being dragged past his ears.

A strange thought occurred to him just then, something about the wonders of plastic.

He'd seen a commercial hailing all its wonderful medical uses. They made it seem as though this one invention could save lives, even lives tottering on the edge of death. The tube in her mouth was hollow, something he could probably break with his fist. Two, maybe three blows. So much for plastic.

He slipped one hand gently under hers while swiping at his eyes. Afraid to put pressure on her hand, he held it gingerly between his own and stared at the slender fingers.

(I know this hand.)

Same as her mother's, except for the lack of jewelry. He thought she would marry one young man a few years ago, but she suddenly broke off the relationship. Never explained why. After that, no one was brought home to "meet the father", so there couldn't have been another boyfriend. Would anyone else ever hold this hand and love his daughter like he did?

The hand nestled in his was the only evidence of familiarity on an otherwise foreign-looking person. He wouldn't have recognized her face— so swollen and bruised—had the doctor not led him to this exact room. How could anyone look like this and recover? The futility was too much to face. Just too much.

"Know that I love you, Sweetheart. …"

It was all he could say. Would his voice make any difference? He would stay and talk forever, if it meant she'd register a fraction of his wishes.

The nurse glanced up at the sound of his voice and then tactfully pretended to adjust the I.V. drip, but he had forgotten she was even there.

"Know that I love you."

***

Lying quietly in the dark tomb, voices rebounded against unseen walls. Movement chased the sounds, disorienting movement, and Donna couldn't tell if she were simply imagining it. Maybe she was the one moving. That spinning sensation still encased her, but she was too tired to sort it out. The fatigue was enormous, as though she'd just hiked the length of the city.

Her brows furrowed at a sudden memory of Jack walking away. Trying to piece together the thoughts and feelings mixed up in her head, she struggled to hold them in one spot and finally succeeded in catching one.

An accident. No, "accident" was too tame to describe the battering she'd taken. She remembered the concrete wall zooming toward her and how she bounced off every hard place inside the car, her mind screaming ... but somehow she was here, wherever *here* was.

Ouch! Donna pulled her right hand to her chest. For a second there, a finger felt caught in something, like the quick pinch of a drawer carelessly closed. As it dissipated, the same pain stabbed her left hand and she pulled it back too. What the hell's going on?

There was the oddest perception of impending encroachment, a stealthy predator circling her. With eyes shut, she could almost hear people talking around her, *about* her. It wasn't frightening, but strange, as if two photographs were transposed to overlap, their separate images distinct yet blended into one frame. One photograph took precedence. It was clear as day; the sketchy edges of the other could merely be sensed.

Donna should have died. The voices around her said so, although not in concrete words. Rather, they registered as a low buzzing with grave tones. Another voice joined the hum and slowly became distinct in its presence. Concentrating hard, she strained to hear the syllables almost out of reach.

(Know that I love you, Sweetheart. ...)

It echoed in her mind with empty sadness, the image of her father.

But then, those racing flash-backs took over again. When death was imminent, they had relentlessly cut through her mind as sharp as a knife. Time had fused them into one compact mixture of logged events and heart-wrenching emotions, and as they blasted apart—fireworks across a clear September skyline—her screams followed blindly.

Trapped in the darkness, the flash-backs steadily softened. A lifetime of experiences haunting her in this dead space. She found it impossible to distinguish seconds from hours. They melded so completely. The past zoomed in close, while the present was barely visible to the naked eye, certainly not to one's senses, which persisted in placing events in some semblance of order, an order now destroyed.

A simple set of digits—307 for example—was nothing special, but the sentiment behind them made her catch her breath and ponder seemingly unrelated concepts: uncontrollable speed, a sad smile reflected across a faded wood table, a love-struck soul turning to meet the eyes of another.

It was buried in the past, where she had no choice but to pull it forward and face it all over again. Thirteen years dissolved to reveal a million details lined up and metamorphosed into a pivotal memory: sunlight reflected so glaringly off the metal crossbar of her bike, wind against her brow, the fabric of those new jeans chaffing her calves, and that worn old knapsack hanging loosely off her back, shifting side to side as she rapidly pushed the pedals in clean circles.

She wasn't in the habit of noticing little things, but that morning so long ago, little things just seemed to jump out and command attention.

Sort of like déjà vu.

***

PART I

SCHOOL YEARS

CHAPTER 1

Her bike smoothly skimmed the pavement. Despite sunglasses protecting her green eyes, she found herself squinting.

(What a bright sky. Too bad I'll be indoors all day.)

The morning was accented with a breeze, lifting Donna's hair from her face. In a couple of months, the air would be cold and callous, but now it was just right. September was a deceptive month, giving the illusion of everlasting summer. No one really wanted to accept the progressively chilling temperatures. So each year, the students of William Aberhart High School firmly set their sights on the following June, a mental target to carry them through the tedium of snow and homework.

Raising her arm to signal a turn, Donna leaned into the curve. The sun was blinding again and she raised her hand to shade her forehead. Suddenly, a moving object appeared directly ahead. White T-shirt, jeans, brown hair, arms carrying a pile of books and a paper bag. In a moment she would hit him. Too late to squeeze the brakes, she saw the collision in slow motion, unable to do anything except register the inevitable.

(Left! Turn left!)

Her front tire twisted madly, but all it did was launch her sideways.

Jack saw a blur of blue coming at him. Instinctively, he dropped everything he was carrying and threw his arms across his face. As the bike skidded out from under her, she fell against him and they tumbled to the ground.

Jack quickly jumped to his feet. Who was this asshole? Just a girl, a stunned girl with blonde hair and sunglasses. Instantly, all the four-letter words that came to mind vanished at the sight of her. A delicate necklace was caught on the collar of her blue polo shirt, now only half tucked into her jeans. His eyes automatically skated across her chest. He didn't know

3

much about cup sizes, but they were enough to make him glance again as he extended his hand to help her up.

"I'm sorry," she rambled, "The sun was in my eyes. Are you OK? Did I hurt you?"

As she hurriedly picked up a few of his books, her shirt fell into place and he blinked at his luck in having glimpsed this girl's bra. Well, it was only a strap and a bit of the rest, but he'd take what he could get.

"No, I'm fine. Here, I'll get that."

He lifted her bike upright and awkwardly traded it for the books. The bike almost toppled over in the transfer. Lunging to grab it, he caught a quick scent of something—her hair or skin, soapy and fresh, a girl smell.

She anxiously checked his expression. His face was long and slender, a little large for a teenager but the length was offset by a beautiful pair of eyes. Donna's preference had always been for lighter shades. In the past, brown eyes as deep as these gave her a feeling of uncertainty, finding them unreadable, but his were kindly, drooping at the corners and framed by slightly wavy hair. At first glance, she assumed he needed a haircut. It wasn't messy, just a little long, especially in the back. There was enough for a short ponytail.

She realized she was staring. There was something about him ... or maybe he just had that kind of face; everyone thought they knew him from somewhere.

"Have we met before?"

(Oh, I did not just say that!)

"I don't think so, at least not this way." His lips turned up impishly.

Donna swung one leg over the bike and slid her shoe into the toe clip, an embarrassed smile spreading shyly across her face while she tucked her shirt back in.

"Well, OK. Sorry again ... Bye."

(Why did I say "Bye" like that, like I know him?)

Riding away, she checked behind her. He was stepping onto the sidewalk, trying to balance his lunch bag with all those books. Then, he turned the corner and disappeared.

***

Donna coasted to a stop in front of Jen's house. As usual, the front door was open, and not bothering to ring the doorbell, she walked straight toward the kitchen. Jen met her in the hallway.

This was a lazy start to a new school year. A huge sweatshirt draped down to Jen's knees, probably one of her brother's. No makeup surrounding her blue-gray eyes, mismatched socks, the shirt didn't even look clean.

Strands of brown bangs hung in her face and she ineffectively swiped at them. They stubbornly fell back into place.

Most people mistook her for jailbait. At this age, it was no compliment, but she suspected she might appreciate it in a decade or two. She was a petite jeans and T-shirt kind of girl, uninterested in anything more formal or compelling. Donna's style was decidedly different, a fact evident since the roots of their friendship in junior high.

Having met through mere alphabetical order, which had determined the proximity of their lockers, there the similarities ended and that was probably the attraction.

Where Donna was careful, Jen stormed through. Observing things big and small, she seldom hid her opinions from the world. The kids who understood this got along well with her. Those who didn't tried to take her down a notch or two by playing her own game. They would point out some harsh truth about her character, but she would either laugh or agree with them.

"It's my destiny to be an oddball," she'd proudly state, "I'll never fit in anywhere."

Donna figured it was the world that didn't fit in with Jen, simply because she didn't try to be anything other than what she really was—fun and witty and often brutally honest. If you wanted a nice diplomatic statement about your outfit, go ask Donna. If you were brave enough to face the unfettered truth, Jen's your girl.

"Just be a minute," she announced through a mouthful of toast.

"Jesus Brammon!" Donna exclaimed in a low voice, "Get your head out of your ass and buy a watch."

A cross face poked out from the pantry. Jen's mom. "What did you say Donna?"

Jen kept her eyes on her toast as though considering adding a layer of jam, but Donna caught her infuriating smirk, which practically screamed, "Showtime! Let's see Carlin get out of this one."

"Got to head out to class by the looks of my watch," Donna answered sweetly.

Rolling her eyes, Jen disappeared down the hall. Screw the jam.

"Oh ..." A slight eyebrow pucker remained and then slid into the kind features of Marianne Brammon's uncertain smile. "Orange juice?" she asked, reinforcing her long-held tenet that no family could function without this much needed fluid to start the day, as well as a mother to distribute it.

(OJ after toothpaste? Gross.)

Donna smiled politely. "No, thanks."

5

She headed into the kitchen and straight to her designated seat at the table, where a united greeting assaulted her. "Don!" called a round of male voices, with the exception of Jen's dad, who was too caught up in the morning paper to speak and merely lifted his eyebrows at her.

Mrs. Brammon plunked down a glass of juice in front of Donna. "Jenny tells us you're the Social Convener on the Students' Union this year. You must have a big job ahead of you."

"Well, it's more like being a glorified tour guide. I'll have to organize some dances and clubs, but today it's just showing the Greeners around."

"That's still a big job. I'm sure you'll do fine," Mrs. Brammon summarized decidedly, her confident opinion of Donna set in stone. Then, the eyebrow pucker returned. "Um, what are Greeners?"

But before Donna could answer, Mr. Brammon bellowed over the newspaper, "Jenny! You're going to be late!"

Jenny. Donna had called her that once and got belted for her trouble. Jen's brothers just laughed, "Jenny ... Jenny!" They were too big to hit and they stuck together like glue, an impenetrable wall against all things female. Well not Jeffrey, the independent firstborn. He had paved the way. Carl and Billy were more complaisant, copying his style. Her brothers were "The Original" and "The Two Clones", although "Clowns" was often substituted by their father. When Jen actively resisted becoming a third clone, she sensed a growing respect from Jeffrey. It reaffirmed her belief that the status quo didn't necessarily apply to her.

Donna had become a master at projecting false patience against this family's chronic disorganization. Given a week's notice, you'd still see them under the gun on day one, but maybe living with five people would make anyone a little scatterbrained. Donna only had herself and her father to look after. She maintained a private respect for Jen's mother, who somehow managed to get the entire lot fed and out the door by 8:30 every morning.

The Brammons were used to having a truckload of people around. Their family was a friendly one with visitors constantly knocking on the door, their house alive and vibrant. They rarely sat in the living room. It was the kitchen or more precisely, the kitchen table where all socializing transpired. Placed squarely in the center, it beckoned those who entered to join their group. Childhood traumas were kissed away, while Jen's mother set out plates for another meal. Donna could almost hear the noise this table had absorbed over the years.

Jen's big family made quite an impression on Donna during her first dinner invitation, after her mother died. The friend of a preteen sister was of little consequence, so Jen's brothers repeatedly bypassed the boundaries of good behavior. Except for Billy. He kept passing her second helpings and practically spoon-fed her.

6

For Donna, the meal was nothing short of chaotic—this house full of sibling rivalry and constant mess—and she enjoyed every minute of it. Mrs. Brammon reminded her a little of her Aunt Gloria: full-figured, caring, worried about her kids, trying to make their home happy. Jen and her rambunctious family were an excellent distraction from Donna's loss.

Her hand brushed the table edge, across nicks and scrapes representing individual moments in time. Jen's mother thought it too old and bulky by today's standards—its steel frame scuffed and marred—but when put to a vote, the rest of the family unanimously agreed to keep it in favor of a new more stylish one. Billy's reasoning was, "We'll just wreck a new one anyway."

Donna was even included in the vote. Though agreeing with Billy, she shrank from offering her opinion until Jen said, "Oh, come on. Your butt's been glued to that chair for the past six months." The statement was mirrored in all of their eyes. That was five years ago, and Donna remembered it as the day the Brammons officially adopted her.

Finally, Jen materialized looking just as unpolished as ever. Donna wondered what she'd been doing for the past ten minutes.

"Couldn't find my runners," she explained unapologetically.

Billy followed the girls to the front door. "They're where everybody leaves them," he scoffed, "In the bathroom … Idiot. She actually does that a lot."

Jen's eyes narrowed. "Oh, you wouldn't be able to find your ass to wipe it if it wasn't attached."

Billy's gaze zoomed from Donna to Jen. He opened his mouth with an equally nasty retort, but instead blurted, "Hey! Is that mine?" Reaching, he grabbed a scrap of Jen's sleeve, which she twisted out of his fingers so quickly, he almost lost his balance.

"Got to go! Gonna be late!" The girls raced to their bikes and pedaled furiously away.

When they were a safe distance down the street, Jen said, "Can you believe it? I walked right in front of him and he didn't catch on. Did you see me yanking at the collar? Too busy making cow eyes at you."

"He was not," Donna protested unconvincingly. Billy's crush was an awkward topic she discouraged by politely overlooking the signs and symptoms, but Jen never politely overlooked anything.

"I told him you love plaid. He's been wearing the same shirt now for three days. It's kind of sad actually—"

It took Jen a moment to realize that she was riding alone and she circled back, where Donna had suddenly braked.

"Stop doing that," Donna said, her eyes hard.

"Doing what?"

"Leave him alone. I don't want him to get his hopes up. Bug me all you want, but leave him alone."

Jen blinked. Donna looked really pissed.

"OK! Jesus, you're in a mood and a half."

Rolling across pavement again, that first pedal push always seemed so hard.

"Besides," Donna grudgingly smirked, "that shirt was hideous."

"That's what makes it so fun … or it did." She made a face and lifted a flat palm. "Oh don't start. What's your first class?"

"Biology. Yours?"

"Don't know. I'll find out when I get there."

"You didn't pick up your schedule?"

"Naw, I had better things to do." Jen flipped her wrist carelessly, cutting a loose line above the front tire of her bike. "Anyway, they don't ding you for that on the first day. So, how was dinner with Daddy's new girlfriend?"

"Oh, the dinner part was fine. It was breakfast I could do without."

"She stayed over?" Jen asked incredulously. The mere suggestion of such improprieties would bring a swift frown of disapproval from her parents, and she relished the existence of such freedom, even if it occurred in a different household.

"Yeah. Talk about a wake-up call. I couldn't wait to get out of there."

"Why? Is Daddy's love life cramping your style?"

"What style? I don't even have a boyfriend."

"Well, where do you expect to find one, in your algebra book? If your life's lacking in glamour, it's your own fault."

Donna pitched a queer look, which Jen promptly returned.

"Oh, please. You know what I'm talking about Miss Little-Bit-Of-Everything. The grades, the safe dress code, Social Convener title elected by a landslide. Judy Pincemin is probably still choked about that one. I loved the look on her face when they announced you won. You upset her idyllic notion that her tight ass would swing the votes. You know she has blue hair now?"

"Blue?"

"Yeah, and not just a few strands across the top. We're talking *Bu-lue*. … It would actually be effectively slutty if she wasn't so short. Looks like a freakin' Oompah-Loompah."

"They had green hair."

"Really? Only you would know that." Jen peered at her, "You know, you should consider a hair change. Shave it and dye it brown or something. Go for a totally new look."

"This, coming from someone who hasn't cut her hair in three years ... but you know, I've been thinking about growing it long."

"Worked for me. Al still calls every night. Anyway, what happened with Paula this morning?"

Rolling her eyes, Donna explained, "For starters, I didn't know she'd stayed over. She came into the kitchen when I was making coffee. My back was turned and I thought it was Dad, so I passed her a cup and the words, 'So, how long is this one going to last?' were halfway out my mouth. You know how you start to say something and before you can stop them, the words are right here?" She held her hand a few inches in front of her face and then jerked her head abruptly. "Of course *you* do. Anyway, it doesn't matter what you do, you can't pull 'em back. I'd gone as far as, 'So how ...' and I covered by adding 'do you take your coffee?'"

"Good save."

"Then, she lights up right in front of me—I mean, Dad should have told her how much I hate that. Anyway, that wasn't the worst of it. Paula is into palm reading. She insisted on giving me the bad news."

"What bad news?"

"Well, I have a weird line—some loop off the heart line—and it's supposed to mean something *terrible*." Her voice trembled in mock fright.

"Like what? You marry some bozo and it triggers the end of the world?"

Donna shrugged impatiently. "She said a loop is a situation that comes back to haunt you, something you can't avoid. ... She's full of shit, unless of course she meant you. Then, there might be something to it."

Jen laughed. "Oh, you haven't seen me in full form yet. I can irritate you in ways you haven't dreamed."

"No argument here."

They glided to the front of the school and after securing their bikes, weaved through several groups of students to their lockers. What did you do all summer? Is she still going out with him? Who's taking French in period six? Snippets of conversations overlapped each other like a radio on scan mode.

Jen tossed her backpack into her locker and pushed it shut with the sole of her shoe. *Bang!* The sound caused a few heads to turn abruptly, tired faces, resentful of the early hour. Jen ignored them and slapped a lock on. *Click—click—click!* She darted through a maze of students to reach Donna, who was clutching a binder and peering intently at her schedule.

She spoke without even a glance Jen's way. "See you at lunch? Same table?"

"Yeah. By the way, your dad isn't the only one getting some action lately."

Donna's eyes went wide. "Did you? ... With Al?"

"Oh, I have your attention now. Do you know you always ask two questions in a row? Gotta get my schedule. See you at noon."

Jen lifted her hand in a short farewell and marched off, leaving Donna gaping. She could have been extracting quality info all this time and now had to wait until noon.

Shaking her head, Donna abruptly turned and took no more than a step. *Bang!* Her schedule went flying across the hallway to glide to a skidding stop against a locker. The binder dropped solidly onto her toes. At first, all Donna could register was the pain of crashing into someone, and then long blue locks. *Bu-lue ...*

Her tactful side fought, but the opportunity was too good. She blurted out, "Smurf's up!"

Laughter punctuated the hallway. Judy Pincemin reciprocated with a deadly look. Regaining her balance, she spun away from Donna as though she were never there.

(Same school, same assholes ...)

***

His name was printed boldly across the top margin of his school schedule—Jackson Petrasyk. He never went by that name. Jack was simpler, friendlier. It was a name you could split a soda with, a name that would shovel your walk in winter and mow your lawn in summer.

"Hey," he said to a passing kid, "do you know where Room 242 is?"

"Upstairs, east wing, first door on the right."

Jack nodded gratefully and stepped quickly toward the stairs. He was like a salmon swimming upstream, as a wave of students moved forcefully down the steps. After a long walk down another checkered hallway *(Does this school ever end?)*, a hanging sign indicated the east wing. The late bell rang and he picked up his pace. First door on the right. He rushed in, then stopped dead in his tracks.

The room was filled with girls. A sound of startled amusement ran through the class and he looked sharply at the teacher. She stood at the chalkboard, which read in bold white letters "Health Education". An unmuffled giggle pulled his focus to the front row, where he was faced with the strangest color of hair he ever saw. After staring dumbly at what he thought was a clownish wig, Jack bolted back into the hallway. The laughter of teenage girls chased his burning ears.

(Different school, same assholes ...)

10

***

Donna sat in the second row of English class, staring down at her left hand. A pen had accidentally brushed against her skin, and she rubbed the streak of blue with her thumb, until it diffused into a general hue across her palm. The color ran parallel to her heart line. She peered at the oddly twisting line etched into her skin from birth. It seemed to fold back on itself.

Paula had been annoyingly enthusiastic about reading Donna's palm. At least, she was until she'd taken a good look at it. Studying each hand over and over, she hemmed and hawed while Donna's irritation grew. Finally, Paula admitted her interpretation of the round line. A few vague niceties about Donna's intellect and perseverance were also added, so absent-mindedly that the words lacked conviction. Not that there was anything to it, but it was weird how the line looped around in a perfect circle.

Minutes before noon, an announcement rang through the school, "May I have your attention please. Donna Carlin, please report to the main office. Donna Carlin to the main office."

The words shot out through the speakers and into the ears of every student there, the third time this morning. Faces turned to her curiously. Flushing at the unwanted attention, she missed the envious looks of classmates when the door shut behind her.

The Social Convener's duties were clear: show new students around and connect them with the appropriate clubs. She checked her list—just one more kid. The first one had been a science whiz. The second, a computer nerd. They were patently uninterested in anything the school could offer, but got the obligatory tour anyway. This last one was supposed to be a jock. His portfolio listed sport after sport, no doubt an ego case.

Her jeans made a steady swishing sound through the empty hallway, and to punctuate the rhythm, her stomach gurgled loudly. Why did she have to be called down to the office so close to noon? She was almost due in the cafeteria to quench her curiosity about Jen's first time. Maybe this next kid would be happy with a school map and a list of clubs and skip the tour.

Quickly stopping at her locker to trade her books for a small paper bag, she hurried toward the main office. While she stood in the office doorway, the noon bell rang insistently. Seconds later, a barrage of noises filled the hallway as students behind her crisscrossed to various lockers.

Donna ran her fingers through her hair impatiently. To the outward eye it was a casual gesture, the false appearance of relaxed confidence. She was a sharp contrast to other students, who were accosting the administrative assistants about their missing class schedules. They all had the same look: young, abrupt, loud. The receptionist was almost at her wit's end.

The vice-principal, Mr. Hansen spotted her hovering in the doorway. A big man with a rough-looking beard and open manners, his size made him an imposing figure, but Donna found him quite harmless. The tornado aftermath in his office matched his disheveled appearance. Even now, he stood unaware that his tie was askew. He had a way of talking with his large hands, punctuating every statement with a gesture or two. Kids often mimicked him by saying a single word, while violently waving their arms around. Donna liked him enormously.

"Come in, Donna."

He swung a big arm out to usher her through. The movement reminded her of some mimes she'd seen in a park once with their ridiculously exaggerated actions. Then that thought leapfrogged into the next: an image of Mr. Hanson dressed up like a mime in one of those tight suits, painted face, swinging his arms madly like a traffic cop to steer students to class. And Donna's smile almost became a giggle.

Then, as Mr. Hanson led her into his office, she saw the boy with all the books. Her smile evaporated.

***

CHAPTER 2

(Oh shit, I've never been in trouble at school and now it's over some guy I don't even know!)

Mr. Hanson cleared his throat loudly and said, "Jack, I'd like you to meet Donna. She's the Students' Union Social Convener. She can give you help with anything you need, special events, bus passes, you name it." A huge hand grandly swept from one student to the other.

Jack smoothly answered, "We've already met."

Donna blushed and searched for a reply, but before anything came to mind, he grinned. "Kind of ran into each other on the way to school."

His sudden smile exposed an air of goofiness and immediately her panic dissolved.

"Oh, good," the large man continued, "then you already know that Jack here has some athletic aspirations. Maybe you could take him to meet Mr. Koshni." Another sweeping arm movement, indicating that Mr. Koshni was elsewhere.

Donna covertly studied Jack, who was surprisingly muscular for a boy his age and perfectly proportioned. His T-shirt emphasized his wide shoulders. Not that his physique was large. It was more in the way his muscles were positioned, each just the right size compared to the others, giving an impression of symmetry.

(So, he's the one trying out for all the teams.)

Her experience with school athletes was mostly negative, but rather than look full of himself, he exuded a quiet energy, a tension just under the skin, something unsettled and wanting. She didn't know where these assumptions were coming from. It just seemed that bits and pieces of his personality were displayed on the outside, like a crest on a jacket. Some people were like that, right out there for inspection.

13

"Sure, it's on my way to the cafeteria anyway."

She was privately glad to have a specific task. Might make up for almost killing him earlier. And that one pit stop would be a lot shorter than an entire school tour. He could probably make do with a map anyway. When Donna turned toward the door, she saw Jen's quizzical look from the hallway.

(What are you doing in there?)

Donna made a face, careful to angle her body away from Jack and Mr. Hansen.

(It's nothing.)

Matching her face, Jen pointed a finger straight down to the cafeteria one floor below. A second later, she disappeared in the flow of bodies.

Donna nodded to Jack and instructed, "Follow me." She was already halfway out the door before Jack turned with his books. Nearly dropping several at once, he scurried out after her.

"Do you want some help with those?"

"No, that's fine," he answered, "I've got it under control," as another shifted with gravity. The pleasant pride in his voice reinforced the quiet energy she sensed earlier. He even opened the hall door, allowing Donna to pass through first. Guys never did that.

Kids lined the hallway, eating their lunches and watching them curiously. Just another senior making some Greener suffer with her books. She realized how much easier it was for kids like her and Jen, who had already absorbed the same faces year after year. Jack was coming in too late to establish a place for himself.

She handed him a map. "Here … don't ask anyone for directions. They'll send you to Sex Ed. So, where do you live?"

"Until a couple of days ago, I was holed up in Motel Village."

"Ah, Motel-Hell."

"What?"

"Twelve motels in two square blocks. Go figure. Where are you now?"

"By the mall. Why?"

"If you lived farther, you'd get a free bus pass."

"No sweat. It's not a long walk … not like this place."

Halfway down the next hall, they reached their destination. Throngs of students were pushing their way out of Koshni's classroom, late for lunch. One student saw a window of opportunity and veered left, clipping Jack's shoulder, and once again his books tumbled down.

Jack surveyed them with dismay. He didn't even get an apology, the climactic finish to an annoying morning. He had gone to the wrong class twice before finding his way around the school, and then his stupid locker wouldn't open. He'd ended up lugging his books around from class to class.

Donna could see that he was having a miserable day. Hitting him on her bike had probably set the tone. As she studied him, their eyes locked and in a strange moment, a feeling of protective concern suddenly washed over her. It was different from the usual fleeting perceptions, a simple truth unobscured by any sort of error. There was a decency about him and this intuition overrode her shyness.

She waited for the last of the students to pass by. Then, with a gentle smile, she impulsively placed a hand on Jack's arm. "Don't worry about it."

His serious eyes relaxed as he saw a compassionate expression reaching straight out to him. It seemed to come entirely from her eyes. They betrayed a distinctly bright mind, but were also kind with understanding. Looking into them gave him a curious mix of ease and strength. Until now, all he'd seen were the eyes of strangers. In an instant, he knew he could like this person. More than like.

They squatted down and picked up the books together. Koshni was arranging his lunch, tuna sandwiches and chocolate pudding.

"Ugh, my internal organs would freakin' shut down to get away from that mess," Jack whispered, as they approached the teacher's desk.

Donna disguised a laugh as a sharply erupting sneeze.

"Excuse me. Mr. Koshni, this is Jack. He wants to know about tryouts."

Frowning at having his lunch interrupted, Koshni waved Jack toward an empty seat. "Which sport are you interested in?"

"All of them."

"All of them? Do you even know what we have here?"

"It doesn't matter. If you sign me up, I'll be at the tryouts."

Donna perked up. Not many people could shut up Koshni for ten consecutive seconds. She wondered how much of this kid's quiet confidence was genuine. All the boys she knew did a certain amount of huffing and puffing, as though required to meet some quota of conceit.

From the time she was five, her dad always said he could see the wheels turning when she was struggling to figure something out. He'd robotically blurt out, "Computing ..." Donna realized she looked like that now. Having delivered Jack safely, was her presence now intrusive? Just two guys talking sports. If she ran out screaming naked, they probably wouldn't even notice. She dragged her fingers through her hair again and half turned away.

Seeing her hesitantly eyeing the door, Jack interrupted the teacher, "Uh, hang on a sec. ..." He walked over to Donna and quietly stated, "Hey, thanks for taking me here."

"No big deal. I get all the strays."

As soon as the words were out, she thought he'd be offended, but his eyes teased her back. "Well, if you're heading to the cafeteria, grab me some Puppy Chow. I shouldn't be long here."

His smile was infectious. Maybe he wasn't so goofy after all.

"Sure, down the stairs, straight ahead, through the big doors. Just follow the noise. I'll get a big bowl ready for you." Then, almost as an afterthought, she warned him, "Oh, and watch out for the pumpkins."

He searched her eyes, but a single raised eyebrow denied anything further on the subject.

"Uh, right ..." he replied guardedly, "See you down there."

***

Jen was seated at their usual spot near the window. A few hundred people could easily fit into "Café-Abe"—a lot of drama potential. Scanning the room, she studied the posturing, gestures, body language. Better than a movie.

Finally Donna strolled up with a bright expression, which was rather unusual for this time of day. Donna was someone who fainted if she didn't eat enough, so she would get pretty snappy by noon. This person looked as though she'd just had the best meal of her life. Taking a seat across from Jen, she set down a steaming bowl of chili and dropped her lunch bag on the table. Something inside the bag hit the table hard and Jen watched to see if anything would seep out. Donna had ruined four thermoses since junior high.

Eyeing the bowl, Jen asked, "What, are you PMS-ing?"

"It's not for me. It's for my tour duty." Donna noticed her friend checking the room for evidence and added, "I left him with Koshni. They're yapping about teams."

"Another fragile self-image for Koshni to destroy over the space of three short years."

"One year for this one—he's in our grade—so he may have a fighting chance. Anyway, you'll have your chance first. He's joining us shortly. Play nice, Jen. He seems OK. So anyway, spill it."

Jen's eyes gleamed. "Spill what?"

"Come on! What was it like? Where did you do it?"

"Well, in case my parents ask, I was at your place."

16

"Consider warning me when I'm the alibi. I was gonna call you. You've known him a whole four weeks now. When's the wedding? Whose idea was it?"

"Mine, but I let him think it was his. I would have jumped him the first night, but I wanted it to bug him a while."

"Well, aren't you the master of control. And this will clinch his affections?"

"Don't be stupid. His affections were clinched a month ago. Just figured it was time."

"Spare me the gooey romantic details. What was it like? Did it hurt?"

Jen twisted one side of her mouth up and Donna already knew the answer. "At first, but then he just went slower and it was OK."

"What did you think of the whole thing?"

A pause. "Oh, sorry. I was waiting for the second question. You tend to pair them up. Well, you *do*. ... It was all right. I mean, it was pretty much what I expected. He was surprised when it hurt. He thought I was way past the virgin stage. I'm not sure if that's a compliment or not."

A brief silence punctuated their expressions of uncertainty. Was the first time that bad? Maybe best not to know after all. Instead, Donna absorbed herself in the task of peeling a hard-boiled egg, cracks already lining its surface.

"Another thermos saved from Donna's brute strength," Jen thought. Leaning her chair back on its rear legs until her shoulders touched the wall, the newsflash began.

"Sheila Groebner fell for the leather jacket trend. And I'll bet once Karen Copeland and Heather Samerson see it, they'll make a beeline straight to the mall. Hey, Jason Kraychy went punk. Didn't see that coming, but it kinda suits him. Trevor Simmons has been eating his spinach. Look at the way he's drooling over Karen."

"God, you're a walking soap opera. They're just talking."

"She is. He's struttin' like a peacock. Don't matter. She spent the summer wrapped around some guy from Kelowna. ... There's a goofy one. He's big for grade ten."

Donna followed Jen's pointed finger to the entrance, where Jack was panning the room.

"No, that's my tour duty." She went to retrieve Jack and led him to the table.

He broke into a huge grin. "Puppy Chow! For me?"

"It's the Welcome-to-the-School lunch special. Jack, this is Jen. Have a seat."

He stacked his books on the table, placing his lunch bag on top, and began emptying it. Sandwich, another sandwich, chocolate bar, cinnamon bun, pretzels ... The girls gaped. "What? I'll eat the chili. I was in a hurry this morning. I packed light."

Jen rolled her eyes from her precarious perch, her mouth full of apple. Not waiting to swallow, she started through her standard list.

"So, where did you move from?"

"Ottawa."

"How come?"

"My mom's looking for work.

"No doubt to feed you. Where's your dad?"

"I don't have one."

"Oh ... Any brothers or sisters?"

"Brother."

"Older or younger?"

"Younger. You done yet?"

Jen smiled. Five questions qualified as a record low. Usually, new kids were so eager to make friends, they let her interrogate them for hours.

"Oh, just getting started, but we can pick this up later."

"Yeah—not likely. What's the deal with the pumpkins?"

Jen turned to Donna, giggling. "You didn't explain the pumpkins?"

Donna shook her head.

"That was mean. How do you expect him to make it past a week here? OK, listen up Jack. Every September, the grade twelves drop a pumpkin off the third floor into the foyer. Usually some melons get tossed in June too. Depends what's in season. They always land about two inches from some new kid's head. Once one hit a kid and knocked him out."

"No," Donna interjected, "It just put his arm in a sling."

"Head, arm, it's all connected. The point is that you have to keep an eye out, or rather, up."

Jack glanced from one to the other and finally asked, "Are you shittin' me?" This was not the city of new beginnings his mother would have him believe.

Jen's answer was delivered with a straight face, "Well, sometimes it's watermelons—better splat range—but pumpkins have a softer shell."

He was still peering at her as if she were a bug in his soup.

Casually taking another bite of her apple, she turned to Donna. "Didn't you warn him about me?"

"Amazingly, the topic of 'You' didn't come up. And unless someone drops you off the third floor and you knock Jack out—or put his arm in a sling—I consider the pumpkins to be a bigger problem, but if it makes you feel better," she turned to Jack, "Somewhere on her is a warning label: The truth, the whole truth, and nothing but the truth, so help you God. ... Run while you still can."

Jen scowled. "Too little, too late. I can't believe you warned him about the pumpkins and not about me. I'm much more trouble than some orange vegetable. ... Are they vegetables?"

A tiny smirk played around Jack's lips as an observation rushed through his head.

(Jen gives the energy, but Donna holds the reins.)

The thought moved as if caught in the middle of a tennis match, darting for cover, and he let it escape with a quick decision to join Donna's team. With playful eyes, he faced Jen.

"Oh, I think if we dropped you and a pumpkin from the same height, you wouldn't be nearly as messy on impact. I'm guessing they have a softer shell. But why talk about it? I vote we test the theory out."

He carelessly flicked some table crumbs to strategically scatter across Jen's lap. With a big grin, she started a full-scale crumb war with his books as their wall of defense: Jack and Donna against Jen, which adjoining tables considered a fair division of power.

At the supper table, when Mrs. Brammon puckered over the casualties evident in her daughter's hair, Jen smiled; her friend's heads were far worse.

***

CHAPTER 3

As the season advanced completely into fall, the students of William Aberhart became resigned to assignments and tests. Donna naturally adapted well to the structure of high school, while Jen rebelled against any and all boundaries. Though consistently late, she completed the required work, often racing in at the last minute with an essay in hand. Since Jen was more cooperative when left to her own predictably unpredictable habits, her teachers turned a blind eye.

Jack struggled more than the other two with school. The teachers considered him well-behaved and full of potential, since he was polite and watchful, taking in everything around him. Even if he didn't get the best grades, his manners conveyed a certain respect for things—school, peers, adults. He just seemed like a good kid, especially since he was spending so much time with the Carlin girl.

In this case, Donna had proven herself a good judge of character— Jack was OK—and Jen set out to complete his education in a way the formal school system couldn't. When Donna pointed out the rough kids, the druggies, the rich ones, Jen translated her descriptions. "Friendly" was really "Total slut". "Well off" became "Won't talk to you without a credit check".

They learned a lot about each other that year. It was especially interesting for Donna, since Jen had long known her history. She was able to share the basic elements of living in a single parent household, a topic frequently discussed with Jack. He learned that Donna's mother had died from breast cancer just after Donna needed her first bra. Her father took over both parenting roles, on top of being an architect for a construction firm downtown. For the first year, she still expected to hear her mother's words from the kitchen.

(Here's your coffee Ray. Donna, do you want butter on your toast?)
That voice grew fainter every year, and her father's grew to fill the void. At least he tried.

Jack had no idea if his father were even alive, since his mother left the marriage when her son was barely a toddler. Pregnant with Mark, she had been determined to support her children alone. They were subjected to a series of baby-sitters, while she worked two jobs, sometimes three or four. Jack used to question her about their father, but his mother made it clear her lips were sealed on that topic.

"No," she would say, "we're just fine on our own."

He often wondered if he resembled his father, since his mother's thick black hair and small face were such a contrast to Jack's features. When he asked to see a picture of the man, his mother curtly replied, "There aren't any." Apparently, she had thrown out anything associated with their marriage. Puzzled to be barred from such a significant piece of his own past, he rallied against her resistance with further inquiries, all to no avail.

A small steel ring was all he had to prove the man's existence. A teacher from his last school had noticed it and remarked, "That looks like my nephew's. He's an engineer." This important clue to his father's identity fueled Jack to wear it constantly. He imagined an impressive man in a suit, carrying a briefcase to his well-paying job. The man worked hard to support his family, whom he cherished above all else. It was a fantasy that had faded in recent years.

Mark had also wanted the ring, but Jack was adamant. Having won their mother's preference early in life, Mark's small dark looks were no reminder of her ex-husband. Within their sphere, Jack felt like a third wheel and relatively alone in the world. He needed the ring.

Jen's full family was a complete antithesis. She favored her oldest brother Jeffrey and her father, two realists who resisted molding her into picture-perfect gentility. Jen maintained more emotional distance from the rest of the family. Marianne Brammon had insisted on having children until a girl came along, but to her daily consternation, Jen was not the daughter she envisioned. Frilly outfits and Barbie dolls alike were repeatedly ruined. On one eye-opening occasion, her mother found her knee-deep in the garden, coordinating warfare in the carrot trenches, as the Barbies battled Billy's G.I. Joes into submission. Mrs. Brammon never determined whether Jen was a product of brotherly influence or the feminism of the era.

Jen griped about her family and all the unwelcome interactions that prevailed in their modest house. Her friends, though mildly receptive to the complaints, found empathizing difficult. Jack would gladly trade his family for Jen's. Unlike Mark, her brothers were not constantly clawing each other in competition. Even those Brammon arguments imparted a rhythm that denoted a caring bond. And Jen's mom was a sweet lady. She made his mom seem scattered and grumpy.

Donna could visualize her own discomfort at living with the Brammons day in and day out, but she loved visiting. And they loved her.

Jen once nailed it by saying, "You know, you're the daughter my mother never had!" She readily agreed with Donna's response, "That's OK. You're the son my father never had, so we're pretty even."

People frequently commented that the three of them made an odd group. No one would have guessed that Jack's athleticism, Jen's anarchy, and Donna's photographic memory were so compatible. Jack was a breath of fresh air to the other two. With their analytical talents exhausted by the same old classmates, here was someone new, who didn't have annoying quirks like most of the student population.

He was different in small ways. The ring on his little finger—deep in thought, he often rubbed it with his thumb as though compulsively checking its whereabouts—that thing never came off. Never. He always prefaced teacher's names with Mr. or Mrs., even the ones earning disdain and even in their absence. Once, when Jen mimicked his show of respect, he cheerfully called her "Miss Brammon" for the next week, until she broke out of sheer exasperation.

Donna could put her in her place efficiently enough, but Jack's quiet tenacity was an understated tactic new to Jen. Despite his friendly approach, he could hold his own in any conversation. He let Jen be Jen, but curtailed her pointed remarks when need be. Upbeat and a little lost at the same time, he was an irresistible combination for the girls, allowing the fulfillment of two vital roles; he became both a friend and a project. Determined to see him safely through the rigors of a new school, they solidly defended him against any criticism levied by other students.

Jen personally took credit for getting him successfully infiltrated, since his initial goofiness made him such an easy target. She was certainly outspoken in her opinions, and this included her immediate regard for him, but Jack also recognized the advantage of being recommended by Donna. People naturally gravitated to her, accepting anyone in her sphere. He suspected she was Jen's saving grace. These girls were smart, unpretentious, and unaffected by peer pressure. Especially Donna. There was just something about her. ... Jack was even grateful for that lousy first morning, because it started and ended with meeting her.

If the girls were his road to acceptance in William Aberhart, he was also a faithful friend and returned the favor with an unconditional ear. In their debates, he frequently found himself taking Donna's side. The support was a boost for her and a delightful challenge for Jen.

For Donna, it was the calm before the storm, that storm so far into the future and yet beside her all along. If only she'd paid attention to the clues lined up. Instead, she'd lived with blinders on, distracted by life's sights and ...

***

... Sounds held a peculiar fascination for her in the swimming darkness. Pounding reverberations of heartbeats filled every corner of her mind, except for the overpowering roar of Jen's car engine. It would abruptly gun into a crescendo and then trail off with a continuous grumble, until the next injection of fuel. The importance of Jen's car was firmly set in her memories, but right now, the sounds associated with them seemed as trivial as most of the things she'd never attempted: crafts, a second language, recreational sports. And Donna's regret ballooned. She should have tried to become ... more somehow, to be enthusiastic and embrace life in physical ways, instead of sliding all her energy into the mental corridor of education.

Funny thing about the dark; dimensions abate, imagination swells. Physical constraints are released and possibilities multiply where none existed before. Concepts like up and down or color lose definition. Only the depths of right and wrong, compassion and despair, clarity and confusion, become assimilated into glaring reality. But this reality gave a blurred border. She could only reach into it so far and no further. If not for the persistent sense of destiny—that pure comprehension would soon be hers—she would have stayed patiently within the undefined sensations assaulting her from all directions.

Like Jen's car engine that always needed fixing and the repetitive echo of her heart. The pounding intensified, but it was almost drowned out amidst the noise erupting again and again. And she felt herself sinking into yet another part of her past. ...

***

Bounce! Bounce—Bounce—Bounce! Jack ran with the ball across centerline. He made dribbling and running look easy. Pass to Ted, get to the outside, catch the ball, dribble it back to the front, pass to Patrick, fake right, lose the guard, move left to the inside, catch the ball, jump shot ... Two points! The crowd on one side of the gym cheered. The crowd on the other groaned.

Donna applauded enthusiastically with the cheering side. Jack was playing well tonight. A year ago, she wouldn't have been caught dead rooting for any jock, but he just made it look so easy, basket after basket.

Standing with cupped hands around her mouth, Jen yelled, "Way to go J.P! Ten more like that and you've got 'em where you want 'em!" Then, she sat down next to Donna and muttered, "We're never going to catch up."

"You don't know that. We could still win."

"Are you kidding? Look at the clock."

"Yeah. Well, I don't really care who wins—don't tell Jack I said that. I'm just glad to get out of the house."

"Daddy and his little love interest?"

"Bingo. She stays over once or twice a week. I lock myself in my room and pretend to have a million assignments due, so I don't have to watch them worry about their bad influence on me, but greeting her in the morning is too weird for words. At least now she smokes outside."

Jen snickered, "If only they knew who your real bad influence is."

"Oh, you're not *that* evil."

"Not so loud."

Two people climbed up the bleachers toward them and Jen let out a low groan.

"Great ... The Velcro Couple."

Tina Jacobson and Steve Tarringer. They were one of those permanent fixtures in every high school hallway, always arm in arm.

With a tilted head, Donna ordered, "Behave."

Jen rolled her eyes. "Well, I just can't help it. I can't identify with anyone who thinks mall is a verb. 'We were *malling*—she actually said that. I swear her mail is sent there. Look at that purse. You could fit a car in that thing. And she uses the word *nice* way too much, like it's her duty to offend no one."

"As opposed to your suicide mission to offend everyone."

"Well, it's a hell of a lot more fun."

"Hell usually is."

Perhaps sensing Jen's disagreeable mood, The Velcro Couple sat on Donna's side. When Tina's enormous purse plunked down on the bleacher, the shaky wood vibrated its response. She promptly dug into a zippered pouch, extracted a makeup compact, and began touching up her face.

Barely glancing up, she observed, "Jack's scored a lot of baskets tonight. He sure is good," dimpling as if they were sharing a secret.

Jen almost gagged.

"I guess he plays every position," Donna answered simply, "and not a lot of guys can do that in basketball."

Donna immediately forgot what she was saying while her head slowly turned. Trevor Simmons was walking across the front of the crowd—going ... going—until he exited through the gym doors. Gone. Trevor had a strong face and no steady girlfriend. He was one of the smarter ones in her calculus class, methodically attending to the course work. Nice butt too. He could have been dumb as dough and her eyes would still be all over him.

"So, what are you doing for your birthday? Anything special?" Tina spoke the word *anything* as if it meant *anyone*, and Donna wondered if Tina had seen her eyes focused off the game.

"We're going to Fioritti's Friday night, the four of us."

She paused, catching a reaction of delight on Tina's face, followed by an intense expression of interest. "Who's the fourth?"

"Al, Jen's boyfriend ... Do you guys wanna come?"

Jen swiveled the ball of her foot, pressing her heel down on Donna's toes. Gritting her teeth, Donna refused to acknowledge the message. Besides, the invitation was already on the table.

"Sure! What time?"

"Seven."

"That's a nice place to spend your birthday."

Steve sighed, his Friday night and cash flow determined. Noting his lack of enthusiasm, Donna volunteered, "It's kind of a dual celebration. It's Jack's birthday too."

"You guys were born on the same day?"

"Yeah," Jen jumped in, "and when you take the time zones into account, they were almost born at the same moment too. They're practically *soooulmates*."

Tina fairly beamed. This time, it was Donna's heel that pressed down on Jen's toes.

The crowd around them roared again. Another basket by Jack, plus a foul shot swishing through the net cleanly. The clock counted down to zero and erupted in a thunderous buzz, leaving players and spectators in no doubt of the outcome. Aberhart had lost by a mere six points. Jack had done much to lessen the gap, but in the end, the final score vanquished all recognition. People immediately started filing out of the gym, some chanting and others indignant at their loss on home territory.

Donna turned to The Velcro Couple. "See you Friday night."

Busy locking lips, Steve and Tina barely heard her. Jen rolled her eyes again, completely annoyed with everyone, and roughly pulled Donna by her shirt-sleeve down to the gym floor. Jack was wiping his scowling face with a small towel. They each slapped him on the arm and he winced into the towel. What, did these girls pull tractors in their spare time?

"Hey, good work out there," Jen declared, "Twenty-eight points just from you. Rather respectable."

"Sixteen," he corrected, angling a pointed look at Donna, "Did she watch *any* of it?"

"Oh, I'm sure she caught the highlights in between the gossip and drama. Honestly Jack, it's a whole other world in those stands. But I must say sixteen is also respectable."

He finished wiping the sweat off and responded, "Yeah, but it was a six-pack light." He tossed the wet towel onto the team bench to land crudely on a crumpled pile.

"So what?" Donna said, "You were awesome. I'm glad we came."

Meeting her eyes squarely, he silently acknowledged her words.

Jen watched them thoughtfully.

(He takes her at face value. He never questions her.)

She had that kind of connection with Al, his sharp intellect coasting through topics like the stem of a boat, or at least she did a few months ago—something just seemed different lately, a lack of energy, enthusiasm, like his missing the game tonight after he said he'd come. Maybe she was being too sensitive. After all, this was his last semester and geology wasn't an easy program. Well, the dinner at Fioritti's would rekindle things.

Jen punched Jack's arm again. "Come on, Sweat-boy. Somewhere here, there's a shower with your name on it. I suggest you two get acquainted."

***

CHAPTER 4

Jack stuffed a handful of chips into his mouth, as Donna tucked one leg under her and gathered a small pile of cards. The other knee was pulled up against her chest and her chin sat perched on it. She peered intently, rearranged them according to suit and numerical order. But there wasn't a lot of sorting to be done, just a pair of sixes. She peered some more.

"You know, Don," Jack explained, "Stare at 'em all you like. If the cards ain't there to begin with, they're not gonna appear."

"I fold," she said, tossing her cards down in disgust.

Jen also threw hers down. "I don't trust you. What have you got?"

Jack laid down an unimpressive hand.

"A pair of fours? I had a pair of sixes!"

"What about this? A straight!"

Jack smiled self-indulgently and scooped up his winning pile of pennies.

"You see how he bluffs?" Jen said, "He stuffs his face every time he has a good poker hand, and this time he did it with his stupid pair. Threw me off."

"Well, learn to bluff better." He faced Jen. "You squish your eyebrows every time you have anything better than a pair. When I see you concentrating, I know to fold. And you ..." He turned to Donna. "You're the opposite. You relax with a good hand, and you sit all scrunched up like that when it's lousy."

Donna protested, "I sit like this a lot. It's comfortable."

"It looks painful. Where'd you learn to be a pretzel?"

"Where'd *you* learn to inhale food? Hey, it's almost seven. We'd better get going. It would be a crime if Fioritti's ran out of noodles before Jack got there."

***

As Jack backed out of the driveway, he faced the rear window, one arm briefly thrown over Donna's headrest. Donna also turned in her seat. Her hair swung around, batting her chin lightly. In an unprecedented move, she had taken Jen's advice and changed her look. All the previously uneven lengths now hung in a blunt cut.

"So, Al's meeting us there? Does he know where it is?"

Jen took a deep breath. Explanation time. "He's decided to opt out of this night ... and every night."

Donna's eyes went wide. "You guys broke up? When did this happen?"

"Today, before you guys came over."

"Why? What happened?"

"Do you realize you always ask two questions in a row?"

"Do you realize you're in the backseat for a reason? Well? What did he say?"

"I'm not sure, but I think that was like two and a half. I'm still counting it as two."

With squinting eyes and pursed lips, Donna resorted to the only weapon at her disposal, a frighteningly accurate imitation of Marianne Brammon.

"Oh Christ, not the Mother-Look! I'm *not* looking. ... Oh, fuck it! He said a lot of nothing, OK? Which probably means he's got the hots for someone else. I should have seen it coming after he weaseled out of the basketball game. And I thought being eighteen would be fun ..." Jen finished the statement with a sour face and an impatient wave of her hand.

Donna turned to Jack triumphantly. Nothing worked on Jen like the Mother-Look. He commented, "You gotta teach me that."

"Years of practice, buddy."

"So, did you ever meet him?"

"Who, Al? Yeah, a couple of times. You?"

"No, after the game, we were gonna—"

"Anyway," Jen interrupted, "speaking of moronic love lives, are we picking up The Velcro Couple too?"

Jack answered, "No, they're coming on their own."

Thank God they'd chosen Fioritti's tonight. It was a short drive, which meant less time belaboring the breakup. "On the other hand," Jen sullenly reasoned to herself, "it's got to be the most romantic place in town."

The interior was as dark as the morose weather, but accent lighting created a strategic ambiance of elegance. Perfectly spaced along each wall were cylindrical sconces in the shape of candles. Had mistletoe been installed, the message could not have been clearer.

At their entrance, a man in a polished black suit sprang to life. He verified their reservation as though they were older and wealthier than their years, and showed them to a large table where Steve and Tina were already seated. A dimly lit lamp hung from the ceiling, separating them from the rest of the patrons. Steve was holding both of her hands under the table, as if preparing to propose on one knee, and Jen summoned just enough diplomacy to refrain from commenting. As everyone arranged themselves in their seats, the lamp embraced them within its limited sphere, excluding all those outside its reach. It also emphasized the empty space to Jen's left.

(Forget about him. Just get into the dinner.)

Tina leaned in to kiss her boyfriend on the ear, a tiny reward for saying something clever. Whatever it was, Tina seemed to consider herself clever by association. Steve's hand sat on her knee and Jack could imagine the rest. In his mind, he skimmed Donna's legs all the way up to her thighs. He could almost feel her velvety skin. Just a belt, a button, and a zipper in the way that would magically unlock at his touch … Then—

As Jen's penetrating gaze fell on him, he quickly slapped on a smirk. "To Donna, for starting automotives without blowing up the school!"

All but Tina raised their glasses. "You're taking automotives? You gotta be joking!"

Jack reached for a dinner roll and slathered it with butter. Donna smiled at Jen and tapped her watch, who had wagered that Jack would start on the buns within one minute of his butt hitting the chair. Jen thought after all those chips, he would wait at least two. She now owed Donna a movie.

Jack explained, "Back in December, we were watching MTV and they were interviewing Barry Manilow. We thought Don looked a little too impressed with him. So, we bugged her to prove she didn't have any Manilow tapes in her house. She finally agreed to a bet and—"

"You totally cheated!" Donna interrupted.

"The bet *was* that if we couldn't find any tapes in her house, then we'd both take sewing with Mrs. Strudland. And if we did find a tape, she'd take automotives. Well, it turned out she did have a private Manilow stash."

"They sucked my dad into hiding this bogus Christmas present for Jen's mom. So, my dad was keeping this thing in his den, and I didn't know about it 'til the day they searched my house and this stupid cassette popped out of his desk."

Tina's mouth fell open. "And you're taking the class?"

"Well, I neglected to check the wording of the wager. It's in writing. They just had to find a tape in my house. It didn't have to be mine. I'll never let that happen again."

"Oh, come on," Jack said, "You like getting in the grease with the other monkeys. How did you do on that exam today?"

"Blew one part of it for sure. I had to assemble a cylinder head and put it back on the engine block. I didn't torque the head bolts in the right sequence, but I did OK on the rest of it. I think I just need to spend some time under my dad's car."

Tina looked as though Donna had landed from outer space, and for a while, her horror was sufficient to restore Jen's good humor.

After settling the dinner cheque, the group huddled beside Steve's car. The temperature had dropped with the sun, seemingly sudden and unalterable, and a fresh layer of powdery snow covered the pavement around them. Though falling steadily from the calm dark sky, serenity was merely temporary; sharp bursts of wind snatched up pools of snow, only to lose its grip just as quickly and recklessly cascade the powder down again. In weather like this, it was hard to imagine the same city needing air conditioners for three months out of the year.

Jen wrapped her arms around herself and envied the grass hidden under its thick quilt. Words echoed in her mind cruelly.

"This just isn't working out," he'd said.

What the hell did that mean? And that's exactly the question Jen put to him. Al had simply shrugged and left as quickly as possible, leaving no explanation to justify all the pain, no nail on which to hang this relationship, but there it was all the same. Looking at it day after day could drive her to drink.

In retrospect, small signs had surfaced daily. They crept into her head tangentially, obvious only to an objective mind. His phone calls lessened. Conversations were punctuated with sudden prolonged silences. His thumb stopped caressing the back of her hand as he held it. Once Al had spoken the breakup words and lifted the camouflage away, her doubts stood front and center. Waving enthusiastically, they called, "See? We were here all along. Fooled you!" Jen knew those doubts were legitimate. Simply ignoring them, she'd talked herself into believing everything was fine. Now, with the wound still fresh, the knowledge accentuated her disappointment ... and the suspicion that Al's heart was elsewhere.

Jack asked, "So, what do you guys want to do now?"

"We gotta go. Other plans." Steve sheepishly shuffled his feet. Jen rolled her eyes.

(Yeah, probably in the backseat of your car.)

The Velcro Couple sped away with an eagerness that sunk Jen's mood further. She turned to follow Jack and Donna to his car, but stopped at the sight of Jack's face.

"Oh, piss," he muttered, and she followed his stare to a pair of dim headlights.

***

A shrill wind masked the sounds of Calgary and surrounded the three with an unfriendly isolation, as they stepped along the straight sidewalk path. Freezing air painted white steam to float up at quick intervals. The two girls clung to Jack for support over the icy patches, and he set the pace, steering them through snow drifting in a mist across their feet.

The diffused moonlight reflected off white lawns to brighten a dreary landscape, but at best, it added a stark illumination. Jen wasn't a big fan of winter. Cold weather made her feel muffled and separate in all that down-filled gear. Al had made her feel separate enough this afternoon.

(Christ, just spark these guys. That'll get your mind off it.)

"OK, let's say Captain Kirk was out of the picture, and someone else had to take over the Enterprise. Who would it be?"

"Sorry, girls. I don't speak Nerd."

"Don't worry. Jen will help you with the really big words."

"Why don't you just paint a massive L on my forehead?" He shook his head. "Oh, fuck it—Scotty."

Donna muttered, "You're such a push-over. Don't give in to her bullying ways. She's like a mosquito. You have to kill it on the spot ... and Scotty's not second in command anyway. Spock is."

"Yeah, but you know how racist the Federation is. Spock wouldn't last two days."

Jen tried not to smirk. These two were so easy to rev up, like dangling strings at cats.

She said, "Yeah, they're big on the human element. McCoy would have him declared medically unfit in no time, but Scotty wouldn't last either. He'd have his ass in a sling the first time he needs warp drive and some engineer lies about the repair time." She cast around for an unlikely candidate. "What about Nurse Chapel?"

"Are you nuts?" Donna blurted out, "They'd let a Romulan pilot the ship before they let a blonde woman give her first command."

"Said the blonde bitterly ... I gotta hear Jen's reasoning. This could be her best argument yet."

"Well, I think Chapel's a good choice 'cause she's the only one with her mind on her job."

"What do you mean?" Jack and Donna asked together.

"Think about it. Spock is way too uptight being dignified. Scotty forgets his own name the moment some babe joins the crew. Chekov thinks the universe revolves around Mother Russia. Uhura and Sulu are good at their jobs, but they aren't leaders. And we can rule out McCoy, just 'cause he's such a flake."

Donna asked, "What makes you think Nurse Chapel would be any better?"

"The only skeleton in her closet is her mad desire for Mr. Spock, and she was smart enough to keep that quiet. Most of the time, she's the one who runs Sick Bay. She always stays calm and looks for answers."

Jack raised his voice over the howling wind, "You think she should be given command over a star ship when the biggest problem she's faced is her Vulcan lust?"

"Jen's got something there. Think about it. What could be more challenging than being in love with someone who doesn't know you're alive?—"

Jack almost interrupted Donna right there, and he may have if it had been just the two of them, but he could feel Jen's eyes zeroing in on him again.

"—Chapel doesn't throw a tantrum or go crazy over the problem. She just does her job and waits to get close to him. You know, she could disguise herself as a Vulcan—someone he could appreciate—and try it from that angle. They've figured out time travel, so she could just keep going back until she gets it right."

Their discussion continued through the snow and ice, voices raised to carry over the wind. As they approached an intersection at the top of a hill, no one bothered to punch the crosswalk button. If they had, the flashing pedestrian lights would have stood in silent warning to a large sedan coming over the crest.

Jen was walking to the left of Jack when she stepped off the curb. With her face still turned toward him, she was splashed in two pools of light, which swung down in a big arc as if searching for an actor on stage. The sudden harsh light made her head jerk, and she was reminded of a time when she was eight and her brother kept shining a flashlight in her eyes.

(Billy, quit it or I'm telling mom!)

A split-second later, the dark metal of the car followed the path of its headlights.

***

CHAPTER 5

Pain, cold face, wet arm … The sensations nagged her one by one until Donna would pay attention. Snowflakes were landing on her nose and cheeks, imposing the reality of her surroundings. Seconds felt like hours before she could catalogue the disjointed sensations properly.

Then Jack's face blocked out the sky, repeating her name. She squinted at him and grabbed his jacket to pull herself upright. A sharp pain shot through her shoulder as soon as she moved her arm. Crying out, she started to fall backwards again, but Jack caught her in time.

They stepped around the front of the car as a man ran toward them, carrying a coat. No, not a coat, a blanket. They followed his path with sudden fear, straight to Jen, who was lying on the ground with her eyes closed, one arm extended beyond her head. A kneeling woman wept openly and reached a hand toward Jen's face, while the man spread the blanket along her legs.

He said, "Someone's calling an ambulance. Gotta keep her warm." He looked up at Jack and Donna. "Are you two OK? I didn't see you guys."

The woman was still crying.

Donna watched as if in a dream. Engulfed in dizziness, she scowled at the swaying pavement. There must be somewhere to sit. … Instead, she leaned against Jack and tried to find a way to stand without her shoulder screaming. He led her to the car, into the warmth of the backseat. That was better. When he jumped out to check on Jen, Donna moved to follow him and her shoulder protested again. Sitting back and gripping it, she could feel a tear in her jacket. Tiny feathers escaped the fabric to land like snowflakes across the seat.

Then, her gaze rested on the woman beside Jen.

(Mom, what are you doing here?)

33

Donna's thoughts moved sluggishly, staying just out of focus. The dizziness was so distracting—spinning movement around a central point. Though she struggled to hold one sight stable, every object seemed to have liquid edges, skewing their shapes to confuse her eyes. Someone was showing crisp movie clips too close to her face, and she was surrounded by rapid violent movement.

(Too fast, I can't see everything!)

Though encased in surrealism, this was too hard on the senses to correspond with any dream state she could remember. It was almost like sleepwalking, authentic yet separated. Things took on a watery look, as though projecting the movie onto the depths of a swimming pool. The film clips had distinct moments of clarity. Then, they would dissolve as other pictures took their place, one after another. Faster and faster ...

She closed her eyes to gather her haphazard perceptions. A weight pressed itself onto her chest, she struggled to breathe, and felt herself sliding away.

***

The paramedics arrived within minutes, but to Jack, it took forever. Two sets of exterior lights from the sides of the ambulance illuminated the intersection. A police car pulled up, flashing more lights. A third car stopped, probably just someone wanting to help.

The paramedics ran their gloved hands over Jen. Fastening a collar around her neck, they carefully maneuvered her body onto a spinal board and then a stretcher. Her parka was open and Jack could see a patch of blood on her chest. When the left side expanded, the right side went in like a perfectly balanced see-saw. Even he knew it wasn't supposed to do that ... but then her chest wasn't doing *anything.*

"Flail chest ... head injury ... Get her inside."

Jen's stretcher slid into the van. The last paramedic grabbed the rear door and swung it shut behind him. The latch didn't catch and the door rebounded ajar. Jack saw the other guy cutting Jen's shirt straight up the middle.

"Sucking chest wound. Get a bandage and pass me the eighteen-gauge."

A needle went swiftly from one pair of hands to another and was inserted directly under Jen's right collarbone. After extracting some fluid, the paramedic frowned.

"No pulse."

His partner finished securing a three-sided bandage on the bleeding hole through her ribs, pushed a button on a flat rectangular box, and the machine sprang to life. He lifted two paddles, rubbing gel between them.

"Defib ... 200."

Two knobs were adjusted. The paddles landed diagonally across Jen's chest, one near her right shoulder, the other under the opposite set of ribs.

"Clear."

Her body jerked upward, stiffening for a second. Then, she collapsed back down.

"Nothing ... 300."

Another shock, another agonizing moment where Jen's body angled up as if being stabbed in the back. Jack stepped closer and he could smell something. It was a scent you didn't smell much in winter—something burnt, but worse. Charred hair, skin, things that weren't supposed to be burnt. Awful.

He leaned into the ambulance about to demand, "Hey! What's happening?" but a firm hand pulled him back before the words escaped. He resisted until he saw the shiny badge on the uniform.

"360 ... No wait, there's a pulse."

Another person was standing nearby, holding something up to his face. Turning sharply, the officer suddenly let go of Jack's arm. He raised his hand to cover the camera and moved forward.

"No way."

Protesting, the man tried to veer around the bulky policeman. Any anger Jack felt at being pushed around disappeared at the sight of the reporter being stopped. In the time it took for Jack to be distracted, another cop had already shut the ambulance door.

A second emergency team attended to Donna *(When did they get here?)* and Jack's heart contracted at the possibility of witnessing the same treatment on her. She was laid on a spinal board like Jen, with a similar collar around her neck.

Once she was loaded safely inside the ambulance, Jack started to climb in after her, but the paramedics pointed to an officer. "No, go with him."

And Jack watched Donna's ambulance drive away, with guilt and worry as his only companions.

***

When Donna opened her eyes, the woman was gone and so was Jen. Donna was inside a room with metal shelves and compartments everywhere. The entire room shook.

Earthquake? There were no earthquakes in Calgary.

She tried to get up once, demanding to know what was happening and who that woman was, the one kneeling beside Jen. Suddenly it seemed important, but she couldn't move her head. She felt a sharp pinch when a man in a navy blue uniform inserted a needle into her arm. Then a mask was placed over her nose and mouth.

The next thing she knew, people in lab coats surrounded her in a brightly lit room, which wasn't shakng anymore. The surface underneath was soft and comfortable. She was warm without the weight of her jacket surrounding her, and spotting it draped over a chair, she felt her neck moving freely now.

"Can you tell us your name?"

Staring at the lab coats as if they were insane, Donna answered, "Of course ..." and was surprised at how thick and heavy her own voice sounded, every syllable dripping with weariness. Then, realizing that they really did expect a response, she told them.

"Donna, do you know where you are?"

"Well, I'm either in a hospital or a really ugly bedroom."

The people in lab coats chuckled, overlooking her surliness. "Either answer works. Can you tell us what month this is?"

She opened her mouth and froze. She knew it was an easy question, that she should know the answer. The date was special somehow. It related to what she'd been doing tonight. Which was what exactly? One by one, the concepts lined up in her mind and she pushed each one over like dominoes.

(Jen ... Jack ... snow ... Rummoli ... bluffing ... The Velcro Couple ... Fioritti's ... dinner ... birthdays!)

"February," she finally answered, annoyed with herself for taking so long.

An officer stepped forward with his pen poised above a notepad. "Donna, I'm Constable McKinley. What do you remember?"

Turning to one of the lab coats, she asked, "Why are the cops here?"

"They have to determine what happened to you tonight."

She squinted. "We were going to Jen's. Um, we were talking about a church or something. There were lights and then someone pushed me down. It really hurt."

"Your friend says you rolled into the curb. Did you see a car?"

"Yeah, I was sitting in one at the drive-in, Jack and me. I think it was Jack. Oh yeah, and a man and a woman were with Jen. She was really upset, crying a lot—the lady I mean."

"What did they look like?"

"I didn't really look at the guy, but she had short dark hair and a red shirt, a nice one. ... Why are the cops here?"

The officer maintained a straight face as he decisively flipped his notepad closed. "OK, I think we're done here."

***

(Why are the cops here?)
Quick panic sparked a surge of adrenaline in Al's chest. A Check-Stop ... in the middle of a damned blizzard! He glanced around, but there were no exits, no way to avoid the cops, who were stopping every vehicle. He steeled himself to show his best face and inched his car forward.

Turning to Tracy, he asked, "Got any mints?"

An impaired charge on their first date would kill the mood real fast. Al had taken her out for dinner and then to a party near campus. Between the two of them, they put away a bottle of wine at the restaurant and another later on. A breathalyzer reading would probably hit the roof.

Tracy fished through her purse. "Here," she said, handing him a stick of mint gum.

Now, the cop was approaching the vehicle directly in front of Al. He bent down close to the driver's side window and then opened the door, beckoning to the occupant. Al and Tracy watched as a woman rose from the car and took a few staggering steps before straightening up. The officer led her directly into the backseat of his police cruiser. A second officer got into her car and drove it out of the way.

Al prepared to stop his car where the woman's had been a minute ago. His heart beat with a nervous rhythm and a light layer of perspiration crossed his forehead. The cop motioned him further. Al complied, closer, closer, now on level with the officer ... but the cop just waved him through. No problem. Breathing a sigh of relief, he took Tracy's hand. Back on schedule.

"Your place or mine?"

"Oh, that was horrible. Do you really expect to get lucky with a line like that?"

"Well, if I don't, that drunk back there was kind of cute. Can you spot me a fifty to bail her out?"

In the morning, cocooned under layers of covers, Al looked to his left and experienced an initial moment of confusion.

(That's not Jen.)

And then, he remembered ending it with Jen yesterday. This was Tracy—the smart girl from his geophysics class—with whom he shared two bottles of wine and a brief scare at the Check-Stop.

Her brown eyes were almond shaped, hinting of some distant Asian blood. Sensuous, they masked her strong practical side. He liked Tracy's

eyes. Jen's lacked feminine disguise. Not only was she exactly as she
presented herself, she could set her gaze on him and he would instantly feel
transparent. It was unnerving. His youth valued things like mystery in a
woman. Jen and her unwavering expressions simply didn't allow for that.

He nuzzled Tracy's neck playfully to lull her from the private security
of sleep. Smiling her silent consent, she rolled her body toward his as they
both thought, "What better way to start the day?"

***

Donna woke up early with the winter sunlight pressing through the
window. At first, she wasn't sure why she was there, except that she hurt
so much.

(What a shitty way to start the day ...)

Her head throbbed madly and the whole right side of her body ached.
A nurse was standing beside her bed. Tall, blonde, short hair, a little heavy
set. She smiled, speaking with soft tones.

"You've been in a car accident. Do you remember?"

Donna scowled.

(Wrong, lady—I don't own a car.)

Then she noticed just how blonde the woman's hair was. She studied the
nurse, trying to piece together some veiled significance, and suddenly ...

The nurse watched the young girl's face give an alert look of
recognition. She waited a few moments for Donna's memory to solidify. It
was still muddy, but now bits and pieces were trickling in.

"You have some cuts and bruises, but luckily nothing was broken.
Just lie still and relax. You're going to feel sore for a while. Your father
and brother stayed here most of the night. They'll be by later to take you
home—"

Donna thought she'd mistaken the nurse's words. Did she say *brother?*
But she was too tired to correct her.

"—don't worry if you can't remember everything right away. For now,
just get some rest. Do you need something for pain?"

"Yes ..." and then the nurse's kind attentions reminded her of her
manners, adding, "Please."

Donna's grogginess covered her eyes heavily. The headache didn't
help either. Images of last night drifted inconsistently past solid awareness.
Just when she felt she could grasp one *(Something about ... a movie?)*, it
would slip away. The painkiller gradually took effect and time passed as
she dozed. When Jack walked in, she was surprised to discover two hours
had gone by. Wasn't that nurse just here?

"Hey, how are you feeling?" His voice was gentle.

"Like I passed out in a dryer," she answered, stirring her finger in the air, "but they seem to have Nurse Chapel on staff. And I think we decided last night she knows a thing or two."

With a groan, she raised her shoulders to sit up. There was a tight sensation on her forearm. She noticed a square piece of gauze secured by tape; it tugged the hairs on her skin when she adjusted her position. She stared down and saw a car seat decorated with ...

(Feathers?)

"Did my jacket get ripped?"

Jack shifted uncomfortably. "Yeah, you ah ... you broke my fall. You cut your arm on some ice on the street when you landed. The nurse said you're gonna be fine, just, you know, sore." He reached a hand across his shoulder, a gesture of sympathy for her pains.

"How's Jen?"

"They think she'll be OK. She's got a broken rib. That's gotta hurt."

"Does she look bad?"

"Haven't seen her yet. Thought I'd wait for you. We can go later, when you're ready to leave."

"What happened? I know we were hit by a car, but ... I don't remember much."

"I practically carried you into the guy's car. You were babbling, mostly garbage. The scariest part was when the ambulance guys couldn't find Jen's pulse, but they got it started again. That was sure tense. The cops brought me here."

Reflectively he commented, "They were nice to the hospital staff, different from how I thought cops act. I told them the driver was right—we went into the crosswalk without hittin' the button, so the guy didn't know to stop. It really wasn't the driver's fault, but they're gonna look into it anyway."

He shrugged sheepishly. They'd stepped straight into an accident that could have been prevented, and he was the only one who wasn't hurt.

Donna asked, "Well, what did the woman say?" Her pain demanded that blame be ascribed elsewhere.

Engaging her eyes directly, Jack answered, "Don, there wasn't any woman. You were just dreaming that. You told the cops about her. Took you off their witness list real fast! It was weird. You gave all these details about her, but you couldn't remember the guy who was really there."

"But ... I saw someone. Short hair and ..."

Puzzled, Donna stopped at the ridiculous image of a woman wearing no jacket. Impossible. She would have frozen in thirty seconds.

"I guess I did dream it. It was so real. She was older than us. Looked like my mother. She was kneeling by Jen and crying. I could have sworn ..."

Her voice trailed off. It was upsetting to discover that such a realistic sight could be as intangible as smoke, especially one embedded in such significance.

Jack stayed until her father arrived. There were shadows under his eyes, and for the first time, Donna could envision him as an old man.

The men waited in the hallway and made awkward small talk while a doctor cleared Donna to be discharged. She dressed slowly, taking care not to move her shoulder. Then, as Jack guided her careful movements, the three of them found Jen's room. Raymond had one hand on the door when a nurse stepped close.

"You're here to see Jennifer Brammon? I'll just let you know that she's sustained a closed head injury and a pneumothorax."

She was faced with three blank expressions.

Donna turned to Jack. "I thought you said broken rib?"

The nurse clarified, "It is a broken rib, but more serious. Her lung was punctured. She's probably not awake, but if she is, don't expect her to make any sense." Observing their hesitancy, she added, "Go ahead. Her parents are in there now. I just wanted to prepare you."

Jen was quite the sight. Asleep with her arms and legs restrained, apparently she had already tried to remove the various tubes connecting her to machines and leave the hospital. A nasty bruise blotting her temple extended well beyond the hairline.

Despite the nurse's warning, youthful naiveté was replaced with stunned silence. Jen really looked hurt. What had seemed like the weight of the world pressing into Donna's forehead shriveled to a fraction of its former size. Unconsciously straightening her posture, she stopped feeling sorry for herself.

With photographic stillness, even Jen's breathing lacked its normal depth. Jack had always wondered at the ability of actors to feign death. How do they hold their breath through entire scenes like that? After one timed test with his brother, he'd almost passed out.

(Must pump 'em full of morphine before each scene. Christ, if Jen died young, this is exactly how she'd look. Creepy.)

Mr. and Mrs. Brammon were seated in the room. She was sipping a coffee as he stared out the window. When the men shook hands, Donna saw something pass between them, intangible but sensed. A father to father message of empathy. But Mrs. Brammon just acknowledged them with a grim nod. Donna assumed that she was tired from being here all night. Then it hit her; this woman's daughter almost died while her friends were able to stroll in with all body parts intact.

(She's pissed at me. He's not, at least not yet, but she is. Why am I thinking this?)

40

Distracted thoughts pulled her concentration restlessly. For some reason, she was reminded of summer barbecues in the hot sun, not the fancy propane ones, but the old-fashioned coals that drove smoke deep into the meat. Sometimes Raymond didn't pay attention and let the hamburgers burn, so her mother had learned to sneak past and flip them in time. Donna remembered her mother's red summer outfit and a matching elastic band, brown hair tickling sleeveless shoulders. In less than a year, they had gone from backyard barbecues to hospital food. There were no outdoor flavors to be savored in this white tiled room, but still, the thought persisted. Why in the world was she thinking about barbecues?

Something else bothered her too; this Brammon picture was so shaded by déjà vu that for several minutes, it completely blanketed her concern for Jen. Even while Raymond and Jack led her through the parking lot, it persisted as if a task had been neglected, an intellectual irritation under the skin. Donna obstinately stifled the feeling. She simply couldn't be thinking straight if her version of the accident differed so much from Jack's.

However, one detail stood out, refusing to be ignored—an intuitive regret that she had lost something forever.

***

CHAPTER 6

Fog shadowed the drive-in again to hang bleakly over hundreds of empty cars, which were parked in obedient rows all around her. No one in sight. Suspended a few inches off the ground, the car shuddered rhythmically while tires clawed the earth in vain for some scrap of leverage. Moving at an alarming speed without actually going anywhere, in her mind this made sense somehow: being surrounded by empty cars, driving in place, while watching a movie.

The screen was huge—taller and wider than any she had ever seen before—and it was showing a familiar movie, some romance. Whoever had set up the projector didn't know what he was doing, because the scenes raced past as fast as she drove.

(Who can follow this? Oh, who cares anyway?)

She'd seen it a million times. Someone was supposed to meet her here, someone she instinctively knew wasn't late, but at the same time, was nowhere in sight.

Maybe they were to meet in a different drive-in. No, the deep part of her mind accepted the situation as destiny. Though conscious of the inherent danger, she unfastened her seat belt and felt it jerk across her lap to stand crisply at attention along the driver's side door. Free now, she peered out the windows for some glimpse of him. Finally, tears of frustration trailed down her cheeks.

Turning her attention back to the movie, she realized the climactic finish was near. There were pictures, snapshots of memorable moments, like the ones catalogued in her father's photo albums. Two stood out. They had been expanded and posted on the movie screen.

(Is that Jack?)

The edges started to melt as they blended into each other, but she could still see their distinct features. A choice was presented. Which one? No time to think—wait! Then someone turned on the lights. ...

Morning sunlight glazed the walls with cheerful intentions. Perplexed by the sheen across her headboard, Donna squinted at the ceiling. A terrible loss hung over her, as if she had failed in some crucial assignment. Closing her eyes, she concentrated. Cars. Where were they? And that person she was supposed to meet? What movie was playing? Her mind insisted these things should be placed all around her, as she reluctantly abandoned the transition phase between dreams and wakefulness. There were no cars, no theater or person to meet. It was just some wild story concocted by her subconscious mind.

She shook her head, coaxing clarity to the forefront. That failure was still bothering her, even though she understood exactly which state was real ... but the other one had been so overpowering with implicit acceptance of details insensible to reason. How could ridiculous constructions commandeer one's head to cause such inexplicable despair upon waking?

(It wasn't real. It wasn't ... but why do I keep having this stupid dream?)

Fourth time this week. Probably from being thrown into the curb. She wondered if Jen's headaches were as bad. No, probably a lot worse. Well, time to get up, shower, make coffee ... join the waking world. She rolled out of bed with a sigh, not looking forward to the day and the headache that would undoubtedly accompany it.

***

Donna's recovery was quick. Within a week, the déjà vu feeling dissolved like sugar in her morning cup, an odd sweet taste, invisible within the enveloping liquid. As her regular life took over, she attributed it to the bump on her head and gradually dismissed it.

The movie dream eventually lessened in frequency and intensity, but the hallucination was another matter. That woman kneeling beside Jen— she stayed in the back of Donna's mind, as if calculating the right moment to leap out at her. Never entirely forgotten, years later Donna could still remember the false value she had placed on something unreal.

For a week or two, they were the talk of the school. Students viewed them with an unenviable awe, wanting to know the details, but not seeming happy once they heard them. Most of the student population hadn't considered the concept of mortality. Normal stresses nudged them along to adulthood, and they didn't relish the morbid potential an unpredictable future held, especially one where they could get wiped out of existence, simply by stepping off a curb at the wrong moment. It was hard enough passing chem. ...

On the other hand, Donna and her two friends had observed another approach to life. Through the accident, they recognized the need to enjoy the people close to them. A solid perimeter solidified their friendship, defining them as a permanent threesome.

Their meetings in Café-Abe became a regular commitment, on par with calculus and physics classes. The absence of one pulled a strong reprimand from the other two. Lunch meetings were noticeably tame during Jen's recuperation, but Donna enjoyed her solitude with Jack. His eyes were not bright and lively the way they were around Jen. Instead, they concentrated on her words with gentle respect. Donna wasn't used to plain conversation untinged by satirical quips. Even with her father, a little teasing was always volleyed back and forth, but Jack didn't do that when alone with her. He listened as if waiting for some important announcement. The way he gave her his full attention boosted her confidence. She opened up with stories of her mother and Jack responded equally. Although melancholy, the conversations were compelling.

Finally, Donna had met someone who understood her background, someone possessing the same streak of lonesome independence, born of necessity. Occasionally catching herself staring at him while he ate, she was glad Jen wasn't there to point it out. In those moments, she'd privately toy with the label of "boyfriend". Those pants he'd worn to Fioritti's had sure made her look twice. Speculation on his feelings would automatically follow, but if he were aiming at a target, it would probably be Jen. He was much more outgoing around her.

Jen returned to school two weeks after the accident. The day she came back, Donna and Jack patiently waited for her in Café-Abe. Donna leaned her elbows onto the table. Jack spotted the gash along her forearm, and every time he did, a fresh feeling of remorse trickled down his back. She caught him focused on her arm and their eyes met.

"That's healing really well," he offered lamely, "You probably won't even have a scar."

Donna sighed. He couldn't lie to save his life. "That's not what the doctor said. What's funny is that I'm almost getting used to it, like it was always there. Anyway, it's pretty minor compared to this." She tapped her forehead.

"Headaches?"

"And the dreams."

"You're still having those dreams?"

"Yeah, some of them don't bug me. Just the ones about that woman. Then I wake up feeling really crappy."

"Why crappy?"

Donna shrugged as the corners of her mouth dipped. "I don't know. It just feels like I did something wrong and she has to pay for it." Running her fingers through her hair, she glanced around.

Jack said, "She'll get here. She's just a little screwed up."

"What do you mean?"

"When I was in gym this morning, she came in and sat down on a bench—just sat down and looked out of it. I don't think she knew where she was. Mr. Myron asked me to take her out, so I found her timetable and took her to her drama class. She was rambling about some dead person. It was weird. And when we were at her class, she asked me where the lady was. I said, 'In drama—in there.'"

Keeping an innocent face, he pushed two flat hands forward abruptly, but his eyes smiled mischievously.

"You just shoved her into the class?"

"Pretty much," and they both started giggling.

Finally Jen entered the cafeteria. Losing weight in the hospital made her sweatshirt seem enormous. The neck opening hung to one side, low enough to give them a quick peek at a red patch of skin below her right shoulder, before the shirt was shifted center again. Her hair covered the bruise on her temple. Otherwise she looked fine, though obviously short of breath.

For someone used to bounding around with spare energy, it was frustrating to pace her breathing before talking.

"Hey, look who's back like a bad nightmare!" Donna exclaimed.

"Sorry I'm late. Movin' kind of slow today. Shit, all those rocks you told me to crawl under and now I can't find one. Just shoot me."

"Only on video. A quiet Jen is a thing to be savored," Donna taunted.

Jen was so subdued, she simply scanned her middle finger at them like a flashlight.

"Be nice," Jack cautioned, "I could have left you at Sex Ed. Hey, you remember what you were talking about outside drama?"

Jen's lips pursed in concentration and finally, she shook her head. "What did I say?"

"Something about dead people."

She squinted across the room. "Oh, yeah ... That was me."

"What?" they both asked astonished.

"I had one of those, you know, near-death experiences, which isn't 'near' at all. It's right fucking there."

Jack suddenly remembered how the paramedics lost her pulse. After jumping into action with a foreign language of numbers and commands, they put those things with handles on her and shocked her back to life. The burned patch on Jen's chest was proof. It was an alarming minute, but after it was over, his concern had returned to Donna with the speed of light. Jesus, Jen had actually *died* and he spent the night worried about Donna's headache. Could he be a bigger prick?

"What was it like? Did you feel like you were moving? Could you hear anything?"

Fascinated, Donna sat holding her breath, but Jen shrugged off the questions as if they bored her. "I don't know. Can't remember."

Donna exhaled in disappointment. Here was the school's biggest extrovert refusing guaranteed attention. Jen's head must be hurting pretty badly to shy away from such a large spotlight.

She muttered, "The invisible brunette would have told us more."

Now Jen squinted at Donna, her eyes hard. "What?"

"Don thought some woman was at the accident, but she was just seeing things."

"Well, she seemed real enough at the time," Donna retorted irritably, "and I keep dreaming about her. ... She was wearing a red blouse and kneeling beside you."

"Did she say anything?"

"No, just crying and hangin' over you, though God knows why—you're not *that* interesting. Anyway, she was totally bogus."

In an effort to distract Jen from the accident, Donna and Jack turned to milder topics, continuing the conversation themselves. Jen fidgeted silently for much of the hour. They chalked it up to her injuries and took care not to pick on her, but they had misinterpreted her mood. The appearance of restlessness successfully disguised a feeling of impending misfortune, the kind that ominously presses on intuitive hearts and is all too often ignored.

***

CHAPTER 7

Weeks passed as the weather gradually warmed. February became March, and then April and May. Snow disappeared, along with Donna's recurring movie dream. She was glad, not because of the monotony, but rather, the adjacent despondency. It was strange how dreams could capture a person's mood and hold it hostage like that.

Jen recovered with the onset of spring. As invigorating as ever, she never shied from speaking her mind, but a bitter side of her peeked out every now and then. Her cutting remarks were laced with an unusual seriousness. Jack and Donna figured the accident, or maybe the breakup with Al had enhanced Jen's testy side.

Sometimes in Café-Abe, she'd just stop eating and stare into space, as if the room had transformed into one big chalkboard with a million dollar question, demanding absolute concentration. Once, Jack waved his hand in front of her eyes and she blinked at him. Then, she dryly replied that she was doing an imitation of his jock friends.

As he dressed before his gym locker, he wondered what kind of mood she'd be in today. He was one of the last ones out of the locker room before the lunch bell rang and he soaked in the silence, until he heard a couple of voices from the next row.

"So, who you taking to grad?" Jack couldn't tell who this was.

"Chick from St. Francis." Definitely Trevor Simmons.

"Catholic girl ... You know who you should've asked? Carlin. Now, there's a good rack."

"Yeah, she's got a handful. Aw, who knows? I might work on her anyway."

"As if you've got a chance. I heard Greg Lorendo's gonna ask her. Anyway, Petrasyk's been doing her all year."

"Like I couldn't get her away from that fag shit-for-brains? I don't even need to take her to grad. I'll just nail her between the dinner and the dance. She'll be dessert."

They laughed coarsely and Jack gritted his teeth. The sound of paper rustled quietly.

"Ten bucks says she blows you off."

"Oh, she'll be blowin' me, all right." More laughter and more rustling. "You're on, Asshole, and after I nail her, I'll be buying drinks with your money."

Jack could hear metal doors shutting and the boy's footsteps fading away.

He sat on the bench seething. With one small opening, he would have made a move on her months ago, but she treated him like a kid brother. If anyone had a crush on him, it was Jen. She was so lively around him. Then again, he certainly would have heard any of Jen's designs by now. He could imagine her jaunty posture, hands on hips, saying, "Well, what's the deal sport? Are we on or what?"

He slammed his locker shut and then roughly kicked it. Part of the orange door folded in. The fluorescent locker room lights now reflected shadowy textures across the bent metal. While Jack stared, it became Trevor's head ... or Greg Lorendo's. What if Greg had already got to her? Straightening up suddenly, Jack hurried out.

***

"Where's Jen?" Donna asked, sitting across from Jack.

"Gettin' some grub. How was your morning?"

"Good. Koshni gets happier as the year goes on. He hasn't given us homework all week."

"He makes up for it in September. At least we won't see him again."

"You know who I'm going to miss? Mr. Hansen."

"Mr. Hansen!" The name was Jack's cue to frantically wave his arms around in large sweeping circles. The distorted imitation always made Donna laugh.

Swallowing his second sandwich, Jack searched for the nearest garbage can. He locked his sights onto one twenty feet away, calculated the trajectory, aimed, and fired. The moment the bag left his hand, his attention went back to Donna. She smirked, wondering at the confidence in someone who didn't feel compelled to check the outcome. He rarely missed at this range.

Donna announced, "I got my letter of acceptance from U of C yesterday."

"Like there was some question? Did Jen get hers yet?"

"Yeah."

"I'm still waiting to hear from U of A. I wonder how long it'll take."

"I heard it can be anywhere from April to the day before classes start."

"Great, me and three thousand other first-years scrambling to find apartments all at the same time. Listen, are you going to grad?"

The sudden question startled Donna, not that she hadn't considered the issue. Back in January, the students began thinking about prospective grad dates, and the dilemma had increased exponentially with every passing month. Those in steady relationships assumed they'd still be in them when June rolled around. Those who were single slotted their classmates into three categories: Preferred Dates, Secondary Choices, and I'd Rather Go Alone. Some minor shuffling occurred between the categories, but for the most part, it remained pretty stable. After all, twelve years of impressions are hard to erase.

She answered, "Yeah, aren't you?"

"I mean, has anyone asked you?"

Jack was casually peeling a banana. Usually, he would just tear the peel off in two quick movements, but he concentrated on this one, handling it gingerly.

Donna didn't notice. Embarrassed, she remembered one of Jen's comments—that Billy would probably pay good money to take her. Other than him, nobody seemed interested.

"No. Are you ...

(... asking me?)

"Going? Or going with someone?" he filled in nonchalantly.

She blinked and mumbled, "Both."

"Yes to going. No to the second part." Part of the peel still dangled as Jack looked straight at her. "Do you want to go with me?"

Her pulse quickened. He was asking her to grad. No one else in school would think twice about it—she knew the rumors—but she recalled something her father once said, that it was easy to ask anyone on a date ... except the person you really like.

"What about Jen?" she ventured, "You know, since Al and her broke up ..."

(... aren't you guys thinking about getting together?)

This was incredibly awkward. How do you question someone's intentions without overtly questioning their intentions? She struggled with the wording, and then making an odd sort of face, gave up.

But Jack was encouraged. She hadn't run her fingers through her hair once. She only did that when something bothered her, and from what she said, her only worry was Jen being left out.

He fired the peel into the garbage can and remarked, "Jen wouldn't care if the grad blew up."

"True," she chuckled and allowed a soft smile at the thought of being his date. Maybe separated from their everyday banter, he would notice a warmer side of her, someone worth pursuing, worth trying for. ... Maybe—

"Well," Jack added, "We'll tell her she can go with us, if she wants."

He missed her smile dropping a notch as his attention became abruptly diverted.

"Go where?" Jen asked, walking up and maneuvering a chair out from under the table. Jack pushed his books out of the way, and she plunked down a plate of macaroni where his books had been.

"Grad. You want to go with us?"

Jen fixed her expression on her friends, bouncing her eyes suspiciously between them. "You mean ... you're going ... *together?*"

They each looked properly uncomfortable. Though it was excruciating watching Jack dance around Donna all year, occasional moments like these managed to temper Jen's impatience. She didn't wait for a response.

"I'm not going to the dinner, just crashing the dance. I'm sure you two can manage to eat without me. Speaking of which, did I miss Jack the great human trash compactor at work?"

Donna chuckled. "'Fraid so. I, on the other hand, was not fortunate enough to be spared the experience."

Jen dipped her fork into the macaroni and commented, "Really Jack, they could use some of that food in Africa," and his sour look was fuel for the fire. "Well, have you ever really watched yourself? It's like those old Godzilla movies. The never-ending gut!"

"Yeah, yeah, yeah," he muttered, peeling another banana.

***

... Every sense was alive, even smell, which resurrected precise memories in her mind, like the sharp flash of a camera to illuminate the moment it captures. Perfume, flowers, food, all powerful triggers. For Donna, it was peanut butter.

The darkness spun around her, but that one scent kept her safe within the tornado. It built a massive barrier between her and the cruel world, allowing her to view the snapshots of her life calmly. With time frozen, she sifted through each brilliant picture. They were a barrage of sights, sounds, and smells, ready for her to catalogue and experience again.

Peanut butter. She could close her eyes, inhale, and almost hear him say ...

***

"Good morning, Pattycake. Bagel?"

"Yeah, thanks."

Pulling up a chair, Donna handed him a cup of coffee, black, then poured cream into her own cup and stirred it absent-mindedly, while scanning the movie listings. Donna considered coffee to be a particularly bitter beverage, but with enough aspartame, it took the weight off her eyes. Raymond didn't have the heart to tell her the truth. Her coffee was horrible—three scoops too many—but he let her be in charge of their morning routine and added tap water whenever she turned her back.

Donna watched him dip a knife into the peanut butter jar, sitting squarely in front of her father's plate. They didn't even bother putting it away anymore.

"You know, you really should expand your repertoire. North American culture doesn't consider that a staple."

"Sure it does. Aren't I living proof? The problem is nobody makes peanut butter bagels. If someone did, then I wouldn't have to put any on."

"Oh, you'd still put it on. Face it. You need a twelve-step program."

He smiled and answered, "Hey, I can quit any time I want ... but I'd quit faster with some mixed right into the batter. Then, I could get off it slowly instead of quitting cold turkey. Why doesn't anyone make them that way?"

"Who would buy them? Yuck!"

"You could. The perfect Father's Day gift to show gratitude for your measly existence."

"Too bad Father's Day just passed and all you got was dinner and a tie. At least gray goes with all your suits. Well, maybe next year I'll harass some poor baker into making you a special batch."

"A fair trade for eighteen years of food, clothing, and shelter. So, when are you writing final exams?"

"Next week, right before grad."

"Oh, yes, that reminds me. ... Here," he said, reaching into his suit pocket. He handed her fifty dollars. "Does this cover the tickets?"

"More than enough. You're only buying two dance tickets," she replied, pulling one twenty-dollar bill from his grasp. He stared at the bills left in his hand and then straightened up.

51

"Do you have a date?"

"Not really. I'm going with Jack. He got our tickets already, so you only have to buy yours. Is Paula coming?"

"Yes, she wouldn't miss it." He added thoughtfully, "My Pattycake has a date. ..."

Donna felt her face turning red. "No, *you* have a date. Jack's just being nice and he doesn't mix with a lot of kids, so it works for both of us—"

Raymond raised an eyebrow ever-so-slightly. Watching that young man in the hospital, the way he'd fussed over Donna reminded Raymond of himself and Patricia twenty years ago. He knew what was in Jack's eyes when that boy looked at his daughter, and the thought made him want to lock her in a closet. Didn't Donna see it or was she pretending a more casual relationship than it was? It didn't matter that he genuinely liked Jack. This was his daughter.

"—and you really should stop calling me that. My days of Pat-a-cake games are long gone." She smiled wryly as she reached for the peanut butter.

"If I'd had my way eighteen years ago, you would have been called Patty. Your mother didn't want two people answering to the same name. Too confusing in one house. I only settled on it as a middle name when I saw her having contractions. I swear, women could rule the world if they just timed their labor better, like in the middle of board meetings and political campaigns. You look more like a Patty anyway."

"But not a Patty*cake*."

"Well, you started it. When you were three, you'd just figured out how to do that little song with your hands and you insisted we call you that. Too bad for you it stuck, but it's your own fault."

Her smile belied the protest, "You're making it up. I never did that!"

"Sorry kid, that's the truth. You made your mother play that game over and over. Pat-a-cake, pat-a-cake, baker's man ... I'd go to work with the rhyme in my head, and come home to hear you two still at it. It got so she hated the nickname, but that's what I remember most about you and her together, playing Pat-a-cake."

For so long, her mother had melded into the layers of the past. Donna only thought about her periodically, usually after one of those heart-wrenching dreams. Her dad had been seeing Paula for a year now, longer than anyone so far. Donna hadn't stopped to think that he might be lonely.

He was someone she considered devoid of regular needs, just went to work, paid the bills, and spread peanut butter on his bagels. Her childish perceptions reduced him to a "Clark Kent" persona, a superman hiding behind the dull expression of an ordinary mortal, with the extraordinary ability to keep her life consistent, and she didn't want to see those other sides of him.

Neither father nor daughter realized the similarity of their thinking. Change was a concept cautiously embraced by both, but resented in the other. She shouldn't grow up and he shouldn't grow old. She saw him as her stronger half, a rational personality to round out her emotions. To him, she was the one reason to stay rational in an ever-changing world. Despite her independence, she was still the three-year-old trying to coordinate her hands. She was just coordinating bigger things now, geometry, hormones, boys ...

Pattycake. That nickname was one of the few links he had to a pleasant past.

"Well, OK ... but not in front of my friends. Deal?"

"Deal. Oh, by the way, Paula is going to join us for supper tonight—"

(And breakfast too no doubt.)

"—what time are you going to the movie?"

"Depends who drives. If it's Jack, they'll be here at seven. But Jen follows a Brammon time zone. It's their trademark."

"Won't you be late?"

"Jack usually applies a little Brammon buffer. You know, lies about the start time? Then we only miss the previews."

Raymond stood up and brushed the breakfast crumbs off his clothes.

Donna glanced up and noted, "Is that new? It doesn't go with your suit. The gray one would be better."

Scrutinizing the tie in his hand, he frowned. "Paula gave me this. I don't want to change it. I'm meeting her for lunch. Oh, I'll just wear it today." He smoothed it back in place and bent over to kiss her forehead.

"Have a good day, Sweetheart."

"Ditto."

After her father left, Donna sighed to herself. Paula's appearances were increasing. Last week, Donna had risen to find the coffee already prepared. It wasn't a task she particularly relished, but it was her task, one of many that served to distinguish yet connect her to her father.

(Oh, well, maybe it won't last.)

***

Sultry aromas drifted through the kitchen, while Paula chopped carrots. Donna handed her a bowl ... tossed carrot shavings in the garbage ... wiped up a spill. It felt odd to be assisting someone in her own kitchen. Sometimes the cleaning lady who came twice a week stayed long enough to have supper started for them, but she didn't count.

Last week, Paula helped her shop for a graduation dress. It was interesting to spend the afternoon with an older woman. Though not overly stylish, Paula demonstrated a practical sensibility.

"That one would wrinkle. ... You'd need a long slip with this one. ... Blue and green are good colors on you. ..."

She didn't gush over the fluffy dresses, or try to steer Donna toward something youthful. Jen complained how shopping with her mother rivaled the car accident, since Mrs. Brammon seemed determined to get her daughter into something pink, the only color Jen despised.

In the stores, Donna admired a sparkly pair of earrings, but balked at the price. Later, Paula presented them as a graduation gift. It was done almost timidly, showing a simple regard for Raymond's daughter. She seemed to know that Donna might not be entirely comfortable with her entrance into their lives.

Paula had never been anything but nice to Donna, which made the unfairness of her own attitude all the worse. If only this woman had bitchy days like Jen, Donna's wariness would be justified. At her worst she was merely on edge, tonight especially. She fiddled with her silverware throughout the meal and kept refolding her napkin.

"This is good. You know, Dad, one of us should really learn how to cook."

"I cook," he responded indignantly.

"What do you cook? You open jars."

"Well, if you want to get technical, the true definition of cooking is the ability to combine any two ingredients."

"That are edible," Paula clarified.

Raymond made a face. "Edible is subjective. Anyway, I do that all the time. A can of soup and water, TV dinners and salt—" He pointed his fork at Donna to emphasize his next example. "—bagels and peanut butter. My culinary talents are endless."

"You're pathetic."

"Can you believe how my own daughter talks to me? Absolute slander."

Paula nodded sagely at Donna. "You're safe. Slander requires a lack of proven facts," and Raymond threw up his hands at her defection.

After the dishes were cleared, they all relaxed in the living room with a pot of tea. Donna curled up in the armchair, tactfully leaving the couch for her father and his girlfriend. Jack and Jen would arrive soon. Raymond must have remembered this as he stole a glance at his watch.

Setting his cup down on the coffee table, he stated, "Donna, there's something we want to talk to you about."

The automatic worry of a child bubbled up.

(What did I do wrong? Wait, they look nervous, not mad. Jesus, the last time I saw that, someone had died. It can't be that bad.)

Donna noted Paula glancing at Raymond through the pause. He always prolonged these things. It wasn't a tactic. He just got a bit shell-shocked in the midst of conflict until someone dove into the conversation. Apparently, Paula hadn't figured that one out about him yet. Donna sat up and leveled a straight look at them.

"OK ... what?"

Raymond cleared his throat. "Honey, Paula and I have decided to get married."

It had happened. Her father was finally going to remarry. Of course, Donna always knew it was a possibility, but possibilities are elusive concepts, existing somewhere out there in their own time and space. In one sentence, Raymond had taken the shapeless concept and given it a tangible strength. Suddenly, it expanded before her, literally blocking her view of her father. Couldn't he see her anymore? Now, only Paula was visible.

Donna's eyes went to her in an instant. She envisioned her father's new wife in this living room every night, a cup of tea in hand. So this was why he wanted to know when her friends would arrive: time to make his announcement, but not enough to prolong a scene. Were the earrings some kind of warm up for this conversation? No, Paula had been genuine that day, but this was a different day and this wasn't about some piece of jewelry.

Donna's concerns were readily apparent; her green eyes had betrayed her discomfort before she could put the mask on. What was more, she knew Paula had spotted those concerns. Acutely shallow and transparent, she should congratulate them, just forget about herself and welcome Paula into her life as her father had done.

But instead, she asked, "Isn't that a little hard to do when she's already married?"

Paula colored at the pointed question, but kept her chin level and shoulders squared.

Raymond's response was patient and firm. "Well, Donna, you know the divorce is just a matter of time. We aren't planning the wedding for a while anyway."

The Wedding. Those words seemed foreign applied out of context to her own someday. Grown-ups get married, not parents of grown-ups. ...

Raymond was staring at her with a combination of understanding and determination. Strange to see. He had always been there for her, and now, here he was divided. Even stranger was his tone. He meant business. She could like it or lump it, but either way, this was going to happen.

Feeling vaguely manipulated, she recognized the callousness of her immediate reaction *(So, are you going to wear Paula's tie for that occasion too? You know, the one that doesn't go with any of your suits?)*, and swallowed it back down.

Raymond was looking at her expectantly. Her relationship with Paula hinged on this moment. It was irrelevant that the tie didn't match his suits—he'd get new suits.

The mask now firmly in place, she smiled at Paula and lightly stated, "Well, I guess we'll have to go shopping for another dress."

Raymond returned a grateful smile. Though Paula's expression relaxed, her shoulders remained stiff.

The doorbell rang. 7:05. Jack must have driven. Donna jumped up, leaving her tea untouched.

"Got to go. Thanks for dinner Paula. That was really good," she called as she rushed out the door.

***

CHAPTER 8

During June of 1987, their graduation ceremony was one of twenty-eight in Calgary, but as much as Jack and Donna tried to downplay it, they felt swept up in the occasion. He worked three extra weekends to afford a suit.

When he arrived in his mother's car, which was running only marginally better than his, it felt like a date. She hadn't been on a lot of them, especially in the last year. Maybe her close friendship with Jack was creating a "hands-off" aura about her. Then again, maybe she just wasn't interested in anyone. Even Trevor Simmon's confidence couldn't compete with Jack's personable nature.

The young man entering her front door presented a previously hidden maturity. Jack had been on every athletic team in the past year and it showed. His brown suit broadened his shoulders, giving him a masculine air. A man dressed this way was terribly sexy.

With heels, they were almost the same height and there was something alluring about this. Their lips were at the same level ... lips, shoulders, hips, as though she could fit into him perfectly.

Her pastel green dress wrapped itself around her body. An enticing line of skin escaped along a side slit of its full length, and at that moment, Jack decided he was a leg man. Her hair, styled away from her face, caressed bare shoulders. Dainty silver earrings completed the ensemble.

Jack's eyes traveled the length of her body to finally rest on her face.

"Wow ... so that's what girls look like."

Reddening, she responded, "Come on, let's go before Dad—"

And Raymond bounded into the living room, waving a camera. "Thought she could get away before this, didn't she! Hold on, the lighting's not good there. Come over here. Turn a bit, Jack. No, the other way. Yeah."

He positioned the camera and adjusted the zoom. Raymond fancied himself a polished photographer, who specialized in candid shots. Being half right, the finished product was usually quite good, but Donna could always hear him a mile away.

"Funny how I keep losing this thing. You'd think it had legs, the places I find it. This time, it was actually in the dishwasher."

A moment later, a sharp flash engulfed two genuine grins. Lowering the camera, his teasing eyes centered on her. "Lucky for you missy, I didn't start the wash cycle."

"Oh, like there was any chance of *that.*"

"Out! Or so help me, this little hide and seek toy will be all you inherit when I'm gone."

As they drove off, Donna noted the expression on Raymond's face from the front porch and she thought, "Relax, Dad, it's just me and Jack." But it wasn't really. It was a grown-up version. Jack could feel her gaze and glanced at her with raised eyebrows. They laughed a little at themselves, all dressed up and driving off to this big affair. This was no cafeteria they were going to.

As they headed south past the university, a cool wind flowed through the open windows, and to Jack it was a pleasantly familiar feeling, triggering some memory. Then, turning into Motel Village brought it right out; last year, his small family had driven through endless miles, crossing provincial borders with the wind flying by. They had landed in this bright clean city, tired and hopeful. Their motel was one of the cheaper ones in Motel Village, but they didn't care. After all that driving, any lodgings felt like home.

Now, he looked at the motels with a swift feeling of envy. The one they were going to tonight was a little nicer and newer than the others, and he thought, "Someday, I'm going to stay there, not just be part of a crowd in one of the conference rooms, but actually *stay* there."

A racy thought followed closely behind—being in one of the rooms— in one of the *beds*—tangled up with this pair of green eyes and long legs beside him. His own eyes narrowed, zooming in on the image ... his hand sliding past her knee and across the smooth skin of her thigh, pulling her leg around him, while his other hand slipped under her unhooked bra. No, make that no bra. She would press the weight of her breast against his hand, and her eyes would glaze over with a smoky appeal. Then, he would feel the warm skin of her hand slide with agonizing slowness down the front of his chest, across his stomach, down to fit him snugly into her. ...

Suddenly, he felt obvious, as if Donna would read his mind and scorn his thoughts. He abruptly pulled his focus back to the present—driving his mom's car, the dinner, the dance later—but his mind stubbornly wandered again.

They seemed perfectly compatible. Coming from single parent families had created a bond of sorts, one of independence. He was not as academic, dividing his time between homework and basketball or football or whatever sport happened to be in season. He knew Donna didn't think much of the school teams, but she still came out to a lot of his games, either with Jen or all by herself, and he was always a little sharper with her in the stands. He wondered if her presence meant a simple show of support or her way of delivering a gentle hint, but ever-present was the worry, "What if I'm wrong? What if I'm only seeing what I want to see?"

This girl looked fantastic and completely unaware, which covered her with a beguiling innocence, begging to be lead astray. Obviously new to dating, she had certainly seen nothing as formal as this evening demanded, and the insight struck a masculine chord in him. It was an agreeable feeling, as agreeable as the wind through the car. Jack resolved to take care of her tonight. He knew she didn't consider it a date, but he was determined to show her that it could be one to remember.

***

... As she envisioned stepping to the beat, she could feel the lights cascading effervescently down her body to pool about her feet. So vivid was their image, she saw his face and felt his hands signaling each turn, each step, and Donna yearned for his touch again.

There was no room in this memory for anyone but him. Even though she knew it was only that—a memory—Donna strained for every nuance that defined it. She had only danced with him the one time, too little to carry forward and cherish. Yet, it had triggered so many fantasies from that day forward.

The voices declared that she would never walk again, which also meant she would never dance again, not with him, nor anyone else. He was the only one who could pull her to her feet and ignite the rhythm.

At that thought, the sparkling lights receded into a dark backdrop and the image of them froze into a single snapshot. Her heart reached out to secure it, but it was already fading like the sparkling lights, and she was left longing for one more dance. ...

***

Smoothly dimming lights drew their attention to the stage. The class president was standing in front of the lead singer's microphone. Around him were a handful of casually dressed people who could only be the band. He introduced them and no sooner had he finished speaking when they immediately burst into song. A large silver ball hung from the ceiling, centered above the smooth hardwood floor. It spun slowly around and cast glittering spots all over the dancers. The bright spots raced with deceptive speed, giving the heightened illusion of movement in those below.

When a slow song started, Jack raised his voice, "Do you want to dance?"

Donna was shy about dancing, but he pulled her into his arms as though they'd done this a million times before. He stepped with a sexy sway, almost too close, his hand on her waist, their thighs brushing rhythmically, and she entertained a short fantasy—Jack kissing her. She would lay a single hand on his cheek, feeling the strong angle of his jaw as his other hand held hers. Leaning in toward her, he would run his free hand along her back. She was careful to keep her eyes low, in case he read her mind like he often seemed to.

(Glad Jen isn't here to see this. She'd never let up.)

As the band was winding down their first set, the Brammons arrived with Jen several reluctant steps behind. But one wide sweep of the room established hope. It was perfect: everyone dressed up, the decorations tasteful and the music loud. By 10:00, her mother would get one of her headaches and go home.

Jen methodically searched the tables, while her eyes gradually adjusted to the darkness. No Donna and Jack. Try the dance floor. The music was slow now, easier to sift through the dancers. At first glance, she didn't recognize Jack. Then, her eyes opened wide at the sight of her two friends in each other's arms. They looked good. Really good.

(Well, he'd be worth a spin or two. Must snag him later.)

As the song ended, Jen made a path to intercept them. Jack and Donna had "couple" written all over them. Ever since the breakup, couples were annoying and she felt like some enormous third wheel.

At least Jack was … comfortable, an extra brother, a cross between Jeffrey and Billy: smart, seeing situations for what they were, yet pleasantly optimistic about life. There was no doubt he identified more with Donna. Usually it was no big deal—comparing Donna and Jen was apples and oranges—but this wasn't the usual situation either. The evening was filled with an excited sort of glamour and it would only happen this one time. As she followed Jack and Donna to their table, she sighed.

(I miss what I had and I'll probably never find it again. These two have it and they don't even know it. This is gonna suck. …)

As it turned out, in comparison, Jen ended up enjoying the evening more than anyone else.

***

The television screen was alive with sparkling costumes. Dancers flowed with exaggerated elegance around the polished floor, every spin carefully orchestrated to impress the judges.

"What the hell is this?" Al asked.

There was supposed to be a movie on, a suspense thriller. Tracy flipped through the television listings.

"Ballroom dance competition from France. Go to channel seven."

A sudden scream emanated from the television, as a serial killer claimed his first victim of the hour. They settled in with their popcorn and beers.

Al wrapped an arm around her, pulling her in close. Tracy tucked her head into his neck and kissed his cheek lightly. She suspected that his European cheekbones and offbeat humor had charmed a number of women into bed. He had intimated that his last girlfriend was a little spitfire, not easily maneuvered into or out of bed, but that was over months ago. He'd only referred to it once or twice, as though discussing the weather. Yeah, it rained last week. So what? His cavalier attitude toward his past was mildly disturbing, but Tracy defined her own situation with him as unique.

Though neither embraced overt romance, they had their geology courses in common ... and the sex was unbelievable. For a man at the relatively young age of twenty-three, he knew how to move with uninhibited skill. That alone created a powerful attraction for her. He was slightly reckless in his ways, unconcerned with politically correct issues or the repercussions of bad choices. His ability to enjoy life as it came in a series of moments was refreshing, even exciting. She could imagine years with this man.

"Al?"

"Uh-huh?" He took another sip of his beer.

"Do you want to get married?"

A momentary pause as he swallowed ... "OK."

It was as simple as that.

***

Donna's table was a busy one. Groups of students kept stopping by, like flocks of geese never straying far from the pack. Donna feigned preening at the attention, since it was more a function of logistics. Their table was directly between the bar and the dance floor.

As always, Jen was fine on her own. Her only unsociable moment was when The Velcro Couple came over, glued to each other as usual. Rolling her eyes, she loudly demanded, "Who needs another drink?" and then rushed off to fill the order before anyone could really answer.

After Steve and Tina wandered away, Donna commented, "Those two should get married."

"Or get a room," Jack answered without thinking.

A second later, he recalled his thoughts about Donna in the hotel and glanced at her self-consciously. An odd look crossed her face. Then she nodded agreeably.

"Probably already did."

His secret was safe. ... Relief pounded in his chest, but he felt cheated in the process. Safety never got you anywhere. Safety gave you a nice view of nothing and let you exist within your own shell, keeping risk and pain on the other side of a glass wall where it could still taunt you. Maybe it was time to take a step out of bounds, take a damned chance for once in his life. After an unearthly long minute, he placed his arm along the back of Donna's chair and opened his mouth to finally voice the questions swimming inside him all night, all year. ...

But then, he felt an insistent tapping on his shoulder. "Let's boogie buddy," declared Jen.

With only the slightest hesitation, Jack removed his arm from Donna's chair and followed Jen, his heart pounding again with anxious relief of the delayed confrontation.

Donna sipped her drink, as the ambiance enhanced romantic possibilities impatiently budding in her mind. ... She knew there was someone for her. She could feel it somehow, the same feeling that reached her during those fast-paced dreams, but when would this person pop into her life and say, "It's me! I'm the one!"

Trevor Simmons suddenly passed across her line of vision, when he approached Donna's table with a beer in hand. Moving as though he had nowhere special to be just then, he took an empty seat next to her and asked, "So, how did you find the math final?"

"Well, I studied pretty hard, so I think I did OK."

"Yeah, right. Koshni will probably use it as the master copy." His eyes ran over her and it felt almost rude, as if he'd used his hands instead. "You look great."

"Thanks. So do you," she replied, teeth gritting behind a polite expression.

His face reminded her of a dirty old man, reducing her to a mere catalogue of body parts. Projecting a subtle SOS, Donna glanced around. Where was Jack? As Trevor lifted his beer, his arm brushed her elbow, folded on the table. Donna resisted the urge to pull away.

A lull in the music bridged the next song, a slow tune. Jack was escorting Jen across the dance floor, holding her hand and laughing about something. Earlier, he had taken Donna's hand, so maybe it was just something he did as a dance partner. This song was the perfect squeeze tune. Perfect for her and Jack ...

Trevor was leaning in again. She pretended not to notice and concentrated her thoughts.

(I can't believe I liked you. Leave, so I can dance with Jack again.)

"Would you like to dance?"

The thought-command failed and her mother's preteen advice echoed insistently.

(When a boy asks you to dance, it's a compliment and all compliments should be acknowledged with courtesy. The polite answer is always ...)

"Yes."

They rose from their seats. As Jack and Jen approached, their hands separated. Jen leaned close to him and said something. He looked quickly at Donna's face and his own lit up with amusement. Were they making fun of her and Trevor? Employ the Mother-Look. Donna squinted and pursed her lips at them.

Jack broke first. "Jen thinks you bear a striking resemblance to a certain Star Trek underachiever."

Trevor peered at Donna and asked, "Who?" Then, a smile spread as he exclaimed, "Don't tell me—Nurse Chapel. You're right, if her hair was shorter, she'd be a dead ringer."

"That's *Ms.* Chapel to you."

She led Trevor out to the dance floor. Jack watched from his seat, his brow puckering. They danced a little too close and Trevor's hand kept snaking up. Was he trying to cop a feel right there?

Raymond set down a round of drinks and handed Jack a beer. It took a moment, but Jack remembered his manners in a nick of time.

"Oh, thanks Mr. Carlin."

"Donna told me you applied to one of the universities for the fall."

"U of A."

With another glance at the dance floor, Jack smiled casually at Donna's father. He knew that this man thought well of him. He even held a deeper awareness of Mr. Carlin's mixed fatherly emotions. Raymond had no son and Jack had no father, but in the end, Donna was this man's *daughter*—the one word encompassing the ultimate barrier to male camaraderie.

As they spoke, Jack kept one eye on his date. He thought back to his joke about Nurse Chapel, and wondered if she was angry. He'd impulsively said it in front of Trevor, an indirect show of the liberties he was allowed with her. Besides, Jen's presence brought out those kinds of jabs, but the words were also a convenient camouflage. Did Donna think he didn't care for her? And more importantly, would it matter?

From under the table, Raymond felt a sudden pressure against his leg, and glanced up to see Paula staring at him. She jerked her head to the dance floor, and then darted her eyes toward Jack.

Raymond leaned over and quietly muttered, "What? I'm supposed to dance with the kid?"

"You're not the one he wants to dance with. Pay attention."

Eyes narrowing, Raymond studied Jack afresh. Paula was right. And Donna was wrong.

Before the song ended, Trevor accompanied Donna off the dance floor, but not toward Jack's table, and a slight feeling of panic bubbled up as Jack watched their path out the door.

(Where is he going with her?)

He excused himself and cut his way through the crowd.

The foyer was filled with people. He spotted Trevor easily, mingling in a group of graduates. Trevor stuffed a folded bill into someone's suit pocket and shrugged good-naturedly. The others around him laughed.

To Jack's relief, Donna was off to the side, sitting with Jen on one of the couches, deep in discussion. They faced a large window with a view to the city.

Streetlights dotted the black landscape. It looked like an immense dance floor. He could imagine leading Donna through the glass and having her all alone out there. If Jen would leave, he could get her outside for "some air". Just them and the June sky, by those trees at the side of the building. He would circle his arms around her tightly and kiss her ... and keep kissing her until she kissed him back. Take the breath right out of her. And then ...

Pushing the thought down, he arranged a friendly face and stepped forward.

***

Jen clutched a drink in her lap, leaned her head back against the couch, and admired the city lights.

"So, what's going on? You look kind of weird. I mean weirder than usual."

"When I was dancing with Trevor, he was trying to get me to leave with him."

"And go where?"

"Well, he wasn't too specific, but the general idea was someplace where we could ..."

"But isn't he here with someone?"

"That didn't matter to him," Donna stated dryly, "God, who is this dense person and what have you done with Jen?"

"Shut up! I'm trying to be nice!"

"Oh, that's why I didn't recognize you."

Jen glanced up and wobbled her head impatiently. "So, what did you say?"

"Well, I'll give you a hint," Donna enunciated patronizingly, "I told him to go find his date. Although 'date' wasn't the only four-letter word I used."

On the heels of this, Donna almost confessed her secret feelings, but she had faced enough disappointment for one night. Jack hadn't acted in any way like a man with a purpose. So many moments tonight could have been spun into an understanding, but he was carrying himself as though the three of them were passing a lunch hour in Café-Abe. He just happened to be in a suit and she in a really nice dress.

She sighed with the frustration of seeing a toy dangled just out of reach. An undeclared confession was hers in some intangible way, but once voiced, the secret would be out of her control, demanding an answer. Losing Jack's friendship on such a special night would be worse than being targeted by someone like Trevor.

Jen saw the sadness on Donna's face and returned a look of honest surprise. Well, if that didn't beat all! Here she assumed her best friend was as infatuated with Jack as he was with her, but it was Trevor who turned her head. How could Jen have missed that one?

As Jack approached from behind, Jen's sympathetic words drifted up, "I didn't know Trevor was so important to you."

Donna didn't trust herself to speak. What if Jack really did want Jen? And what if Jen felt the same? Donna's feelings would certainly be irrelevant and by declaring them, she risked losing two friends for the price of one.

Jack stopped in his tracks. Standing directly behind them, Donna's reflection in the window clearly held a look of distress, gazing at the floor resignedly while Jen studied her. If he could see them, then a mere glance up would reveal *him* listening in. He quickly pivoted around and the sudden movement in the window caught Jen's eye. Her mind sped over the past minute. Judging from the slump in his shoulders, he must have heard a lot. A quick look sideways verified that at least he was safe from Donna's downcast eyes.

Jen bit the side of her mouth. Why does the happiness of one always depend on the unhappiness of another? She wanted to drag Jack back to Donna and say, "Here, forget Trevor! This is the person you should be with." But that kind of help had a way of backfiring. Swallowing frustration at being an unintended witness to the dilemma, Jen suggested, "Let's go back inside. I'll buy you a drink."

She bought one for Jack too, a double.

***

Leaning against the cold third-floor railing, Donna opened her yearbook. An acrid printing press smell escaped the glossy pages. Brand new.

She studied her picture, nestled among rows of graduation caps and gowns, and smiled. It was a good shot, capturing something she couldn't put her finger on, something youthful but aged at the same time. Sex appeal.

(Pretty good for a virgin.)

Flipping forward, she stopped at the sight of her long green dress. It took up half a page. Dancing in Jack's arms, it was a flattering image, his shoulders broad, an arm around her waist, smiles toward the camera. No wonder everyone thought they were screwing.

There was something else too; Jack's leg was raised to take a step. It was certainly normal in the context of a dance, but Donna frowned.

(It looks like he's walking away. No it doesn't. Why would I think that?)

A fist suddenly batted her shoulder. "Hey Don, checkin' out the pics? Have you seen page forty-two?"

Donna suspiciously turned pages while Jen smirked at Jack.

"See there? That's my butt!" Jen proclaimed, pointing dramatically.

"Wow, what they say about cameras is true. ... Which one's yours?" Donna asked, knowing full well that Karen had thirty pounds on Jen.

"The *smaller* one."

Jack patted her shoulder consolingly. "Sure Jen. Who's the other one?"

"Karen Copeland, but she'd never have done it if she knew the yearbook crew was gonna be there."

Like Trevor wasn't enough humiliation without having her butt immortalized. He'd gotten Karen in bed grad night and was now avoiding her at all costs.

"Yeah," Jack remarked, "It's funny how their cameras caught the top bleacher instead of the three foul shots I made."

Jen puckered her lips. "Well, rumor has it our friend here made a call."

"You gave them *my* name?" Donna exclaimed, horrified, "So they think that's *my* butt?"

"Oh, relax. I said I was Karen. So did you get them?"

"Yeah, they're in there." Donna gestured to the swollen knapsack at her feet. "You guys owe me. They're freakin' heavy."

Looking around covertly, Jack reached in and pulled out three medium-sized watermelons.

Jen protested, "Where are the pumpkins?"

"You find a pumpkin in June, I'll put an eight by ten of my butt in the Herald. Here, take this one, Don. OK, ready?"

One last look around for teachers.

"One, two, three! Heads up!" Jack screamed.

Splat—splat—splat!

"Go! Go!"

Racing to the far exit, they pushed roughly past pockets of kids lingering in front of the school. Donna squinted at the bright sunlight, which shot off a glossy page of her yearbook straight into Jack's eyes. As he turned away momentarily, that curious part of her imagination saw him walking away from her again. She looked down to find the yearbook open to the picture of them dancing.

Snapping it shut before Jen could point and comment, Donna declared, "Mission accomplished! Let's go get Jen hammered and sell her for sex."

"Excellent suggestion," Jen concurred.

But Jack didn't laugh and Donna wondered if he'd seen the picture and if that's why he'd turned away.

***

CHAPTER 9

Jack spent the next four years in Edmonton. When he first arrived, college life was new and interesting. He knew it would be hard to attain the grades Donna did year after year. He also knew he'd need a hefty student loan and a part-time job. Maintaining an apartment without a roommate was costly, but after living with his mother and Mark for so long, a secluded lifestyle was appealing. If it meant delivering pizzas three nights a week, so be it.

Other activities filled his time too—sports and women—which followed in exactly that order. There were certainly enough women around campus and several would drift a subtle message in his direction, but they never seemed very interesting next to Donna and the effervescent Jen. He'd asked a few out and even perfected the one-handed bra release, but women had uncanny radar about these things. The more determined the hands, the quicker they were deflected.

His friends chided him about his James Dean magnetism. Girls started conversations with Jack in an open-ended way, while being patiently polite with his friends, who futilely mimicked Jack's approach by acting aloof to women. They even named it: "The Slack Jack Attack." He wasn't consciously employing "an approach". He was just very watchful before making any sort of move on a girl, but if the guys interpreted that as sexual strategy, then at least it kept his virginity hidden.

Jack heard his buddies refer to girlfriends and one-nighters—some referring to both—and he tried to talk as though he'd been laid as much as the next guy. One time, he described the difficulty in separating ideal qualities from those merely acceptable, and he was almost laughed out of the room.

"Tits are tits, Petrasyk! Who gives a shit what options are in the package? Get in the fucking car and go for a ride!"

Jack laughed along rather than clarify the struggle between loneliness and standards. And he was often lonely.

The campus gym helped, thanks to a small set of students who traded muscle-building secrets. "Plate-heads", as Donna called them. The effort showed in his shoulders and chest. Gratifying to see the shape of a full-grown man in the mirror, it reminded him that somewhere another man existed who probably resembled him. Sometimes, Jack stared into the mirror, imagining an older version of his face, the steel ring prominent on his finger.

His other social outlet was a group of people from his psychology class, who met every Wednesday for coffee and poker in the Students' Union building, among the old dusty chairs. Between card hands, they moaned about their difficult courses and how each professor claimed the highest priority. They were an eclectic group with one thing in common; no one was close to graduating.

Only Jack. One more semester of criminology and he was home free, just figure out where to take this education. Most of the crim grads were steered toward probationary work, but that often entailed counseling offenders, not his thing. Despite this dilemma, Jack was looking forward to getting out of school entirely. The academic stuff didn't come as naturally as it did to Donna.

Four years had done little to offset his preoccupation with her. He saw her whenever he drove to Calgary, only to return cursing himself for not taking the bull by the horns and declaring his feelings. At prime moments of opportunity, something always stopped him, a hesitation with no discernable roots, nor purpose. It wasn't the fear of rejection he experienced in high school. It was more like ill-timing, as if a particular tempo piloted his affairs, a rhythm that would eventually settle into a perfect cadence, and only then would success be his. Too many times, he'd been staring her straight in the face with the words at hand, when an inner voice whispered its advice *(Not yet. It's not time yet. ...)*, and the words would stop in his throat.

Occasionally, a girl would catch his eye because she shared Donna's facial structure or shapely curves, but the differences always outweighed any similarities. The one trait that seemed to turn his head most was a certain style of hair. His base image of Donna came from the first day they met, when her hair only reached her ears. In his mind, that was how he'd always see her.

One girl in the poker group actually came close. Michelle, a second-year student, was a petite brown-haired girl with a soft voice to mask the decisiveness of her opinions. She stood out because of her eyes, Donna's shade of green. She tended to take a backseat in the conversations, as though daydreaming, until she would unexpectedly contribute an astute comment.

For the past year, Jack had never seen her with a man. Maybe she was a dyke like some of the guys claimed. Would explain that gal she brought to poker last week. ...

In Michelle's absence, the other guys strategized getting her in bed, which effectively meant none had succeeded, but the mere subject caused Jack to hesitate for fear of becoming just another guy on the make. He imagined her reaction: Couldn't any of them hang out without spotting a potential lay? Safer to shuffle the cards and talk course work.

Recently, there was a lull in the numbers showing up—a combination of Christmas finals demanding a minimum study time, and the unseasonably warm weather in Edmonton through December. Today, Michelle found Jack alone, sipping a flavored coffee and perusing a textbook. Comfortably settled into a ragged couch with his feet stretched out on a low table, one would almost think he slept across from a big screen TV.

She placed her knapsack on the concrete floor and plopped down beside him.

"Hi Jack."

For a brief moment, his eyes went wide. Then he exclaimed, "Geez, I didn't recognize you. Your hair looks good."

His smile had been weary when she first sat down, but now he studied her face with an unabashed alertness. It was one of the many small signs she had been waiting for.

Playing self-consciously with the wisps of hair along her neck, she said, "Thanks. It feels kind of weird. It's been down to here since I can remember." She placed a flat hand at waist level. "You get stuck in a pattern. You know, boys have short hair, girls have long."

"Well, I'm proof that's not written in stone, but I suppose I should chop it when I start going for interviews. Employers are a little squeamish about guys with ponytails."

Jack finished the last of his coffee and looked longingly at the empty cup.

"I'm gonna get a refill. You want one?"

"Yes, please. Medium, loaded." She started to reach for her wallet.

"Sorry, I only deal in large doses of caffeine. It's on me."

She smiled. Another sign ... "All right, thanks."

A few minutes later, he handed her a warm cup. She watched him settle back into the ratty couch and her thoughts fell into place.

(He could be at a Parliamentary dinner or a kindergarten picnic and this is exactly how he'd look, like he's just supposed to be there.)

The ease he exuded, that uncocky confidence gave her a feeling that whatever he said was the exact truth. It was something in his eyes. She took a chance.

"Jack, there's something I've been meaning to ask you."

"Shoot," he replied, uselessly blowing the heat off the top of his coffee. It would cool when it cooled and not a moment sooner. He hoped she didn't want to borrow his calculator again. He was sick of everyone wanting it all the time.

She lowered her voice. "Well, I was wondering ... I mean, I've wondered for a while ... if ah, you've ever thought of asking me out?" As her hands grasped the cup evenly in her lap, she scrutinized his face, but despite the uncertainty in her presentation, he saw determination in her eyes. Not a dyke after all.

A familiar fantasy flashed through his mind: pressing her into the back of his car and tearing her underwear off. It was even easier to envision with her hair like that. She'd struggle against his strong arms, a dark sparkle to her eyes, but she wouldn't be able to help herself. He fast-forwarded through the foreplay and skipped to the main event. She probably wouldn't hold back, her quiet gasps intensifying along with his thrusts, and he would push harder in response.

His fantasies of Donna often took on a rough edge, tempered by mutual raw passion. With Michelle, the fantasy was simpler. He would overpower her and she would give in, happily of course. This scenario frequently traveled through his mind with little hope of fruition, but her proclaimed interest immediately painted the fantasy with potential. He hoped his reddening face would escape her sharp eyes.

When would she give in? How long did it usually take? Judging from his experience, women couldn't get their shit together on that score. They'd be giving every conceivable signal and then snub the man's logical attempt at sex. You had to be careful what you tried and how you tried it. Assumptions were tricky, but maybe if he made more of them, he would get somewhere faster. Maybe Michelle was the answer to all his frustrations. Even if she wasn't Donna, he could close his eyes and almost believe she was.

Within five seconds, he answered, "There's nothing I'd like more."

Jack took her dancing the next night. When he ordered a beer, she maintained an unreadable face and declined any alcohol herself. He sensed that she was watching him disapprovingly, and switched to soda for the remainder of the evening.

Despite her uncertainty of two-stepping, she was an easy partner to lead.

"Two right, one left. That's all it is," he explained.

"It never changes?"

"Not unless we spin or dip."

And without warning, Michelle found herself bent backward over his arm, looking at walls upside down. Her sharp laugh disappeared into the music. Just as quickly, he pulled her upright and continued around the floor.

Only one drawback tarnished their date. Even though the room and music were totally different from his high school graduation, looking into her eyes aroused bittersweet nostalgia. There was a piece of Donna here, stepping lightly from side to side. As much as he knew who was here at this moment, Michelle's presence was glossed over with the likeness of another.

***

For Donna, university life was merely a step up from high school. She devoted summers taking on more courses to complete a biology degree in three years. The course work required a lot of time and effort, but she maintained a consistently high grade point average, high enough to allow early entrance into the medicine program.

The fall of 1990 was also a time of new beginnings for Raymond. He married Paula in a quiet ceremony. Then, they departed on a three week honeymoon, leaving Donna the run of the house. Unfortunately, she didn't appreciate the peace until their return. Now, Paula was there permanently, moving about the kitchen, trying to quit smoking, making coffee in the morning.

With the sudden expansion of the family, the morning routines ceased to be solely under Donna's direction. Small alterations in the household started occurring at Paula's hands. A garage sale made room for a new living room suite. When the three of them rearranged furniture, Paula seemed bent on finding some combination to best cover up the memories of Raymond's past, and Donna could barely contain her annoyance. But the real line was crossed when she discovered her old storybooks in the garage sale pile.

"Those aren't for sale! My mother used to read those to me."

"Oh, sorry. Why don't you keep them in your room?"

"Because they don't just mean something to me."

Lifting one off the pile, Donna thumbed through it.

"For example, this one has a story behind the story."

As she glanced through the Pat-a-cake rhyme, a memory came to life on the page. Two pairs of hands—one large and one small—connected and separated in concert. Donna didn't know if the memory was real or just a moving image created from wishful thinking. Ever since her father had explained the origin of her nickname, she could imagine her mother's part with perfect clarity. The hands came together, the hands came apart, but they always returned to continue the connection. The book made it possible.

Donna expected her father to support her on this one conflict, but Raymond stepped in and said, "I think the books would be better kept in your room."

It was a strange turning point. Squeezed into an uncomfortable corner by the two of them and put to the test, Raymond chose the title of "husband" over "father". Donna started looking for an apartment the next day.

***

As a girlfriend, Michelle turned out to be both more and less than Jack expected. Mature for her twenty years, she maintained her own space and resisted publicly clinging to him. In private, she was affectionate, although still reserved. She had a roommate, but they hardly interacted, which Jack considered a little odd. Compared to Donna and Jen, Michelle presented a cautious manner as though she carried secrets of national security. Trust no one! Jack wondered about her unexcitability, but recognized the benefit of having a girlfriend who kept the details of her personal life quiet.

Her fondness for board games was a big point in her favor. They often invited people over from the poker group as a stress release. Exuding a natural sort of charm, she suggested activities like tobogganing and backgammon and similar pursuits that sported good clean fun.

If Michelle's appearance and personality shared elements of Donna, then she also contained some of Jen's traits subdued. Though honest, her observations were not as blatantly worded as Jen's. She seemed unafraid of the world, striding through her university courses and other commitments with calm focus.

Jack admired Michelle, who carried herself with purpose, since he was still undecided about his own future. He attributed it to the difference in their upbringings. His was an inconsistent childhood with a single parent and frequent location changes, while she was raised in a typical middle class home in Red Deer. Jack imagined how the stability of one home would have shaped his personality, especially with a father around. Michelle was so mature.

(She may be quiet, but this girl knows exactly where her ass starts and ends.)

This became readily apparent early in their relationship. At first, he thought they would end up in bed in a matter of days, a few weeks at the most. When he kissed her, her whole body responded, melting bit by bit into his, but just when it would get steamy, she'd pull away and say, "No Jack, I'm not ready yet." Over and over this happened and he started to wonder what the problem was. If she were eager enough to be his girlfriend, why delay the inevitable? Finally, he learned the truth.

It was the first night they were watching a movie in his bed. With only a candle to overpower the dark glow of the television, Jack gradually maneuvered them into a comfortable position. His hand caressed her arm and waist, until she completely relaxed. He started kissing her mouth, her neck ... but when he slid his hand across her chest, she abruptly pushed him away and sat up.

"What's the matter?" he asked shortly as his arm fit around her waist.

She let it stay, though her back remained rigid. "Look, there's something I should have told you before."

Several fears sped through his mind at once and he almost regretted asking, but curiosity prevailed.

"I was really hurt by my last boyfriend. I don't even know if he was my boyfriend. When I wanted him to do different things with me, he always found an excuse, except if we were going to be alone like this."

She swept a hand across the romantic lighting of Jack's bedroom.

"I kept asking him if he'd come to my church, 'cause that was kind of important to me, but he never would. I don't know why I gave in. Right after it happened, he was so distant. It's like we were never a couple in the first place. I don't want to be with someone who's just trying to get me in bed all the time."

Jack leaned back against the upholstered headboard and ignored the scratchy fabric across his shoulders. Although relieved he wasn't the problem, she was equating his actions with her past. How fair was that? And to add to that, she was cutting off his chances of sex. At least he finally understood why she was so skittish.

Now, how to get around this ... Ten different options were instantly analyzed, all ending with Michelle shutting down and putting him even further from that ultimate goal.

Then Jack remembered a story from one of his lifting buddies. This guy had tried every trick in the book to swing his girlfriend into bed, but she was locked up tighter than Fort Knox. It wasn't until he pretty much gave up that she gave in, and quite willingly too, all because a few choice words passed the reins of control.

Just be convincing.

"Look, I'm not him," Jack responded gently and he lightly stroked her back, "It's no big deal. I can wait."

Her contented smile was so adorable that he almost fell in love with her right then and there. It was the kind of soft accepting expression Donna would give him. Michelle's green eyes crinkled in at the corners and she snuggled into his arms, abandoning the earlier stiffness and separation.

And promptly fell asleep.

With a sigh, he stared at the television and gritted his teeth. He felt badly for her experience with the other guy, even jealous, but the real annoyance was his reverse psychology backfiring.

The church part was no surprise. However, he'd underestimated its importance. Daily prayer and Bible reading put her beyond a simple Sunday worshiper. In time, Jack came to attribute her charismatic strength to these beliefs. It was what really set her apart from other girls.

This combination of femininity and intellect was sexy, but they were qualities founded upon a deeply focused spirituality that elicited his grudging respect. He decided to keep his hands to himself, at least until she would loosen up a little. Often sharing his bed, she cuddled up to him maddeningly, while fantasies of force plagued him.

(I should have just picked up someone in a bar. ...)

***

Donna found an apartment near the university, about a twenty-minute walk away. The solitude allowed an effective study routine, and through winter, she adjusted to the monotony of late nights and early mornings. Jen tried to drag her out to various parties on campus, but Donna's nose was firmly planted in her books. Finally in April, Jen came over unexpectedly and threatened to make noise outside her apartment unless Donna agreed to a drink in Motel Village.

They sat at a tall round table on two bar stools. Jen leaned over and shouted, "I love this place. Everybody's totally shallow." She pointed three tables over. "See that guy in the yellow shirt?" He's here all the time and uses the same line on anything in a skirt. Last Monday, he did his little song and dance on me. Then the next day, I curled my hair. He didn't recognize me and tried the same routine all over again."

"What was the line?"

Jen slouched and adopted an empty expression. "Do you have a map? Because I'm lost in your eyes ..."

"No way! What did you say?"

"That it sounded better last night when I was drunker. Then he says, 'Hey, you *looked* better last night when *I* was drunker.'"

Donna's eyes quickly narrowed. "Oh ... you didn't. You went home with him!"

"I didn't go home with him," Jen grinned as she popped upright again, "*He* went home with *me*."

"For Christ's sake, the guy throws you an insult and you lap it up! If he gave you a left hook, you'd probably rush him to the altar."

"Hey, if I'd had to sit through another evening of pathetic lines ... It wasn't 'til he showed some balls that I wanted to see his. I mean, where's the intellect? Speaking of which, I'm amazed you're here without a stupid book super-glued to your hand."

"Yeah, well, I haven't been out anywhere since Christmas break, and even then I felt guilty. I thought pre-med was tough, but it's nothing to this. Today we got into this long debate about coma states. Half the class felt a person isn't really alive. You know, brain function is next to nothing and why keep people on machines? The other half argued that brain function shouldn't be the prime determinant. One guy made an interesting point: What if unconsciousness produced a better state of being?"

"And this guy made it into med school?"

"I thought you'd totally get off on this. Think about it. What if you hit your ultimate potential there, like the relaxation of hypnosis? You could—"

Jen made gagging sounds. "You know, there *is* a world beyond school."

"And what a world it is when the highlight is taking home offensive drunk strays."

"Well, it beats a coma. God Donna, loosen up! You really need to get hammered."

A waitress in a short skirt and low-cut blouse stopped at their table, and gave them a lukewarm smile. She saved the warmer ones for single men, who always tipped better than women. For the hundredth time that night, she asked, "What can I get you?"

"Rye and water."

"A draught, thanks."

The waitress scribbled it down and moved to the next table.

"Hey, I got a letter from Jack," announced Donna.

"Yeah? How's old J.P?"

"He's in the middle of finals. He's gonna be in town this weekend."

"Why's he coming here if he has finals?"

"I don't know. Maybe he needs a stress break."

"By driving for three hours? Some break."

"Maybe it is for him. You drink, he drives, and I ... Well, OK, I don't really do anything to escape. Maybe I will get drunk. Anyway, the point is that everyone's different."

"Spoken like a true diplomat."

"Well, somebody has to cushion the world from you. Do you want to have lunch tomorrow, the three of us?"

Looking off to the side, Jen smiled slyly. "If I have it my way, I'm going to *be* someone's lunch tomorrow."

She jerked her chin toward the entrance. Two guys, one tall with sandy blonde hair and a wiry build. His friend was shorter and stockier with black hair.

Donna covertly checked them out. With her eyes still on them, she leaned back toward Jen and determined, "The short one's my type."

"Why do you always like the shorter guys?"

"'Cause you can see a face when you dance ... Yes I know," Donna added, rolling her eyes, "When you're doing the horizontal hokey pokey, no one's tall!"

The two newcomers were still scoping the room, apparently looking for someone in particular.

(Hope it's not their girlfriends.)

The waitress arrived with their drinks and waited impatiently while they dug for their wallets. Waving at the ten-dollar bill in Donna's hand, Jen instructed, "Put that away," and gave the waitress her own bill with a moderate tip. The waitress didn't look impressed.

They watched the two men join a group along the wall and Jen smiled, noting the lack of women there. She confidently stated, "Betcha I go home with the blonde."

"Must you have all the toys? Besides, how do you know he'll pick you?"

"Because they don't have any choice in the matter. Haven't you figured that out yet? The only reason they approach you is because you send the Welcome Signal."

Donna raised one eyebrow.

"Trust me. You have all the control here. And this should work well tonight."

"Why? What do you mean?"

"Well, look at us. We're dressed good, sleazy—me more than you of course—but not so sleazy they'll wonder who's been there before. I have the sexy drink. You have the friendly Hey-I'm-a-Girl-Who-Likes-a-Beer drink. I send the signals and you keep them here with that med school shit. Guys love it when the girl has a career. You're a potential jackpot. Just don't start up with that coma crap or they'll run for their lives."

"No, we certainly wouldn't want something as silly as an IQ needlessly trampling over your orgasmic potential."

"Exactly."

They finished their first drink and the waitress was quickly on hand with another round. The place was starting to fill up with people shouting to each other over the music. Donna watched as more bodies filled the dance area.

The dark-haired guy was walking toward them. In her peripheral vision, she saw his large shoulders moving through the crowd. Closer and closer he came, weaving past tables. Had he noticed her?

But at the height of the moment, he breezed past with no more than a glance. Disappointment and relief mingled uncomfortably within her. Safe now, she leaned over to catch a back view of his jeans and once he disappeared from sight, Donna grinned at Jen.

But Jen was looking across the room. "Well, that should get back to him quick enough."

"What?"

"His buddies were watching you watch him. It was a test. Congratulations, you just sent out your very first signal, although we may have to work on the subtlety angle."

Donna's eyes darted across the room, where three guys were openly grinning at her with beers raised in a salute. Closing her eyes tightly, she shook her head. One hand delivered a short wave. The other hid her face.

The blonde said something to his buddies. Then, coming directly to Jen's side, he asked her to dance. Jen smiled at Donna as if to say, 'See, I always get what I want,' and hopped off the bar stool.

"Hold the fort," she commanded, as she strode to the dance floor.

Donna sat awkwardly and sipped her drink.

(Just hang a big "Pathetic Single" sign over me with an arrow pointing down.)

Pounding music reverberated at steady intervals, punctuating the buzz of the crowd. A hazy mist of smoke glazed the dance floor. As it thickened to a rolling pooling depth, it scurried and swirled around the dancers' feet. Donna was transfixed at the people seemingly moving through clouds.

(Why is dry ice such a fascinating sight? Glad Jen's guy didn't ask me to dance. Zero rhythm. Do I move like that when I'm drunk? How drunk should I get toni—)

Suddenly, she felt a distracting sensation as someone touched her shoulder. Automatically turning to greet Jack, instead Donna was faced with the black-haired man.

***

78

CHAPTER 10

"Hi, I'm buried under a mountain of books right now, but if you have the means to clear my student loan, I'll call you back. Please relay all relevant information, including last year's tax return after the—" *Beep!*

"Hi Don. I just got in. I'll be at my mom's house tonight. Uh, call me between chapters. Bye."

Jack lowered the handset with quiet aggravation. The one time he wanted to catch her at home, she had gone out somewhere. She never went out. Must be at the library. She was always studying.

He went to the privacy of his old bedroom and lay on the bed, stretching his solid arms comfortably above his head. A week ago, he'd been lying in a bed like this, deep in the recesses of a dream, when he felt a jab in his side.

"Jack, wake up."

"Huh?" he squinted.

It was her … here in bed with him. Her green eyes drew him closer and he took her face in his hands firmly, fearing that she might disappear. Readying his lips, he realized something was wrong. Her hair—it was supposed to be blonde, not brown. Instantly, he stepped completely out of the dream and let his hands drop from Michelle's face. His shoulders and head fell back heavily against the pillow, and the hands that had held her face so lovingly now rubbed his eyes.

A pained expression paled her face.

"Who's Donna?"

"Donna?" he responded with surprise, "She's just a friend. Someone in Calgary. Known her for years. Why?"

"You were talking in your sleep. Friend, eh? Could have fooled me the way you said her name. You thought I was her just now, didn't you?"

"No," he said in exasperation, "It was just a dream. I have about a hundred of them a night. In any case, she *is* just a friend, which is more than you can say about Colin. I mean the guy's still in your head. ... You didn't think I knew that, did you?"

Michelle's mouth almost dropped open. Watchful, she sat back against the headboard.

Savoring the way he'd deflected her suspicions with his own, he ungraciously stated, "Yeah, you got nothing to say now. Tell me—if he called you tomorrow, would you even bother with a 'Dear John'?"

The expression of stiff fortitude abruptly left her face as her chin quivered. Bending her face down into her hands, she started sobbing quietly.

(Oh, crap. Women's tears. No fair.)

Her experience with Colin had made Jack so cautious with her. Now, he realized just how much and it had nothing to do with sex. Maybe he'd sensed this all along. Maybe it was what made him hedge his bets and keep Donna in the back of his mind. There was also the knowledge that he would be graduating soon and moving back to Calgary, while Michelle would return to her parent's house in Red Deer for the summer, possibly for the next year. She was considering taking time off school to work and build up some cash reserves. Though closer to Calgary than Edmonton, Red Deer was still a hefty drive, which served to keep his urges in line, even if the thought of Donna didn't.

Michelle's tears made him feel callous, despite the complexity of their situation. Was it really that complicated? He was with her because she was a little bit like Donna, and a little bit is better than nothing. She was with him because she was on the rebound. ...

Her disquieting resemblance to Donna satisfied needs built up over the space of five years. He knew Michelle deserved more and debated confessing this, but after her declaration of celibacy, a piece of resentment had been planted. He never conceived of a girlfriend who would refuse that side of him. His friends would certainly raise an eyebrow if he told them, so it put him in a strange position. To the outer world, he was the guy who was nailing Michelle, but the truth of her physical refusal was nothing short of rejection. It was the way people made him feel for most of his life—his mother, his brother, kids in school after school.

Donna and Jen were the only people who seemed to care without question, without conditions or intricate problems to unravel. They didn't require kid gloves. They just accepted everything about him, pulling pieces of his personality out for inspection and allowing him to do the same. Michelle wasn't like that. Though strong-minded and sweet and countless other great things, she was unattainably private. Jack knew how to embrace everything she had to offer, everything except what was most important to her.

After her tears tapered off, she peered at him with red eyes, as though he had just slugged her. Then, she got out of bed. The mattress shook like a brief shiver. The movement jostled him to protest her departure, but her squared shoulders allayed any words he could have added.

"Jack, you don't know what you want. It isn't just about saying a name in your sleep. I've known for months that you aren't really with me. I think you should take the summer to figure it out."

As she dressed, he only watched in silence.

Michelle's parting words were still fresh in his mind a week later. When she left his bedroom, it felt like he'd lost his best friend, but after sleeping on it, he concluded that his real best friend was Donna, and she was someone he'd never had in the first place. That was the root of the problem. Michelle was a mere substitute, a square peg being shoved into a round hole. This realization became the catalyst that sparked Jack to settle things with Donna, once and for all. The decision set in his mind, it would have to be followed through.

If only Donna would pick up the phone.

***

"Hi, I'm Ric."

His buddies must have signaled him that he'd passed the Walk-by Test. He looked even better close up. He was probably her own age, maybe a little older, with a clean-cut face and very straight teeth. Donna's first thought was that in another time and place, he could have been a pirate, strong and ruthless against gales of wind snapping past his broad shoulders.

She barely stopped herself from responding, "Ahoy there matey!" and instead, looked him squarely in the face and answered, "Donna" as she put out her hand. The corners of his lips turned upward. He was either amused or impressed at her concise formality—she couldn't tell from those black eyes—but he shook her hand strongly. No weak grip there.

They exchanged their specifics over another beer: Ric Guzzo, Italian, student in mechanical engineering, fourth year. In fact, all of them were engineering students. It was funny how these guys shared the same look: rugged, masculine, and arrogant. Dave, Tony, Mike, another Mike, and some foreign name she couldn't pronounce. The guy with Jen was Peter. Donna would forget every name by the next beer.

Ric sat beside her, asking polite questions about her studies, while staring straight into her eyes with his own dark ones and nodding at her assertions. At the intimate sight of them, she couldn't remember what

she'd been saying. Whatever it was, she just hoped it made sense. He was
awfully attractive.

Ric bought Donna another beer and asked for a slow dance. Replying,
"Sure," she colored as though an entirely different question had been
discussed.

The possibilities in her smile coaxed him closer, and he circled his
arms tightly around her waist. As they swayed rhythmically, he leaned in
as though to whisper in her ear. She could feel the heat of his breath glaze
her neck.

Then déjà vu swept over her again, a dichotomy of the familiar coloring
the new, and she startled at its intensity. The pattern of his shirt, the smell
of this nightclub, even the song playing was somehow already logged in
her brain.

She seemed to experience an inordinate number of déjà vu episodes,
although they had decreased in recent years. It had happened often during
grade twelve. Usually she could explain them away, but she couldn't
attribute this one to anything in her past. Donna had never set foot in this
place before. And Ric was a complete stranger ... but he sure didn't feel
like one.

She arched her neck just enough to look in his eyes, and suddenly
everything was new again, new and uncertain.

There is a point during a song like this that an understanding takes
place. Ric's lips pulled her to that point and beyond. He kissed her once,
twice, and one more time.

"What's your number?" he asked, taking her hand firmly.

She stepped close, lifted a pen from her purse, and flicked open a
button on his shirt. After printing her phone number backwards across his
collarbone, she instructed, "Just don't shower tonight."

Jen congratulated Donna all the way home.

***

Donna tried to hide from the train thundering around the corner. She
had slept longer than usual for a Saturday. There was always so much
material to study; it easily filled her weekends. Finally, the shrill noise was
too much and rolling over, she reached blindly. And missed. A weak groan
escaped when a sudden pain dug into her forehead. Her free hand tried
ineffectively to suppress the throbbing and she reached again.

"Hello?"

"Hi, this is Ric ... from last night. Did I wake you up?"

Bolt upright now, Donna rubbed her eyes. Her voice immediately
acquired a woven coherence, although her mind was still a step behind.

"No, um … I was … I was just studying." Grabbing a magazine off the nightstand, she rattled it a few inches from the earpiece. "Time for a break anyway."

"I've been studying too—mostly my mirror. Your threes look like eights. I've called four wrong numbers so far."

"What do you know? A numerically challenged engineer."

"On a good day. But seeing as I passed in only five tries, what do I get for my effort?"

"How about an eye exam? Those were clearly threes."

"No fair. I was distracted by your long brown hair."

Donna tried to contain a giggle. A small laugh wouldn't hurt her head too much.

"OK, enough small talk," Ric decided, "Come for lunch."

"Today?"

"No, next year. That way, we'll be real hungry."

This time the laugh couldn't be contained and it shot a nasty pain through her temple. She took a moment to answer.

"And a smart-ass to boot. How can I refuse?"

"When should I pick you up?"

"I thought you did last night. … Oh, give me an hour," she said, her tentative commitment with Jack and Jen swept aside. "Do you want directions or can you overcome that reading problem long enough to decipher a map?"

"And she calls *me* a smart-ass. I'll take the map. I'm assuming it was written by someone sober."

For those few minutes, Donna almost forgot about her exploding head, but once the phone was reconnected to its cradle, the unhappy task of separating herself from this warm quiet bed was before her.

Every step to the bathroom felt as though wading through mud. With squinting eyes, she misjudged the dresser and slammed against its side. A set of picture frames toppled over, clattering to the floor. One clipped her toes. Closing her eyes to the noise and pain, she blindly carried on.

The shower helped, but that reluctant heaviness taunted every move, "Don't go too fast. Don't do it. OK, just for that, I'm going to give you a great big spiky pain right *here*." And she would wince, pressing the spot across her eyebrows. It was akin to ice cream spikes … or the accident. Getting hit on the head was like being drunk and hung over at the same time.

She stood in front of her closet.

(What should I wear? I should call Jen. No, Jen would say go sleazy.)

Donna thought she'd made enough of an invitation on the dance floor last night. And then scrawling her phone number across his chest—a nice slutty touch. Better go with damage control, casual and conservative. A beige sweater and her favorite old pair of jeans. There, fine. Some makeup, but not too much. She wondered if Ric would be equally impressed with her today. The latter part of the evening was hazy, but she distinctly remembered his lips on hers and the thought made her catch her breath.

Time check—he would be here in twenty minutes. God, her head hurt. She resolved never to drink more than one beer and popped back some aspirin. Closing her eyes, she commanded the pills to work.

The phone rang. She considered ignoring it, but what if it was him calling? Maybe he was having trouble finding her place. No, he couldn't be that numerically challenged. This was stupid.

"Hello?"

"Hi Don! How's it going?"

"Good! Did you just get in?"

"Last night. I left a message, but it didn't include my tax return."

Donna saw the flashing light on the answering machine and muttered, "Oh, I forgot to check messages. ... Jen got me loaded in Motel-Hell. Just why do we need twelve motels lumped together like that? Anyway, what are you doing later this afternoon? Wanna meet at The Bean?"

Jack was quick to reply, "How about lunch?"

"Can't. I met a guy last night and thanks to Jen's coaching, that meal's spoken for."

"Oh ... OK ah, how about The Bean at three."

"Sure. See you then J.P."

As her headache diffused, Donna relentlessly channel-surfed while time puttered along.

Time check—11:50. Anytime now.

Studying would be a lost cause today. The excitement of seeing Ric negated that kind of concentration, but hey, she deserved a day off with the mental marathon she chronically ran.

Instead she called Jen, who recommended a tight skirt and gave Donna strict instructions to phone on her return. If Jen couldn't witness the date herself, a prompt and detailed—if not embellished—post-game synopsis was in order.

11:57 ... 11:58 ...

Two polite knocks on the door and there he was, standing in her living room, similarly dressed in casual clothes, the same smile as last night. Without hesitation, he kissed her lightly and immediately, something in his eyes, a dark swarthy confidence reaffirmed their attraction. She wanted to stand there and kiss him some more, but her rumbling stomach urged her out the door. As they descended the stairs, Jack's blinking message on the machine remained unheard.

***

CHAPTER 11

The Greek restaurant was a busy place to be on a weekend. Between the red checkered tablecloths and hanging plants, the décor appeared bright and homey.

New to Donna, it was a rather out-of-the-way place, small and run down, but very friendly. The staff all seemed to know Ric by name. They catered to him and fussed over her as if she were on the arm of royalty.

She secretly wondered how many other women had sat with him at this table, making small talk. Verbal foreplay. She could imagine them: attractive, charming, but somehow not charming enough to hold his interest, and a moment of sharp anxiety took over.

After last night, Donna couldn't stomach any alcohol, but he drank two beers. He held her hand every second it was free. In the past four years, none of her dates had ever made her this nervous. Sometimes the guy approached it like a simple outing, but this one was definitely a date. He seemed to study her as though openly appraising the swiftest way to melt off her clothes. A conspicuous sensation kept running through her: the unnerving feeling that if he decided to, he would end up in her bed. It was like a flicker of a memory which hadn't happened yet, just crouched around the corner with some mysterious certainty. He would be her first and she would be helpless to resist him.

Small talk. Just focus on small talk.

"So, does anyone call you Richard or Rich?"

"No, it's Ricardo, but my parents are the only ones who call me that."

It suited him. His face was classically Italian with an exotic appeal, perfectly balanced except for the slight curve in his nose. He noticed her staring and explained offhandedly, "It got busted in a volleyball game."

Last semester, she'd studied fractures. Lifting his chin for a better look, she commented, "It must have healed well. It's hardly noticeable."

She welcomed the excuse to stare at him. When she took her hand away, his eyes narrowed and he pulled it back toward him, palm up. He traced one line with his index finger, and at his touch, she almost jumped right out of her seat.

"That's different, that loop here. Is it on your other hand?"

"Nope." She extended her right hand for him to compare.

"I thought lines were the same on both."

"No, I think the way it works is that one hand is what's destined to happen in your life, and the other is what'll happen if you follow the course of action you're on now. I guess it's not all set from birth, but I don't know which hand means what. My stepmother talks about it a lot. She's kind of odd. Do you believe in that stuff?"

"No, do you?"

"Not really. I think lines are just lines, like fingerprints, but maybe I'd believe it if I knew more about it."

She liked how he kept holding her hands while he studied them. His touch was warm, his fingers strong and smooth-skinned. Her reaction to it reaffirmed that something was smoldering from last night.

In front of her apartment building, he asked, "Are you free tonight?"

Her smile was sweet as she nodded. This girl was absolutely lovely. They walked up the two flights to her apartment arm in arm and slowly kissed their way to the couch.

Ric took his time, hovering over her face, drawing in her eyes. As his mouth followed a path along her neck and just behind her ear, small sounds escaped from the back of her throat, carried on heavy breaths. It felt so good to be tangled up with this man, who was all lips.

Reckless thoughts *(I should have found an Italian long ago!)* spun through her mind. The minutes seemed to fly by, yet there was a sparkling quality framing each moment in slow motion. In one of those moments, Donna became conscious of his hands wandering and she stopped them with her own. He didn't seem bothered. Just carry on.

The phone rang, which they willingly ignored. With the answering machine left on high volume, Jen's voice boomed out across the room. "Hey, you there? Pick up. Peter called and we're going out tonight. Oh, who am I kidding? We'll be staying in! So, how was lunch with Ricky? Yoohooooo! Don-ahhhh! Is he there? What are you guys doing? Playing scrabble? Well, spell this: C-A-L-L-M-E!" *Click.*

Every so often, Donna felt his hands getting carried away and she would break the mood, confused as to whether she really wanted them stopped or not. Part of her said, "Go ahead, it's about time anyway." Another more cautious side advised, "Wait, just wait."

Caution prevailed and she breathlessly pulled away from Ric's lips. "What time is it?"

"Two-thirty."

"I have to go. I'm meeting a friend in half an hour."

"Call her. Tell her you can't make it," he murmured in her ear.

"It's not a 'her' and he's from out of town. I can't cancel."

He raised his head.

Noting his suspicious expression, Donna added, "He's an old buddy from high school. I haven't seen him in a while."

The terse look vanished, almost. He kissed her neck, until she relaxed in his arms again.

Ten minutes later, she said, "I really have to go, Ric."

Resignedly, he lifted her to her feet, dizzy and stiff. They stood in each other's arms a minute longer, she to regain her balance and he to prolong the embrace. At 2:50, Ric left her apartment with plans to return in five hours.

***

The Bean was a rustic cafe. Rustic appealed to Jack. It matched the rough taste of coffee and made him think of mountain air, pine trees, backpacks filled with trail mixes and water bottles. If a tent were pitched in the middle of the room, nobody would have thought twice about it. Floor to ceiling windows offset the mahogany tables. Soft jazz enticed the customers to stay a little longer. It was a place that welcomed anyone to sit and read or catch up with a friend. The staff, in jeans and matching T-shirts, served steaming coffees of every kind.

Donna, Jack, and Jen had spent many summers there drinking pot after pot, debating everything from politics to cartoons. After Jen switched to decaf, the discussions lost some of their edge, but for all the good it did, the change still resembled the miniscule difference between a storm and a tornado.

Jack had chosen a sunny window table, small and comfortable. Placing two mugs down, he looked for some fake sugar.

(She'll bring her own anyway. 3:05, she's not coming.)

He cursed his timing. It bugged the hell out of him that some guy could get a date with her in one evening, when it took him months to ask her to their high school graduation. And what was he offering? Coffee seemed paltry, after another man was taking her out for a whole meal. The past week had been rough with school and Michelle. And another rooster in the henhouse didn't lighten his mood any, but at least they would meet now. After five years, he should be able to handle a few more minutes.

His plan was to come clean and see what happens, but ... Donna had met someone. That threw a big fat wrench in things. He hadn't considered that card coming into play. She was always studying, except the one night he wanted to have with her. It was like their graduation all over again. Hearing her prefer Trevor Simmons had crushed Jack, and then the prick didn't even hold her interest. How could someone so smart be so oblivious to shit right under her nose?

Time for Plan B: Find out exactly where she stood with this new guy. If Jack got the right tone from her, he'd speak up. Heads or tails. She'd be flipping a coin and wouldn't even know it.

(3:07, she's not coming.)

Donna rushed in, draping a denim jacket over the back of her chair. "Sorry I'm late. I kind of got sidetracked with that date." She pulled a small jar out of her purse and shook some powder into her coffee.

"You know you're gonna grow horns from that stuff."

"Yeah well, they'll be horns without calories."

She had never looked better, not even on their graduation night ... or was he just imagining brightness to her eyes, an untamed look of adventure across her face? Gone was the sedate girl, and in her place sat a beauty bursting at the seams. Someone had touched her spirit and it wasn't him.

"Sounds like your date went well."

"Yeah, it did. In fact, I think I've acquired a boyfriend. The restaurant was really good, not like Fioritti's, but the food was amazing. You should go there sometime. ..."

Her mind kept stealing away to Ric's lips. The faint scent of his cologne had lingered on the neck of her sweater and it was distracting. Did they really stay on her couch for over an hour?

"The baklava was about ten-thousand calories. I can feel my ass expanding as we speak. Ever had it?"

Jack shook his head distractedly and kept his eyes on his coffee. She stared at his blank expression, sensing something she couldn't put her finger on. Though always a bit reserved with others, he was never this stiff with her. If she didn't know him so well, she'd think he was utterly bored, but they never bored each other, no matter what the topic. Maybe school had him preoccupied. The last year of any program was exhausting and Jack didn't take as well to the grind.

"Jack, is everything OK?"

A glimpse of deep sadness came out of his eyes and straight through to hers. Then just as quickly, it was gone. He waved his hand absent-mindedly and replied, "Yeah, I'm fine, tired. Hard week." Then, the old Jack was back with the old Jack's smile.

In a flash of half-correct insight, Donna attributed his manner to some romance gone awry at U of A, and suddenly she felt selfish for monopolizing the conversation. Pointed questions perched eagerly on the tip of her tongue. Though tempting to pry, it was really his business.

(Oh, hell. Send in the artillery.)

"Do you want to get together with Jen and me for lunch tomorrow?"

"No, I ah, have to get back to Edmonton early. Got an exam Monday."

The lie came easily. Hadn't he been lying for five years already? He had almost spoken up and destroyed a friendship. Thank God, she'd stated her news first.

Donna's brow momentarily furrowed. He was the worst liar. What was he not telling her?

Standing beside her car in the spring sunshine, they avoided the growing puddles around their feet.

"Maybe I could introduce you to Ric the next time you're here."

"Sure—"

(Then I could introduce him to the pavement ...)

"—that would be great."

"Good. Well, have a safe trip back. Good luck on that exam."

Peering carefully, she thought her expression might entice him to open up, but he merely answered in his usual casual tone, "Yeah. See ya, Don."

They drove off in opposite directions and the literal irony was not lost on Jack.

***

That night, Donna's date with Ric was a continuation of their session on the couch. It was exhilarating and uninhibited and a little scary. After twenty-four hours, this man made her fantasies run wild. Curiosities plagued her relentlessly: what it would be like to wake up next to him, to feel his lips on other parts of her, to lift her hips against his ... but she resolved to hold off until she knew him better.

During the first two weeks, they saw each other every day, which cut into Donna's precious study time considerably, but she was happier than she'd ever been, which her fellow classmates noticed immediately.

There was no formal "Will you be my girlfriend?" question. None was needed. He called with a complimentary consistency every night. Looking forward to hearing his voice, there was something erotic about lying in bed with his words caressing her from the phone. She imagined his muscular body under the covers and his hands sliding over her skin with delightful leisure.

Ric was highly physical. Always touching her in some way, holding her hand or her waist protectively made her feel small and feminine ... and curious. It put her at odds with her shyness, but she reveled in his constant touch. After two weeks, she could barely keep her hands off him.

With his roommate devoid of a social life, privacy was exclusive at her apartment, which was exactly what made her nervous during the heat of his kisses. There were one or two close calls when she barely stopped him in time, and for a moment, she was completely powerless. That moment was as exciting as it was scary, but to her relief, he did stop and she felt an unsatisfied separation within the safety. She wondered if it would have happened any differently had they been lying in bed instead of on the couch.

Tonight, they were sitting in his car outside her building. Ric secured one arm around her back, his free hand stroking hers, but he didn't seem like himself. He looked like Jack did in The Bean, all antsy.

Usually this was the most awkward part of a date—ending the evening. Kiss him? Wait to be kissed? With Ric, those questions didn't exist. The evening automatically entailed hundreds of kisses, but tonight she wasn't sure if this would happen. Why was he so restless? Was he tired of her already?

"Are you OK?"

He lowered his eyes sheepishly. "Yeah, I just ... I have a confession to make."

"Those are always good to hear," she commented dryly.

(It's not you, it's me. I need to focus on school. I got a job in Manitoba. I met someone else. I'm sick of you not putting out. I—)

"Oh, sorry. No, it's not that bad. Well, maybe you'll think it is, being in your field and all." Carefully watching her reaction, he reached under his seat and pulled out a pack of cigarettes.

Donna almost laughed. "Is that all? God, I thought you were going to show me a picture of your wife and three kids!"

He wove his fingers through hers and squeezed her hand. "No pictures, just smokes. I don't really smoke much, just when I'm driving around, so I keep a pack handy. I didn't want to tell you. I didn't think you'd like it."

"Well, I don't, but as long as you don't do it around me, it's not my place to preach. So, what do you want to do now? Stay down here and play chimney all by your lonesome?" She batted her eyelashes with ridiculous exaggeration.

"I could stay the night."

Again he searched her face, which clouded over immediately. Explaining her lack of experience was uncharted territory. What did men think of virgins? Was it a hassle to coach a girl through her first time?

His eyes still on her, she leaned back and ran her fingers through her hair. After a minute, she began stiltedly, "Look, I have a confession to make too. ... I mean, um, I ... I'm a virgin," she finally blurted out.

"You are?"

"Are you?" she countered, suddenly feeling as though she were under a microscope, just a little chemical specimen whose sole purpose is to be studied.

"No."

Donna didn't know whether to feel relieved or disappointed. She assumed sex was no different than any other new experience—the best teacher is one who has honed his craft—but would he silently compare her to the others? Should your first partner be someone you're madly in love with or someone you'll never be madly in love with?

She was aware that they were at the point of decision, right here in his car. With a lifetime of fears boiling down into the here and now, apparently her face was transparent, because a look of comprehension came over him.

He took her hands and explained, "It doesn't matter. I'm not someone who isn't going to be there the next day." Staring into her eyes solicitously, he added, "It doesn't have to be tonight."

Donna saw him in all his sweetness and at that moment, fell in love. The sudden alteration in her face was unmistakable. Seeing only Ric, her eyes softened as she fixed a calm expression on him.

"Maybe I want it to be tonight. ..."

Surprised at the ease following those words, the fight with herself had vanished. It washed over her, settling somewhere in her knees, and gave her strange peace despite the excitement of this new commitment. But she brought herself back to earth.

"Do you have anything on you?"

"Oh, yeah, I guess you aren't on the pill, eh?"

"The pill doesn't stop everything."

"I don't have AIDS."

"Oh, were you tested recently?"

"No," he scoffed.

Donna sighed—as if a disease would simply skip over him to infect someone else—but she pushed the irritation aside, wanting nothing to affect her mood.

"Well, we still have to use them."

He smiled slyly and pulled her close. "Yes, the plural is definitely in order!"

Flushing with embarrassment, she resisted matching his grin, opened the car door, and jumped nimbly out of his grasp.

"Come on. Hurry up before I change my mind."

He chased her to the front of the building and caught her in a tight embrace. They kissed again, enveloped in anticipation.

Something surrounded her as they climbed the steps to her apartment, the feeling that something important was imminent. There was a fascination to it, like her dreams covered by a surrealistic veil of déjà vu. Every step she took drummed the words into her head *(I'm finally going to do it)* with a steady rhythm, but buried within the beat, she wondered exactly where this would lead her.

***

CHAPTER 12

"We need to talk."

As Tracy sat on the edge of the couch, Al mentally braced himself. Perfect posture only meant one thing—pissy issues to unload. Why did she always have to do this when the good shows were on? Her pinched scowl was nothing new. Their eighteen-month old daughter was getting to an energetic age, and by this time every evening, Tracy was worn out.

He remembered how they used to hit the bars before they had little Ashley—getting smashed and avoiding the Check-Stops on their way home. Those were fun days, but now they were both twenty-seven, and he was slugging it out on the oil rigs. He would go for two to six weeks at a shot, and then come home to rest before the next job out.

This last one had been long, almost seven weeks. Now, he could enjoy a whole month of holidays ahead of him. Curiously, despite the bags under his eyes, Tracy seemed to think that he should take Ashley off her hands and just let her dick away the time. Why should she be tired? She wasn't slaving the rigs.

He brought the beer up to his mouth before asking, "What's up?"

"I'm pregnant—"

His mouth spread into a wide grin and he made a victory fist. "Yay team!"

"—and I'm getting an abortion."

Al's grin evaporated. His arm fell back to the couch. "What? ... I thought you wanted another baby. I have no say in this, my kid?"

"Not while you have a beer in your hand. You said you'd to go to a meeting two months ago."

"Come on, that's just your hormones talking."

"You creep! My hormones are nothing compared to your drinking problem. It used to be a beer at the end of the day. Now, it takes a six-pack just to keep you level. You think I don't know how much you drink? You have a problem Al, but I'm not going to let it be mine ... or my kid's."

He sat silently wrestling with layers of truth. He didn't used to drink so much or so often. It was just something he did, like other people play squash.

Back in university, parties were everywhere and everyone drank. Well, almost everyone. He remembered this one girl he was seeing then. On her eighteenth birthday, she wanted to go to a movie and then play some lame board game with her friends. You were supposed to get sauced the minute you became legal, but she said it was the one day she wanted to be coherent—she had the rest of her life to get sauced. Imagine that!

Yes, looking into his wife's eyes, he could imagine that. There was a life beyond the booze, but not a comfortable one. It was like being squished into a tight little box. Zero space, certainly not enough for his family *and* his beer.

He realized he was clutching the neck of the bottle and consciously loosened his grasp.

In a deadly quiet voice, Tracy stated, "It's scheduled in four weeks. I'll give you that long to prove you can stay dry and go to meetings. If you take even one drink, I'll know ... and I'll get it done."

Al's chest sunk as a shaky sigh escaped him. This was a different world from those bar days—wild and fun, lacking the constraints of his present responsibilities. Back then, life made few demands. That time held a particular nostalgia, but now he took a careful inventory: Tracy, Ashley, work, house payments, and the possibility of another child, maybe a boy.

He suspected he was what they called a functional alcoholic, still able to keep a job and not fuck up too much, but what if that changed? What if he lost his job while Tracy was pregnant? As it was, he needed a drink just to get through an interview. He envisioned the inevitable spiral downward, and compared it to the lifeline she offered him. A meeting, a simple meeting. Twenty others like him, drinking coffee and confessing their alcoholic sins. He licked his lips slowly and made a decision.

"Trade you for a phone book," he said, holding the beer in his outstretched hand.

***

Jen was correct in her prediction—she and Peter ended up in bed. If forced to choose one word to describe it, she would say "thorough", but more than anything, he was fun. No cajoling her into bed with well-timed lines or overpowering kisses. With such a relaxed guy, they seemed to fall onto the mattress without much effort from either.

Later, they settled in to watch TV and shared a bottle of white wine amidst the twisted sheets, alternating between feeling excited and silly. When she went to retrieve the bottle, he expected her to produce two ordinary drinking glasses. Instead, the wine glass she handed him was delicately crafted. This tiny piece of elegance contrasted with her straightforward manner. He had assumed a simple affair with Jen. Wine was something on level with other romantic gestures putting him on his guard, and he hoped he would enjoy this night without a complicated aftermath.

Noting his hesitation, she arranged two pillows and reclined back with her knees bent.

(Oh, relax. You're hardly marriage material.)

"Are you graduating right away?"

"Yeah," he answered, "You?"

"No, I have to redo a couple of courses in the fall. I missed a lot of classes. Didn't like the other Artsies. They just sapped me of all the energy I had, so I got behind."

"It's like that in my program too. You're in the same classes with the same guys all the time."

"How long have you known Ric?"

Peter lay flat, doubling a pillow under his head, and curled the back of his neck to taste the wine. "About a year. We've had to partner on some labs."

"Oh, I thought Donna said you play volleyball or something."

"Like we have time for that? No, I just needed a ride to the bar. I wasn't thrilled either."

"Why?" Jen quizzed, her interest suddenly peaked, but Peter shook his head as if tossing something aside.

"Just don't like hanging with him. When Ric gets set on something, there's no changing it."

"Like Donna?"

"Yeah, he told all of us to stay clear of her. Don't know about you, but I don't like someone telling me who I can pick up."

"I thought I picked you up," Jen sniffed.

"We just let you think that to stop the cat fights."

"Over a bunch of drunk engineer wanna-be's? I don't think so."

She stroked his arm lazily. Up his forearm, around the elbow, over his shoulder, down again. Lifting his glass, Peter finished the wine in one large gulp.

"Don't matter. I wasn't looking at your friend anyway."

He sat up, poised on one elbow, and leaned over to kiss her. When his lips became more insistent, she suddenly pulled away.

"Would you like some more?" she asked innocently, lifting her glass between their faces. The wine swirled in circles to reflect a diamond shine around the glass.

Peter grinned wickedly and slid one arm across Jen's bare waist. He looked like a cat ready to pounce. "Well, since you're offering ..."

She started to say something smart, when he abruptly grabbed her hips with both hands, and dragged her body to the middle of the bed. She yelped as wine splashed on her chest. A cool line sped down to her stomach, another toward one shoulder. He snatched the glass out of her hand, swallowing the remaining liquid in one dramatic movement.

"More! I need more sustenance!" he cried to the ceiling, his arms spread wide.

Then, he let the glass fall from his fingers. It bounced off the bed to roll on the carpet, as he buried his face into Jen's stomach. She giggled and squirmed under him.

Suddenly he stopped, his face a few inches below her chest.

"What's this from?" he asked, running his thumb over the oval patch on her ribs.

Though appearing rough, the scar was strangely smooth. Only something really traumatic would cause this. He knew because his brother had suffered a campfire burn. After a big ember floated down onto his arm, the solid red section was prominent for months until it faded to white. His brother's scar was a lot like this one.

Enthusiasm escaped Jen's face. A barrage of confusing images filled her mind, bright lights and faraway voices, and somewhere nearby, a woman crying. Of all the details, that was the most disturbing—that mysterious woman. After four years, her desperation still permeated Jen's dreams.

"Fell off my bike when I was little."

He frowned at her simple explanation, wondering what she could have landed on, but there were more appetizing things before him. His tongue slowly followed the crease of her breasts straight up to her neck, and he lingered there, tasting the wine on her skin. He met her eyes with a delinquent look.

"Ahhh sweet, yet tangy with a light aftertaste, aged to perfection while still maintaining the youthfulness of its fruitful labor. A good year."

He bent his head back down.

"Definitely vintage."

***

... A warm salty taste filled her mouth and her heart jumped at the sensual thought of his kisses. She felt the soft skin of his lips trailing across her shoulders, his hands strong, maneuvering them closer. Then pleasure mixed with pain. She'd forgotten how close the two could be. The memories pulled at her insistently, both extremes commanding equal attention, and Donna reached for only the good, the safe, but she could do little to control them because ...

***

Ric held her face as he kissed her. With foreplay dusted by commitment, Donna felt locked in this decision. Her nervousness was only mildly tempered by his smooth hands and lips. He seemed to know exactly what to do. She had fantasized about undressing a man, but he held her too closely to do this. After pulling her clothes off, he stood undressing himself with his dark eyes on her, while she lay on the bed. Their caresses took on an alert flavor, heightened with every minute.

When he started to enter her, she made a small sound at the pain, instinctively retracting her hips. She thought he would ease off and go slower, but firmly gripping her shoulders, he said, "Don't worry. It won't hurt long," and suddenly pressed into her hard. Crying out again, tears formed in her eyes. The pain was sharper than she expected. After several seconds, it gradually subsided.

"There, now it'll be better," he whispered comfortingly, though this did little to alleviate her spiked anxiety.

He moved steadily, kissing her skin, securing her under him. Finally sinking into the new sensations, her hands slid over the rounded muscles of his shoulders and down his arms. He lifted his chest up, took her hands, and placed them above her head on the pillow. When she brought them back around his shoulders, he did it again and she realized that he expected her to just lie there. Wasn't it supposed to be better for him if she were doing some of the moving too? Apparently not—he started going faster with closed eyes and panting breaths. ...

Afterward, his voice possessed an unusual tone, absorbed and distracted at the same time, as though savoring a perfectly executed tumbling routine or the exuberance of Mozart, something fascinating and beyond dissemination.

Tucked in beside him, she pondered whether she had given her body willingly, or if he'd simply claimed it for his own. She was filled with questions. Had he kept her contained to make her first time less demanding? Were most men like this in bed? Would Jack be? Imagining his disapproval of Ric, it disturbed her that the thought of another man swam into view right at that moment.

She had long since given up on a relationship with him. If he hadn't confessed an interest in five years, it likely didn't exist, but she still looked at him with words on the tip of her tongue. Jack was like a comfortable old shirt she took for granted, but would never part with. She wondered if he'd become a habit and if *she* was one to him, habits naturally being overlooked in their consistency.

(Maybe I've been hanging around Jack too long. Maybe I don't know how to relate to another guy, except to compare him to Jack. I really need to get out more.)

"Are you OK?"

Donna abandoned her preoccupation with a private guilt. Strangely, the guilt was more for her friend than her lover. Smiling up at Ric with her head cradled on his shoulder, she stole an arm around his waist.

"I'm fine."

She tried to relax within Ric's arms. They felt lovely, though not as calming as she expected.

Somewhere inside, there was an awareness of an unbreakable connection, existing beyond the parameters of the present, a pairing of spirits, too correct to ignore. Lying in the circle of his arms, the idea swam closer to the surface than ever before. If she could bring it near, she would really see, understand.

Certain elements boasted clarity: that there was a difference between her fantasies and what she had just experienced. Not unequivocal disappointment, more like shooting an arrow at a target and hitting the very edge of the bull's-eye. Her vision drawn from center, the achievement lacked a balanced measure of all sides. A recognizable face was supposed to be on that target, a face with old eyes, reflecting the perfect connection of souls having met and married before.

She was in love with Ric, wasn't she? A tiny voice from deep down reminded her just how little she knew this man. Struggling with the feelings, she finally let them slide back into her subconscious, barely aware of being close to some sort of enlightenment.

Ric was softly rubbing her arm. Donna sighed again as his touch distracted her from her deeper thoughts, but for some reason, Jack remained in the back of her mind.

***

99

CHAPTER 13

For a full three years, the University of Calgary Medicine Program was extremely tough. Warned not to take on any part-time jobs or extracurricular activities, the students were force-fed information. To ignore this advice meant certain failure, even for someone like Donna, whose photographic memory was an enormous aid.

Donna's timing in starting her sexual history was poor, given that she wrote exams every six weeks and Ric was writing them now. Torn between keeping her nose to the grindstone and exploring this new relationship, she agreed to meetings on campus if he respected her study time.

Their favorite place was a sunken lounge called "The Pit." Located half a flight of stairs down in the Social Sciences building, between Biological Sciences and Engineering, the chairs were tattered and grubby, but it was private. They relished their limited time, all the more because those limitations enhanced its inherent value. Ric always begged for a few more minutes, another evening, another hour in bed. His consistent attentions complimented her with the primal thought of being wanted.

As a take-charge guy, his strong body and manners were overwhelming. He lessened the work of the relationship by making most of the decisions, when they would meet, what restaurants to go to, what movies to see. She felt pampered and appreciated … but there was school, relentless school, morning to night.

In May, she almost failed an obstetrics exam. The scare prompted her to curtail their meetings. After requesting a few days to concentrate on an upcoming exam on the immune system, he reluctantly agreed, but showed up at her apartment anyway, wine and his mother's lasagna in hand. It was hard to stay annoyed with the thick aroma of oregano filling her apartment, but she insisted on finishing her chapters first.

Most of Ric's friends started sending resumes out before their last school term was finished, but Ric was too caught up in his new girlfriend to attend to it. There were many ads for engineers in rural areas of Alberta and British Columbia. Very little in Calgary. Donna circled job ads for him, but he dismissed most of them, especially the ones elsewhere in Alberta. At times, he was frustrated with the whole process and sat in her apartment simmering in silent annoyance. Donna thought he equated that dented up engineering ring with magical job security, and by June, she knew he wasn't really trying.

When she suggested he apply for a temporary research position like Jack, his sensitivity on the subject jumped out full force. After barking at her, silence weighed heavily for the rest of the evening. Later they made up, and it was almost worth that first fight. So contrite with the fear of losing the other's love, their solicitations were doubly passionate.

The medicine program gave students six weeks off between their first and second year. In July, Donna enjoyed this well-deserved break from her classes. The first two days were spent with Ric, mostly in bed: careless hours, unconcerned with assignments and exams, just two people excited about each other.

Occasionally, he would leave to go out for a smoke. "A smoke" often took twenty or thirty minutes and Donna suspected that the extent of his habit had been grossly misrepresented. Then, he would dive back under the covers as though absent for weeks. Staying holed up with Ric was cozy, but she had an uneasy feeling that he would completely do without the world, if it meant he could bury her away with him. He hadn't seen any of his friends since their first meeting in the bar.

Families, however, were not as easily deterred. With school keeping Donna so busy, meeting Ric's parents had been continually delayed, but under their pressure Ric finally convinced her to come to Sunday dinner.

"Hello Dowona!" Mr. Guzzo exclaimed in a heavy Italian accent as he rushed to the front door. "Welcome, welcome. This is my family, my wife Maria, my daughter Grazia. Come in, come in. Maria take her coat. Grazia move out of the way."

Mrs. Guzzo hung up Donna's jacket. "Ricardo," she scolded, "you should be more prompt. The dinner is waiting. Dowona must be hungry."

"Sorry, ma."

Grazia's eyes narrowed slyly at the absence of an explanation, and with an unwavering expression, Ric added, "Had to stop for gas."

"Well, it's good they are here now. Good, good," Ric's father extended a meaty arm to usher Donna into the dining room. "Let's all sit down and Dowona can tell us about herself. Oh, Ricardo, you picked a beauty. Bella, with hair like the sun. Yes, sit here by me. Maria, get the kids something to drink. Bring the red off the counter. Ricardo, you open it for her. So Dowona, you are in school, no?"

"Yes, I—"

"Good, school is important! My Ricardo worked very hard, but this economy …" He clucked his tongue, "There are no jobs, but we must be patient, eh Ricardo?"

Mrs. Guzzo placed several steaming casserole dishes on the table and fussed about the seating arrangements, before finally sitting down herself. Was the sun from the window bothering Dowona? She could sit here instead—Grazia could move. She was sorry the chairs were not more comfortable. They were being recovered next week. And that serving spoon was much too small for the cannelloni. She could get a better one while Grazia filled the water glasses. Somehow amid the endless courses, the conversation abated little during the meal, Mr. and Mrs. Guzzo asking and answering most of the questions themselves.

Donna subtly studied each one around the table, and took particular note of Grazia's reserved demeanor. She was as timid as a rabbit and picked at her food, seldom bringing it to her mouth. Then Donna noticed how slender Grazia was, not just slender, but downright skinny.

(No wonder she's so tiny—she doesn't actually eat anything. Boy, if I lived here, I'd be as big as a bus. … I wonder if they know this teenager's anorexic. Look at the way she's sitting, like she's trying to shrink on the spot. What's up with that?)

"Dowona, have some more. Your plate's almost empty. We can't have empty plates. Maria, pass her the cannelloni."

Donna gestured to her plate, which still sported an ample helping. "No thanks. I really—"

"Here, my wife makes wonderful cannelloni. Have some bread. And some bruschetta. You need some bruschetta too. Wash it down with the wine. It finishes the taste properly. Just right." He smacked his lips on his fingers.

"So Grazia, are you in school too?" asked Donna, trying in vain to deflect attention from her plate.

A large spoon tapped her decorative stoneware resolutely, as Mr. Guzzo deposited another serving of cannelloni squarely in the center.

"Oh, there is no rush. After all," he announced, returning the spoon to the enormous casserole dish and patting his daughter's hand, "she is only twenty-one. She doesn't know what she wants. She would do well to find a man like my Ricardo."

So, she wasn't a teenager. Her size had been deceptive. Was it Donna's imagination or did the girl pull away at her father's touch just now?

Donna tactlessly responded that she herself was merely one year older and on her way to a medical degree. Grazia's face lit up. Ric's parents simultaneously scowled. It was his mother who attempted to regain some good cheer by asking about Donna's family.

"My father is an architect. My mother passed away several years ago. I don't have any brothers or sisters."

Scowling became mortification. "How terrible!" they both exclaimed sympathetically.

"Your father must be so lonely."

"How could you manage without your mother?"

"It happened a long time ago. My father's remarried. Besides, we were always pretty independent."

Sympathy returned to scowling. Donna knew she'd won no friends at that meal, save Grazia, but the evening gave her some fresh insight into her boyfriend.

Meeting Donna's family was tamer. The combination of school and Ric had prevented her from visiting home much, but she eagerly arranged an introduction.

On entering the house, she could see that Paula was still renovating Donna's childhood home. It was strange to see new wallpaper in the kitchen. And where were the cups and saucers now? Suddenly, these irritations were minor in the face of showing off her handsome boyfriend.

Donna had to admit that her father seemed happier than she could ever remember. If not for presenting a prospective marital partner, she would have continued to feel displaced in an infantile way, but her own glow covered those feelings with a soft layer of distraction. It was so effective that Donna missed how no one shook Ric's hand.

***

The phone rang again; third time in an hour. Barely managing to hold her tongue through the first two calls, Jen could feign no more patience. This was her evening with Donna, or maybe it would be if that lugnut would stop calling. Holding back was difficult, since a tacit agreement allowed Jen's opinion on any issue. Well, maybe not this issue, at least not without express invitation. She sensed that Ric would like to drive a wedge between them. And wouldn't her big mouth give him just such an opportunity! Best be careful.

Glancing over, she caught Donna shaking her head sullenly. Her voice was too low to hear, but there was no mistaking that body language. A minute later, Donna was finally off the phone, muttering to herself.

Jen suggested, "Let's go to my place. Ric doesn't have my number, does he?"

"With the way you go through men, my concern could be timed with a stopwatch. Where are my keys?"

Ten minutes later, they were wading carefully through Jen's small and cluttered living room. Donna considered it an extension of the crowded Brammon household, complete with that soothing chaos, a lack of precision and pressure that ordered living engenders. Jen used every conceivable space and never threw anything away, but apparently this habit of holding on to things didn't include people. Still the loner. No roommates and no steady boyfriend to check up on them.

Donna pointed this out while fishing through Jen's cupboard for clean glasses. "I don't think you really want a relationship. You purposely choose men who aren't good for you, or they're tourists, or moving to some other city." She pulled out two glasses and smirked at the Flintstone characters etched into them.

Jen's denial was succinct. "You're full of shit. Rye or rum?"

"Rye."

"Fred or Dino?"

"Dino. Fred's a blowhard."

"He's just stale. You really think Wilma puts out? Ice?"

"Yeah, thanks. Well, at least he's in a long-term relationship. What's your excuse? And to be clear, I mean something longer than a week. Why do you choose guys you know won't call the next day?"

Jen almost laughed, "Oh, they call, but it's too easy. Why should I settle on someone with so little sense, as to sleep with me the first night? Hand me Fred. Besides, Donna The-Oh-So-Experienced-One, I haven't met anyone I'd want to keep around for longer than a week. Look at you. You hooked up with Larry Latino and now you have to sneak out with me, just to get some peace and quiet."

Jen dropped one ice cube too many into Donna's glass and a line of dark liquid escaped over the side. Opening an empty cutlery drawer, she frowned at the pile of dirty spoons in the sink.

"Here," Donna offered, flipping up her middle finger, "Use this."

They traded sneers, then stepped over and around things to get to the balcony, where a heavy curtain obstructed the entrance. Jen shoved it aside and slipped through in one clean movement.

Behind her, Donna froze. Something about this ... the precise hang of the fabric, the width of the glass door, dividing balcony from living room ... elicited the creepiest presence of danger versus safety between the two. And out there was not safe.

She blinked, clutching her drink tightly. Ice danced against its sides. And just as quickly, that ominous feeling simply disappeared like a shadow into the night. All-encompassing and then just gone.

Maybe seven seconds had passed. Jen hadn't even noticed her hesitation. She was setting her glass down on the railing and scanning the skyline. Had she turned, she would have caught a confused cross between a smile and a frown on Donna's face.

(Ridiculous. I gotta get more sleep.)

This view was worth the rent, especially on an evening like this, dimming summer twilight to transform an ordinary sky into something exotic and untouchable. Standing tall from the downtown core, the Calgary Tower pierced potent colors across the horizon and stubbornly refused to be overshadowed by surrounding buildings.

It was one of Donna's childhood triggers. Skyscrapers pushed upward, and in her mind, they suddenly took on the bright colors of candles. She saw a table full of children with cone-shaped hats on. A round cake with seven candles sat in front of her, begging a breath of air and a wish. After her mother died, she stopped making wishes on birthday cakes.

She said, "I remember going up the Tower for dinners when I was young. My mom put a lot into making my birthdays special. That's one of my most vivid memories of her."

"Must have been hard when she died," Jen stated between quiet sips. The Fred glass clinked as she set it down on the balcony railing.

Donna squinted at the distant buildings. "Yeah, it was. She'd always been around, but I was getting to the age when I didn't want her around so much. I remember one time, Dad fell asleep on the couch and Mom put a blanket on him. It seemed like such a 'Mom' thing to do, it just bugged me. So, I got all the blankets in the house and piled them up on him. Blankets, quilts, anything I could find. I even got this filthy one out of the garage. He had this one little space for an air hole. Didn't even wake up. Blankets became a thing after that. We started hiding them in each other's rooms and stuff like that, and she'd play along, but I think she knew she was the butt of a joke."

Donna was tapping her nails on the railing. Normally, it was the sort of thing she would do just to see how long it would take for Jen to snap at her, but she didn't even seem aware that she was doing it.

Tap—tap … tap—tap—tap.

"Then, she got sick and I hardly saw her before she died. The last time I did, she kept saying how cold she was. So, I went home and got a bunch of blankets ready to bring the next morning, as if the hospital wouldn't have enough of those—I don't know what I was thinking—but she died that night. I remember I was standing in the laundry room when my dad told me we didn't have to go back to the hospital anymore. I kept insisting we did, 'cause I had to bring her this pile of blankets fresh out of the dryer. You know, so they'd be *really* warm. The look on his face ..."

Peering straight at Donna, Jen stood solemnly with fingers grazing her drink. She almost forgot it was there.

Tap—tap—tap.

"It was pretty bad. I felt kind of responsible, like I'd wished her dead somehow, you know, 'cause of never appreciating her when she was around. Anyway, I was messed up for a while, angry, the whole bit. I think Dad was really worried about me, but I snapped out of it eventually."

(No you didn't, not really.)

Until that moment Jen had never put her finger on what made Donna different. She just carried this invisible cross that weighed nothing, but it was always there and no antics from Jen could ever heal a scar of this depth. Distract yes, heal no.

"I thought about taking her name. She never changed it to Carlin when they got married, pretty unusual for a woman in the sixties. I think she just liked that it was different, the name I mean."

"What was it?"

"Slobodian—" Donna didn't even wait for a response, though she could see Jen's smirk twitching, "—but Carlin is more me anyway. It's ..."

"Anal?" Jen volunteered, "Well, it is. Listen to the sound. *Donna Carlin.* Makes you wanna plant potatoes. But Donna Slob—what?"

"Slobodian."

"Slobodian, now that's a name. That girl would do it naked."

"Actually, I think some of Mom's relatives did. From what I'm told, she was some kind of tame throwback. So if you believe in genetics, there's hope for me yet."

"What do you remember about her?"

"She was ... a typical mom I guess. I only really knew that part of her. Dad says I'm a lot like her. She was a private person, smart, you know, got things done. One time, Dad said she didn't enjoy life as much as she should have. I don't know what he meant exactly. ... This is going to sound strange, but sometimes I feel like she's watching me. I get these weird moments when, well, I feel like someone's there, and then I turn around and it's gone. It started in high school. I think it's just some kind of guilt about doing fine without her." Donna mumbled, "Ric's parents couldn't identify with that at all."

"If you could go back and meet her now, would you?"

"Sure. There must be things in me that maybe come from her, and I never had the chance to see them. I'd meet her, but not as a kid. As an adult. Parents don't show their whole sordid histories to their kids, and it's kind of bad. You never know just how normal you are 'til you see how abnormal everyone else is, especially your parents."

Jen nodded. "What if you could go back in time and change something?"

"You mean, *would* I change anything?"

"Yeah, well, I'm assuming everyone would change something in their past."

"Hmmm, that's a tough one. Well, besides ditching the Barry Manilow tape, I'd probably warn her about the cancer early and try to save her. But maybe not. I mean, what if I didn't warn her in time and only prolonged her suffering? She had a really aggressive type, only got diagnosed a few months before she died. If I got to her sooner and it was still irreversible, she'd just have longer to be miserable. No, I don't know if I'd change anything, except taking more time to get to know her. What about you?"

Jen didn't hesitate. "I'd go back to the day Al dumped me and dump him first! And then I'd stop us from going out the night that car hit us. Christ that was a shitty year. I think I'd just go back and give myself a humungous sleeping pill and wake up the next year. Avoid the whole mess. What about Ric? Would you still choose him?"

"I think so."

"That was convincing."

"I just don't know if he's Mr. Right or Mr. Absurd. I'm crazy about him, but well, it's like he doesn't want to share me with anyone. He even interrogated me about Jack earlier. It was unreal."

(Bingo! There's my opening.)

"Really? Sounds like Mr. Insecurity, if he can't give you one night on your own. If you have doubts, then something's not right. What do you guys end up doing? Besides the obvious."

"The 'obvious' is now about even with him beering and watching me study."

"Beering?"

"It's a Ric-ism. Guys have an amazing way of having any non-word to do with drinking or sex make sense somehow. Anyway, I've been wanting to have you and JP over now that he's back in Calgary, but Ric acts weird whenever I bring it up."

"About both of us or just Jack?"

"Just Jack. He hasn't even met him. I've explained that he's a buddy and I've owed him an invitation for a while now."

Jen spoke slowly and pointedly, "So ... you've talked to your jealous boyfriend about wanting another guy to come over to your place?"

"No, I've suggested that two friends of mine come over for a game of Rummoli," Donna replied, just as pointedly.

"Until he meets Jack, how's he supposed to know the difference? Look, I'm not saying he's right—he's as wrong as people with penises can be—but if he has a problem with Jack, the only way he'll get past it is if he gets to know him. Otherwise to him, Jack will always be some other guy you talk about."

Donna started to answer, but there was a certain plausibility in Jen's words. Every time Donna mentioned Jack, Ric would hold her hand a little tighter, or change the subject, or charm her into bed. She hadn't completed two sentences in a row because of these tactics. On the surface it was flattering, but sex could only go so far to distract her from friends of countless years.

"Well, why don't we do Rummoli next weekend? Bring Peter."

Jen scoffed, "Oh, he's long gone. I'm seeing a guy I met at the bank. Actually he works there."

"Then it must be true love. If he can access your account, you know he's not a gold digger."

"Well, he's not digging for much of anything, so I'm already on the lookout. I'll use the old standby—bad timing."

"You're so mean. Imagine the therapy bills for these guys every time you chew one up and spit him out." Donna shook her head, "Bad timing ... Ric's timing was good. I think I just happened to be ready when we met. He makes me feel swept up in something that's right out of my control. All my life, I've been in control of things, but maybe that's just been a big illusion all along. God's ultimate joke. I'm starting to think most things happen the way they're meant to."

"Like we can't decide the final outcome? I don't buy that. I'm proud to say that all my mistakes have been completely engineered by me. I think fate's a bunch of crap, in the sense that we can't take charge, but yeah, maybe things happen for a reason, which makes time travel a bit of a challenge. You know, messing with karma and all."

Donna nodded, adding, "It's a dead issue, not to mention overanalyzed by people wallowing in regret. You can't rewrite the past. Just accept it and get on with your life."

"How do you know it isn't possible? If you watch the news on TV, aren't the film clips a look at the past?"

"Sure, but that's not the same as being there."

"OK, then, what if you look in a mirror? By the time the reflection gets to your eyes, it's already in the past, and you're right there."

"But it's still unchanged. There's just a microscopic delay bouncing off the mirror before it reaches your eyes. I think the only way time travel is possible is if you're an observer. Period. Suppose you changed the wrong thing? You could screw up your whole future."

"But according to you, it isn't possible to change what already occurred, so you're safe. Maybe the changed version was the correct one all along."

"Then you never would have known the original version anyway. Pardon the irony in this, but rewind thirty seconds. Did I not just say that this has been overanalyzed by complete losers?"

"Speak for yourself," Jen countered undeterred, "I'm visionary. What if there are two dimensions—a current one and a possible one—and you had the power to flip one into the other? Why should the past be irreversible when the future isn't? We all carry around distorted views of the past anyway. We have these little versions of what happened, and they never match anyone else's. In a way, that shows the past is as unpredictable as the future."

Donna was reminded of her palmistry lesson to Ric, one hand representing fate and the other potentiality. It was similar to what Jen was saying, but there was a huge difference between the enormity of someone's past and a few lines on a hand. The hands could exist simultaneously, while a future could only exist in relation to a particular past, already creating the foundation of itself. Even one change to that past could splay the dominoes irrevocably. But don't the lines on our hands change with time as well, etching our history into us as we go along?

This was a much more complicated debate than Donna bargained for. Weren't they all? Compared to Jen, med school was a breeze. Best to get out now.

"You're not *visionary*. You've just been watching too much Star Trek."

"I know what I'd change—I'd go back to 1969 and force the NBC executives to keep Star Trek on the air! And I'd put Spock in charge. You'd like that, Donna. He has no imagination either."

***

CHAPTER 14

Push, pull, push, pull, shift, angle, push, pull, push, pull ... Was that a knock? Donna clicked a switch and listened while the vacuum geared to a stop. Ric, early as usual. Too early. She faced a quick choice: refuse to let him in or put him to work. Reluctantly opening the door, she gave him a kiss and pointed him toward the machine.

"That's women's work!"

He wrapped two arms around her and steered her toward the bedroom. Four months ago this would have been cute, but she hadn't showered yet, the place was a disaster, and Jack and Jen would be here in an hour.

Twisting out of his grasp, she implored, "Ric, let go. I'm not done yet."

"Oh, come on. We have time for a quickie. Hell, we have time for three or four." He kept maneuvering her closer to the bed.

"*I* don't have time for anything. ... Ric, Ric, quit it. *Ric* ... Jesus Christ!"

In a sudden lunge, she broke free and stomped back into the living room. The whirring vacuum filled the apartment, though only momentarily. Out of the corner of her eye, she saw him yank the cord from the wall outlet and toss it sideways. The motor faded to silence, pulling Donna around to face a stranger.

Through clenched teeth, he growled, "What's your fucking problem?"

Staring, she froze at the sight of his clenched fists. The seconds stretched painfully as Donna took a careful breath.

"Please plug that in," she calmly asked.

When he didn't move, she stepped face to face, reached down, and did it herself, keeping the vacuum nozzle between them. He stared at her darkly ... and then turned and walked to the couch. Continuing the chore, Donna kept one eye on his hands. It wasn't until she saw them relax in his lap that she exhaled.

***

Vacuuming was an inherently dull task, but Tracy threw herself into it with fervor. The nesting urge was starting early this time. With Ashley, she was cleaning the weirdest things about a week before the delivery, but this baby still had two months to go. Two long months. She felt heavy and awkward with her stomach defiantly pushed forward.

Compared to the first pregnancy, this one was exhausting. One discomfort after another: morning sickness that volunteered for afternoon and evening shifts, achy joints, terrible fatigue. She could just sleep all day.

Finally finished with the main floor, she propped her hands firmly on her hips. The weight had been pulling on her back all day, creating intermittent knots, and she calculated the earliest possible bedtime for Ashley. Maybe in another half-hour. Then, she'd gratefully escape to her own bed.

Ashley pretended to help by pushing a toy broom around. She bore a strong resemblance to Al and Tracy wondered whether her own features would be stamped onto this new baby, though it would be fine if they both looked like him. His strong cheekbones and piercing blue eyes could make a woman melt.

And he was doing much better now. The drinking seemed to be under control. In fact, he was at an A.A. meeting tonight, the one at seven. When in town, he hit as many as possible. On the rigs, he kept to himself and avoided the after work pressure to toss back a few. Yes, Tracy believed the label "Alcoholic" and the recovery process were being handled very well.

Her friends warned her, "There will never be a day when he can say 'I'm cured. I don't want a drink.' Every day he'll want one, and every day he'll consider lying to get one." Even his sponsor verified this. Brad was an older man, who had been through the recovery process for twelve years, so he should know.

Those words sat ill on Tracy, as the depth of the addiction unfolded before her. It wouldn't go away like the flu. He would wrestle with it until the day he died. The last five months were hard on him, but the effort nurtured a seed of hope.

During her first trimester, she hadn't been that convinced. She kept the appointment for the abortion until the day before it was scheduled, though she could never have gone through with it. But the threat alone worked on

Al. He attended a ton of meetings in those four weeks. He knew the scrutiny was diligent and deserved, and each day he talked himself out of drinking, sometimes each hour. Though proud of making it through the thirty days, he embraced his addiction with a gritty and methodical realism. Just a big fat gun pointing him toward two simple choices: Ugly and Uglier.

Pressing her hands into her low back again, Tracy tried to coax out the soreness. Then, she felt a strange sensation: wetness, running down her right leg.

(Did I pee myself? No, I couldn't have. I just went a little while ago.)

When she raised her leg at an angle and saw the dark red fluid, her heart contracted painfully.

(Blood. Back labor, not knots. No, it's not time yet! Oh God, where's Al? What do I do with Ashley? What should I do?)

In a crazy moment, her first response was to get a towel and clean up the drops on the floor. If she removed the sight of the blood, then she wouldn't really be in labor. Just deny that it's happening, the way Al hides his addiction. The similarity of the comparison was brazenly before her, and it was the closest she would ever come to understanding the desperation of her husband.

Grabbing the phone book, she quickly scanned the list of A.A. meetings. The one he always attended was only a mile away. Punching the numbers on the cordless phone, she snatched a tea towel off its hook.

"Alcoholics Anonymous. May I help you?"

"I need to speak to someone in your meeting right away. His name is Al."

"I'm sorry, the meeting ended at 6:30."

"No, it was supposed to start at 7:00. Please, just look around for him. It's an emergency."

"I'm sorry, there's no one here except the coordinators and I know them by name. They're not the person you mentioned."

With overwhelming helplessness, she muttered, "I must have the wrong number," and slowly placed the phone on its cradle. He had lied to her. There wasn't any meeting. He was probably out drinking with his poker buddies, while she was vacuuming and bleeding all over the floor. She stood there stunned, uncertain if she should risk driving to the hospital.

(Maybe the people next door could watch Ashley—or take me to the hospital—or both.)

Her thoughts stumbled about incoherently. Picking up the phone again, she strived to recall the neighbor's number when the front door opened.

Al took one look at her and his face turned white. He rushed toward her, but when he stepped close, she slapped him clear across his face—a crisp handclap, echoing in the bright clean kitchen. Utterly shocked, he stood unprepared for the second slap, and the third. ... Ashley started whimpering behind them. They were barely aware of her.

Grabbing her wrists, he shouted, "Trace, stop! What are you doing! Come on, calm down! You're bleeding."

"I know damned well I'm bleeding! I was the one here to see that in the first place! Where were you?"

He still held her wrists, which were fighting against him. Pushing at him futilely, the pregnancy tipped her weight off-center, and he tried to steady her at arm's length.

"I was at the meeting. You knew that. How long—"

"No, you weren't! I phoned them. The meeting ended at 6:30. You were drinking at Doug's! Drinking and playing poker while I've been bleeding and—"

"Trace, listen to me. Shut up! Which meeting did you call?"

She stopped fighting, but still sounded hysterical. "The one by the mall."

"I didn't go to that one, remember? I went to the one close to Brad's, 'cause he didn't have a car tonight."

As she stared into his face, she saw the honesty etched deep in his eyes. His words struck a familiar note in her memory, something about having to leave earlier to get there in time. Anger gave way to frustration at her dependency on this man, who could just as easily have been belting back shooters instead of where he claimed to be.

Her eyes filled with tears when another spasm of pain crossed her back. The reality of premature labor and the associated fear filled her head with singsong words.

(Not knots, back labor, not knots, back labor ...)

She was too frightened to express it, but he saw her half-hearted acceptance of his story. Then, the feeling of being misunderstood and persecuted was suddenly enveloping. Presumed guilty.

Beyond the fear in her eyes, he recognized something she kept hidden most of the time, a wary gaze that came out when she thought he wouldn't notice. She was waiting for him to slip up and disappoint her. In fact, she considered it inevitable, like a plane that will nose-dive to earth when it runs out of fuel, unable to fight the laws of nature and certain destruction. He never felt so unfairly summarized. Tracy had assumed the worst and she wasn't even right.

If the crisis hadn't been imminent, Al would have considered making her assumptions real, but they didn't have time for this.

(Where's Ashley? Oh God, she's crying in the corner.)

113

For a second, he didn't know who to help first. Scooping up his daughter in one arm, he led his wife out the door with the other.

Their small son was born forty minutes later. They named him Kevin Albert Morin, Kam for short.

***

CHAPTER 15

The Rummoli game lasted two hours. For Jen, it was two hours too long. At first, she thought Donna was on stage, saying the useless shit people do when hosting things. But Donna didn't play at roles like that. If you wanted a beer, you just marched into the kitchen and got yourself one.

Reminiscent of Jen's mother, this host was fussing about the potato chips and whether the dip was fresh enough to serve. It was mildly annoying. And then Jen noticed Donna's shaking fingers raking that blonde hair. She stopped being annoyed and started watching.

Despite her babbling, Donna wasn't talking to Ric a lot. In fact, Jen couldn't remember one sentence uttered between them in the last hour. Ric didn't look particularly happy either. Dealing the next round of cards, he kept scanning the table surreptitiously as though sizing up the poker competition, especially Jack, who was engrossed in his usual banter with Donna.

"I see you took my advice. You haven't sat like a pretzel all evening."

"I need all the coin I can get. Student loan from hell."

Jack offered a sympathy pout as he lifted his beer. The steel ring clinked against the bottle and Ric all but glared. Wasn't this guy in detective school or something?

(You don't wear a badge you haven't earned, Asshole.)

Ric didn't realize how tight his expression was until he felt Jen's eyes on him. He glanced up at her, while Jack and Donna continued their easy rhythm. Jen had old eyes, the kind that could see into people, and he didn't like the look in them right now. It wasn't the first time she'd stared at him this way, but this expression contained more, full of suspicion and doubt. Unnerving.

(He was here first. You'll never have that part of her.)

Ric couldn't interpret the precise message, but sensed that her insight into his relationship with Donna surpassed his own, which caused a queer mix of vulnerability and anger. Refusing to acknowledge her silent statement, he distributed the last of the cards and asked, "Anyone for another beer?"

"Nope, need all my wits to out-bluff this guy," Donna answered, gesturing to Jack.

Jen volleyed Ric's deflection by fixing her expression on him even more solidly. "Not me, thanks." The politeness was empty, but Ric was the only one to lift his head at her tone. The others were busy studying their cards.

Jack didn't even attempt politeness as he shook his head and grunted.

"OK, just me then."

Donna frowned when Ric got up and turned to the fridge. He must have put away six bottles already. Jack noted the ease with which this guy conducted himself, offering drinks as though it were his name on the lease. Then, he would suddenly disappear for several minutes. On his return, the acrid smell of smoke would follow. Frustrated, Jack wanted to yell, "This isn't what you're all about. What are you doing with this guy?" Silently stewing, he reminded himself that he had no right to say anything and focused on the game.

They opened the bidding at nickels and Donna quickly tossed hers into the pot. "OK, you guys. I've got like seven aces here—all spades—so fold now if you know what's good for you."

Ric smiled briefly at her and then transferred his gaze straight across the table. "Raise you a dime."

Everyone complied. Jack noted Donna sitting up properly and shuffling her cards around more. People never really gave up their tells. She had nothing.

"Raise you a dime," Ric repeated.

Donna tried not to scowl at her cards and dropped another coin into the pot. *Clink!* Jack followed with two more. *Clink—clink!*

Jen snarled at Jack, "You are so full of crap. I know you've got zip. ... He rotates his signs, but I've been keeping track. And I'll raise you another nickel." She added her money.

"Raise a quarter." Ric tossed thirty cents in and glanced across the table again.

Now, Donna really was scowling. She pulled one leg under her and started to lift the other knee up, but then returned Jack's smirk with her own and tossed her cards down instead.

"Oh, forget it. You three duke it out."

"Dr. Pretzel has left the building!" Jack declared, "Now, let's see what you two are made of. I'll see your quarter and your piddly-ass nickel and I'll raise you another piddly-ass nickel."

Clink—clink—clink!

"Why don't we really see what we're made of?"

Three sets of inquisitive eyes looked at Ric. Reaching behind, he pulled out his wallet, placed it on the table, and leaned back in his chair. For a brief moment, that one inanimate object had seemingly stifled all conversation.

Jack could see Ric staring just over his cards and right at him. Two dark eyes, separate from that sleek smile. He smoothly replied, "No bills, Ric."

But casually leaning onto his elbows, Ric opened the wallet and plucked out a fifty, pinching it in the air between two fingers. "Bills? ... Or balls?"

Jen dropped her cards as though they were scalding. "There's no way I'm going there."

Jack chewed his lip thoughtfully and quietly asked, "Isn't what you're holding worth more than that?" Clenching his jaw, Jack could envision leaping over the table, cards flying everywhere, and ramming Ric flat on his back. His toes even unconsciously curled into the carpet for better leverage.

"Here, I'll make it easy for you." Ric flipped his cards onto the table face up and carelessly dropped the bill as well. It landed beside a full house, queens and sevens. "Can't you match it?"

"Not your wallet, no, but the thing about this game is you never know what the other guy's got. Or at least, *you* don't."

"I don't need to see what you got. I know what I got." Ric leaned back with eyes leveled on Jack, who fought to keep his voice light.

"See, I think it's more about how you play what you got. Law of averages ... Time tends to balance out good hands. Well, maybe not to Don. She couldn't see a good card if it came in a gift box."

"Bite yourself, Bud! I didn't do the pretzel once."

"She says with her knee stuck up her nose." Jen snickered.

Donna looked down to discover she was indeed pretzeling, and her twisted expression broke the spell pulling their attention quizzically back and forth at the guys.

Jack forced a pleasant smile. His cards landed face down as he rose from the table. "But tonight, you're right. Can't win this time, just two pair. Come on, Brammon. Don't you turn into a really nice person after dark?"

"Yeah, she rivals Mother Teresa." Donna stood and started randomly scooping up the deck, except for Jack's cards, which she discretely slid to the bottom of the pile. While Ric and Jen were clearing bottles off the table and Jack was tying up his shoes, she flipped the pack over to skim through the last five cards.

He did have two pairs, both nines.

***

Jen followed Jack out of Donna's apartment building and into a gentle evening. Tonight presented a brilliant dusk with jagged mountains silhouetted to the west, Jen's favorite time of day. They walked through the August evening with only a slight breeze to accentuate the sunset that bounced off each car window they passed. Shiny and calm the way only true summer can be. Alive.

Jack remained silent all the way to his truck. After roughly unlocking the passenger door, he ignored Jen's marked stare following him around to his own side. He slid into the driver's seat, and pulled his door closed with an excessive tug.

"Come on, you're not rattled by that cork-head, are you?"

Glowering, he stared at his keys poised in the ignition.

"Fuckin' blow-hard. He's the kind of guy who would pick a fight 'cause you looked at his girlfriend funny."

As he turned the key, the engine responded sluggishly. Needed a tune up or something. Donna would know. Donna, Donna, Donna. Were no thoughts unconnected to her?

"And did you?"

"What?"

"Look at his girlfriend funny."

Jack's hand fell into his lap, while he scanned the roof of the truck. He opened his mouth, but before he could answer, she leaned back in her seat and made a low sound, "Hmmm ... Listen Jack, I know you've had this crush on her since Café-Abe, but—"

"You do? Does she know?"

"I don't think so. If she did, she wouldn't let that interfere with your friendship anyway. She just doesn't see that kind of thing sitting in front of her face."

"Unlike you," he replied caustically.

She gave him a bright smile and raised one shoulder coyly. "Yeah ... but I'm not the one you're flipped over. It's always easier to spot when you're not the target. Anyway, I think she likes his confidence, though I wouldn't call it that. You know these engineer types."

118

"Think they're God's gift to the economy."

"And everyone in it." Jen shifted in her seat. "She may be with him now, but that doesn't mean she'll marry the guy. In fact, I'd put money down they split up by Christmas."

"Why?" he asked, trying to pace the hope swimming to the surface.

Jen's mouth screwed up and her eyebrows came together. "She can do better. You're right about him, about his ego I mean. He's got that Little-Man syndrome, makes him pompous. Maybe he's intimidated by you."

Jack's voice was doubtful, "We're the same height. I'm not any bigger than him."

Jerking her head, Jen said, "Yeah, I forgot—size is everything. ... He may be her first, and for now it probably gives him an edge, but you've been her buddy forever. Imagine how he feels. She talks about you enough and he's pretty possessive. They even had a fight about it last week."

A sharp disappointment tugged at his heart, hearing that this prick had taken her to bed. It was the same masculine indignation in learning that Michelle was not a virgin either, but the idea of a guy in bed with Donna was worse and Ric's displays of ownership pushed that fact into Jack, over and over. The guy constantly had his arm around her or her hand locked in his.

Part of the problem for Jack was his own loneliness. Somehow, Ric's message emphasized how he'd let Michelle walk away. He called her periodically, just polite conversations tinged with hopelessness. They were two people who carried similar heartfelt pains, but regardless of Michelle's side of it, he knew the balance of the problem rested on him.

After wrestling with this for so long, here was Jen condensing five years into a few sentences. It was disconcerting to be read so easily. Jen and Donna knew nothing about Michelle, nothing at all, but suddenly he feared it painted on his face. Jen seemed to smell lies and she'd just dig deeper until all secrets were divulged. He had this comical image of her in a Nazi uniform, torturing people with nothing but words. They would be begging for freedom in seconds, ready to confess all.

But could Jen predict a breakup? Now that he thought about it, he'd witnessed some strong tension between Ric and Donna. A few months ago, she had shined from his attentions. Jack remembered her talking endlessly about their first date, until he'd almost put his fist through the window. Tonight, Donna seemed restless and annoyed. She could do better, a lot better, and maybe she was starting to gauge her unbelievable talent for picking assholes.

If he'd spoken up sooner, then Donna wouldn't be with this jerk who wanted to keep her on a leash. ... The distance didn't help either.

(Hell, three hours of road was enough to kill any relationship. Oh, get real. Three hundred hours would be nothing if she were on the other end.)

The problem was she just wasn't on the other end. If not with Ric the Prick, then she would probably end up with someone else. For now, Donna would likely plug along with that loser, thinking he was some great guy, while Jack beat his head against a wall.

Taking a deep breath, Jack sighed. Jen was fiddling with the radio dial, but unable to find any song to suit her mood, she clicked it off.

"Buddy, in a weird way, she's closer to you than me or anyone really."

"Then, why am I the last one to find out they hit the sack already?"

Her eyes narrowed. "Did it ever occur to you that maybe she's afraid of what you'll think of her?"

"She's not the asshole, he is."

"Well, for now that's not how she sees him. Look, if you want my advice—and of course you do—I would prescribe a strong dose of casual sex ... not with me, Stupid. Don't give me that look. Just go out and find someone who looks like her and bop her silly."

(Already tried ...)

"Not my style Jen."

"Oh, bullshit! You're a guy. Chasing tail is what you people do best. Now take me home ... in the non-sex way."

He pulled away from the curb and drove down the street. When they arrived at her apartment, he asked, "I don't suppose you'd keep this conversation between us?"

"Don't be a doorknob."

He felt a little more secure then. Jen wasn't the most sensitive person in the world, but if she agreed to a code of silence, she could be trusted to honor it.

"OK ... accessing my Jen / English language dictionary ... Oh, that means 'yes'. You really do turn into a nice person after dark, don't you? Some kinda reverse vampire."

"It's no big deal. So I ca—"

"You care? Jen cares!"

"Shut up." Jen rolled her eyes and stepped out.

"I bet you practice being polite too," he added, "So *nicccccce! Nice—nice—nice—nice—*"

Slam!

As Jack spun a U-turn, he continued calling through the open window, "*Nice—nice—nice—nice—nice—nice—*"

He could see her tugging smirk below the finger salute held high and proud.

"That's my girl," he nodded.

***

A few days after the Rummoli game, Donna started the second year of her program. Professors didn't waste any time coddling students who still had summer on their minds. They made it clear that the Doctors-To-Be were to eat, sleep, and breathe medicine, but Donna didn't object. Just as she was excited to share her summer break with Ric, she now looked forward to diving back into her studies. She felt so antsy, bordering on hyper.

That week, a strange series of dreams filled her nights. They were choppy, fast moving scenes prompting contradictory feelings. Though always difficult to recall the particulars, there was an overwhelming mood of anticipation and simultaneous loss. It was the same every night—the feeling of being swept along an exciting current of events, which inevitably led to some sort of betrayal.

Upon waking, a mix of erotic and sad thoughts would creep through her mind, leaving her exhausted after a full night's sleep. Most bothersome was their vague familiarity, especially one prominent image—her mother's face—but it was different from what she remembered, younger with beautiful skin and a glowing smile. Mystifying was the incongruity of this lovely image creating such despondency.

Donna thought the dreams represented her fizzling relationship with Ric. She spent several days determining how to address it, but she was terribly inexperienced in the etiquette of breaking up.

Within days, the words became necessary.

***

Michelle waited nervously. Playing with a spoon, she stirred it in her water glass, then let the current grab hold and toss it about. Small bubbles chased the spoon, disappearing as soon as they made contact. One second they were there, the next they were gone. The sight was peculiarly lonesome.

It had been four months since Jack left for Calgary, and in all that time, he had only called a few times. She often picked up the phone, but never seemed to finish the number sequence. Instead, she would stare at it, frustrated with her own stubbornness.

Last night, it had rung and she'd jumped up with high hopes.

"Hello?"

"Hello yourself."

Colin. He was the last person she expected to hear from. How many months was it? Almost a year. And he sounded as if they'd never missed a day. Through an uncomfortable pause, she suddenly found herself sitting down.

She should say something. What?

(How are you? Are you in Red Deer? Why did you dump me last year? Did you think of me even once since then?)

But he spoke first. "Hey, I'm in town tomorrow. Are you free for lunch? I can be at Zoria's Deli at noon."

Before she could collect herself, she meekly agreed and hung up bewildered. Shortest conversation they'd ever had. Why did he want to see her again? She considered the possibilities and concluded that he was just looking to get laid. Their short-lived relationship couldn't have meant much to him, not with the fast way he'd left it. She'd be sure to steel herself against his charms.

The next day, Colin arrived right on time, looking much like he did a year ago: jeans, brightly colored rugby shirt, freshly shaven. His sandy brown hair was short like Michelle's, except for the straight sweep of it across his forehead. It fell into his eyes and he had a habit of brushing it out of the way with his hand. She remembered sliding her fingers along its length.

Though not large, he was tall, his lean build giving off a friendly energy. Of all his traits, it was this quiet intensity that had attracted Michelle the most. In a world where people were most interested in talking, Colin listened and accurately determined what made them tick. He was observant, noticing the stitching on her sleeve becoming unraveled or the exact cologne from someone five feet away. Was he seeing into her right now?

"Hi."

"Hi yourself."

He had a funny way of throwing greetings back at her, but he was so cute about it, Michelle didn't find it annoying at all.

Bending down, he kissed her cheek before sitting across from her. The gesture was a gentle one and enticed a cautious smile. Catching a faint scent of his aftershave, it automatically brought back a barrage of memories: sitting close on her couch, against him in bed, stealing a kiss at a traffic light. She released a quiet sigh.

As soon as he sat down, he picked up a fork and stood it on end. It swiveled from side to side between his fingers. She was reminded of all the little things he used to do, gestures and mannerisms unique to him. Unable to sit completely still, he fiddled with things, a pen, his keys, salt and pepper shakers. Always something in his hands. She imagined it might really bother some people, but this habit was almost fascinating, the way a magician deflects attention with the little flourishes of his fingers.

At first, their conversation was sidetracked through the usual small talk areas. He was back in school, the Faculty of Commerce. She spent the summer working at a bookstore. She had been considering staying in Red Deer to work for a year, but recently decided to head back to U of A, finally set on a political science major. They'd probably see each other around campus. Yes, she still attended church. His parents were fine, but his sister broke her leg water-skiing in the summer. A nasty spiral fracture. He had just bought a Scottish terrier. It was a pleasant meal and she was a little surprised at her own calmness through it ... at least, until his compliment.

Studying her, he suddenly proclaimed, "You look amazing."

Michelle swallowed uncomfortably.

"I mean it."

"Colin," she stammered, "I um ..."

"Look, I know you're wondering what we're doing here, but I didn't come down for kicks." He was watching her closely and caution swept over her.

"So, why did you?"

"I've been thinking for a long time. I've missed you."

Blinking, she finally responded, "The past year would beg to differ."

"Well, something happened." Colin leaned back and for once, his hands completely relaxed, which betrayed his true nervousness. Those hands were never still. "My cousin died. Stevie."

"I know," she replied softly, "I saw the obituary. Cancer at what—fourteen? His folks must have been devastated."

"Very. Anyway, we were all at his funeral. You know, me and about three hundred people packed into this church and they were singing this hymn I didn't know. And Hanna was totally off-key—"

"Hanna?"

"Oh, you guys never met. Just someone from school. The point is that when I look back, I realize that I was alone. I just felt ... *alone*, and I couldn't figure out why. And then it hit me. It didn't matter what I was doing in my day, school or work or fartin' around or this funeral, I was alone. A situation like that, you start to think 'What matters at the end of the day?' It's not what you do, it's who you do it with. I should have been there with *you*. I should have spent the past year with *you*. I was just so fucked up."

Michelle's heart skipped a beat and then she suddenly frowned. "Wait a minute. Why was she there?"

"Who?"

"Hanna. Did she know Stevie?"

"No." He peered at her, perplexed.

She suddenly nodded. "You were *seeing* her. ... A funeral is personal, Colin. If you don't know the deceased, then you're there for someone you care about. That was right after you broke up with me. But you had to have been seeing her long before that for her to be there with you. Nobody takes a new relationship to a funeral."

His silence seemed to confirm the worst.

She was looking at him wide-eyed. This was a stunning revelation to her Christian mindset. When he'd ended it with her, she assumed that he left her for someone else, but for there to be an overlap? She felt ridiculously naïve. A hundred signs probably showed what he was doing and she'd ignored them all.

"When did it start?" she asked and was surprised to hear her words whispered.

Colin sighed at the cold look in her eyes. "A few weeks before. I didn't know how to tell you. It was stupid ... and didn't last long."

"All this time I thought you dumped me after the classic cheap score, but it was just because of some other cheap score." Her voice had risen sharply and he patted the air with hunched shoulders while glancing around.

"Look Mitch, I screwed up. I did want to be with you. You're the whole package—I know that sounds cheesy—but it kind of freaked me out. I mean, look at you. You've got everything, plus this spiritual stuff. I understand how important that is now."

(You're playing me. You're just playing me all over again. God, how stupid do you think I am? ... God, how I've wanted to hear this.)

Michelle leaned back in her seat, softly biting her lip. Assuming he actually was sincere, there was still that big hole in her heart from the last time he walked away. She would need a game plan, one to protect her. But that was exactly how she'd messed it up with Jack ... because she didn't need to be protected from *him*. She should have played it oppositely: connect with Jack on his terms and force Colin to meet her on hers.

Her eyes narrowed and it was a look Colin had never quite seen from her before. Scrutiny, layered with light confidence. The look of a candidate with a job offer, who only needs to negotiate salary.

"This package has changed. It's now served with God, not sex."

"That's exactly what I'm looking for. Consider it trading up, no offense."

She stared at his sincere face and grappled with the conflicting urges of head and heart. He still knew how to smooth her over, a trait both endearing and worrisome. One man had earned a place in her past, which was comforting in its familiarity, and the other could earn a place in her future if she chose.

Colin was her first, her only ... and along with that went the memories of crying in despair when it fell apart. Jack never made her cry in despair, only she'd been the cause of that, always staying reserved around him. Maybe she kept her distance because beneath the stamina of her values, she was comparatively weaker. He was the one who could pick up the pieces of his life and carry on, and if she let him, he would carry on without her.

She remembered dancing with Jack on their first date, closely but not crowded by his body. He had a wonderful body, the product of hours spent in the gym. It was an indication of the kind of person he was: hard-working, steady. There was nothing unreliable or cruel about him. He had questioned her heart with savage demand, but now she concluded that it was probably deserved.

She'd been strict with Jack all year, keeping his hands away, setting up those physical boundaries, even though she yearned for the touch of a man. Michelle already knew Colin's touch—playful and exciting—but Jack was so much more. He held an inner strength and a sweet innocence of that strength.

She had accused Jack of not knowing what he wanted. If anyone was indecisive, it was her. Until this very moment, she hadn't understood the extent of her confusion, but seeing the choices set before her dissolved them into a simplicity.

"I'm glad you want to find God, but that's something you've got to do on your own. I can't be your spiritual aspirin."

"Spiritual aspirin?"

"Maybe you're just associating me with a time when you felt better. How do I know if any of this is really about me or not?"

As she spoke, Colin had been shaking his head. He gazed intently at her and leaning forward, gripped her forearm firmly, which lay folded politely on the table. Though her heart leapt at his touch, she pulled her arm away and tucked it into her lap.

"It has everything to do with you. ... Mitch, when I think of who I want to be, what kind of person, I can't see myself being that without you."

She stared, speechless. That was a big compliment, probably the biggest compliment a man had ever paid her.

"Well, I thought that too," she stated quietly, "I mean about myself when I was with you. But a lot's happened since then. You think I've been sitting in one place waiting for you to come back?"

"No, I just ..." Colin stared. "Are you saying you've got a boyfriend?"

Michelle sighed, uncertainty renewed. "Yes, thank you for assuming I didn't. ... To tell you the truth, I don't know, but he's put a lot more time and effort into it than you did, plus I'm pretty sure he's not screwing around on me, so excuse me if I need more than words to be convinced." The tears were too close to the surface and her voice broke. "I gotta go."

Wanting no obligation between them, she quickly dropped a bill on the table and rose, but he took her hand.

"Wait. Listen, I'm gonna be here for a couple of days." He pointed straight into his chair. "Right here ... eating corned beef 'til I puke. I won't move. OK? I'll be right here."

She almost relaxed and smiled, but instead, twisted out of his grasp and hurried out.

At home, Michelle thought for a long time, and after a sleepless night, made a decision.

***

CHAPTER 16

Jack glanced at his watch. Eight-thirty. Work wasn't until nine. Carrying another cup of coffee, he walked to his bedroom, where boxes lined the walls. Until he found a steady job and moved out of his mother's condominium, those possessions would stay packed. It was strange living out of a suitcase in the most permanent home he ever knew, but last month, Mark had mentioned an interest in his old room. Jack definitely wanted to avoid sharing space with his brother; maintaining a transient layout was an effective reminder that time was short.

Picking up a black marker, he put a line through yesterday. Tuesday, September seventh, now in the past, never to be seen again. Only six more days until his research job was slated to end. There was a marginal chance funding would be extended for another six months, but it seemed unlikely. He needed a career. Lately, he was considering the police force. Maybe if he made some inquiries this week, it might take his mind off Ric and Donna.

For days now, he'd been contemplating those two.

(Donna must have strong feelings for that prick. Girls always do about the first one, and she doesn't go through men like Jen. If she felt anything like Michelle did about Colin, then I got no chance with either one.)

A big gulp finished his coffee. As the cup lowered, his line of vision opened on a picture tacked to the bulletin board across the room. A younger Donna and Jack smiled laughingly at him. Her pale green dress and his suit reflected five years of unreturned affection.

"This is bullshit," he muttered to himself.

It was never going to happen with Donna. Even if Ric took a hike tomorrow, Jack would be off in the wings while some other guy jumped onto center stage. He had put Michelle on hold to chase an elusive fantasy,

127

based partly on fact and mostly on pure fabrication. Donna had become someone unreal to him. No longer a woman with a balance of beauty and bad habits, his obsession had reduced the negative aspects, so that only a lovely image remained with soft lights to surround and support it. If she chose to sleep with Ric, then Ric had forced her. If she stayed with him, he must have twisted her thinking.

Jack began to realize how much he'd strayed from seeing Donna as a mature person, responsible for her own failings, and it wasn't fair to either of them. Nor to Michelle. Having patiently given him the summer to consider their relationship, there he was, squandering his time waiting for Donna to leave Ric. When Michelle's face crossed his mind, she was miserable, the way she was when she left his apartment that night. By now, she was likely lost to him. A star quarterback in a no-win game. Maybe Jack had been playing for the wrong team all along, his attention fixed so far afield that in the back of his mind, Michelle was already in the past tense.

With reluctance, Jack reached a turning point. Maybe it was this frame of mind that set the stage for the next segment of his life. On his own, he wouldn't have seen it through, but later that day, the woman he'd needed all along came back to find him, and in no time at all, she solidified his resolve.

***

Donna often disappeared during class breaks to shut her eyes and clear her head before the next blast of information overload, but today, she was enjoying a coffee with Dennis Fontaine. Having shared immunology with Dennis, she was glad to see him in her neurology class now. He was a good study partner, that is, when he wasn't trying to set her up with his friend. Sometimes, he went a little overboard.

"You'd like him."

"Why? What's so special about this guy?"

"You know you always ask two questions in a row? ... He's just like you—well, besides his stunning skill of listening to an answer before moving on to the next question and making drinkable coffee—all he does is study and ace his courses."

Donna laughed, "Wow, I counted three slams in that delivery. Bonus points for couching them in compliments. Do you practice that? ... Or is it a natural talent since birth?"

"Nice try with the conjunction, but that was still two questions. Jesus! Is that your leg? You're gonna spill everything."

Sorry, I'm just frazzled. I'm not getting enough sleep and it's making me weird. I'm running on fumes."

"Well, pace yourself. That's not supposed to happen 'til exams."

Donna pushed the coffee away and tried to relax her hands.

"OK, enough about you," Dennis said, "Back to Brian. Just think about it. He's seen you around and he's asked about you. He's a good guy. Look, there he is—blue plaid shirt."

"What are you on, cupid commission?"

But curious, she turned to see a slender man with brown hair walk steadily across the foyer. Unrushed, he carried a paper cup and a knapsack stuffed full, balanced on his shoulders with ease. Although he lacked Ric's powerful presence, he seemed attractive and relaxed. She could definitely use some relaxed people in her life.

"Maybe if he loses the plaid … Come on, let's get to class."

She rose and followed Dennis toward the Biological Sciences building, deflecting more of his barbs. It was like dealing with a male Jen, though Jen never played cupid. In Donna's mildly flattered mood, she missed Ric skulking behind the stairs.

***

Jen walked fast for someone of her small stature. Her car kept stalling on the way to school and the only parking spot was beyond the Bio building. It was always crapping out when she needed to be somewhere.

(Not another repair bill. Never should have bought this piece of shit.)

This was the first week of school and her last semester before graduating. Normally, she didn't place much importance on attendance, but her profs were already organizing them into groups for upcoming theatrical productions. She could miss her first class if late, which occurred more often than not, but she couldn't miss her production meeting at 9:15.

They were planning to divvy up all the unpleasant stage tasks, and if Jen didn't show up, Dean would probably delegate the bulk of work to her. He was such a dick—trying to be an actor and only one very blunt prof had dared burst his bubble. In a weird way, he had switched to the director's chair by dominating group assignments. Everyone knew that was Jen's job.

A gentle breeze caressed her face as she picked up her pace through the parking lot, zigzagging between cars. She liked fall weather, that spicy mix of crisp morning air and summery afternoon warmth. The sun had risen early today with cheerful promise for the morning ahead, but for some reason, Jen felt keyed up … and then her car stumbled all the way here. A superstitious person would probably deem it ominous, but what would that change? She'd still be strung out with a useless car.

At least the shortcut connecting the buildings was clear. In winter, students could spend the whole day going from building to building without ever putting a jacket on. Dozens of tables lined the Social Sciences foyer, an aptly named building. Jen skirted past a long row of tables, automatically scanning the area for familiar faces.

(Hey, there's Don having coffee with some guy. Good thing Ric's not here to see that!)

Jen debated stopping, but already late, scooted down the stairs and past "The Pit" to the lower-level classrooms.

(Damn, which room is it?)

Scurrying along the curved hallway, she looked for signs of her group in the classrooms. Not here, not there, not in that one ... Then suddenly, her classmates were strolling casually out the next door right in front of her and Jen barely stopped her feet in time.

Skidding haphazardly, her shoes made a high-pitched squeak against the smooth tiled floor. It sounded like runners in a basketball game. Her brown knapsack was thrown from its safe shoulder perch and the strap caught on her forearm, swinging its weight across her stomach. She twisted herself to avoid hitting both her classmates and the floor, but it was in vain for as soon as she regained her balance, she was violently shoved from behind. This time, the knapsack dropped to the floor with a blunt *thud!*

Jen fell straight into the group, then down to the floor, followed by the swiftest reminder of something terribly unpleasant, the sensation of flying uncontrollably through air ... but there was hardly time to think about it with the wind knocked out of her. A few seconds passed before she realized that someone was at fault. She looked around, sharp accusations in her eyes, but the guilty party was already disappearing. A glimpse of dark red was all Jen saw.

Her first impulse was to chase down the woman, but instead she yelled, "Hey, what the hell are you doing! I know what you look like! You'll be seeing me again!" Too late, the maniac was gone as quickly as she appeared.

Dean pursed his lips as though whistling. Staring down the hall, he said, "Whoa, I'd get flattened by her any day."

He was such an ass. Jen started to glare when she saw his absorbed expression: no leering quality in his eyes or tone, just honest admiration. It was so uncharacteristic of him, it stopped her biting words.

"Here, this is your share." Dean handed her a lengthy list of duties for their next project.

130

Taking the paper, she rolled her eyes and bit her tongue. What a lousy morning, the kind that augers a disastrous day ahead. Every little thing seemed so inflated. Maybe she just needed some coffee ... and someone she could stand to drink it with.

Upstairs, she searched the tables for Donna. Nope, must be back in class already. But there was always Jack. His office was just around the corner.

As she passed through the foyer, her brow furrowed.

(Did I forget something?)

A feeling of despair suddenly enveloped her. The accident in high school. That woman ... that dark-haired woman who bent over her. She was here somewhere. Jen could feel it.

Spinning abruptly, she scrutinized every face in sight, logging and sorting features with the speed of a computer hardly knowing how or why, but since the mystery woman had never been seen by Jen's eyes, accuracy was impossible.

So instead she stood calmly, and with closed eyes, turned her search inward. The woman was still here somewhere ... somewhere. And then it faded away like a radar signal moving just out of range. Gradually, the despair also faded until there was nothing but Jen's own questioning thoughts to fill the space. After a reflective minute, she pushed them aside and walked to Jack's office.

***

Neurology had been tough today. Mountains of material to get through. Donna debated skipping her afternoon errands in favor of studying with Dennis, but she really needed to go to the bank and get groceries. And it was time with Jen. In the thick of school, sometimes running errands with a friend was her only social outlet.

Dennis reiterated the virtues of his friend all the way to Donna's locker. Brian this, Brian that ...

(God, he's worse than that snoopy matchmaker from Fiddler on the Roof.)

Did he really think she was going to wrap her legs around another guy before ending it with Ric? As she extracted her knapsack from her locker, she paused to zip up the front flap, securing her wallet and keys.

(I didn't leave that open. ... Did I?)

It was so refreshing to step outside after being cooped up all day. A gentle breeze balanced the sun's heat and Donna inhaled deeply. Thankfully, Dennis's car was the other way. She wasn't up to introducing him to Jen;

the two of them together would make her run to that matchmaker with open arms.

Donna found Jen at the far end of the parking lot, brushing something off the passenger seat of the Valiant.

"Look what some asshole did!"

The passenger window had been smashed in and Jen was using a rag to clean off the seat.

"Did they take anything?"

"Like what? My breath mints? Who would break into a shit-heap like this? OK, I think I got all the pieces. Now for part seventeen of Jen's Shitty Day—The Car That Wouldn't Start."

But to her surprise, it started fine.

"I barely got it here this morning," Jen muttered perplexed.

"Sounds OK now. Do you want to just get it home in case you can't start it again? I can walk."

"Naw, let's get our stuff done."

"Well, what about the window? You don't want to report this?" Donna pulled out her cell phone.

"There's no point. Here," Jen instructed, tossing a blanket onto the seat, "Sit on this. Where to first?"

"Mall."

Donna considered making "mall" a verb somehow just to bug her, but the phone suddenly beeped. She muttered, "Oh, it's probably Ric." After a pause, she tucked the phone away. Jen glanced over enquiringly and Donna made a face.

"Not up to it right now ... Hey, were you in my locker today?" The words were sharper than she'd intended.

"Dial it down! I'm the one having a shitty day. You PMS-ing?"

"No, I'm just trying to figure something out. So?"

"So what? Oh, no I wasn't in your precious locker. But I did go by. I saw you having coffee with someone in the foyer this morning."

"What were you doing in Social Sciences?"

Most of Jen's classes were in the Fine Arts building, clear across campus.

"I was meeting my stage group. We're putting on that all-important production at the end of the month."

Donna strained to recall the all-important production and finally gave up. She had been too busy getting into courses and out of relationships to pay attention to Jen's dealings.

(When in doubt, change the subject.)

"Oh hey, guess what?" Donna announced, trying to make her tone lighter. "Did you know The Pit's gonna be flipped into a study area? No more lounging around on bad furniture and choking on cancer sticks."

"It's not a puffer zone anyway."

"Like they cared. It was out of hand. Classes down the hall were complaining about the fumes. So, now if you want to do a Pit-Sit, you have to be quiet and read a book."

"Well for you, that's a match made in heaven. So, what are you doing tonight? Reading six or seven hundred pages on diseases?"

"Almost as good—I have to see Ric."

"Don't you sound excited," Jen responded dryly.

(And therein lies the bitchiness. Can't wait 'til this guy's gone.)

"Trust me, I'm not … and I'm sure he won't be either, when he hears what I have to say."

"Uh-oh, I assume the end is near?"

"Oh, the end came for me a while ago. That's my bank. Park here."

The bank was sandwiched between a shoe store and a post office. At the sight of some boots, Donna knew Jen would be gone for the next half-hour. She drove salesclerks nuts, trying on everything in the store, only to say, "No, I'm really just browsing."

Donna was lucky. Usually there was a big line-up at this time of day, but the bank machine was devoid of customers. She dug into her wallet and found her card.

Insufficient funds available.

For some reason, the machine kept repeating this stupid message.

Donna stepped in line for the next available teller. Wasn't the point of a bank card to avoid these line-ups?

"Hi. There's something wrong with my card. It won't let me take any money out."

"Let me check. Do you have it with you?"

Donna passed it over the counter and the teller swiped it through her machine.

"According to our records, you withdrew one thousand dollars today. That's the daily limit on this account."

"I haven't used my card today."

"Well, this shows that amount was taken out."

"It couldn't have been. OK look, where was the withdrawal?"

"Through the machine at this branch … at 8:42 a.m."

"That's got to be a bank error. I was in school."

"Does anyone have access to your card?"

"No." Wait a minute. Her wallet was in her locker all day. Did someone take her card? Ric and Jen were the only ones who knew the combination. A thousand dollars. She peered into her wallet.

(This twenty isn't going to go very far. Debits won't work until tomorrow. No point borrowing from Jen. She never has any money. Crap ...)

Donna dragged a protesting Jen out of the shoe store, while mentally deleting most of her grocery list.

When Jen dropped her off, Donna made a second discovery. Her key was sitting in the front pouch of her knapsack, off the key ring. Another odd occurrence, but the money was a bigger problem. Huge.

After putting groceries away, Donna stepped into the bathroom. The toilet seat was up.

Standing there frozen, it all came together. The money, the key. Ric was playing at some kind of control game. Clean out her account, gain access to her apartment, dissuade her from her friends. He'd practically moved in here himself. But he'd gotten careless with the toilet seat. What the hell was he doing in her apartment today? The thought was totally creepy.

(What should I do? Well, for starters, he's history. He was anyway. I could get a big burly roommate. No, I like the quiet. ... Shit, I'd better check if anything's missing.)

Donna quickly rifled through her possessions, but everything seemed accounted for. She returned to the bathroom and stared at the toilet, deep in thought. Could she be wrong? Tired with school and jumpy as hell, maybe she had started to clean the toilet this morning and just didn't put the lid down. She had been so out of it lately. No, Ric had been here and he was going to see his mistake when he came over tonight.

***

Later that evening, Ric arrived at Donna's apartment. She opened her mouth to speak, but his entrance threw her off. After setting a simple kiss on her lips, he simply breezed through the living room, the way he had breezed past her at the bar, as if she didn't exist. Take her or leave her.

He barely said, "Hi," before getting a beer out of the refrigerator. In one movement, he managed to swallow half of it and then strode directly into the bathroom. Donna stared at the closed door nervously.

When Ric came out, he leaned against her balcony door with an unreadable expression. Then, flipping the latch, he swung the door open and stepped outside. Following reluctantly, Donna watched him carefully and tried to gauge his reaction. Ric must have seen the toilet seat and realized he'd been caught. To be honest, she was still uncertain about his guilt, but independent of that, there was a frightening air about him right now. He looked like a dog kept on a tight leash, just waiting for the next irritation to set him off.

Nursing his beer, the silence was unbearable.

Finally, she decided to start the conversation herself. She asked about his day in acidic tones that left no doubt of her intentions. The argument quickly swelled, and in the heat of the moment, Donna told Ric she never wanted to see him again.

***

... Everywhere her mind went, the sounds followed, even in this nothingness. Inflated, each memory became that much stronger, rougher, and more desperate. You'd think a place that black would allow for quiet repose, but Donna could barely think amidst such noise.

Big terrifying crashes and small frightened whispers all pressed in on her equally, giving her no room to move. Just wait it out until it passes ... but, oh God, the interminable stretch of time until it did. Waves of smashing, weeping, ringing over and over again. If only she would ...

***

(Pick up, Jen. Pick up! ...)

"Hello?"

"Call Jack and come and get me."

"Don, why are you whispering?"

She was shocked to hear Donna crying in shallow gulps, but her voice was so muffled, Jen had to press the phone tightly against her ear. There was also the steady sound of water running. It reminded her of the relaxation tapes her mother listened to. A trickling stream to calm one's nerves.

"Where are you?"

"Home, bathroom. Call Jack and get over here fast."

"Don, what happened?" Silence. "Donna! Has he hurt you?"

A small voice, not wanting to speak the answer. "Yes."

"That stupid fuck! OK look, Billy just walked in. Hang tight. We'll take his car. ... You *what!*" Jen screamed away from the phone. "You won't believe this, Donna. The first time in five years he rides his goddamned bike!"

Donna heard what sounded like a pile of coins in the background and she realized that Jen had thrown her keys to Billy. "See if it'll start. Just go! I'll tell you after."

A dull sound came through on Donna's end, knuckles on wood. Jen strained her ears over the running water. She expected awful sounds—thuds, screams, breaking glass.

Donna slid a knife out from the folds of a towel and gripped it tightly in her free hand. "Just a minute," she called, "I'm still washing up." She sounded amazingly calm, a complete transformation from a minute ago.

"I'm going home," Ric announced.

"OK, I'm gonna get to bed. I'll see you tomorrow," Donna responded agreeably.

"Sure."

Jen was flabbergasted. What kind of psycho pounds someone and then makes conversation to bore your grandma? And how was Donna able to play along so well?

Donna could sense him leaning into the bathroom door. Her eyes bore through the wood, knife pointed, willing him away. Finally she heard the front latch. Opening the bathroom door a crack, she scanned an empty living room, then put the phone back to her ear. The knife stayed glued to her hand.

"He's gone."

"Lock the door."

"It won't matter. He's got a key."

"Why in hell did you give him that?"

"*I didn't*," Donna spat out the words, "I think he made a copy today, and I think he got into my bank account and took some money." She went to the window. "Oh Christ, he's still there. He's smoking in his car. He's not leaving!"

"What? Look, just get out. Go out the back door."

"I already tried. It's stuck."

"Call the cops now or else I will."

Donna spoke with a bitter combination of high-pitched stress and helplessness. She had already run through this a million times in the last ten minutes.

"Don't you see? Even if he didn't copy my key, he could still grab me anywhere. I tried to break up with him tonight and he went nuts. I need someone to deal with him or I'll have to live in hiding until he finishes what he started!"

Jen remembered the comment Peter had made in bed.

(When Ric gets set on something, there's no changing it.)

And a disturbing image followed. She could see Donna's bruises multiplied, her body limp on the living room carpet. There would be things strewn about to indicate Donna's futile defense against Ric's strength and determination: books, broken dishes, furniture knocked over, and in the middle of it all, she would lie with a glassy-eyed stare at nothing.

"Here's what we're gonna to do. Get your things together. You're staying here tonight. ..." A pause and then Jen spoke away from the phone again, "Yeah? Oh, finally something good ... Don, the car's running. We're coming now."

"OK. I'll call Jack."

"No, keep your line open. We'll call him on the way. Meanwhile, get into one of the other apartments there."

"I tried. No one's home. Just hurry."

Donna was loath to hang up, but Jen was right about keeping the phone line open. Punching in 911, she hung up before the connection was made. One little redial button was all it would take.

Still clutching the knife, she grabbed some things at random: three shirts pulled straight off their hangers, underwear, pajamas, another shirt ... She couldn't catalogue necessary items through her shaky tears. Clothes? This weapon was all she needed. She almost cut her ear with it, while wiping her eyes with the back of her hand. The effort was pointless. Many more tears waited to fall, and not only tonight. The realization brought on a sad depth of hopelessness.

She would never feel safe again.

***

He watched the front of the apartment building intently, just sitting in his car, blowing little rings of smoke out of his mouth. He appeared relaxed, as though enjoying the replays of marvelous sex. After jamming the back door—the front would have been better, but someone could have seen him—Ric expected her to tear across the front lawn. Her lights were on. Must still be in the bathroom. Girls could fucking live in that room.

At least her only escape route was a badly lit one. These older apartments had tons of trees blocking the streetlights. And they were built narrow and tall, creating lots of shadows.

Movement straight ahead: Two people with a dog turned the corner and crossed the street, cutting just behind his car. Ric slid down in the seat. Their voices sounded clipped and terse. Probably arguing. Seemed to be the thing tonight.

137

The dog, sensing something, dragged his owners to sniff at the driver's side door. He started to growl, but a stern yank on the leash pulled him away.

Ric stayed hunkered down for minute. When their voices grew faint, he shifted upright. The cigarette was still poised between his thumb and index finger.

As he inhaled deeply, its red tip burned brightly. Smoke escaping his lips briefly veiled her only exit. Couldn't watch two, and he congratulated himself on his ingenuity. Ma would be proud. "You gotta have a plan, Ricardo," she'd say, "A plan will get you the important things."

He took an inventory of his assets: Donna only had three neighbors in that building, none home. It took a full month to get their schedules down pat. He had jammed the back door, disconnected her phones—one of the benefits of an engineering education—and taken care of the cell phone. Jen would take the heat for that and the money too.

But then, he had almost blown it when Donna started the argument. Making sure he saw the toilet seat. Obviously, she'd already moved on with some other dude. Must be Jack the way she was madly cleaning her place for Rummoli.

(Damn well wouldn't have bothered for me.)

He understood plenty, but the one thing he hadn't counted on was getting dumped. It bumped up his timeline while there was still daylight and a witness would be disastrous. So would leaving evidence. He'd have to remember to take the beer bottle fragments. Fingerprints on table tops? Explainable. Fingerprints on broken glass? Not so easy.

No, the key was to make it look like a suicide or an accident. A fall off the balcony could explain the black eye and post-mortem blood work would confirm everything, but he was prepared to go with Plan B. Once she bolted, a few strategic blows delivered between the buildings could simulate the exact bruising from a fall. Then place her body at a spot right in front of the balcony. It was almost dark enough. If she didn't come out soon, it was back to Plan A.

(Just make sure she's passed out this time and goes head-first. No crying your way out of that one.)

A memory perched on the edge of his mind: his mother holding a bag of ice to her swollen lips to muffle tears. She didn't see Ric watching in the dark, halfway up the stairs.

It started when he was small: a low voice spewing threatening words, punctuated by another blow. It went on for years, but one night Ric fought back and blind luck landed a punch to reverse the pattern for good. Though not trained to aim, he was big for twelve. He could still remember the thrilling spark of revenge at the splintering sound of that rib breaking, and the heavy-handed man whimpering on the kitchen floor.

There was a similar appealing taste of control when he swung at Donna. Announcing it was over, as if her decision was the only one that counted. Fuck that. She'd leave all right.

Ma almost left too, for about eight years. Bag packed and hidden so pathetically, the only person stupider than her was Dad for not finding it, tucked behind the flour in the pantry all that time.

(A plan is only as good as its execution. Execution! Fitting ...)

The lights went off in her apartment. And it was dark enough outside. Ric stepped out of the car and looked carefully down the street. Those people were still in sight, but far away. No one around.

Time to finish this. She had no way out. It really was a perfect plan. Just sneak back in.

But someone else already had.

***

CHAPTER 17

Donna paced through the apartment, glancing constantly at the front door. When she heard an insistent knock, her heart practically jumped out of her chest.

"Donna, open up. It's Billy."

With a shaky hand, Donna opened the door and Billy's face fell. He cautiously stepped in and shut the door behind him. Her left cheek was swollen enough to press one eye half-closed, and the start of an ugly bruise was forming. Tears kept sliding in a slick path down her cheeks from bloodshot eyes.

But Billy wasn't looking at her face. She confusedly watched him reach out as though to shake her hand, but instead, he gently opened her palm and removed the knife pointing straight at him. Her face crumpled.

He set it down out of reach and took her hands.

"Take a deep breath. ... Donna, look at me. Are you sure about the cops?"

"He did this because I broke up with him. What do you think he'd do if I pressed charges?"

"OK," he said reluctantly, "Jen's got the car in the alley."

"He must have seen you come in."

"No, he was looking the other way. I'll take care of this. You shouldn't be here."

Billy swiftly took in the layout.

(Door opens left ... visible in the mirror on that side ... smart of her turning the answering machine off ... prick won't get to her through the phone ... knife ... broken glass on floor ... ornament on bookcase ... hairbrush near lamp ... all potential weapons for him ... grab the knife too ...)

He scooped up the larger pieces of glass and collected the other items.

It was now dark enough for the apartment lights to block their view of the street. When Donna flicked them off, the living room was bathed in shadows. She stepped to one side of the window and peered out between the blinds.

"Jesus, how long can a man smoke? How do I go without him seeing? ... Oh God, he's coming back in!"

Billy thought quickly. "Is there a laundry room on this floor?"

"Yes." She grabbed her bag.

"Go. Stay there until he comes up. Then, get out to the car as fast as you can. Don't wait for me. I'll stay here tonight."

She handed him her cell phone. "Take this. My phones are dead."

Ushering her into the empty hallway, he closed the door and she heard the sharp click of the latch separating them. Now she was on the same side of the door as Ric. A bright light hung from the ceiling, which seemed to point her out with all the piercing accuracy of a spotlight. Here she is! Come and get her! She stood frozen under its beam, until heavy steps beat rhythmically up the front stairway.

Donna turned white. She stood stupidly under the hall light, unable to run as each sound carried an echo, amplifying and stretching it out. *Step—echo, step—echo, step—*

Move! She dove into the laundry room, closing the door as quietly as possible. Soapy smells circled her with stifling warmth. Standing against a loudly churning washing machine, Donna couldn't hear where Ric was. Coin-operated, no off—button. Her bag dropped to the floor with a muffled *thump!* Reaching behind, she pulled the cord out of the wall and the washer obediently went silent. She flattened her ear against the wall. She heard a key open her apartment door and then ... nothing.

Donna's eyes jumped around. What was happening in there? She peaked into the hallway—empty—and ran as lightly as possible down the stairs, out the entrance, around the building. Jen was waiting where Billy said she would be.

The Valiant was idling. God, don't stall now. Duct tape bordered up the smashed passenger window. As Donna shut the car door, she could feel bits of glass shifting under her runners.

Jen's eyes went wide. "Oh, Jesus! He did that to you? That big fuck." She gritted her teeth, pressing her foot onto the gas pedal hard, and the car lurched into gear.

"Wait!" Donna exclaimed, "Ric's nuts. We can't leave Billy there."

"Yes, we can. He's a second-level black belt. Pity Ric."

They sped away through the dark alley.

"Tomorrow we'll get your locks changed. You should also get your bank account switched ... but how did he get in it in the first place?"

"He took my card today when I was in class. He must have figured out my PIN number. Maybe he saw me punching it in or something. I never told it to him. I just know there's a thousand dollars missing, and my key wasn't where it was supposed to be when I got home. Did you call Jack?"

"Yeah, he wasn't home."

Donna moaned, "Oh, no."

"What?" Jen asked, alarmed.

"I left my bag up there."

Jen angled her head in exasperation. "You want to go back and get it?"

Donna shook her head, as more tears squeezed out from between tight lashes.

With anger leaping from her eyes, Jen glanced at her broken friend and muttered, "Where the hell is Jack?"

***

She led him into the hotel room. Barely inside the door, she reached up and started kissing him. Her hands slid along the row of buttons, finding the top one, and slowly undid it.

As the smoky smell of the bar drifted up from their clothes, she snaked one hand under his collar and over the swell of his shoulder. His musky scent overlapped the smoke. Very masculine.

Stepping closer, she said, "I want to feel your hands on my skin. I want to feel everything. ..."

Jack resisted tearing her clothes off and forced himself to match her pace. Her light touch was amazing. He let her undo each button, until she slid her warm hands around his waist and up his back. He pulled her shirt off and leaned down to kiss her neck. One hand held the back of her head and he could feel just how silky her short dark hair was. Then, he felt her fingers tugging on his zipper and he kissed her hungrily.

Clothes were scattered everywhere, making a direct path to the bed. Her sighs became heavy breaths that flowed lightly across his chest, and gone was the familiar ache of emptiness as if it had never plagued him. From that night on, his heart was released from Donna's hold and delivered into the hands of another.

***

When Billy phoned Jen's apartment, he calmly announced that Ric would no longer be a problem. Donna grew quiet at the implication and slept poorly on Jen's couch, seeing Ric's face in her dreams. He snarled maliciously as his arm stretched back for another blow, but then he changed into Billy and she was no less frightened.

Her mother was supposed to set things right somehow. Donna knew she was somewhere close, ready to help, but she wondered desperately if her mother could find her in time. Opening her mouth to scream, Donna's voice was gone, cut off with sudden searing pressure. Gales of wind swirled around her to steal every ounce of oxygen as she clawed the air. She woke up with a sheen of sweat on her skin, clutching her throat and reaching out to the woman she could still sense in those waking moments.

The next morning, Donna took a cab home. Determined to recapture some piece of independence, she refused Jen's equally determined offer to drive her. Even if the cab driver was protection of a sort, it wasn't the same as being guarded all night. The steps between Jen's place and the cab returned an element of confidence, of freedom she had taken for granted, but back in her apartment, she was reminded how scary it all was ... would always be.

Two rumpled blankets and a pillow lay on the couch. That couldn't have been very comfortable. She should have told Billy to sleep in her bed. There was a dark bloodstain soaked into the living room carpet, a good foot in diameter with a sticky thickness meshed into the carpet fibers.

She wondered exactly what Billy had done to Ric to leave this kind of mark, but an even more alarming thought weighed in.

(That stain could have been mine ... and if it had been, it would have been a lot bigger.)

With effort, she turned away and gestured to the kitchen table. "I'll make some coffee. Sorry, I only have instant."

Taking a seat in one of the chairs, he fidgeted so awkwardly that she finally remarked, "Don't believe Jen. My coffee isn't *that* bad."

They both smiled at the weak joke.

Then, Donna quietly stated, "Thank you. It must have been hard."

"No ... it wasn't."

They stared at each other, but after the intensity she'd just escaped, the message was too much and she dropped her gaze abruptly. She also didn't want attention on her face. It wasn't so much the unsightliness of the bruise as the aged misery in her eyes. He seemed to understand this, blinking uncomfortably and conveniently closing the subject for her.

He even called a locksmith. "We need someone as soon as possible. ... That's fine. Yeah, second building in from the corner. Apartment 3. We'll be waiting." Hanging up, he turned to Donna. "Someone can be here within the hour."

Donna busied herself with preparing coffee, feeling confused by her simultaneous relief and wariness of Billy's presence. He was a man, a large muscular man who had done something to draw blood, not a few drops by accident, but an ugly pool of it. Even across the room, it appeared huge. She dragged her eyes away to rest on the answering machine.

(Why's the power off?)

Her hand automatically reached out and touched the "on" button, and a tiny red light blinked up at her. *Beep!* All systems go. She stared at the little red circle. It was bright, like a fresh drop of blood. In her mind it expanded, erupting into one big pool. She could see it spilling over the counter and down to the floor, spreading the color everywhere, and she closed her eyes to the image.

One eye was still swollen, despite all the cold compresses Jen had prepared. It still hurt, a stinging don't-move-any-part-of-me hurt that speaks as though it were alive. A good-sized bump decorated her temple, where it had met the wall. This was one headache that wasn't going to leave any time soon.

What was she supposed to be doing? Coffee. Make coffee and then make it to school, make it through seven chapters without her head exploding, make a life without fear. ...

When the coffee was mixed, she placed a warm cup in front of Billy, bent down, and kissed his cheek. He smiled and suddenly, he was just Billy, Jen's harmless brother. She smiled back a little crookedly, trying not to wince at the pain this caused.

"I have fake sugar if you want," she offered, digging into her knapsack. No aspartame jar. She must have left it on the table after having coffee with Dennis yesterday. After the trauma last night, one missing jar was trifling, but it was one frustration too many and she had to fight back tears.

"That's OK. I use the real stuff," he said graciously. He stirred a spoonful of sugar into his cup and tasted it. When she wasn't looking, he quickly dumped two more heaping spoonfuls in.

They sat in silence until the locksmith arrived. Though it took mere minutes to install a new deadbolt, Donna found the short interval almost excruciating. Until the lock was in place, she could envision Ric storming in, grabbing her arm painfully, and spinning her around to face him. And then that fist coming out of nowhere ...

After Billy paid the locksmith, he offered, "I'll go with you to school. I don't start work 'til ten."

As if she'd be able to concentrate on a lecture after last night. No, Dennis could cover for her today. And tomorrow. And then the weekend would give her a couple of more days to let the swelling go down.

"I'm not going to school, but let me drive you home."

As she reached for her keys, the stain caught her eye again. Just this patch of liquid was enough to turn her stomach. Looking at it reminded her of Ric's fist skating across her cheekbone. Everything reminded her.

Billy muttered, "Uh, I think you're gonna need a steam cleaner. It's soaked in pretty good."

She simply nodded as if he just suggested it might snow today, and with one big heave, dragged the couch over to cover the evidence. Then they stepped out the front door, locking it solidly with her new key.

***

September crept along. Donna moved into a different apartment building with a security system, and a new phone with an unlisted number. Driving home now entailed several detours through side streets. Jen often accompanied her to necessary errands, scanning the crowds like a formidable bodyguard after parking in well-lit lots. Donna also started carrying her valuables with her, instead of leaving them in her locker. With these precautions in place, she was able to concentrate on her studies. The bruise faded and so did the questions from well-meaning classmates.

She deferred visits home, for fear that she wouldn't be able to hide what really happened. In part, it circumvented reliving the violence and also preserved her peace of mind ... as well as her father's. Every glance into the mirror was an acute reminder of the distress that surely would have radiated from his eyes.

A sad feeling of responsibility sat squarely on her shoulders. On the surface, Donna knew Ric's actions were unprovoked, but the weight of being victimized overshadowed any attempt at logic. Underneath it all, she kept wondering what she should have done differently. Perhaps because there were no real answers, it was easier to hide in her new apartment and study, than face the worry of family and friends.

Jen had asked her, "Why did you call me and not your dad or Jack?"

"Dad would have called the cops and then Ric would have killed me for sure. And without you there, Jack would have killed Ric for sure."

"When did you think all that through? During or after the guy was choking you? Jesus!"

"I don't know. These things just hit me on the spot. Listing the options probably kept me from panicking. Anyway, I wanted Jack to come, but I knew if you took charge everyone would get out of it alive."

I don't know. If I'd been up there, I probably would have killed him myself. You were rolling the dice on any of us."

"I suppose."

(But I'd gamble on you any day, Jen.)

***

During the last week of September, Raymond came over unannounced. The bruise was now at a point where some elementary makeup skills camouflaged it, but regardless Raymond seemed to be wrapped up in his own good humor. He set a large paper bag down on the kitchen counter.

Donna eyed him suspiciously. "Since when do you deliver Care Packages? Let me guess—the Jiffy Special?"

"Close," he answered with a gleam in his eyes, "It's just a little something I was introduced to recently. Thought I'd share it with you."

Donna peered into the bag. Bagels. A distinct whiff drifted up, bringing to mind breakfast, just the two of them.

"Are these peanut butter? Where did you get them?"

"Well, it took a little detective work, but as it turns out, the bakery by my office is willing to make them. I happened to receive a batch and they were the best bagels I ever had, exactly what I've been wanting to start my day with."

She returned his teasing inflections with a smirk, despite a feeling that she didn't quite understand the whole joke. Either he'd talked someone into making these or someone else did—probably Paula—and now he was giving Donna a baker's dozen. She felt an initial reaction of ruffled fur at her stepmother's intrusion. The bagels represented the quirky untouchable bond between father and daughter, a bond so private, she had never voiced it to a soul.

But as her father stood before her, she recognized the care behind his effort. He didn't arrange to have them prepared for Paula; he was giving them to *her*. Even if Paula had got the ball rolling, the heart of it could still belong to Raymond and Donna.

"Well, let's see how these things taste."

They were better than she expected.

After Raymond left, she was tired, not the kind of tired she felt from studying, but the kind that would surprise her after an adrenaline rush, as though every bit of energy suddenly evaporated into thin air and would never return. Alone, she was calm. Around others, she was on stage, even with her father, and it was draining.

On some surface level, she was cognizant of being safe, but that surface was as sheer as tissue. It couldn't hide the gnawing worries of "What if he finds me?" and even worse, "What if they're all like that?"

Billy's persuasion was the deciding factor in her safety. Unfortunately, his title of "protector" had been accomplished on Ric's terms. At the time, it simply had to be done, but she didn't know how to react to Billy after seeing that bloodstain.

Jen knew Billy had sacrificed his meager chances with Donna by acting in the only way that would save her, and for the first time in Jen's life, she sympathized with him. She also resented Jack's absence that night. If he were so hot for Donna, where was he when she needed him most? He didn't even return Jen's call and that wasn't like him. Within days, her resentment cooled off and a quiet worry took its place. Where could he be?

Donna secretly wished Jack had been involved instead. Still carrying a fantasy of him rising to be her greatest champion, she wanted to unburden herself of this appalling event, but as time passed, Donna believed the topic was better left on some remote shelf of her memory. Soon after, she learned that Jack had abruptly left Calgary, and with him went the disturbing dreams that had pestered her all week.

A haranguing vulnerability shattered her stable life, but she would have felt worse to discover several small items missing from her apartment. With the memory of Ric's fist too prominent, fear painted shadows over everything and created an inability to decipher the most important details right in front of her.

Most frightening was that the strictest precautions could not prevent the nightmare from starting all over again the moment Ric wanted it to. Donna didn't know that time was on her side, at least for now. Only much later would she learn how situations in life have a habit of going full circle. Like those recurring dreams of despair, the threats of her past were destined to return, intent on a second chance.

***

PART II

WORK YEARS

CHAPTER 18

... The spinning had subsided, though only by degrees. The true change encompassed those emotions swirling around, which had shifted from spiking fear to methodical routine. Her heart calmed despite the noise, an uplifting tumultuous noise, and Donna remembered being propelled into steady monotony before the pain started.

A pattern emerged of childhood overlapping working years. They were playing Pat-a-cake and Donna smiled at her mother's hands. Coming from everywhere, the hands multiplied and created such deafening applause, she was filled with wonder. It was a moment of honor, of pause, to catch her breath and prepare for the next phase. And all her thoughts funneled through the noise, back to ...

***

The Jack Simpson gymnasium at the University of Calgary had been built in time for the 1988 Olympics. Designed to double as a convocation site, the two-hundred meter running track on the upper level was being used as a reception area, overlooking the 1993 graduation ceremony.

Two huge bleachers flanked the graduates, who were seated in rows in the center of the gym. Donna's father, Paula, Jen, and Jack were halfway up the bleachers. Three hundred men and women in black robes eagerly awaited the degree presentation. Applause trailed each name as, one by one, they received their diploma.

"Robert Kent Anderson"

"Rod Leo Peter Boychuk"

"Alysha Gayl Burton"

"Terrence Douglas Cabriossa"

"Donna Patricia Carlin"

Raymond watched his daughter walk gracefully across the stage, where the university president shook her hand and passed her a scroll. The camera was positioned, the focus automatically adjusted. Raymond snapped off three good shots of her smiling broadly. Just one of fifty proud parents of new doctors.

As she stepped down the platform stairs, Raymond kissed her cheek and whispered, "Way to go, Pattycake!" Then he escorted her back to her seat with the other graduates. He took one more picture before returning to the audience.

The past danced before Raymond. Twenty-four years ago, Patricia had delivered Donna by cesarean, after hours of pain. As a premature baby, she was small enough to fit in one hand. Another complicated labor was too risky and the waiting period for adoptions became so long, Donna ended up an only child. Those early years were good, full of growth and humor, still feeling young and climbing the ladder at work.

A myriad of images flashed through his mind: her first steps, Donna crying because Patricia refused her a cookie, the chronic Pat-a-cake game, Donna playing "doctor" on her dolls, the plastic stethoscope carefully pressed against her doll's knee ... and then his wife discovered the lump in her breast, and their lives were full of alternating hope and fear. How much should they tell Donna? Conflicting advice from people only served to compound the stress.

There was the biopsy—positive malignancy. Hospitals, radiation, and chemotherapy took over their lives, and they hardly noticed when Donna's grades dipped. Between juggling work, his wife's illness, and the uncertainties of the next few years, Donna was inadvertently neglected in the process. Patricia was dying.

When she was gone, all the relief Raymond thought would be his was engulfed by the shock of her sudden absence. The mountain of pain she'd endured simply skipped over to him. His sister Gloria stayed with them for a while, but her own family needed her back in Vancouver. It was hard then. Donna was only twelve. The life insurance payouts kept them going until Raymond returned to work. Hiring a cleaning lady was a move designed to keep his daughter from growing up too fast, but she seemed to anyway, retreating into herself without a female influence.

Later, Jen befriended her and Raymond marveled at how this brazen girl picked up his daughter's spirits so effortlessly. He never knew that Donna had actually picked up Jen. Her meddling had cost her best friend a guy and the girl had dropped Jen for good. Donna's sad state was a moral diversion for Jen, who needed to feel properly placed in someone's life. Ultimately, the banter just became routine for both. Sometimes Jen still crossed a line with her meddling, but at least now, she could gauge how far that line could reasonably stretch.

Donna looked up and waved her scroll at them playfully. Her minute of glory was over, a minute to be savored a long time. How did that little girl in the black robe get all the way across that big stage by herself?

The band played a powerful song while the graduates filed up to the second-level reception area. Swarmed by family and friends, the air was filled with excitement, "Congratulations" everywhere. For Donna, it meant a lot: no more deadly exams every six weeks, no more exhausting nights with books. As she stepped up the stairs, she left those tiresome days behind.

One by one, they all embraced her. The last hug came from Jack, who she hadn't seen in two years. A new military look accentuated the square cut of his jaw.

"Jack, who stole your hair?"

"Job requirement, no tails allowed."

Donna rubbed his stubbly head and for a moment, he grinned. The goofy expression sat at odds with the rest of his appearance, but then it was gone, replaced by mature cordiality. His body was larger than Donna remembered, but he'd stopped growing in height a long time ago. Still about 5'10", the added muscle gave him a solid masculine outline, particularly contrasted beside Jen's petite frame.

Jen had lost some weight and on her, a little was a lot. She was battling an annoying cold. The tissues clutched in her hand caught her rasping coughs. She had legitimately called in sick to be here. Stage managing for a small theater group didn't pay a lot, but the right to bully actors was a definite perk, almost as good as bullying Jack.

After the last Rummoli game, Jack had disappeared like smoke. Donna learned from his mother that he'd left town, and completely puzzled, she kept expecting a letter to arrive, but none did. Then just as abruptly, he reappeared a few weeks ago. He waited a long time to let them know he was back. Today was the first time they'd seen him, and with his detached countenance, Donna wasn't sure how to act toward him, though Jen's example seemed to work: just bug him as usual.

Jen handed Donna two wrapped gifts and said, "This one is from my parents ... and this is from Jack and me. It's for all the free medical advice we're going to expect from now on!"

Donna turned to her father. "My first bribe."

Jack scratched his chin and gave a wide smile. "It's ... advanced payment."

"It's a bribe," Raymond mirrored deadpanned.

"Hey," Jack retorted, "We're the ones taking a risk here. She might be a really crappy doctor."

Leveling a look at him, Donna pulled the wrapping paper off the squat box. "A coffee maker! Well, that's worth a flu shot or two."

"We thought it was time you had some help from technology," Jen said. "Look, there's even a measuring spoon! Something to think about." A series of hacking coughs escaped, and she bent over miserably in an attempt to control them. Finally straightening up, she announced, "I have to be off. Gotta get to work. We're rehearsing 'Death of a Salesman' until late tonight. I can't wait 'til the play ends. It's got me totally run down. I wouldn't mind if the story wasn't so bloody depressing."

As Raymond watched Jen thread a path to the exit, he remarked, "Colorful as always ... Here," He plunked another box into Donna's hands. "These are stimulant free, but they may have other uses."

From the box, he lifted a white lab coat and waited for her to remove her graduation gown. After she stepped into the coat, Paula placed a stiff new stethoscope around her neck. They all stared admiringly.

"Wait," Jack said, taking a pen and sliding it into her breast pocket, "There. Now all you need is really bad handwriting."

"First course they make you take! ... Thanks, Dad. But you know I'd have been just as happy with bagels."

She shared a private smile with Raymond. For the past two years, they had coerced the bakery near his office into adding the extra ingredient. Actually, the baker had complied quite willingly. Paula must have prepared him to expect the odd special order. The first time Donna walked in and made the request, the baker eyed her peculiarly before chuckling and nodding his head. Though he seemed outwardly agreeable, she always left feeling a little creeped out by the guy.

Another graduate strolled up behind Donna and she kissed him affectionately. Jack noticed that his arm stayed around her waist. She leaned comfortably against the man and her fingers stole across her waist to stroke his hand. It appeared to be an unconscious gesture, done a hundred times before.

With a hand extended to Jack, Donna stated, "Brian, this is Jack Petrasyk. Jack, Brian Landrew."

Jack was faced with a tall fellow with light brown hair and matching eyes. As they shook hands, he asked, "What did you graduate with?"

"Biology."

Jack nodded politely. Raymond and Paula congratulated Brian and more hands were shaken.

"Where are your folks?" Donna asked.

Brian scanned the crowd and pointed to the far end of the room. "Over there. I'd better get back. See you tonight."

He gave her a kiss before walking off, his black robe flowing out behind him.

***

Donna glanced around at the new décor.

(The Bean must have changed hands. That scraggy old owner would never do pastel.)

Yellow arborite had replaced the dark wood patterns, but the staff still wore jeans. The place evoked neighborly kitchen friendliness, much like the Brammons. Baked goods and soups were added to the menu, producing an inviting mix with the coffee aromas. Though cozy, there was still something disquieting about their old haunt changing its appearance.

As she studied the other tables, a man across the room rustled a newspaper and gentle waves of familiarity niggled her. He sat alone, a slight figure sipping his coffee quietly. His shoulders slouched forward with an unassuming presence, almost sad. Holding the cup with two hands, he carefully brought it to his mouth.

Donna tried not to stare, but this guy ...

(An undergrad class? One of the bank staff? That asshole in the Pontiac last week?)

Finally, unable to place him, she shifted her gaze to the window.

She watched Jack walk from his car and scan the restaurant; the other man was instantly forgotten. When Jack approached her table, Donna met him with a hug. Their embrace felt formal, with a distance that had never existed before, but then, he'd never disappeared for two years before.

And again, déjà vu ... almost as though she were watching this scene elsewhere, while acting in the middle of it, being in two places at once and completely aware of both views. Impossible to dismiss, too many unique details were concentrated in this one moment, sights and sounds all new and yet old somehow, like watching a movie seen twenty years ago.

"Hey stranger!"

Jack agreed, "Yeah, it's been a while. I've been busy with training. There's still two months to go before we hit the streets."

"Do they just throw you right into it? Here, go chase bad guys!" She moved her hands carelessly as though brushing crumbs off the table.

"Sort of. It's more like here, you and Officer Been-Here-Forever go chase bad guys. So, do I call you Dr. Carlin now?"

"Technically yes, but I still have to do two more years as a med-slave before I actually get to *be* a doctor. Ridiculous process really. You have to apply to different schools for your residency and be interviewed by each one, so you're spending mega-dollars flying all over the country. Then, you get this little scrap of paper in the mail that says 'Donna Carlin has been placed at such and such a school.' That's it. After all that effort, it's very impersonal."

"Did you want to stay in Calgary?"

"Yeah, everything I know is here."

"Including Brian. Seems like a decent guy. How long have you two been together?" he asked with only a hint of prying. It covered his question like a transparent layer of plastic wrap, so effectively that Donna failed to notice it. She glanced up at him, and in a split-second, he knew Brian was not a contender.

"About a year, but I've known him longer. We were first introduced by a mutual friend. It was a total set-up. Then, I started seeing him around more, and finally he asked me out."

Her voice conveyed a genuine respect for her boyfriend, though lacking the ignited spark once shown for Ric. As Jack scanned the tiny laminated menu, he wondered how that relationship had ended. Probably just the way Jen predicted—they'd fizzled out by Christmas.

A waitress stopped at their table to take their order. Coffee and muffins, heated. She was a perky high school girl who smiled a lot, a bit more at Jack. Donna realized that Jack's well-defined physique must provoke attention like this all the time. It was briefly irritating.

With a tilted head, she remarked, "You look good Jack. Catch me up on everything."

Jack's eyes widened and he exclaimed, "Where should I start? Well, you know I was in Red Deer for a while working on different jobs, restaurant stuff and some construction."

"Did you like it?"

"The restaurants were OK. Couldn't stand the construction. I always had a book on breaks instead of sucking back a pack and a half, so I wasn't real popular, but the money was good. It paid most of my student loans off. I still owe a bit, but the police force pays during training, so it'll be wiped out in a couple of months."

The coffees arrived, steaming with crisp flavor. Donna poured some milk into hers.

"Where's your pound of fake sugar?"

"Oh, I kicked the habit. It was making me kind of weird. Why did you move away? Your mom wouldn't give me your address."

"She didn't have it. I guess she was too embarrassed to admit that." He paused, his face contrite. "I needed some time away from Calgary. I was dealing with something ... and there were too many reminders of it here. I just didn't want to talk to people."

Donna's brow furrowed, "When was this? And why didn't you tell us about it?"

Grinning sardonically, he commented, "I see you still ask two questions in a row. Isn't there a pill you can take for that?"

"Nice try. Come on," she beckoned with fingers.

His smile dissolved with a quiet sigh. If it were Jen, he'd play at deflecting her for a while, but Donna automatically pulled his truthful side to the surface. He turned his coffee cup around slowly as if sizing up its diameter.

"Well ... it was kind of personal. I met a woman and it just didn't work out. Anyway, the long and the short of it is that I became a Christian."

Donna laughed, "You did not!" before seeing the honesty in his eyes. She stopped laughing. "You did?"

He nodded.

"How did that happen?" He'd never been into that. She thought with his body, the gym must have been his church. She opened her mouth with a second question and then abruptly closed it.

With downcast eyes, Jack didn't notice. He leaned back in his seat and crossed his ankles under the table.

"I'd been searching for her. She was supposed to be in Red Deer. When I got settled and started getting regular paycheques, I spent all my extra time looking in places I thought she might be. She was big on religion. I must have hit every church in the city two or three times, but no one ever heard of her. Then, I got into this one church. The pastor was a young guy who helped me out when I was pretty low. Well, it was more like a breakdown and he got me through it with some counseling. A lot of counseling. He got me reading the Bible too. Now, I read it every day."

Donna always had a little trouble believing in Bible stories. How relevant was a book written two-thousand years ago? But there was a gentle strength in Jack's voice that was good to hear, even calming.

"What denomination is it?"

"Baptist, but not the severe kind. No throwing you in a river," he smiled.

"Oh good, so my Saturday mornings are safe?"

"Yeah, we don't go door-to-door. Just do our own thing and save the brainwashing for the truly unredemptive."

"I'll warn Jen."

Religion had never held a secure place in Donna's past, but she recognized a common thread of satisfaction in those who embraced it. Jack was shining proof. He seemed to accept where his life was going or was he simply resigned? Either way, Donna could see Jack's personality mixing well with church services and Bible study groups. Surrounded by instability, his childhood had boasted no father figure, and of all the candidates in the world, God was hard to beat. Into rules and procedures, a male-oriented belief system would soothe a lot of strife for Jack.

Donna had never craved the constraints of organized religion. At best, she felt a vague belief in a higher power, but couldn't describe this power if her life depended on it. How did Jack manage that transition?

Three huge muffins were deposited between them, toasted and steaming, two of them for Jack. Hungry, Donna bit into hers right away. Jack spread butter on his and waited for them to cool.

He remarked, "It was a good move for me. I'm finally getting things done I always wanted to do."

"Like what?"

"Well, there's the police force, which is an endless pile of friggin' hoops. I'm not sure I would have had the patience for all the entrance requirements a few years ago."

Donna was about to interrupt with an articulate comparison of med school hoops to stop his complaints cold, but his next comment took her by surprise.

"I also decided to look for my dad."

"Really?"

He had never expressed an interest in searching out his roots before. Next, he would announce a sex change. Automatically glancing at his pinkie finger, she frowned. His ring was missing. Jack never took that thing off. Maybe they didn't allow cops to wear jewelry, some job rule.

"Why now, after all these years?"

"For starters, I didn't know where to begin … if he would even be alive, but mostly, I just didn't have much to show for myself. I mean, at least now my degree's done and I've started a career."

Donna's heart went out to him. In some ways, Jack was still the affable high school kid, proving he could get on every sports team, but he was also a fully grown man with muscles and pride and a mind of his own. It was a new side of him. Healthy, determined, yet still a bit reserved, an intriguing combination. Donna was glad he was back and she told him so.

His polite smile was quickly swallowed up as a series of unidentifiable feelings crossed his eyes. He plainly held a carefully contained sadness, the look of a beautiful wild animal the moment its spirit is broken, and she wondered what his ex-girlfriend had done to make him so unhappy and distant. Glancing around rather than meet her eyes, a subtle barrier was now erected between them, as if all women were to be approached with caution and she was included by simple categorization.

The thought was upsetting. So many layers overlapped their history that she had a hard time isolating the exact nature of her reaction, but it reminded her of the first time they met back in high school. That moment their eyes locked made her wonder if they'd known each other in a past life. Some undercurrent of connection had fueled a gentle concern for him, unwavering with time.

In a weird way, she was a little jealous of this woman in his past. Previously, there was only room for Donna and Jen, and then he left, leaving a void in their friendship. With the last two years of school so busy, the hole sat camouflaged behind the pages of her books. Now with the books shelved, she saw how much she had really missed Jack.

Apart from Jen and Brian and his circle of friends, the people in her life were few and far between. The close ties she had acquired in school were all being placed in other cities for their residencies. They were people she could easily live without, their absences creating comparatively tiny holes. Jack's return suddenly brought his value into perspective and simultaneously diminished the others. She realized that despite his return, the void he left was still there and she resolved to repair it.

When they finally rose from their seats, Donna noticed that the man with bad posture was still sitting across the room, clutching his cup protectively. Donna was certain she'd seen him before, that his name was catalogued in her distant memory, possibly someone from school or a friend of a friend, but she didn't bother mentioning it to Jack. As he followed her out the door, she dismissed it with the assumption that neither of them would likely encounter the man again.

***

Just sugar. The shakes were distracting Al from the black and white print. He hated this part of the withdrawal. Two hands were needed to steady the cup or it might spill again.

At least the antagonism was low. Last week, he had almost hit his son. Kam had been fussing, trying to get at a toy just out of reach, and Al heard the whining with escalating annoyance. He shouted at the boy and raised his hand. Instantly his wife sprang to life, pushing him off-balance. Then, in one quick movement, she snatched up the boy and ran into their daughter's bedroom.

Al stood in shock at what he had almost done. Should he follow her or not? He had never made a woman run away in fear before. Eventually, she came out and announced that if he took another drink, she would throw him out of the house and change the locks. Determined to stay sober, for four days he made good on his promise.

Then, the cravings started again. Had they ever left?

He knew his wife was serious about kicking him out, but that insistent urge kept nagging him. Thoughts of it snuck in all the time. He chewed aspirin like candy and almost called his sponsor fifteen hundred times. Al knew it was what he should do, but embracing the badge of failure was utterly demoralizing. His family already saw the extent of his addiction. Why broadcast it further? Even if someone understood the whole process of recovery, the problem was still his.

Finally, the depressing feeling of being controlled became too much. Al walked into a bar and sat nervously wrestling with his needs. The bartender was so busy with the after work crowd, she didn't notice the struggle on Al's face. When asked what he would like *(another bottle of pills, my sponsor, a sledgehammer ...)*, he almost responded, "I need a minute to decide," but the decision had been made before he entered the bar.

"Vodka, neat."

Later, he came home straight and strong with minty fresh breath as his accomplice. His wife saw his sloppy gait and cheerful mood. The next day, his key wouldn't fit the front lock. He didn't become violent by kicking the door or yelling at her through the peephole. He'd always been pretty tame under the influence. Instead, he rang the doorbell repeatedly until she opened a nearby window.

"Fuck off, Al! You're not coming in. I told you I'd change the locks."

"Come on, Trace. It was just a little one."

"They're all just little ones. Get a grip. You're an alcoholic."

"I'm just a drunk. Alcoholics go to meetings."

Slam! Jesus, she was really pissed off this time. Even his offbeat charm wouldn't help smooth her over.

That was a long night at Motel Village; desperately Al put his kids in the forefront of his thoughts. The first couple of hours were tolerable. Then, the vodka started leaving his system. By midnight, those familiar symptoms of withdrawal were challenging his senses again, but he took them in and dealt with them, one by one.

In the morning, he found a friendly-looking coffee shop with pastel arborite and stayed for five hours. Seven cups of coffee and two hot chocolates. His hands kept shaking and he could hardly concentrate on the newspaper, but in the end, he was proud of himself.

He whispered a little prayer. Maybe she would let him in now.

***

CHAPTER 19

Jen was floored at Jack's religious conversion. And she stated this in no uncertain terms to Donna, who was lying under the Valiant with various tools scattered about. Donna groped for a wrench propped against a greasy bucket, until Jen handed it to her.

"I just can't see him crossing himself and saying a bunch of Hail Mary's. Well, I don't intend to change a thing. He's going to get all the same four-letter words from me!" She laughed sharply, suddenly remembering, "I told him dirty jokes at your convocation!"

"Not the one about the priest and nun in confession."

Jen averted her eyes. "I hope he didn't try to sell you a Bible or something."

"Of course not. If anything, I got the feeling he was a little embarrassed about it. He's changed in a small way. More private but more strong-minded too. He never was one to swear like a sailor, so overall not much is different."

"Except his arms. Huge pipes on that boy."

"Yeah, he might even fit into your clothes now."

"What do you call those weight lifters?"

"Plate-heads. Don't you ever wear anything in your own size?"

"Not unless Billy shrinks someday. His closet is still the cheapest choice, and offers the best selection of plus-size clothing. Besides, he's not that swift. He thinks they get lost somewhere between the spin cycle and the dryer."

"All done."

Donna shuffled her body out from under the car and sat up, wiping her hands with a rag. Jen smiled at the black smudge on Donna's face and decided to keep quiet.

Donna cocked her head. "Smile, Jen."

"Where is he?" Jen conspiratorially whispered.

"Around the corner."

As they turned, Raymond's camera clicked to capture another candid Carlin photo. Smugly exclaiming, "Ha! Gotcha, girls!" he retreated back into the house.

"Is there anything your dad doesn't have a picture of? I mean, it's kind of creepy how he pops out of the woodwork and documents your life like that. Here's Donna making pancakes. Here's Donna watching cartoons. Here's Donna doing an oil change."

"Only child," Donna shrugged.

"The last of four. I'm sure the only pictorial evidence of me can be found in your dad's camera just now. ... Hey, could you look under the hood? This piece of shit wouldn't start again the other day and I had to take it in."

"But it started for you to come here, right?"

"Yeah, but lately my luck is fifty-fifty, so if you want this driveway clear, you'd better check it out. The guy at the garage seemed to fix it, but then it conked out again yesterday. Probably should have checked his credentials."

Standing up and stretching her legs, Donna remarked, "Like I have any? I mean, the patients I'm used to can at least form words."

"Hey, you're the Grease Queen of William Aberhart. I have total faith in you, probably more faith than our Christian friend does in the Almighty. ... You know, Jack didn't mention anything about religion at your convocation. Isn't that kind of a major thing to leave out?"

"Well, like I said, he seemed pretty private about it. I guess he met some woman, and after she dumped him, he got into this church."

"That's typical. Hey, my cousin—you remember Evelyn?"

"The skirt-aholic?"

Jen pointed her index finger straight up. "The very one. She went bug-eyed religious when her parents died. No makeup, no pants. And God forbid her dresses sport anything resembling an attractive pattern."

"I seem to recall an unhealthy amount of plaid."

"Is there a healthy amount?"

"Point taken."

"Anyway, she was into cutoffs and halter tops until this thing happened. And then it was the Church of Plaid all the way."

"And you would have preferred the Church of Mai Tai's?"

"Well the altar boys look a hell of a lot better. Definitely a funner crutch."

Donna stared at the engine. Jen, watching her intently, was about to ask how high the repair bill would be this time, when Donna responded, "I don't think it's a crutch now. I mean for Jack. Maybe it was at first, but he really seems to have his shit together. To tell you the truth, I've wondered if I could do with some churching."

Jen threw her head back, exclaiming, "Oh, Lord, two of you. You'll be dragging me off to some barbaric service. They'll be waving their hands in the air and begging God to save my *wretched soul!*"

"Like they'd let you in with your track record."

In an uncharacteristically prim voice, Jen said, "That's hardly Christian of you Donna, or were you considering some other religion? I could find a nice-sized Buddha for your coffee table."

"I take it your agnostic sensibilities are alive and well?"

"Of course. I've always thought there was something out there, even before the car accident, but I'm not arrogant enough to try to define it."

Donna hid a smirk and reached around the battery.

(Here we go.)

She said, "Hey, the spiritual stuff helps people cope. You know what the suicide stats are among churchgoers versus the rest of the population? A fraction. Religion can do a lot of good."

Jen scoffed, "Yeah, it does tons of good. The cruelest acts against humanity are routinely committed in the name of religion."

"That's a bit dramatic, even for you. ... Look, here's the problem—the wire is off the ignition coil. All you have to do is tighten it up. ... There."

"You mean that's what I paid fifty bucks for?"

"Probably, but on the other hand, this isn't exactly my forte. Tell you what—if it explodes, I'll keep my day job."

Donna let the metal hood slam shut with a *bang!* She reached down to pick up her soda and hopped up on the hood. Nothing dented in with her weight. Manufactured in an era of inviolability, it was a mobile suit of armor, designed to encase its occupants to every destination. It had certainly been that the night Billy took care of Ric.

Jen sat behind the wheel and slid the key into the ignition. When it roared to life, she delivered a sideways expression as if to ask, "Was there ever any doubt in your diagnostic abilities, my friend?"

Donna bent over in a gracious bow. Turning the engine off, Jen stepped out and leaned against the side of the car, cradling her chin in her hands.

"I don't know why you still have this piece of crap, Jen. That window's an eyesore. Get it fixed already."

"Naw, it has character. The solid tape look's gonna catch on, trust me. ... So, does Brian know about your Barry Manilow fetish?"

"Romance is best maintained with a bit of mystery."

"Apparently friendships too. I mean, I don't get it. Why would Jack throw himself into religion, when he's got two people right here who are perfectly capable of administering guilt?"

"He went through a bad time. I think it was so bad, he's still going through it. If a book and a prayer help get his head straight, what's wrong with that?" Donna paused thoughtfully. "I mean, he could have chosen a thousand self-destructive crutches to limp past his problems, but he chose a sin-free lifestyle. There are worse options—like the Church of Mai Tai's. People who have something to believe in tend to have healthier lives. They eat better, live longer. ... Just look at the Mormons. They don't drink caffeine or alcohol, their babies are typically healthier at birth, and they have fewer incidences of cancer and infectious diseases."

"Oh, listen to you. You talk like such a doctor."

"I *am* a doctor you moron, and just for that, all the coffee makers in the world won't make me save your sorry ass with free medical advice."

"Well, be that as it may, pull the stethoscope out of yours and think about someone like Jack, who really likes his coffee. Wouldn't he make a great Mormon? Do you think he's going to pick a religion that doesn't allow for his vices? No, he's going to pick some package of beliefs that'll conveniently fit over them. Someone doesn't choose a religion to make him a better person. He chooses it to reaffirm that he's *already* a better person."

"So what? Take two guys on the verge of suicide. My money's on the guy in the front pew."

"Give 'em a pew or a Prozac, they're both still fucked up."

"Oh, ye of little faith. You're the one who needs a pill. Trust me, the ones who think they don't usually need the biggest dose."

"I got a big freakin' pill when that car hit me—I was clinically dead and I sure didn't want to come back. Anyone who's experienced that wouldn't look at it in terms of societal good and crap like that. You can't take that kind of feeling and stick some labels on it to explain your life."

"Good for you for being more enlightened than the rest of the world, but just because you can't define what you experienced doesn't mean others can't ... or shouldn't. People need parameters and definitions to understand how they fit in."

Jen lifted her head. "Parameters are exactly why people are going crazy to begin with. Too damned many parameters boxing us in all the time. We don't need another one telling us how to demonstrate our spirituality."

"Oh Christ, next you'll be spouting off conspiracy theories about the government. Did it ever occur to you that the things boxing you in give other people stability? Security? An understanding of their place in the world?"

"Jack's fooling himself if he thinks he understands God 'cause he goes churching every Sunday."

Donna retaliated, "You're just annoyed he made a decision in his life and didn't report it directly to you."

"Well ... yeah! And tell the truth—so are you. What the hell's up with that?"

"It's just something he needed to do. Leave it at that. You can't criticize people for defining their beliefs in different terms than you do."

"Oh when you boil it down, everybody's beliefs are pretty much the same. They just don't know it."

"OK, I'll give you that, but why are you so warped-out about Jack?"

"He got dumped and then fell headfirst into the arms of religion. It's not your normal kind of rebound."

If Jen had only seen Jack's unhappy eyes at The Bean. He seemed like someone dragging a frightful load across the world. Donna had always considered him a slightly fragile soul, needing care despite his strengths. He didn't need to deal with Jen too.

Donna didn't presume to judge Jack's life until she heard his story, and even then she was hard-pressed not to accept him for what he was, for what he had become. Who was Jen to judge? Besides, it was time Donna got the last word in for once.

"People rebound in lots of ways that don't make sense. ... Broken heart or death, in the end they all reach out to something, religion or the next girlfriend, anything for a connection. You forget, I've seen a lot of people die."

(OK, argue your way past that, Brammon.)

"Oh, so you understand human motive 'cause you've watched death? I'll see your bedside manner and raise you one actual death experience. When you've got something real to wager, then we'll talk."

(Damn, how does she do that?)

***

1995 was a year of changes for Dr. Carlin. She completed her last year of residency—a demanding experience, even more than all the years leading up to it. Every type of ailment presented itself during month after month of long shifts. People exhibited life-threatening diseases, contrasted by cases of hypochondria or denial. Each day provided a new perspective and the career she had chosen grew closer to reality.

It was much more tiring than expected. Not only were there long hours of monitoring cases to completion; the weekly shift changes broke up her sleep cycles, and this hypocrisy of tending to the ill while chronically exhausted prompted her to join a fitness club. When the sign-up fees were paid, she vowed to complete four workouts per week, and most of the time, she stuck to her promise.

Brian also signed up, since it was the only way he could get time with her. They spoke the same language of scientific analysis, reviewing his lab experiments or Donna's hospital politics while pedaling stationary bikes or climbing stair machines.

After two busy years, the next five weeks promised no commitments. So accustomed to long shifts, she found free time foreign. Brian prescribed absolute relaxation, but plagued by restlessness, she kept feeling as though important deadlines were being missed.

"No books," he'd command, "Nothing heavier than a magazine!"

He unplugged the phone so she could sleep, filled her refrigerator with groceries, and prepared bubble baths of rich oils to soak in. It was heaven to be this cared for.

Their third-year dating anniversary had been in August, at the tail end of Donna's obstetrics and pediatrics rotation, which proved an unpredictable area for her schedule. Complicated deliveries routinely prolonged her shift, and Brian wasn't sure if she'd even show up for their workout, let alone the grand evening he had planned—including dinner and the key to his apartment. Moving in together was something he'd suggested before, but she preferred having her own space. At least, that was what she told him. He suspected she was holding out for a ring.

When her shift interrupted his romantic plans, he settled for a video and a big bowl of popcorn at her place. Her apartment: should he move in here or could they fit into his? No, they'd need more space—at least a two-bedroom—but keep her furniture. His was in bad shape, especially the couch. Hers was lined with plush cushions. A person could sink into them and never escape. It was a comfortable couch, a comfortable apartment, decorated simply yet still offering an air of hominess.

She surrounded herself with warm colors as if in a chronic state of healing. Shelves of books framed the television. There was an order to them, each one displayed according to subject and convenience, the ones she still used stationed at eye-level. Then, there were those children's books curiously earning a place between Grey's Anatomy and The Merck Manual. Brian asked her about them once, but she gave him such a strange look that he dropped the subject immediately. Chalking it up to a bad study night or PMS, he soon forgot about it.

The books were not the only oddity in her place. There was a distinct lack of small appliances, except for a microwave Brian gave her for Christmas, and a coffee maker, which mostly sat as an ornament. Her father's visits heralded the only occasions he'd witnessed its use. She made the worst coffee, though Ray Carlin seemed perfectly happy with the stuff.

Brian envied their relationship, two people who had lived under the same roof and still liked each other. From growing up with two sisters, he was inherently suspicious of all the unpredictable moods women could have, but Donna displayed fewer than most. She was as comfortable as her apartment.

Suddenly, he switched off the television. Donna blinked at him, as he stood with his hands shoved deep into the pockets of his pants. Her feet were crossed on the coffee table, a handful of popcorn halfway to her mouth. He stared at her, at the floor, at the wall, at her again. ... What was he doing?

Finally she quipped, "If you're planning to replace the TV, you'll have to be livelier than that."

He smiled briefly and then looked hard at her.

Her brow furrowed. "What's wrong?"

Skirting around the coffee table, he sat beside her, took her free hand in his, and blurted out, "Marry me Donna."

Donna stared at him. The popcorn dropped back into the bowl. She had envisioned this before and now the moment was literally at hand. The room froze while her mind raced.

He was someone she loved. They shared common goals and interests. They both wanted children. The sex was good, not exciting like Ric, nor as scary. He would be the perfect choice. It's not as if she hadn't considered him before, but every year of medical training brought a fresh set of stresses that continually demanded attention. Marriage was something for later on, after exams and hospital rotations, not now.

Time slowed down as the analysis swam through her head. A lifetime's worth of considerations competed for her attention at this very second. Would she be happy with this man? Yes. Would he care for her the way Ric had not? Definitely. Would he be a good father? Yes, he would certainly be an excellent father ... and husband ... and son-in-law. Her own father thought the world of him. She saw Brian in five years, ten years, forty years, and knew she would be loved by this man. More importantly, she saw herself living alongside his love ... and her answer was crystal-clear.

Time sped up again.

"Brian, I can't."

He shook his head slightly as if retrieved from distraction. "I don't mean right now. When you're comfortable in your job and I'm done my thesis. Let's move in together and plan for it a year or two down the road."

This wasn't the way he expected it to go. This felt like he was trying to convince her, but they were great together. Everyone knew that. During his explanation, he stared nervously at her hands and finished his sentence with his eyes back on her face. Then, he saw her expression.

"God, you really mean 'no'."

Donna could barely look at him. Brian was exactly the right person to follow Ric, to restore her faith in relationships, and she was grateful for that. He offered her a safe life, pleasant, everything she desired. Almost everything. His love was a gentle cloak of soft cotton, soothing warmth wrapped around her just right, letting her breathe and move in whatever direction she chose.

He never pushed her to the edge of her emotions—that cliff overlooking torrential waves, exploding against a thick wall of rock. It was a connection beyond physical dimensions, a fusion without loss of individual parts, a machine that only comes to life with flawless articulations and a precise timing to scatter the wave off the rock, returning an incoherent spray to the sea. She had always sensed those waves, but never felt that perfection in the arms of a lover.

There were dizzying times with Ric. Being in bed with him was like spinning recklessly through uncontrollable currents—not knowing which way was up. Though exhilarating to feel such helplessness in a man's arms, Ric fashioned her submission to such a degree that the excitement transferred completely to him. He coveted the heart of her emotions, while Brian would never dream of stripping away pieces until she was an obedient shell. It was the fear that a man could do this that created her reluctance, but their relationship had progressed without incident. Compared to the chaos Ric generated, Brian had grown on her, like loving a cloudless sky or the delicate skin of a newborn. It was just easy.

Soft-spoken and intellectual without pressing her into hard debates, he was thoughtful, remembering names and events meaningful to her. Most importantly, he expected her to be her own person, defined independently. She respected him for all those things, but still there was something missing.

Why was there always a difference between desire and possession? Before her was a solid relationship, built on everything decent, but she craved a deeper connection: something as equally powerful and obscure as tearing through an ocean of water. Someone was there swimming in the currents, his outline obscured by the murky depths. He would always be there, always create a careful distance between her and other men; she couldn't just walk away from him and have a life with Brian.

The person in the water was mesmerizing. It wasn't Ric buoyed up by intimidation which held her back. It was Jack. ... It was always Jack.

Brian had never garnered her care like Jack did all through high school. He didn't have that special drive deep in his soul, or that look about him that made her want to go out and conquer the world. Though good and honest and real, whatever wonderful qualities Brian possessed, he wasn't her soulmate.

He wasn't Jack.

Despite her initial refusal, Brian did his best to change her mind, but he could see the futility in her eyes. Reflected in them was the worst kind of hesitancy, not wanting to cause the pain that would surely occur, and it was this that finally convinced him of her decision.

She sheltered the exact truth; since Jack's return, a seed had been replanted in his favor. Growing from deep inside, it appraised him with an old set of eyes. And it was these eyes now turning toward him and away from Brian.

With this gentle man so nervous in his proposal, she was wrapped comfortably in cotton, but cotton held no fascination when the smooth caresses of silk could tip her over the cliff's edge to spin through the waves.

***

CHAPTER 20

... For a brief period, those images fell into the sequenced rhythm of a complicated play, with characters treading on and off stage, the lights dimming in preparation for another scene.

This time, everything was illuminated in fluorescent white: clothes, files, faces. ... A parade of them marched across the stage, some changing countenance for the better, and some leaving by a mysterious side exit, never to be seen again.

Donna could hear voices, so many voices, compliant and needy, and she saw herself stepping forward to attend to the next bunch. There was never a moment alone and yet, this was exactly how she felt, so necessary and contrarily insignificant. When would this all end? She was almost afraid to see, but the lights were starting to brighten again to that time in September, when ...

***

Dr. Carlin finally entered the workforce as a full-fledged physician. A modest practice in southwest Calgary was looking for a general practitioner to build a clientele, under the existing ownership of Dr. Gene Shonberg. Nearing retirement, a young energetic doctor was needed to slide in and eventually purchase his business.

Dr. Shonberg interviewed several competent graduates, who all seemed intelligent and prepared to practice medicine, but lacked a knowledge base in other essentials, such as pharmaceutical inventory control and business planning. He was impressed with Dr. Carlin. Apparently, in preparation for this interview, she'd interrogated every doctor in her residency about the insurance system. Anyone who could so smoothly direct an interview toward the prospective employer's business operation was bound to be an excellent diagnostician. After an hour, Dr. Shonberg had the odd feeling *he* had been hired.

At first, Donna only took the overflow patients. Spending much of her workday shadowing her boss, she introduced herself to everyone who walked in the door and, if allowed by the patient, assisted with treatments.

As a result, Donna's clientele was slowly expanding. She would soon require a nurse to schedule and organize patients. Gene's assistant handled both of their bookings, but she would be retiring soon. So in her first managerial move, Donna placed a job ad in the Calgary Herald with a short deadline.

One hundred and fourteen resumes arrived.

Donna waded through them in between patients and short-listed them to seven. She needed someone with strong organizational skills, experience in difficult health issues, and above all, tactfulness. Anyone could learn how to set up appointments. Paramount was the ability to calm down a frightened child and put people at ease the moment they arrived.

After Donna and Gene met with the candidates, they reviewed their impressions and agreed that one would be the sort of assistant required. Gene was supportive of her choice, explaining that Donna's efficiency rode largely on her support staff. If blue toenails would make her a better doctor, then that's what she should look for!

The following month, Anne McLauren came on board as Dr. Carlin's assistant.

She was a little shorter and younger than Donna, with dark brown hair and chameleon eyes. They seemed to change every hour. Her extensive experience in pediatrics and palliative care was an asset, but mostly, she just had a friendly air about her. It complimented Donna's seriousness and Gene's fatherly appeal. She suggested giving fun little toys to children, and always wore odd jewelry that served as conversation starters. One necklace separated into two parts that she blew through to make bubbles. The kids loved her.

Within a year, Donna was a busy physician, in no small part due to Anne. It was an excellent way to distract her from her stalled love life.

***

There was no convincing her. "No," he answered politely, "just the usual, one loaded, one black."

The clerk brightened her smile and tried again. "We just made them. They're really fresh. The banana nut ones are my favorite. Are you sure? No charge."

"No, just the coffees, but thanks anyway."

She gave up trying to tempt the officer with muffins and handed him two steaming cups. Grateful for his presence, The Bean staff never charged Jack for his orders.

This clerk was particularly friendly, to the point of making Jack slightly uncomfortable. Flirting was not his strongest suit. Well, there was one time several years ago when he'd flirted and it worked like a charm, but it was the only time he felt that kind of confidence. There had just been something smooth about it. The whole thing flowed into place like water. *She* flowed like water.

For a split-second, the warm paper cups he held became shiny white porcelain with perfect little handles on each one. The woman in the hotel room cast her lovely smile and his heart jumped, and then ... she was just the fresh-faced clerk at The Bean.

He thanked her again and stepped toward the door, conscious of her eyes on him. Out in the car, he passed a cup to his partner.

Officer Kennen inquired wryly, "When's the wedding?"

"After she graduates from high school."

"Hey, she'd make you good coffee in the morning."

"Yeah, I live for a woman who can percolate." Then, he muttered, "Where's a good robbery when you need one?"

"Petrasyk, King-of-Deflection. Set up a speed trap on nineteenth?"

Jack appreciated that Kennen was no babbler. She had a habit of speaking in slightly clipped tones, and only when absolutely necessary. Sometimes he even forgot she was a woman.

"Pawalek's already there, but I don't think anyone's at the playground zone on thirty-second."

"All right, let's go."

Jack pulled out of The Bean parking lot and turned toward Crowchild Trail. Kennen determinedly sipped her coffee in spite of its scalding temperature. She asked, "How is your search going?"

"You mean Ontario?"

"Yeah. Any leads?"

"Well, there are about twenty Petrasyks in Ottawa alone. Already eliminated fourteen of them based on age, but this guy could be anywhere in Canada or in some other country ... or he could be dead. So, I'm not holding my breath. It's tedious, but I'll keep trying all the major cities until I exhaust them."

"And yourself."

"Yeah, and then I guess I'll start on all the eastern townsites. He's got to be somewhere."

"Can't imagine it," Kennen stated, "Two parents, four grandparents, five brothers and sisters, all in tiny Krydor, Saskatchewan. I escaped them first chance I got."

Jack chuckled. It was strange how he and Kennen got along so well. Except for this job, they shared virtually nothing in common, kind of like Jen and Donna. Those two were polar opposites, and he was a third point of the triangle to balance the weight. Donna had called him a few times lately, but he hadn't seen Jen in a long time. If anyone in this world came close to Jen, Kennen would be it. She wasn't as outgoing, but she conducted herself with a no-nonsense approach. With her, he knew exactly where he stood—a partner and subordinate officer—no more, no less. She'd probably take to Jen, if she caught her on a tame day.

Donna was a safer bet. She'd create a good impression on anyone. Jack hadn't seen her much since moving back to Calgary, certainly not like he did during their school days. Though still able to disarm him with a simple look, Donna was painfully naive about those things. Completely oblivious to the power right under her thumb.

If only she didn't remind him so much of that time years ago, when he was open to new avenues, open to taking a chance. The research job, his ex-girlfriend … Before that, Donna stood a chance, but now it was all done with. Maybe it was for the best. He had solidly entered his career and she was now doing the same. They could get all caught up in work instead of each other.

***

Brian took the breakup badly. Unsuspicious of any rivals, sadness could seek no outlet to trade for closure. By the fall of 1996, this pair, who began as the closest of friends, ended as virtual strangers. If it were only Brian dropping out of her life, she would have coped with seeming impropriety, but along with him went all of his friends. Most of them were pleasant couples, who genuinely liked her. They'd thoroughly expected an engagement announcement within a year. Donna hadn't considered that walking away automatically meant losing them too, and it was this absence that made her lonely, much more than Brian's. That alone validated her decision, but it was a comparatively large price to pay for the knowledge.

Breaking up threw Donna into the untamed world of the singles. At twenty-eight, an insistent voice in the back of her mind sounded eerily like Aunt Gloria.

(You do want to have children don't you? You know you're going to be thirty soon. Why don't you get out and meet some men? …)

She dreaded the idea of dating: the small talk, first impressions, worries. How did Jen do it so effortlessly? Well, Jen wasn't really doing a lot of that lately. The last time they spoke she was suffering from some awful chest cold.

Donna couldn't imagine walking up to someone and flirting, at least not with Jen's brash style. Her relationships with Ric and Brian seemed to evolve all on their own. The men she knew back then were more assertive. The older they got, the lazier they became. Although it forced her to rise above her inherent shyness, avoidance was an easier option. She wanted to talk to Jen about it, but the next time she phoned, Jen sounded sick again.

"Not again—" she clarified, "—still. I never got over the bronchitis from two months ago."

"Jen, have you been checked for asthma? I can get you a referral to a specialist. Isn't this your second bout of bronchitis in the past year?"

"Third, but if we count this as pneumonia, then it's only two." She held the phone away as a painful batch of coughs forced their way out. "Don't bother. I'm dealing with it. On the bright side, I lost my job the other day. They got tired of all the days off I needed."

"And this is the bright side because ...?"

"I got wind of it beforehand. I gave notice that I was going on sick leave, so I get unemployment payments for a while."

"How long is 'a while'?"

"About six months, if I don't find another job first, so I'll be all right. By the way, you'll never guess who I ran into last week—Tina Jacobson."

"Oh, what's she up to? I haven't seen her since grade twelve."

"She got married last year."

"To Steve Tarringer?"

"No, she said they broke up right after high school. She married some guy from Winnipeg. An electrician. They live out there. She was just here visiting her folks."

Donna experienced a moment of disorientation. One of her chief memories of high school was Steve and Tina attached at the hip. After her own breakup with Brian, it seemed fitting that other people's lives were equally inconsistent, though the discovery was still mildly disturbing. People left cities and relationships all the time. Why should it be monumental when it occurred to her and people like Tina?

"So, did William Aberhart hold a memorial service to mourn the disbandment of The Velcro Couple?"

Jen laughed, "Oh, there was probably a pumpkin dropped in their honor."

"Hey, did you hear? They banned the pumpkin drop—liability. Now they do a pajama run."

"What's that?"

"I don't know. Jog around in their undies and try not to get molested. No liability *there* ... You probably would've liked it."

"That's because I'd be the one doing the molesting."

"True, we all have our skills. Well, call me if you want some company. I'm not really looking forward to the holidays this year."

"Have you seen Brian?"

"No, he's avoiding me like the plague. I can understand that, but I still miss the whole relationship thing."

"He's a nice guy," Jen stated agreeably.

(Yeah, that was the problem. ...)

***

(I wonder if she'll say, "So, what seems to be the problem?" Every doctor I ever saw says that when they walk in.)

Tracy sat in her gown playing nervously with her ring finger. She just didn't want to explain all the details to her own physician, not someone who had known her from her youth. A new doctor at the other end of Calgary seemed a wise choice. Too frazzled, too scared of the complexity her life was taking, maybe a different doctor in a different office could help.

It was a clean little building with soft blue paint on the walls, a few toys in the corner to occupy the kids, up-to-date pamphlets on topics like breast-feeding and diabetes. There was a pleasant feeling about this clinic, starting with the nurse who booked the appointment. She sounded friendly, in a way that suggested how much she still liked her job. And when Tracy saw her at the reception desk, she thought the voice on the phone perfectly matched this buttony sweet person.

(This is someone who will meet Mr. Right and it will actually be Mr. Right, not a man who spirals into a struggling fraction of himself. No, this girl will find a nice guy who needs a little tender care, just a little fixing to round out his life, and if she's lucky, he'll realize the value of the jewel that he holds ... how much he really needs her.)

Finally, the door opened and a well-dressed young woman stepped in. She stood tall in an open lab coat, holding a fresh file folder. "Morin, Tracy" was typed clearly across the label. Shutting the door behind her, the doctor extended her hand and introduced herself. It was a friendly gesture, but also crisp with professional courtesy.

(I'm being treated by the nurse on Star Trek! Jesus, she's young. This girl must have graduated from med school yesterday.)

But Tracy also noted her serious, though soft expression. On level with a priest, this face would certainly defend secrets of the confessional.

Tracy sensed it was an entirely different approach than the nurse used, but somehow between the two of them, they got the job done. A calm began to subdue her nerves.

Gazing at the file in her hands, the doctor marked down the date, October 29, 1996. She summarized, "I understand you've had a fever for a few days. Let's check that right now."

She lifted the thermometer away from a holder on the wall, and placed a fitted plastic cover over its narrow end. Tracy tilted her head sideways as the doctor gently pressed the end into her ear. After a second, the thermometer beeped its answer.

"Your temperature's a little high, but not excessive. Do you have any other symptoms?"

Tracy burst into tears. Her partner, she explained, had used a condom and it was right after that when she noticed the symptoms. She was wondering if the condom could have torn and she'd developed some horrid disease.

"He's married. If he has to get checked out, then so does his wife."

After an examination, the doctor assured her that it was likely just a reaction to the spermicide in the condom. A simple cream would solve the problem, but she did a test for the more common sexually transmitted diseases.

"The results will take a couple of days. If anything turns up, my nurse will call you. Meanwhile, use the cream. You can pick it up in any pharmacy."

She wrote the names of two brands on a prescription pad, and handed the piece of paper to Tracy. Pointing to the first brand, she stated, "This one is less expensive ... and try a condom with no spermicide on the outside. It's a fairly common reaction some women have to it, some men too."

Tracy nodded calmly, but her eyes still gave off a frightened look.

The doctor paused, watching her patient closely. "Did you have any other concerns?"

More tears and then the resigned voice of truth. "I have a friend who is an alcoholic ... and I don't know what to do about it."

"Is this person you?"

"No," she answered surprised.

"Do you live with this person?"

Staring at the floor dejectedly, Tracy said, "Not right now."

"Are there any children involved?"

"Two."

"Well, you probably know the basics of alcoholism. He has to want to stop himself. You can't make him. If he's not in recovery, it's a positive thing he's not around your children. Is he attending A.A. meetings?"

"I think so. … I don't know. He goes for a while and does really well, and then something starts him up again."

"Nothing starts him up. He starts himself up. It's important not to endorse his choices, even in your wording. It's a tough love thing. You have to be strict about it. I know it feels petty, but it works." The doctor smiled empathetically, though her eyes sharpened. "Do you feel safe with him?"

"Yes." But the word sounded forced.

"Do you think your kids are safe with him?"

Tracy paused. "Once, I thought he was going to hit one, but he never has. I know he loves them. And me, I guess … but I just don't think it's ever going to get better." Tracy shook her head slowly. "And now, there's this other person. It's just so complicated. I don't have a job. I'm totally dependent on him, on the alcoholic, I mean."

"You may feel that things are out of control right now, but if you think about it, you're probably making some very logical decisions. You're forcing him to deal with his addiction on his own. That puts you and your kids in a much safer position. Any time you increase your sexual partners, your risk of STD's also increases, but at least it sounds like you're taking precautions. If your life feels complicated, that's a pretty clear sign that you need to determine how you feel about these men and make some decisions. You need to be safe and your kids need to be safe."

Scribbling on another small square of paper, she tore it from the pad in one quick movement. For a split-second, the sound amplified in the tiny room and then disappeared right into the walls. Not even an echo to chase it. Tracy mechanically reached out to take the paper.

"Here's the number of an abuse center. Keep this handy or just memorize it. Some other things you can do are to have a bag ready with a change of clothes and some money in it. Keep tabs on your children—always know exactly where they are—and tell people if you don't feel safe. You've told me what's happening and that's a good start, but it's important to tell other people too. Can you do that?"

She'd totally underestimated this doctor. No way she was new at this.

"Yes." This time, the confidence sounded genuine.

In the end, Tracy was glad the whole situation had come out, not that she received any earth-shattering words of wisdom, but it was heartening that the doctor understood the depth of the problem. Through simple sound advice, she'd motivated Tracy to regain control.

That was the worst part: not knowing when Al would start drinking again, not knowing if her lover considered her just a creative outlet for his marriage, or even if that was all her lover was to *her*. Too many uncontrollable variables here. And her kids … Is a drunk father better than no one at all?

In her anxiety about sexual diseases, she had lost sight of the big picture. The doctor had focused Tracy's thoughts on protecting her kids and herself. This was her second separation from Al. It was hard on Ashley and Kevin for the same reason it was hard on her; they were robbed of their stability every time Al picked up a bottle. She just couldn't continue in this marriage. Not like this. She wouldn't, she vowed, suddenly filled with her first solid decision in months.

(That's it. No more. This separation is strike two. Three strikes and you're out!)

As Tracy left the clinic, she was surprised to be able to shake the doctor's hand and look her in the eye, determined to reach the New Year with resolutions of stability and peace of mind.

***

CHAPTER 21

Through the winter, Donna hardly saw Jen. Neither paid much attention when 1996 slid into 1997.

Jen was still ill, and Donna was trying not to associate the Christmas holidays with Brian and his flock of friends. They presumed that Jack was knee-deep in playing cops and robbers, or maybe he was camped out in his church. At least Jen couldn't accuse him of trying to convert her, but they missed him. Jen wanted to pick on him and get picked on back, and Donna wanted to satisfy herself that she hadn't made a stupid mistake by dumping Brian.

By February, Jen was sufficiently recovered to meet Jack and Donna at Fioritti's. Still managing to raid Billy's closet despite living under separate roofs, an oversized turtleneck hung limply off her shoulders. The pneumonia had left her pale and weathered.

If Jen looked bad, Donna's appearance made up for it. A day of pampering—starting with a facial and ending with a new outfit—gave her skin a glow, her face framed by long hair. It was a glamorous contrast to her burgundy sweater. An evening with Jen would hardly have prompted such effort, but Donna felt inspired knowing a man might appreciate her appearance.

Jack, however, didn't seem to notice. The obvious signals between strangers were comparatively easier. Years of proximity caused those same signals to become lost in their everyday jargon. He wasn't one to flirt anyway, and she spent much of the evening wondering who the bigger fool was. At least the food was good and the conversation almost made up for her confused feelings toward him.

Jack reached for a dinner roll with one hand and lifted his soda with the other. He didn't drink alcohol anymore, presumably due to his religious beliefs. Jen, on the other hand, had a beer. Donna stuck to water, claiming that she didn't feel like a drink, but the truth was she was leaning toward Jack's way of life. Maybe she had been anyway. During her residency, twelve pounds had thickened her frame and the gym was keeping it under control. Alcohol wouldn't make that any easier.

After their drinks arrived and meals were ordered, Jen raised her glass in a toast. "Happy birthday, you two. Do you guys realize the last time we were here, we got knocked over the hood of a car? I'm glad Jack drove. This time we have God on our side."

"Yeah, just think, God *and* a cop," Donna added, "We're surrounded by spiritual and physical security, especially with his headlights off. Should be absolute Nirvana."

"Well, don't get too secure. God may love you unconditionally, but I on the other hand, have some taste ... and I can be bought too. For the price of a good steak, I'll protect just about anybody. Even you two."

Jack's grin reminded Donna of their first triangular conversation in Café-Abe, ten years ago. Jen had given him a strong blast of her personality and he had returned fire. He was always able to hold his own with her, using words that were often just as direct, but delivered with a softer style. He wasn't as quick to initiate the first verbal jab, or as cutting once he did, and regardless of the severity of his discourse, those deep brown eyes always stayed friendly.

"So, are you done training yet?"

"Yeah, I'm working the streets with a regular partner. Training lasted about six months. We went over driving maneuvers, shooting, law, self-defense, other stuff. ..."

He flipped his hand over abruptly in a dismissive gesture, but they didn't seem bored. Jen's blue eyes studied him across the table in her blatantly piercing manner. Donna's eyes were more subtle in their analysis, her head tilted slightly toward him. As the dim table lamp cast appealing hues across her face and darkened her green eyes, he momentarily lost his train of thought. Donna always did that to him, if he looked at her too long or too hard.

"They put rookies with a partner, until they think they'll be OK on their own. I have a pretty good partner right now."

Donna asked, "What's he like?"

"*She's* been on the job for seven years. She's better with people than I am, so I follow her lead a lot. They tell me she's an easier partner than some of the other women, less uptight. You know, a guy will put up with another guy being a slob in the car until he smartens up, but the women officers don't have much patience for that. If he doesn't clean up after himself right away, she assumes he never will and it becomes A Problem."

He placed his hands about six inches apart, as if holding A Problem between them. It never occurred to Jack's friends that police were real people, who had to find a way to work together just like everyone else.

Jen remarked, "So, the same people who are breaking up domestic disputes are dukin' it out over who left the cookie crumbs on the front seat?"

"Yeah, basically. Anyway, I'm not too slobby, so we get along pretty well. Actually, I'd trust her with my life. I know that sounds pretty serious, but really, it's a fun job."

Jen and Donna exchanged a quizzical look.

"Fun?" Jen declared, "Police work is fun? Don't you put up with the scum of society?"

"Well, yeah, you don't tend to see people at their best, but every day is different, which I like, and there's a strong camaraderie among the officers. You learn a lot and I've been getting good feedback on my evals. For the most part, I like it."

Sensing his ambivalence, Donna asked, "What's the downside?"

"Two days ago, I told a family their father died in a work accident. Giving bad news is hard, but I'm toughening up. The worst is when you see little kids in accidents or abused. You want to punch the parents out. Then, there's just little stuff, like getting caught up swapping war stories with other cops. It's good to get out with real people ... and the shift work was hard at first."

"I hear you," Donna nodded knowingly, "I sure did enough of that, just not with a thirty-eight."

"We carry forty-calibers. And the way you guys keep those stethoscopes in the freezer, you're just as lethal."

"We save the really cold ones for snarky cops."

It was almost like old times, only they were older and busier with bigger things in the world. For Donna and Jack, the repercussion of a poor decision could kill someone.

"You know, as a cop, you see a lot of different stuff, how people live. Not just civilians, but other departments too. At serious scenes, everybody's there, even the press."

"The press? How do they know where to go?"

"They monitor radio lines and tail ambulances." He shook his head and scowled. "You're trying to help a paramedic so he can save this guy, and you end up spending more time holding back the reporters. It's my job to keep everything under control, but man, I can barely stop myself from decking them."

"So," Jen probed, "when you say 'everybody' who's that?"

"Police, fire, and ambulance. It's called a Delta Response. It's for serious accidents. There could be hazardous materials around or the scene might need crowd control. You never know."

"*Boring*," Donna interjected, "Hey, I've always wondered—when you read someone their rights, do you have to have that speech memorized?"

"No, we keep it on a little card in our shirt pocket. It's different from what you hear on TV."

"How?"

"It's not, 'You have the right to remain silent. Everything you say can and will be used against you in a court of law.' Blah, blah, blah. That's the U.S. In Canada, it goes, 'You have the right to retain and instruct counsel without delay. You can call any lawyer you wish or get free advice from duty counsel immediately. If you wish to contact any lawyer ...' There's more, but I don't know it off by heart."

"But you could recite the one off TV, right?" Donna asked, smiling.

Jack gave her an impish grin. "I plead the fifth. So, how's your job going?"

"Pretty well. I have a good boss. He doesn't really act like one and my assistant is wonderful. I'm glad I'm in a small office. Med school was so grueling. The sheer volume of material getting stuffed in my head was insane. There was always this feeling that I didn't know enough. Now, I see people all day long who think I know *everything*. Talk about positive feedback."

Jack returned her earlier question, "What's the downside?"

"Some people are hard to read. I get the odd hypochondriac and these people can manifest actual physical symptoms."

"Then, how do you sort out what's real and what's not?"

"Well, basically, I take a step back and go with my gut feeling. Yeah, I know—sometimes it's not as scientific as we'd like it to be. Anyway, I started treating a man with a paranoid personality disorder. ... I shouldn't be telling you guys this. Ethics and all. Well, I'll just explain this one example. He thought his wife was causing him to have small M.I.'s."

"What?"

"Myocardial Infarctions. His left arm would even ache. I was doing every test that exists on him, until I just stepped back and considered how he made me feel inside. Whenever he was there, I felt confused and put upon, like he was purposely out to get me, and then I realized that this was exactly what he was feeling all the time. Since then, we've made progress. Now, he doesn't get the chest pains anymore, although he still thinks his wife is planning to do away with him in more dire ways."

"I don't know," Jack commented, "I think a heart attack would feel pretty dire while it's happening."

MEETING JACK

"It's actually tame compared to some other ways. A strong one can kill you in seconds."

Jack leaned back in his chair and almost laughed at Jen's face. She looked like someone who was witnessing an ugly car accident, hating the sight before her, but unable to turn away. It wasn't like her. Jack's eyes sparkled as he relished the opportunity to make her squirm.

"Yeah," he added, "but imagine how long those seconds are. The stabbing pain right in the middle of your chest, the desperate gasps for breath. An easier way to go is a razor blade in the tub, but all that blood? If you're efficient, it'll spurt out pretty fast and that would be hard to watch. I've been called to a few of those scenes. Me, I think I'd rather go quicker, except that the quick methods are just as gross. A bullet, knife wound, high speed collision, all pretty instantaneous."

Donna countered, "Oh, I've seen some sadly lingering cases of attempted suicide using every one of those means. One wrong move and you're in a coma instead."

Jen snapped out of her discomfort at the opportunity to steer the subject sideways. "So who says that's not a good thing?"

"Because you don't go anywhere in Limbo-Land," Jack answered, "You know, the tunnel, bright light, you miss out on all that. You just sit there."

"You mean the tunnel and light that people *claim* to see in near-death experiences?" Donna asked, one eyebrow raised.

"What do you mean near-death?" Jen exclaimed, "It's death-death. It doesn't get any nearer!"

Jack smiled, automatically preparing for the onslaught. One hand extended to Jen, "First-hand experience versus—" then it flipped toward Donna, "—medical science. Let the games begin!"

"Look guys, it's all just a chemical reaction. When you stimulate the visual area on the frontal cortex, people claim they see a light. They actually feel the sensation of squeezing through a tight space and see a light that isn't there. The same area is stimulated by a chemical that's released at the moment of death. Nothing more."

Jen asked, "So, you're saying dying entails nothing more than a brief hallucination before you kick off?"

"A realistic one ... but yeah, that's basically it."

Jen's eyes searched between the cutlery on the table to find the best response, and then gave a short sigh. "Well, if dying is no more than a vivid high, imagine what possibilities a coma holds."

Donna barely stopped herself from gloating at Jen's pout. Though rare to illicit uneasiness from this sparring partner, a wary part of Donna recognized an inherent lack of sportsmanship in the topic. No matter what

183

scientific facts Donna knew on the subject, Jen's direct experience was infinitely more applicable. In any case, Jen had managed to open a new channel of discussion without really surrendering her position.

"Well, as far as anyone knows," Donna explained, "nothing happens in a true coma. There are varying degrees of consciousness, but when someone is right out of it, there aren't any measurable chemical reactions to suggest that they're experiencing any real sensations ... but who knows? I've had dreams that feel incredibly real. Maybe a person is capable of living more fully through a coma state, because their experiences happen in their head."

"*Boring*," Jen mimicked, "She's got that doctor-talk face on. Just let her ramble for a minute so we can move on to something that's actually interesting."

Jack retorted, "Hush, little one. The adults are talking," and Donna almost choked on her water.

When she stopped coughing, she faced Jen. "I do not ramble, you flippant little turd."

"Well Don," Jack sheepishly interjected, "You kind of do. ..."

"God, five minutes with you two and a coma starts to look pretty good. OK now focus, you tedious peons. If the mind is the most powerful part of us, why couldn't it create bizarre situations when it has total control? I mean, when you're unconscious, it has nothing to compete against. You're not aware of anything around you, so there aren't any distractions. It can design the best fantasies and make them all seem real."

"Yes, thank you Dr. Ramble, but I'll go you one further," Jen said with a defiant lift of her jaw. "What if your mind made it so realistic, that it went to the people around you too?"

Jack stared curiously. "What do you mean, like they could see the same things that were happening in your head?"

"See them, feel them, totally interact with whatever's coming out of this one person's mind." She paused, noting their expressions of disbelief. "Listen, you've heard of out-of-body experiences, right? Think about all that unused brain-power while you're just lying there. What if you could take yourself right out of that coma state? Step out and mix it up with other people telepathically or something."

She swung her hand smoothly across her plate, sliding from point A to point B in one straight line.

"I mean, what if that unused brain-power could take your body with it and physically place you with other people, people that maybe aren't even there now, but were there at some point in your past ... or would be in your future."

This time her hand swung from point A to a spot directly above point B.

Donna noticed Jack's eyes narrowing without their usual softness. There was a curious look about Jen too, or maybe it was just her typical sparkle as she crossed swords. It made Donna think twice, but not wanting to be drawn into one of Jen's far-fetched debates, she decided to ignore it.

"And you say *I* ramble … Come on, Jen. I was talking about unconsciousness—meaning *not* conscious. No matter how realistic dreams are, they can't bounce from head to head or affect the physical environment around us."

"Then, let me ask you something. Sleepwalking is a fact. I mean, there are people who walk in their sleep, aren't there?"

"Oh, no you don't—"

"And if one person who is sleepwalking meets up with another person and they interact, isn't the sleepwalker in fact affecting the reality of the other person, not just intellectually, but physically?"

Once again, Jen had maneuvered the conversation into a line of reasoning that was equally illogical and irrefutable. There were serious holes in Jen's argument, but in a swift communication from one pair of eyes to another, Jack and Donna agreed to bypass the challenge.

Donna stated, "Well, I wouldn't be too eager to dive into a coma. It's often just a short prelude to death. It may be painless, or maybe as you suggest full of life, but there are ramifications that go way beyond the victim, especially with a botched suicide attempt. Don't forget the pain of the person dying eventually ends, but the family gets to feel it forever. There really is no easy way to go. In fast ways, the pain is terrible, like when someone falls or asphyxiates, but it's over within minutes, and then there are slow ways like cancer, where the pain grows over months or years."

Jen frowned. "I forgot what it is you two do for a living. Remind me never to eat with you again. The closest I get do death is when I show some guy how to fall on stage so the audience can see his fake blood. Let's get back to office politics before the entrees arrive. Don, tell us about some of your strange patients."

Donna and Jack exchanged a mischievous smile of victory and Donna considered side-stepping the question. She could see that Jack would have willingly played along; there was a message in his eyes connecting their eager conspiracy, and for a moment, she was caught in their color. So brown, they possessed a strength to hold the world in their steady gaze. They were eyes that would stand by the people he cared about, that could completely envelop a woman, dividing her into sensual sections of herself and yet, still keep her wrapped up in one piece. Donna spent no more than a couple of seconds thinking about this, but it was enough to wash away their little attack on Jen.

"I told you I can't do that."

"I don't mean names and dates."

"It's still not right."

"Oh, who cares! Just tell us the general stuff, like the paranoid guy. Is he the weirdest one you've had?"

"No," Donna almost laughed, "There are plenty weirder."

"Like what?"

"You're just not going to drop this are you? OK, well, I don't know if I'd call this one weird. It was just kind of complicated. A few months ago, a woman saw me who was in a tough situation. She was wondering if she had an STD—"

Jen rolled her eyes. "STD? What is it with you and these acronyms?"

"Slut of the year and she doesn't know Sexually Transmitted Disease."

"Oh, I thought it was Spank The Doctor."

"Well that only applies to really cute patients. Anyway, the real problem was this woman's home life. She was sleeping with a married man—I think she was married too. She must have slipped her ring off for the appointment, because I could see the mark on her finger. And if that wasn't enough, her husband suffers from alcoholism. She thought he might get abusive, but she wasn't ready to leave him. Well, it turns out the married man and his wife are also my patients. During one of his appointments, he confessed what he was doing and let her name slip, so I knew it was the same woman. Luckily, she didn't actually have any disease, but even if she had, I wouldn't be able to tell the other couple to check it out, because of my confidentiality with *her*. … I have a hard time being empathetic when people knowingly take risks."

Jack nodded in agreement as Jen watched her two friends pass judgment on the world. This time, she changed the subject so smoothly, the others didn't even notice.

***

CHAPTER 22

Calgary summers are everything from pleasant to miserable. Especially accurate was the old adage, "If you don't like the weather, wait ten minutes". 1997 was particularly erratic. Winter made a last ditch attempt to hang on with a sudden cold snap late in March. Snowflakes floated down to accentuate the winter hold, but they were gone as quickly as they fell and a long stretch of mild spring weather followed, promising a comfortable season ahead.

Donna was biking home from the gym. Mid-evening, there was a window of opportunity to catch the sun and fresh air before dusk stole the heat, a perfect balance of summer tempered by the pull of the horizon. Soft sun.

She wove carefully through the next flock of runners, the shrill sound of her bicycle bell preceding her. A few raised their hands when she passed. Lifting hers in return, she sped on. Long in place by city developers, the recreation paths hadn't predicted the growing territoriality between bikers and joggers. In recent years, rollerblades were adding to the confusion as well. Who was entitled to be where, when, and how fast?

Pedal, pedal, pedal ... *ring!* ... swerve ... pedal, pedal, pedal. More runners ahead.

(Nice butt.)

Then, she smiled and slowed down next to him.

"Hey, J.P!"

He took his stride down to a fast walk, breathing hard. Glistening sweat dusted his arms and legs. With his tank top stuck to his chest and back, outlining every curve, Donna was suitably impressed.

"Hi," he said, "I didn't know you toured these pathways too."

187

"I just finished doing weights and thought I'd get some cardio done while it's still nice out."

"Ha! Don becomes a Plate-head at last! I knew it was a matter of time."

"Resistance is futile to the will of the Plate-head."

They veered off path, Donna pushing her bike, until they found a soft-looking patch of grass to stretch on. On one side of them, the Bow River flowed past. On the other, cars matched its meandering trail along Memorial Drive. The bike path and grassy slope offered a buffer between river and road, nature's resilience and man's mechanical encroachment.

Jack started with a calf stretch and Donna followed, pressing her heel gently into the ground behind her.

(Dorsiflexion.)

Her mind automatically catalogued the anatomical ankle position. It was hard not to be so aware of bodies, even on her off-hours.

Jack's body was wonderfully developed. He had kept up his size and it gave him a powerful air. Donna remembered when she first met him eleven years ago. Did she really think he was goofy? She predicted that he would have a manly appearance when he finally grew into his looks, and she was right. A perfect fit. His facial structure was still long and serious-looking, but now it complimented his rough and tumble body. Even those brown eyes were strong. Donna knew breaking up with Brian had been the right choice, the only choice.

"Hey," she asked, "Are you going to church on Sunday?"

"Yeah, but not the morning service. I'm on days 'til next week, so I'll be working until 3:00. Then, I guess I'll catch the evening one. Why?"

"Well, I've been thinking of doing a little church shopping. I thought I'd start with yours."

Jack began untying his shoelaces, the movements slow with deliberation. Though his face was unreadable, his back seemed to retreat within itself and those broad shoulders rounded, as though a sudden weight had fallen from the sky and landed squarely on them.

She ventured, "New people are allowed to come, aren't they?"

Sure, but ..." He slipped his shoes and socks off and let the light June breeze drift through his toes. Averting his eyes, he explained, "See, I don't go to be with people. It's a place where I can get my head straight."

Donna asked, "You haven't gotten to know anyone there? Isn't the point to feel connected?"

Jack shrugged, tilting his head in a response which conveyed nothing.

This brief exchange chaffed her mind for several weeks. Maybe he doubted her sincerity about attending services. Part of her wondered if he saw through her veneer of religious interest to the honest core underneath. She did want to find a church and give it a try, but she had to admit that she'd be quicker to try one where he was a member ... especially after seeing him with perspiration running off his hard body.

Meanwhile, his discomfort with the idea of accompanying her was upsetting in a nagging way. If she were Jen, the topic would have been extracted, examined, and filed quickly, but Donna decided to sift for more clues. She chose to overlook his reaction to her request, and instead try a smaller request. She asked him if he would show her the Bible and explain how to get started reading it. Again, he diverted her.

"I'll get you my pastor's number."

"Well, I don't need a thesis on the subject."

Her irritability was difficult to subdue. She wasn't asking him to go streaking at the local football game, but he avoided the Bible study opportunity as if she were presenting him with just such a demand. Should she be offended? Laugh and go on as usual? Confused and miffed, she sensed a chunk of information missing, as though she were walking into an exam unprepared and forced to do every equation by hand. And Jack was sitting next to her, refusing to share his calculator.

***

Dr. Carlin, a woman, and a crying boy stepped out of exam room three.

"I know you're ears hurt Sweetie, but you make sure your mom gives you these drops OK? Tomorrow, those ears won't hurt." She bent down and whispered, "They're magic drops."

The boy's eyes went wide, swimming in great big tears.

"You know, that nice lady at the front desk has a whole box of Ninja Turtle stickers." She leaned in close with a serious expression. "And she gives extra to the really polite kids. Just so you know. Do you remember her name?"

"Annie!" the boy exclaimed, tears suddenly forgotten.

"Excellent. Go see how many you can get out of her." Donna turned to the mother. "Keep him home for another day or two, even if he seems better. This infection can rebound so it's better to play it safe."

"Dr. Carly?"

She bent toward the boy again. "Yes, Sweetie?"

"My brother says you're real hot."

"Good to know. Get a sticker for him too."

189

As he trundled out after his mother, Anne remarked, "Another happy customer. I need to get some girl stickers. Barbie or something. You know what he told me? His brother thinks I'm hot!"

"How many stickers did you give him?"

"Eight ... and two for his brother."

"Hmmm, we've been played by a seven-year-old."

"Well, I'm sure it won't be the lowest point in our careers."

"Speak for yourself. Apparently I'm *real* hot." Dr. Carlin glanced down at the next file folder. And looked again. "Is this a joke? Is she really here for an appointment?"

Anne nodded. "She called yesterday. Wanted the last slot before lunch, and luckily, Louise Kaufmann had cancelled. She was very insistent, but she wouldn't tell me what it was about."

"She's an old friend. Hope she brought burgers. These sandwiches are getting boring."

But when Donna entered the room, Jen was seated on the examining table, swinging her legs nervously with no burgers in sight.

"Hey! What are you doing here?"

"Well, you are a doctor, aren't you? You didn't just bluff your way past seven years of university."

Donna's smile evaporated. The sharp wit was there, but something was biting in Jen's voice. Her words were delivered impatiently, beyond a mere bad mood, her eyes hard and unhappy. She looked as if she'd been forced to run a marathon in the middle of the night.

"All right, what's going on?"

"I want you to do three things for me. First, I want you to be my doctor."

Donna's eyebrows pressed together. "I can't Jen. Ethics—no family or friends. I can work on whatever you need today, but then I'll have to recommend another doctor for you."

A moment of tense disappointment sat clearly on Jen's face, but she wiped it away with her next question.

"What if it's complicated?"

"Well, technically by seeing you today, I'm obligated to follow up on treatment when ongoing treatment is warranted. ..." Her voice trailed off. "Are you pregnant?"

"First things first. Are you my doctor?"

Donna peered as though Jen were speaking a foreign language. Then exasperated, she exclaimed, "OK, I'm your doctor. So what do you need?" turning to a cupboard to extract a pregnancy test. She lifted one off a small pile, sandwiched between the glucose strips and HIV pamphlets.

But Jen just gazed stonily and replied, "Well, not *that*. Try the one on the right."

Donna blinked at the tidy stack of pamphlets. "You—Jen, are you OK?"

The words tumbled out impatiently, "No, no, I'm not. In fact, I've already had a test done and it's positive, which is fucking ironic wording. I just want you to do one so you'll be convinced."

"What? Wait a minute, who did the test? I can call and confirm it with them." She couldn't digest this.

"No, you'll just talk yourself out of believing it. You'll always doubt it a little unless you authorize the test."

She was right. This was one truth Donna would avoid at all costs, but Jen had asked her to take on the burden of that truth. And in effect, Donna had acquiesced by agreeing to treat her, even if only temporarily.

"All right," she said, maneuvering her fingers into a pair of gloves. "Pick an arm."

Jen pulled up her left sleeve.

"Make a fist."

Swabbing the skin, Donna noticed a black lesion near her elbow, probably one of many Jen was painstakingly hiding. It was only the size of a dime. Donna couldn't remember the last time she'd seen her friend in a short-sleeved shirt. A year or more. All those bouts of pneumonia. She should have figured it out.

Jen barely startled at the needle prick, though Donna's worried thoughts were ruining her normal finesse. You could jab some people with a poker and they wouldn't even notice.

"Don't you make the nurse do this?"

"Usually, but sometimes I do it. Keeps my skills up."

(I've got to do something. Oh God, if it's AIDS, I won't be able to do anything.)

She had no idea how to act. Should she be detached? Break down in tears? What?

"OK, relax. Press here. … Listen, do you want to talk about it?"

"No, just call me with the results. And don't say your nurse will do it if anything shows up. That's such crap."

She walked out, leaving Donna in the examining room gripping the blood sample. Donna's hands felt numb, as though they couldn't bear to be touching the glass tube.

She spent the next hour in her office. Staring blankly at the desk, uninterested in the sandwich in her hand, her thoughts funneled into one neat line. Jen might be HIV positive. She may already have AIDS.

(So this is why it's unethical to accept friends as patients—you can't separate their medical condition from them.)

The moment Jen revealed her intentions, Donna's objectivity had fallen by the wayside. She could imagine her approach to the problem in one of two ways. She would deny the legitimacy of the test results, just as Jen predicted ... or leap to the rescue with heroic determination, ready to do battle with the virus. Neither approach would solve anything for Jen. If she really were infected, it was just a matter of time. Donna recognized the small blessing of having the next week to get used to it, but what about after that? Someday, would she be forced to continue their friendship through memories? There were a lot of memories after all these years. Little snapshots in time, eventually fading like the details of a dream.

Several minutes passed, until she remembered that there were supposed to be three requests, but Jen had only stated two. Donna shook her head, realizing she'd spent the last twenty minutes clutching the sandwich deep in thought. Ham and low-fat cheese on whole wheat, no butter. So much for healthy food. She turned to the wastebasket, and in one sharp movement, tossed it in.

***

Wearing a bed sheet and a bright smile, she opened the door slowly and beckoned Jack into the room. He followed in a daze, amazed to have found her after all these years. She looked exactly as he remembered: tall, slim, appealing curves, those eyes ...

With fingers trailing along a shiny lunch tray, she offered him a sandwich. They sat precisely arranged all ready to eat, but he ignored them.

Jack reached out to pull the sheet away and draw her naked body close. He wanted to feel the smooth skin of her arm against his in another dance. He could even hear the band somewhere in the distance. With only one dance, the rest would follow. He would have it all ... but in the time it took to notice the sandwiches, she was already across the room. She moved like the thinnest of clouds, drifting with fluid grace. She had the kind of body that flowed. If he were to place his hands on the small of her back, he imagined her slipping right through his grasp like water.

"Let's have our coffee out here," she said, turning to the balcony. Her voice floated carelessly toward him. The sensual tones reminded him how she'd whispered his name in bed.

She stepped out as a breeze lifted the sheer curtains lightly across the balcony doorway, and he could see her standing against the railing, gazing at him invitingly with those eyes. The curtain lifted again, briefly covering her dark hair like the veil of a young bride. Then, as it gently fluttered down, she disappeared. He ran across the room and searched outside, but the balcony was empty. A familiar desperation filled him.

(If only I was quicker ...)

Jack stared at the sunny sky, willing her to return, but she was gone like smoke. Was she ever really here?

The sandwiches were gone too. Instead, money lay scattered near the dresser, twenty-dollar bills decorating the floor in a circular patch and, as he stared down at them, saw the empty bed sheet clutched tightly in his grasp. Raising his face to the mirror, Jack crumpled at the sight of his haunted eyes.

That was usually when he woke up, embracing a pillow as if it were the pliable contours of a woman.

***

CHAPTER 23

The following week, Donna asked Anne for a few minutes uninterrupted in her office to review Jen's lab results. The printout confirmed the presence of the HIV virus in the patient Jennifer Brammon, dated August 10, 1997. The numbers would remain in her memory forever. She read it again. And once more.

How long had Jen known? How long had she been infected? Behind the privacy of closed doors, Donna's face contorted. Although she had been braced to expect the worst, the confirmation still took her by surprise. Now, there was nothing but bitter reality to wade through.

After collecting herself, she dialed Jen's number. Donna's voice was all Jen needed to know that her temporary doctor was convinced, and another appointment was set for that afternoon. As they sat side by side in Donna's office, none of their usual banter prefaced the conversation.

"How long have you known?"

"One year, four months, twenty-two days. It came up on a blood test, when I had that chronic pneumonia last year. Sorry to just dump it on you. I didn't want to believe it myself, and then I didn't know how to tell anyone. No one else knows yet."

Jen's statements were unembellished with any gestures, her mannerisms muffled. Donna had seen this stiff behavior before. The anger people felt about having a terminal disease would sit like a big rock on their shoulders. That was the moment when life really left them.

"So, you haven't been referred to an infectious diseases specialist?"

"No."

"Well, we should get you in right away. There's a waiting list, but I'll see what I can do about getting that sped up." Then Donna remembered, "You said you needed three things from me. Was that the third?"

"No."

Whatever it was, it couldn't be any worse than the second one. Nothing could compare to discovering the death sentence of her oldest friend.

"I want you to tell my family for me."

Donna gaped at her. It was definitely as bad.

"You realize ... Jen, they don't hate me and they deserve the right to despise the person who tells them. I'd be making it worse by taking that away. Why don't you have your regular doctor do it? I can still be there."

But even as she said it, Donna knew how cowardly this offer was, and she dropped her eyes in the face of Jen's unshakable gaze.

"You are my doctor, remember? It says so right there. Listen, you know they'll go into denial faster than hell. Well, maybe not Jeffrey or Dad, but the others would cling to a whole bunch of crap if it came from anyone else. They'd claim the doctor was a quack and send me for ten-thousand other tests. If they heard it from you, they'd know it was real. ... Don, I can't keep a job anymore. I'm too sick. I have to move home soon. They have to be told and I don't want to do it myself. I need you to deal with their questions and keep them from getting weird on me."

An uncomfortable pause hung between them. Jen leveled a pair of sharp blue eyes on her and Donna knew she had no choice. Her own eyes radiating sorrow, she answered, "Yes, of course I will. When?"

Jen visibly relaxed, now clear of the dreaded refusal, but how could Donna refuse her friend this simple request? Was it simple? The word was a classic understatement.

"My brothers are planning to work on my parent's deck Saturday. They'll all be there and," Jen emphasized, "it's no one's birthday. I don't want to turn someone's special occasion into 'The Day They Got The News'. ... Look I know you've done this before—"

(Yeah, on relative strangers, not on people who borrowed my lip gloss in junior high ...)

"—and I know you'll do it right. I make no excuses. I don't want you to lie to them, but I don't want my past to be put on the table."

"Why would it?"

Jen made a face, "Well ..."

"That's only one possibility. Think about it. All it takes is a speck of blood through a hangnail. And ten years ago, you must have had a transfusion after that car hit you."

"Oh yeah, maybe ..." Jen replied thoughtfully, "Well, I still don't want it out in the open."

Donna stated firmly, "It won't be," and with those words, agreed to rally to the defense of her oldest friend.

***

At 3:30 on Saturday, Donna arrived at the Brammon's house to find Jen's brothers diligently working on the backyard deck. They greeted her with salutes of their paint brushes, "Don!" The final coat looked good, rich with glossy depth. Another thirty minutes and it would be done.

"Unless," Billy suggested, "you decide to add your muscle. Got extra brushes!"

Jen agreed, "Yeah, what do you say, Nurse Chapel? Add the commanding presence of the woman's touch?"

Donna lit up. "Damn it Jen, I'm a doctor, not an engineer! ... I've always wanted to say that!"

As the young men completed their finishing touches on the deck, it reflected the sunlight brilliantly, but Donna and Jen were becoming too nervous to appreciate the sight before them. Then, Jen's brothers were putting their tools away and appraising their clothes. How did that stain get there? And this mark? And that one? Carl sported more paint than the wood.

Jen pulled Donna out of earshot. "I explained that you had something to tell them and my mom immediately thought you were getting married. Of course, Billy was devastated. So, I told them that it's serious and now they think you're pregnant. Anyway, Billy will probably marry you, but Carl thinks you should seriously consider suicide over marrying Billy. ... It was quite the discussion over lunch."

Donna shook her head and they smiled bleakly at each other.

Finally, the family was assembled around the kitchen table. Cool drinks of iced tea and beer were set out around a plate of cookies centered on the table. Every symbol of home and family gave Donna a special little ache inside. She was about to upset this idyllic kitchen scene. It had been her home too, but after this, it would never be the same. None of them had ever known anyone with AIDS.

She took a deep breath and started her speech. "Jen told you that I need to discuss something of a serious nature with all of you. I need you to be as caring and strong and open-minded as possible. I'm going to be talking like a doctor, because it's the only way I know how to describe what I have to tell you."

The Brammons listened intently. A vague uneasiness spread among them. This didn't sound like a conversation starter for an announcement on Donna's marital or maternal status.

"As you know, Jen has had a number of episodes of pneumonia. The particular organism responsible is called pneumocystis carinii. It indicates the presence of a more serious disease."

At the word "disease", startled faces tuned into the severity of the topic. This was not about Donna at all.

Jeffrey filled in the blank, "Lung cancer?"

Catching his expression squarely, Donna explained, "Not directly ... but yes, lung cancer will be present sooner or later. The actual disease Jen is facing is AIDS."

Silence. The drinks were frozen on the table, the cookies untouched on their colorful ceramic plate.

No, this was a joke, a stupid joke. There was no way. ... Jen was pulling a horrible prank, getting them back for—well, any number of things—and Donna was in on it. Any second now, Jen would slap her hand down on the table and exclaim, "Gotcha, you twits! I'm gonna live forever, just to pull this kind of shit on you!" But Jen and Donna just looked deflated ... and patient. Those were two things they *never* looked.

Mrs. Brammon covered her mouth with one hand. A single tear dropped from her enormous eyes and trailed slowly down her cheek. Donna followed their stares to rest on Jen, whose eyes darted back and forth among them defensively. Donna realized the magnitude of pressure that required deflection right now. She struggled to keep her voice steady.

"I'm here as Jen's friend and physician, and as your friend too. This is going to be a very confusing and difficult time for you. You need to understand that whatever you're feeling is completely normal. I can answer some of your questions now ... or I can leave you alone to talk."

She turned to Jen and asked, "What do you want?"

The answer was swift and certain, "Stay."

Smiling reassuringly, Donna tried to transfer some of her composure, which seemed to work. Jen straightened up in her chair and showed a glimmer of those blue eyes of steel.

Then Donna addressed the group again, "There are sources of support for families of AIDS victims—I hesitate to use that word—but it's important you understand what you're facing. Jen is a victim and that makes you victims as well."

At this point, Marianne Brammon burst out, "Wait a minute! How can this have happened to her? She's not a drug user. She's not—"

Jen's eyes took on a sudden frightened shade. Recognizing the danger of letting her mother's questions steer the discussion, Donna quickly interrupted.

"There are a lot of ways someone can be infected. The HIV virus has an incubation period of somewhere between five and ten years, maybe less. We don't know when she was infected or how. In fact, that information would be useless anyway." She looked carefully at everyone around the table. "If you focus on that part of it, it will only drive you crazy. What is important is to know that you can live with a person who is HIV positive. At this point, Jen's reached the disease stage. She'll need to live here and start seeing a specialist."

Carl asked, "Can't you help her?"

"I wish I could, but she really needs a specialist."

"Aren't there drugs she can take? I mean, something right?"

Donna nodded conservatively, "There are some experimental medications, and the sooner she has them, the more time we can buy."

"You're saying there's no hope," Mr. Brammon summarized quietly.

Her voice equally soft, Donna answered, "Even with the medications, there's no cure. You have to accept that."

Marianne Brammon's hard gaze zeroed in on Donna. "How long have you known?"

"As Jen's physician, I can't answer that."

"How about as her *friend*?" Mrs. Brammon icily added and Donna faced the same expression that she did back in high school, when an accident rendered Jen the only one seriously injured.

Billy shot a look at his mother and her eyes dropped to the table. A painful pause filled the room. Mr. Brammon pushed away from the table, placed his hands on the sink, and stared stonily out the kitchen window. Lacy yellow curtains framed his body. Donna remembered his silhouette in the hospital window years ago, when she was a patient instead of a doctor. She was just Jen's friend then, whose biggest worry was her father's encroaching love life, not a physician giving a family the worst news they could ever hear.

Everybody was waiting for her to present a solution, to fix this unfixable thing. In those moments, Donna had to concede that Mrs. Brammon had a point. Which role weighed in more right now? One contained the power to heal and the other could be destroyed with a few choice words. Sitting there amongst this family, *her* family, she couldn't hide behind the medical training. It seemed less and less meaningful as her emotional side gained ground. Tears welled up.

"I wish I could tell you different, but I can't make this better."

(We're talking about this right in front of her, like she's already dead! This is what it will be like, sitting around the table, except we'll be shooting the shit with "Remember When?" stories. Why did you make me do this Jen? I can't do this. I can't. …)

For a few seconds no one moved. Then, Jen put her hand on Donna's wrist and quietly whispered, "Thanks."

In showing her emotions, Donna thought she'd ruined a delicate situation, but Jen had calculated correctly. The Brammons understood the severity of the situation, because this news came from someone who had been in their lives for fifteen years. Her mere familiarity proffered an air of competence they could trust, and her emotion gave them permission to be human, while pulling the core of the tension off Jen. It was the impetus that forced the family to talk. In the midst, Donna rose to make a discrete exit.

Jen and Billy followed her to the front door. Pulling Donna to him, Billy held her tightly, the way he wanted to the night of her attack. It was an embrace she didn't expect, tender and protective: the only time he had ever braved the gesture and the only time he was exempt from his sister's teasing.

Instead, Jen watched sadly, realizing that this embrace marked the end of Donna's place in this family and she was the cause of it.

***

CHAPTER 24

During the fall, Jen's pneumonia worsened. Donna referred her to a specialist and made a point of calling every week. Now that Jen was living with her parents, screening her calls wasn't an option. Mrs. Brammon was always at home. She answered the phone, as if expecting the caller to have a miraculous drug that would save her daughter, that is, until Donna would speak and then her usual motherly tone would stiffen. The conversations were always the same.

"Is Jen there?"

"Yes, but she's sleeping", "resting", "in the bathtub", etc. "and can't come to the phone."

"How is she?"

"She's the same," or "a little better," never "worse".

Mrs. Brammon had an amazing ability to fill an entire conversation with no real information whatsoever. Donna thought she was avoiding her daughter's impending death by making everyone else avoid it too.

Since Jen's condition was announced, the whole family had maintained a cautious distance. Donna warned Jen that this would happen. Quiet animosity was the worst kind. Though upsetting, it was expected, so she tried to take it in stride and hoped it would pass.

Jack's distance bothered her more. Under strict orders from Jen, Donna was limited to disclosing her condition to those with a Brammon surname. Though unsure if she was held to the promise as a friend or a physician, she honored it just the same.

Despite the prime importance of confidentiality, she longed to unburden herself to Jack, to curl up in his arms and describe how hard it had been to face Jen's family. She could envision the fit of his arm around her waist and her head on the high part of his shoulder, and she told herself she was just being a friend, the way she had been in Billy's embrace.

When summer was over, it discouraged her that she'd only seen Jack a handful of times. She had yet to visit his church or share a Bible passage. He was so busy; his job alone was a big deterrent to a social life. Understanding the rigors of shift work, she carefully timed her calls lest she interrupt a precious sleep cycle.

Sleep—that was another issue. Despite her own stable schedule, she found herself lying awake at night, usually thinking about Jack, but not just about him. Her mind would race as though on a treadmill, not deciphering anything of value yet running toward it just the same. The futile restlessness claimed her attention night after night, as a foreboding undercurrent applied its pressure. In the recesses of the dark, just at the brink of sleep, a part of her sensed that time was running out. It was ...

***

... falling into disarray. She could sleep forever here, but the images kept calling, one after another, tumbling in circles against a night sky.

Dizziness almost sent her into a panic. If she could stop herself from spinning, then she would be able to focus on his face, the one she needed to see so badly. He would be at The Bean, sitting beside Jen, drinking his coffee—black like the sky surrounding Donna, without so much as a snowflake to cut into it.

The images were enchantingly lifelike, but though she wanted to reach out and caress them, it was his voice she craved more. That soft low strength in his tones, as melting as his arm across her hips. The darkness added to the nuance of the fantasy, just like before, and sighing, she finally heard him say ...

***

"Hey, Don, glad I caught you. Can you tear yourself away tonight for some sledding?"

"Tobogganing? I haven't gone in years! Geez, I don't even know if I still have my sled."

"Maybe Jen has one. I'll call her."

"Oh, don't bother. ... She's got something happening tonight. Should I pick you up Jack?"

"No, I'll come get you in about fifteen, OK?"

"Give me twenty. I got to find my snowsuit."

201

She put the phone down and exhaled. She was going to see him. Where was that snowsuit? Would it even fit? Rummaging through an old box, she was pleased to discover that it fit so well, her shapely curves were hard to miss.

(Guess that membership paid off after all!)

Donna had never done things like this with Brian. He'd tried—there was just no time then. Now, Jack and Donna tobogganed enough to compensate for years of stale studying. Up they trudged, avoiding other people zooming on their way down. Jack always hauled the toboggan and gave her first choice of where to sit. She most often chose to sit in front with her back secured against his chest. His arms would then be around her.

Once, they miscalculated a mogul and flipped sideways, tumbling over each other as the toboggan slid away on its own. Jack was still clutching her when they stopped rolling and laughing. There was a moment when their eyes met, a moment of snowflakes against a starry sky. Then, he helped her to her feet and dashed off after the runaway sled.

As she watched him, it occurred to her that this was exactly what she needed. Fresh air, snowball wars, snowsuits to make even the most graceful person bumble about like a diapered toddler. The most fun she'd had in ages. It was too bad Jen was missing it. Jen would miss a lot of wonderful experiences, but Donna didn't want to think about her tonight. Being with Jack was such a lift from her stresses.

After two hours, they were sick of the wet snow and craved hot chocolate in a warm house. No one ever complained about her hot chocolate.

Their cheeks were shiny and red when they entered her apartment and peeled off their outer layers. She changed into a pair of biking shorts and a T-shirt, before bringing two pillows and a blanket to share. Taking positions on opposite ends of the couch, they sipped their warm drinks. It was almost like being at The Bean.

"So, how's life in police-land?"

"It's OK. I still like it. I get annoyed at people sometimes, but it's a good job."

"What's annoying?"

"Well, you know how it is. You're driving along and suddenly, you see a cruiser. What do you do? ... You instantly become Joe Model Citizen—shoulder checking, signaling, and driving just slightly under the speed limit, waiting the full three seconds at a stop sign before proceeding. I swear, the best driver in the world is the one who's right in front of the cop car. And then I see these people when I'm off duty. They're barreling along, cutting people off, driving like there's no tomorrow. ... I've gotten a little pessimistic from seeing how two-faced people are."

She colored self-consciously, remembering the creative U-turn she'd pulled yesterday.

"Do you still consider it your career?"

"I don't think I'll be in it forever, but for now it's all right. I'm not like you that way. You knew what you wanted to do right out of high school. I didn't figure this out until I was already finished my degree. And even now, I have my doubts."

"What do you mean?"

"Well, I'm not OK with some of the duties. Here's something—this is real. There's this other Born-Again cop I know. He was told to monitor the abortion clinic on his shift. He said he wouldn't do it, so the supervisor gave him an ultimatum. Do it or get suspended. He didn't come out and say it like that, but the guy knew what he meant. See, I haven't been faced with that kind of choice yet, and I'm not sure how I'd handle it if I was."

"I guess it's a little extreme when your ethics get scrubbed, but you know, there are lousy things about every job. I mean, if you took up something else, you'd probably find just as many frustrating things in that."

"It's not frustration exactly. It's more like ... nerves."

"Nerves?"

"Yeah, you know how you learn something and you get to be good at it? Well, the longer I do this, the harder it is to relax into things. Should be the other way around. It's like walking along no problem, and then realizing the whole time, you've been walking along the edge of a cliff. Just nerves getting the better of me, but why now, years into the job?"

"Maybe that's what makes you good at it, not getting cocky. What else would you do if you left the force?"

He shrugged indifferently. "Ah, I don't know. Some guys leave and take up a trade. I suppose there are a lot of things I could do. Always wanted to start my own business. Maybe a restaurant ... but it would have to be a healthy one."

His voice trailed off and Donna watched as his mind went elsewhere, somewhere sad. There was a peculiar look in his eyes that reminded her of his distance at The Bean. He had sat at the arborite table, his face purposely self-contained, describing his time in Red Deer. At this moment, he was still there rather than four feet away. And she wanted to be wherever he was right now. The image of the two of them abandoning their careers together was charming. Fantasies, by their nature, thrive on charm. And where there is charm, deceit is usually a close companion, but she stubbornly embraced both.

"What would you do if you couldn't be a doctor anymore?"

Donna glanced around as if the answer lurked on the living room walls. "No idea. I've never considered another field. I worked so hard to get to where I am, it would take a pretty serious situation to make me consider anything else."

"At this point, I can deal with the stuff I don't like ... but if something serious happened, I'd probably walk."

"Like what? Don't you deal with serious stuff all the time?"

"Well, sure. Most of it's intense for the people involved, but I can still keep myself removed. You need a sense of humor about what you see and not let your emotions affect your judgment. That way, it's not *my* stuff. So far, my life hasn't been in any real danger and I haven't had to use my gun. I don't think I could anyway, not that I'd admit that to my partners."

It hadn't occurred to Donna that Jack's religious beliefs could be a detriment to his work. Such a prominent part of him, they enhanced an attractive strength of character. He seemed more capable with them than without, but she realized the difficulties he could face in being defined by those beliefs. How confident would a fellow officer be in a partner who refused to take a life, even in self-defense?

As the night progressed, Donna became lulled by his deep voice—relaxing, almost hypnotic—and by midnight, she was fading rapidly. Coming off a row of night shifts, Jack's internal clock had transposed night and day. For him, it was more like late morning.

The automatic lights in her apartment turned off, leaving them swimming in the glow of the television. Jack saw how tired she was, how her half-lidded eyes took on that sultry depth. She cocooned her body into the couch. Her voice became low and breathy. He placed his hand on her shoulder and gently pressed her down. As she let herself be settled into her half of the sofa, she was surprised to feel the fit of his body behind hers. He slid one arm under her neck. The other came around from overhead, and comfortably wrapped in his arms, she hardly knew how to respond. It was something she had fantasized about for months. It was lovely.

Neither one spoke, just relaxed in the comfort of each other's bodies. With the solid curve of his biceps against her cheek, she felt the way she used to with Ric: small, feminine, and excited about something in life. When was the last time those feelings had called out her name and made her stand tall? Must have been years.

Despite the uplifting sensations running through Donna, she was exhausted. She wanted to feel every inch of him nestled against her, but finally allowed her eyes to close.

The television continued to throw gray shadows against the walls.

In the flickering dark, Jack studied her. She exuded a familiar scent, not any discernible perfume or lotion, something else distinctive. It was *her.* Imagining her smooth body under his, her skin, her breasts ... the memories came alive inside him and old feelings crept back, hidden under years of dust. His ethical side reminded him that he shouldn't mix up their current relationship with one which had left such pain. It wouldn't be fair to her. He should leave. He should just go and let her sleep in peace.

His hand rested on her arm. Gently raised and lowered by the hypnotic rhythm of her breathing, Jack's fingers lightly moved past her elbow to her wrist, and slowly returned to their starting point. Skimming his hand across the length of her arm, he paused over the scar on her forearm: a two-inch line of skin, whiter than the rest, a battle scar from a bad night. It was the only interruption in his touch, but she didn't stir. He mistook her sighs for deep breaths of slumber.

His thoughts stole back to the smooth skin of a young woman's arm brushing against his, as they swayed to a slow sad beat. All these years, the image had stayed alive in his mind, every part of it, the translucent sensations of sight, sound, and touch existing in the dark folds of his memory, haunting him in the face of his old friend.

Distracted by the past, he let his hand cross the connection where her elbow rested on her hip. His fingers slid along the slippery material to the skin of her thigh and then her knee. Back they traveled, past the hip and onto the shoulder. He didn't know what felt more erotic, the sleek biking shorts or her bare skin ... and he kept exploring the side of her body.

Donna couldn't believe how wonderful his caresses felt. If any doubts about their suitability persisted, they were erased the moment he touched her hip. She wanted to feel his hands everywhere. She wanted to sigh loudly and let him know how it was for her, then twist around in his arms and face him. Most of all, she wanted him to kiss her. Something as simple as a kiss would envelop her the way air rushes past a falling body, invisible fingers skimming over it protectively.

Jack's fingers passed over the sensitive part of her waist. As it tickled, she let out a small sound and his body stiffened up.

"I thought you were asleep."

She turned a drowsy face toward him. "I think I was."

Here was his opening. He could kiss her easily. It was a matter of inches, the invitation clear on her lips.

"I should get going and let you get to bed. You work early, don't you?"

Lifting his body off the couch, his eyes tried to veil guilt. She almost sputtered in disappointment. He could have kissed her just now. Why didn't he? Standing beside the door, she drew the blanket around her shoulders, her hair tousled, her face tired but bright.

It had been so long since anyone caused that kind of sensual alertness, the kind that goes straight to vivid fantasy. She hoped he would kiss her before he left. And then, maybe he would stay. She would feel herself falling over the edge, the one keeping her stable and sane, the one keeping her from feeling every part of herself.

His lips were visible through the romantic shadows cast by the television. She knew he was thinking about it, and almost held her breath against the mounting anticipation.

But Jack said his farewells without any such contact. Slipping into his heavy winter jacket, he stared at her strangely. Donna wondered if his shift work could be playing tricks on his mind; he peered as though she were someone else entirely. A shaken element clouded his eyes, like a person waking from a dream and still expecting the dream people to be there, gazing without seeing the actual dimensions right in front of him. The moment only lasted for a second or two, but it was enough for her to know that his heart was elsewhere.

He quietly slipped out the door and she was alone.

Leaning heavily against the wall, her head rested on the wooden doorframe. She peered up as if expecting a message from God. The blanket stayed around her. Although it seemed she would never feel cold again, Donna pulled it close and slept wrapped in the wool fibers that should have been his arms.

***

He slept alone these days, usually in front of a snowy screen. Otherwise, it would just be him and the black night, an uncaring companion. It never used to bother him, but now there was something sinister about overlapping charcoal shadows—lifeless untouchable apparitions, and yet real to at least one of his senses. Al knew the phobias were groundless, but they were no more controllable than the flow of blood through his veins.

This was not the first time he was on his own. There had been two other trial separations, but this one was for real. No false sense of security to carry him through until they would get back together again. This time, Al knew his marriage was over.

He could do without her, but it was several weeks since he'd seen his kids. Even on Christmas Day, Tracy whisked them off to Saskatchewan to be with her parents. They didn't even stop by for Al to give them their gifts, but they called on New Year's Eve. Over the phone, Ashley talked about Grandpa's German shepherd in the back yard. They spent most of today playing with him. Then, she gushed about the great board games Grandma gave them, and how they were making ice cream right out of snow. Grandpa used to do that when he was a boy.

Al could tell that the concept of her grandfather once being a child was beyond her imagination, as though all adults were born with their present size and characteristics. It would likely surprise her that her own father had once learned to make ice cream out of snow. He'd gone to elementary school, and executed somersaults on grassy slopes, and watched girls like his daughter grow tall and curvy. No, she didn't have any real understanding of what change was all about. She probably still thought he and Tracy would get back together. "When Daddy comes home ..." was a well-known phrase around the Morin household.

As his eight-year-old daughter spoke, he stared at the brightly wrapped gifts decorating his kitchen table. He waited for a break in her animated descriptions and mentioned, "Pumpkin, you'll have to call me when you get home, 'cause I've got some presents for you and Kam. Would you tell him that for me?"

"Kevin!" she shouted, right into the mouthpiece and Al winced, "Dad says he's got presents for us in Calgary!" Al heard an excited holler in the background.

"Give Kam a kiss for me."

"Yeah, right. Kevin! Dad says to give you a kiss, but I'd rather kiss a frog's butt!"

Al heard his son laugh.

"OK, Sweetie, I should go now."

"Kevin! ... Quit it! ... What, Dad?"

"I said I have to go. I'm glad you're having a good time at Grandma and Grandpa's. Say 'hi' to everybody for me and remember to call me when you get home."

"OK. Happy New Year."

"Happy New Year, Pumpkin. Bye-bye."

Click ...

Al sat at the kitchen table, hearing that sound over and over. *Click ...* A person could seem so close through a phone line, but it was a lie. When they hung up, that last little sound pulled reality in fast, the way a movie camera zooms in on a close-up. His family was playing with Scampy the German shepherd a province away, while Al was sitting at his kitchen table, hearing that sound. *Click ...*

A large bottle of vodka had remained unopened in the cupboard since Al bought it on Christmas Eve. Occasionally, he thought about the sound of the cupboard door swinging open, and about the transparent drink pouring into a glass. He even thought about it sliding down his throat. But tonight, those things hadn't entered his mind. Instead, he kept hearing the sharp sound of the phone hanging up. *Click* ... Such a small sound, really.

The gifts for his kids were not small. The boxes covered much of the kitchen table, so much there was barely any room to put his new gun down. Al just held it thoughtfully in his lap, pulling the trigger back occasionally. *Click* ...

After an hour, he risked hearing that little sound by calling his sponsor.

As morning slid toward noon, Al woke to the permeating smell of coffee and a gentle shake of his shoulder. Brad was pulling him upright. His wife set a pillow behind his back. He liked Joanne. She had soft eyes.

A haphazard collage of hours-old images fluttered through his mind: holding a drink, holding the gun, holding another drink, holding hands, yelling, sobbing, too many hurdles for one man to leap.

Brad said, "There's a meeting in half an hour. We're going. Jo's staying. She'll have lunch for us when we get back." They were standing over him with square expressions that meant "Don't even try to argue your way out of this."

As Al gazed bleary-eyed at their tough-love compassion, he almost said, "You shouldn't have bothered."

***

CHAPTER 25

The cold month of January passed by with no word from Donna's friends. Tired of calling the Brammons and having one-way conversations, she let the effort temporarily lapse.

Jack also seemed to be in hiding. Donna hadn't seen him since the night he almost kissed her. It was eight weeks and every day felt more lonely than the last. She went through each one with a monotonous attention to her job. The one spirited aspect was Anne, who continued to organize patients with an efficient happy ease.

She was a good employee, and wanting to keep it that way, Donna made a point of limiting their social outings to the occasional lunch. Without confiding in Anne, all those conflicts about Jen and Jack craved an outlet. Instead, she listened to Anne's problems with outward sincerity, but considered her own dilemmas weightier.

Donna was turning twenty-nine soon, on February seventeenth. Jack would be twenty-nine too, which was a good excuse to call him. They decided to go out for dinner on their birthday, and finally she knew she would see him again. For weeks, she could feel his fingers sliding down her thigh and see his lips hovering inches away. The curiosity was maddening. What did that episode on her couch mean? Was it just a normal occurrence for him? If someone held his heart, she should know it somehow. She'd known him too long for something that meaningful to slip by her.

Donna thought about what she would say in the restaurant, but every plot of words adopted the varied tone of her moods, so when the seventeenth arrived, she was no closer to securing an approach. As it turned out, she was diverted from her original topic anyway.

Jen called her at work to wish her a happy birthday. She avoided the subject of her health, except the one meaningless phrase, "holding steady". Bound by the principle of confidentiality to a patient who didn't seem to exist, Donna told herself that Jen had every right to seek medical attention at her own discretion, but the stress was starting to outweigh her patience.

"What a good doctor I am for my healing powers to reach you through the phone cord all these months."

For once, Jen just ignored the sarcasm and made a strong effort toward conversational ease. They spoke as only two people do who have known each other well for years. It shaved off a layer of frustration and served as a reminder that, in comparison, Jen's problems were infinitely more concrete. Donna could live with her own, but Jen faced no such option.

At one point, Donna told her about the tobogganing invitation from Jack and how she had supplied Jen's excuse.

"I think it's time Jack was told about this. It's one thing to refrain from offering information, but it's another to lie."

"Yeah, you shouldn't have to do that. ... OK, go ahead and tell him."

"Me?"

There was silence on the other end of the phone ... silence to command an audience the way no shouting words could, silence to chastise, to completely reverse a person's opinion in the space of a few endless seconds. It was unheard of for Jen and that in and of itself told Donna how badly she needed the support. There was so little Donna could do for her. This would certainly be a minor chore after having faced the Brammons.

Donna sighed, ashamed. "All right, I'll tell him tonight."

"Thanks. Um, let me know how it goes," Jen answered meekly.

Jack picked her up promptly at 6:00 to try a twenty-four-hour Chinese food place some co-workers recommended.

They sat at a booth with high-backed seats. The window beside them was etched with winter's frozen signature; its edges framed cloudy swirls of snow briskly circling outside. When people entered the front door, stubborn bits of white powder would chase after them and cling to the carpets. The host kept fretfully sweeping it into the corner.

Surreptitiously studying Jack's body language, there was no indication of anything out of the ordinary, but his mannerisms were hard to read. Ever since returning from Red Deer, he'd carried himself with caution. Tonight especially, it was a little disconcerting.

Along the top border of her menu, a movement caught Donna's eye. The inquisitive little face of a child peered at her from the next booth. Donna wiggled her fingers in a tiny wave and the child waved back. Matching her eyes, baby blue hair ribbons trailed along her round cheeks. She slid out of sight for a few seconds, and then popped up as though to scare them. Long blonde curls swung over the seat to land beside Jack's head. When he pretended to snap his jaw like a dog, she squealed gleefully, and with a low growl, he nipped at them again.

Donna's smile deepened. Nothing compared to the sight of a muscular man playing sweetly with children, especially when that man held a woman's heart.

When a waiter stood respectfully at attention beside their table, Jack whispered, "I have to go now," and the little girl nodded seriously. She waved at Donna one more time before disappearing into her own booth.

"Ginger fried beef, vegetable egg foo yong, and steamed rice please."

The waiter courteously repeated their order and turned to the next table.

(OK, now there's nothing to do but talk. Get it over with.)

"Jack, there's something I have to tell you."

Concern flashed through his eyes before he could mask it. "What's that?"

"You know Jen's been sick a lot, right?"

"No, I haven't seen her in a long time."

Donna swallowed. This was never going to be easy.

"Jen had some tests done last year and ..."

She stared at her water glass as Jack peered at her gravely.

"She's HIV positive."

Jack's mouth dropped open. He leaned back in his seat, while his eyes panned the room and landed hard on Donna. Although she knew it was not a reflection on her, she paled under his gaze. Would he do what the Brammons had done, shoot the messenger?

"Does she have AIDS yet?"

"Yes ... She'll be lucky if she sees another birthday."

***

On the way home, silence seemed to fill every corner of the car. Donna debated with herself, while Jack carefully maneuvered over the icy patches. Balanced precariously in her mind, like snow perfectly centered on a fence, it could fall to either side. Falling left, it would belong entirely to her, but falling right would place it forever within sight and out of reach. Though due to the most abject circumstances, they had connected at a new level, and with such gravity, pure honesty was a breath away. She knew he would face her with the truth. And that was what worried her most. Where would the snow fall?

Parked in front of her apartment building, she squared her shoulders and engaged his eyes. "Jack, what are we doing, you and I?"

It seemed an eternity before he answered. "I wondered when you were gonna bring this up."

Donna colored at her apparent predictability. "Gee, I didn't realize the subject was so *distasteful*. I was just wondering what that little incident on my couch meant. Or is the memory too awful to face?"

He sighed and put up his hand as if warding off blows. "I didn't mean it that way Don. I just ... shouldn't have been on the couch with you. I thought I might be leading you on. The truth is, I don't think we'd make a good couple."

She wanted to crawl under the seat. That was the worst thing to hear, that she'd been led on like a dog on a leash. Could this get any more degrading? But even worse was the disappointment. He had refused her, built up her interest and then tossed it aside. She'd seen all the signs and ignored them, one by one. And now, she felt like an idiot.

Jack watched her run her fingers through her hair. After a terribly long pause, he explained, "Don, my beliefs are important to me, but I have a hard time staying focused. They're a house of cards. One wrong move and it falls flat. I've been celibate a long time and I know I shouldn't have done that. I saw you in those shorts and I couldn't help myself. I'm sorry."

His downcast face finally raised, she saw the sincerity in his expression, the soft eyes, slack jaw. They shared an embarrassed smile. It was easy to acknowledge his compliment; it served to dissipate her anger and also nurtured a tiny hope.

There seemed nothing else to say. They parted awkwardly with Jack perhaps having greater insight into her pain than she did. Hadn't he felt that way once? When she opened the door, he offered a last attempt at making the evening pleasant.

"Happy birthday."

She looked straight at him, answering, "You too," and her eyes pleaded one more time.

(Kiss me.)

(I can't, Don.)

She stepped out of the car determined to remain friends, and unaware of the unhappiness plainly written on her face.

***

For five months, Donna did her best to stay platonic with Jack. She even went on the odd date. The bike paths were a good place to meet people. At least one hobby was guaranteed in common and there was no need to dress up.

She saw Jack occasionally and whenever she did, her latest date went completely out of her head. The sight of his hands and lips still enticed a feminizing effect from her. He never strayed far from her thoughts, especially when alone in bed. Amidst a sad ache for his arms, she had cried in frustration too many nights since his refusal.

The biggest problem was no one to confide in. Jack was hardly a topic she could broach with her father, and Raymond's marriage also emphasized her mother's absence. The understandable reality of prioritizing his new wife felt as if Donna had lost him in the process. In looking around for sources of support, she was solely to blame, having ranked school over people. For so long, there was simply no time.

Now, strange barriers prevented new relationships from forming. As a physician, ethics barred personal involvement with the patients. Anne was a professional associate and Jen was still barricaded in her parent's house. Often wondering about Jen's condition, Donna hoped it was better than she theorized. She had stopped calling, partly from being too wrapped up in fantasies of Jack and partly from fearing the worst. Never was the phrase, "No news is good news" more applicable.

Finally, on a bright Saturday evening in July, the Brammons contacted her. For once, Donna heard the chirping sound of the phone, hoping it was anyone but Jack. He was supposed to come over right away to watch a movie, and fears of him canceling swelled with every minute.

She filled the coffee maker with a mocha blend, timing its preparation with his arrival. Donna knew she made terrible coffee—Jen told her often enough—but she wanted to offer him something. He never drank alcohol and she didn't have much else on hand. Flipping the switch on the coffee maker, she turned to pick up the phone.

"Hi Donna, this is Jeffrey."

"Hi Jeffrey. How are you?"

"OK, but I need to tell you something."

Donna stood frozen to her kitchen floor, as a tiny chill crept up her spine. For a quick second, she envisioned putting the phone back on its cradle, but her arm refused to comply and the phone stayed against her ear.

"About Jen?" she asked solemnly.

"She's in the hospital. The doctor thinks she has a few days. She wants to see you and Jack whenever you can get there. Don't bother going tonight. She got a big shot of something a while ago."

"I see. ..." Time was short. A quick sigh released her contradictory feelings of relief and anguish. Quietly confused, she couldn't determine which was stronger, but drawing her focus back to Jeffrey, her voice matched his steady sentences.

"I'll tell Jack. We'll be there tomorrow."

She wanted to add her condolences, but thought it would sound hollow. Jeffrey was the realist, the one most capable to undertake the morbid details, like letting people know his sister was going to die any day now. This call was just one more chore for him to complete that night. It was what Donna represented to the Brammons, an unpleasant reminder that they were going to lose Jen. She wanted to say something to reach them, to let them know she was hurting too, how much she needed them, needed someone—there were six of them and only one of her—but the difference was that Donna was alive and healthy, and that was a world more than Jen would ever have. Whether the Brammons were conscious of it or not, it was a difference beyond forgiveness.

He relayed the name of the hospital and Jen's room number, and they hung up. It was finally here. She was going to have to say goodbye to Jen. *Goodbye.* How many times had she rattled off those syllables without considering the potential enormity of the word, the finality?

Mechanically, she sat on the couch, staring at the memories in her mind, as if they were happening right before her eyes, existing only in the present tense. Ric seducing her here. Brian proposing. Jack teasing her heart. And through it all, Jen sat here throwing humorous truths in her face. Of anyone in her life, Jen was the cleverest, the funniest, the most consistent.

A hundred scenes reenacted themselves on the dark surface of her coffee table, while the rich husky smell of coffee slowly circled her senses. Jen at The Bean ... They'd spent hours there with Jack, arguing impractical points across the dark tables. She always started conversations that couldn't be properly finished. Over the years, they had discussed a lot of things, important things, silly things, mostly how to put up with each other, playful verbal jabs, given and received in jest, but they never once discussed how to leave. Jack's two-year disappearance was the closest they ever came to that topic, and even then, he eventually returned. How would she adjust to Jen's departure? How?

Donna's tears fell just as the doorbell rang.

She told Jack plainly with naked pain detailed in her eyes. He held her, comfortably knowing he wasn't the cause of her tears. Supporting her in his arms, he stroked her hair. It felt wonderful. Slowly, his close presence took over and her emotions shifted gear.

(Don't leave, not tonight when the thought of people leaving is suffocating.)

She looked up, keeping her focus on Jen, and asked, "Would you stay with me tonight?"

Jack searched her eyes for a motive, and not finding any, he searched himself. Donna watched him sift through various worries. He must have decided that her needs outweighed his concerns, because after an eternity, he quietly answered, "All right."

***

CHAPTER 26

The bedroom was normally dark. Back in Donna's residency, shift work had prompted the purchase of special blinds to minimize light. Open now, the glow of the moon gave the room a gentle tone, almost like that night on her couch. Just enough to veil the walls in mystery.

Rather than being in complete darkness with Jack, she wanted to look to her left and see the man in bed with her. She was amazed that he'd agreed to stay, amazed he was there now, beside her as if he had always been in this exact spot. Lying shyly on her side away from him, she listened to his breathing deepen, the start of detachment.

(Hold me. Fold your body into mine and make me feel covered and cushioned from the world. Take my pain away.)

Only Jack's arms could do this. Only his skin with that particular musky smell could caress hers and evoke something other than frustration and despair. Her mind cried out at him, commanding him to stay awake, to hear her thoughts and comply ... but he was drifting off.

Donna felt achingly alone, even more than in the nights spent without him. Here he was next to her, this man who had the power to change the weight of her soul. Without even touching him, she could feel the heat from his body drifting over her, the way coffee had circled her all the way from the kitchen. Every breath teased her ears. It seemed to say, "Even when I'm with you, you don't have me. I can lie close to you and still not give you any of me."

Losing her friend was terrible, but lacking the confidence to speak her heart was like losing herself. Jen would never stand for that.

Donna's tears swelled until they found a small escape. Pressing her face into the pillow, she quietly cried, not for Jen, not even for her unanswered prayers, but instead for the person she couldn't be. Someone to draw him near, open his heart, someone to make him hear her pain and force him to respond. Who couldn't respond to this depth of emotion?

Hers were embarrassed tears, the type that expects more grief for being noticed. And it didn't take long.

Jack's low voice came out of the darkness, "You know, I'm still here. I have a couple of ears if you need them."

Donna could tell he was speaking to the ceiling, as if she were up there and not six inches to his right, and suddenly she recognized his error. He assumed her tears were for Jen. The deception was easy to allow; she was desperate for a way into this man.

"Would you hold me?"

Would he say no? Get up and leave? After a pause, he extended an arm across her pillow. Donna turned her body to face him and rolled her head onto his shoulder. Cradling an arm around her back, they lay there quietly.

Never so aware of another human being as she was of Jack right now, all her senses tuned in to him and soaked up the sensations: his warm skin, his smell, that dark profile against the moonlit window.

(This is what I want. This is who I want. This man.)

The minutes rolled by while each relaxed. With increased courage, Donna let one hand move along his chest to rest gently on his shoulder. She felt calm in his arms, the earlier tears forgotten, but still there was that urge to run her hands all over his body. She shifted her arm slightly and let her fingers explore a small area of his chest. With little hair to interrupt the flow of her fingers, they trailed an aimless path. She could tell they were both focused on the sensations, but Jack didn't react, or maybe he was fighting as hard as her to appear innocent. Despite his stillness, there was a slight tension in his arm around her.

His skin was as soft as his muscles were hard. Donna could name every muscle in the human body, their location, purpose, but this knowledge paled at the grace of their orchestrated placement. Where one tapered, the next swelled to lift the skin across another powerful curve. And another, and another. Oh, to feel that strength against her entire body ...

Her leg slid over and between his, slowly molding herself to him. Knee over knee, the front of her chest against his side, and now he became conscious of her hips also softly pressing against him. So far, the fit was perfect and both maintained the delusion of naiveté. She wondered if he could feel the weight of her breasts. Her hand moved along his stomach to the far side of his hips. Jack inhaled sharply, expanding his chest, and slowly let the breath out. She wondered if he would make her stop, if *she* could stop.

The tension still ran through his arm, but now a hand caressed her back and side. There was her answer and all of a sudden, years of barriers fell away. As inhibition and courage traded places, she surprised herself by slipping over him. Legs straddled, she began kissing his neck and shoulders as his arms secured her hips against his ... but still she sensed the space between them.

Her mind cried the words, "Please kiss me. ...." It was when Donna felt him pull back that she realized she had spoken out loud.

"Don, I can't."

He pressed his head into the pillow and laid the back of his hands above it. The words were senseless to her, overshadowed by the way he'd removed his arms, which felt like a splash of cold water. Just five seconds earlier, he had been letting go of whatever it was between them. Now, she was awkwardly lying on top of this man who refused to touch her ... but he wanted to. She knew he did.

"I can't go through it again."

Through what again? Having to turn her down? His eyes must have been full of guilt. What was shaded in the dark was clear in his voice. He had remained her friend these past five months out of obligation, trying to soothe his own conscience. Feeling responsible for leading her on, he had no idea how much she wanted to be led on. She should have internalized just as much guilt and remorse, but desire was stronger.

So instead, guilt became courage, remorse became effort. Nothing had ever pushed her to act like this, against such obvious resistance. Jack had taken his arms away and replaced them with the old familiar ache of yearning, empty and wanting, thinking this would get them back to an amiable place, but there was no amiable place left.

Somehow, with her still lying over him, she would have to convince him of her invulnerability. In the space of a second, her mind sifted through a hundred angles and settled on one.

Donna summoned her most natural voice, the one she used on patients unprepared for bad news, and said as if comforting a child, "Jack, we've been friends a long time. This isn't so wrong is it?"

She could see him shaking his head in the dark, widening the soft dents in the pillow.

"Look," she smiled unaffectedly as she lied, "for the record, I think we'd make a lousy couple."

Chuckling softly, he placed his hands gently on her back again, but then replied, "I just can't Don."

An intense feeling of failure washed over her, while her mind grasped at straws of self-respect. She would have to let him leave, probably for good. A line of moonlight betrayed her expression and he watched her eyes swimming in sadness. Donna didn't know how close he was to seeing his precious house of cards topple down, or that she was pulling the key card out from underneath. All she knew was that despite being braver than ever in her life, it was in vain.

(Why? Oh, please don't pull away. I've needed this for so long. I've ached to feel your hands on me, your skin, your lips, your all of you. Please ...)

This time the words stayed inside, but when Jack searched her face, her eyes leaped out at him. The resemblance was spellbinding. They were a mirror to a time years ago when he felt just as incomplete and brokenhearted. Everything she couldn't say was written there, the simplistic summary of a thousand words in one look, and in the next moment the decision was made. Donna shifted to move off him, but catching her face in his hands, he put his lips on hers. They were soft and firm at the same time. Just right.

(Oh, God, they're so right. I wondered about this for years and now here it is. I can't move. I can't breathe—Jack ...)

When he finally released her face, she couldn't separate any part of her from him. She sought his lips and kissed him again and again. His arms were around her back, her fingers sliding across his shoulders and hair. The world dissolved into a tangle of desperate caresses and for a brief while, nothing else existed.

Donna became conscious of the thin layer of clothes between them. She raised herself up and he followed. His shorts were off and she wondered in a disoriented way when that had happened. While slipping her shirt over her head, she suddenly found herself leaning backwards, until she was lying under him.

For a minute, Donna thought it might happen, that they would finish what had been brewing for so long. She wondered with faint desperation about condoms, but the concern faded as their excitement increased. It didn't matter that she wasn't on the pill. Nothing mattered except Jack's hands on her breasts and thighs. It was such a luxury to finally respond to them.

At one point, gazing up with smoky eyes, her hands circled his neck as though he were an ornamental vase that would break at her touch. She spoke his name lightly, delivering the word with just enough sultry weight to reach his ears.

"*Jack* ..."

It was then that he opened his eyes. Even through the dark, she saw the same momentary confusion which had crossed his face during their evening on the couch. He was thinking of another woman, someone from his past or even someone unreal. Her voice had dragged him from his fantasy with the equivalent shock of a slap across his face.

Donna stopped moving under him. Her eyes filled with fresh tears and she put her hands over them. She had gone up against God and some invention in his mind, and failed.

Jack felt the change in her shaking body and gently pulled her hands away. She offered no resistance. As his concerned eyes ran over her face, he asked, "Are you crying because of Jen?"

"Yes," she answered, too exhausted inside to speak the truth.

(Yes, you fool. I'm crying about Jen, because she will never feel what I do when I'm lying here under you, with your hands on me and your excited breath floating over me. She'll never feel alive and carried off into this kind of passion ... and be this desperately in love with a man.)

He held her, believing her pain to be something else, something he couldn't change, and she fully gauged his relief at being free of the burden. Donna would have voiced those thoughts, had her inner strength outweighed her anguish, but she couldn't risk losing the small comfort his arms provided. It felt like all she had in the world. She needed him in her life on speaking terms. Wasn't that equally important to him? Rather than openly challenging the question, silence was the safest choice.

For Donna, sleep was delayed as long as possible. At some point, the sky would lighten, invading their privacy, and she wanted to keep him secluded in the dark. The world and all its problems would be far away. Later, morning would come ... later. Sleep would sneak up like a slick thief and steal her time with him, but for now, she could tuck her body into the curve of his arm and claim the tiny space as their own.

***

When she woke, he was gone. If not for the indentation in his pillow, she would have thought it a dream. The covers were tucked around her securely. One arm stretched out across the bed, remembering the man lying there just hours before, while her mind struggled to piece the night together.

That acute sense of failure softened its shape in the morning light. He had touched her body and caressed her heart. Had he really reached down into her soul like that? With eyes closed, it was more real, and she relived every detail consciously excluding his absence now ... but that didn't matter. Those recent sensations were fresh in her mind and she ran through them again.

(How had it all started?)

Jen's situation gradually pushed itself in front of the scenes. Donna realized she was clinging to the comfort of the bed in order to delay the inevitable visit. With reluctance, she raised herself from the pillows that still held his musky smell and pressed her thoughts to the day ahead.

Donna arrived at the hospital late that morning, tired and wide-eyed at the same time. She didn't bother with makeup or attempts to tame her hair from the night before. In the bathroom mirror, another woman looked back at her, a woman carrying something too big to handle. She stared at herself, after catching a sliver of the natural beauty enticed out through Jack's hands. In that tiny moment, she understood what had finally made him kiss her, but it was only there for a split-second, and then she was left searching her eyes for that mysterious element.

Somehow, she knew that neither Ric nor Brian had ever touched that part of her. She would have felt its existence at once and held onto it willingly. Jack was the only one. If she died tomorrow, at least she would have experienced her soul at the surface of her skin. It was a terribly vulnerable feeling, a dark beauty drawing out her deepest self-awareness, surrounding her inside and out. And she desperately craved it all over again.

When Donna entered the hospital room, she understood in an instant that Jen would die soon. She looked awful.

Though always a small-bodied person, now her limbs were mere sticks. A few black lesions spotted her arms and neck, probably more under her hospital gown. The one near her elbow had doubled in size. All her muscles appeared to be pressed into her belly, which was bloated into a huge ball. It reminded Donna of the little starving children from third-world countries, all stomach and nothing else. The cancer must have spread to her lungs, digestive tract, and skin.

Propped up in bed, Jen was flanked by parents, guarding their daughter against further harm. Mrs. Brammon's voice was light with small talk. Mr. Brammon barely spoke. Donna suspected that of anyone, this would wound him the deepest. A father should never have to watch his only daughter die.

Finally, Jen's parents excused themselves. "We'll be back later, Honey." Her mother kissed her forehead tenderly. Mr. Brammon squeezed her hand and Jen returned an appreciative look.

Once alone, Jen asked her, "Who called you?" Her voice was weak, punctuated with painful coughing fits.

"Jeffrey … and I told Jack myself. He came over last night."

"Good, then everyone who matters knows about it."

"Why did you keep me away?"

Jen stared at the opposite wall and sighed. "Oh, I don't know Don. I really don't. … I know I should apologize. There's just too much to deal with. When I couldn't keep my job and my apartment, it was like my life was over right then. Knowing I'd never meet anyone or do any of the things I wanted to do. I think I was mad at anyone who still had a life. And then living with my family, the looks on their faces all the time. It wouldn't be so bad if they'd just talk to me … or you. The day you told them, I really didn't think they'd be like that, but you were right."

"Never thought I'd hear you say that. You *must* be dying."

That did the trick. They were both able to smile.

"They're scared Jen. We all are. Their anger is normal. Look, none of us feel we have as much right to hurt as you do, but we hurt all the same. Not talking about it shows a respect by allowing you to do the talking instead, so you can work through this."

She shook her head at Donna. "Work through what? I have a few things to say, but I'm not going to babble regrets about my life. They're waiting for some big deathbed confession. You know me better than that. Don't do that to me, Don. I could stand it from anyone, but you."

Though spoken weakly, Jen's words—neither exaggerated nor superficial—left no response necessary.

Donna's eyes welled up with tears and she dropped her head into her hands. She'd spent all morning preparing to be strong for Jen's sake, but in two sentences, Jen had stripped her of that option.

In eight years of medical training, she'd experienced all sorts of deaths—slow lingering ones and fast unanticipated ones—never once encountering a patient from her own past, no one from high school, not even an acquaintance to bring home the concept of death. No one but her mother, and until now, Donna had kept that association separate, maybe because the dreams brought her near.

Finally, Donna raised her head and stated frankly, "I … just don't know what to do. What do you need?"

Jen replied, "Let's just talk. Tell me what great trouble has befallen you."

Donna studied her friend's gaunt face and Jen answered her silent question, "Well, something is written all over you. Get it out, but I'd better warn you I just had some more drugs, so if you want me to be conscious you'd better hurry."

And so Donna talked … and what was supposed to be Jen's confessional became Donna's therapy. By the end of it, she was exhausted.

Jen responded in a floating voice, "Well, I can't say I'm surprised. You two have been avoiding this for a long time, but there's always been something missing with you guys, like a piece of a puzzle or something. Know what I mean? You can see what the picture's supposed to look like, but you keep looking at that hole in the middle where that one little piece got sucked up by the vacuum." Her hand lightly moved in the air to show the piece flying away.

Jen had no idea how close she was to the truth.

"You know a few years ago, you told me I was purposely choosing bad men."

Donna's lips curled up. "I remember that. I think I got your standard subtle answer, 'You're full of shit.'"

"Well, normally you are with all that doctor-talk, but this time you nailed it. I was never happy with anyone since Al."

"That geology guy? That was years ago!"

"Yeah, I was more hurt than I let on, and I've never met anyone like him. Probably could have if I'd just opened my eyes. Wasted a lot of time thinking he was some soulmate I let slip through my fingers. Maybe he was, or maybe I could have made someone else my soulmate just as easily. But now that I know I'll never see him again, he's the one I'm seeing clear as day. Don't give up on Jack, not if he's the one you'd see at the end."

"Maybe I *should* just give up," Donna ventured resignedly, "but something inside me says I was supposed to be with him a long time ago. I can't shake the feeling that we're right and wrong for each other at the same time. I can't stop wanting him. ...."

She felt guilty talking about herself so much, but it probably didn't matter anyway; Jen was pretty giddy now. With her face deceptively relaxed, it was easy to gloss over her advice. Cloaked in reflections of Al, the intended meaning was almost irrelevant, but mostly, the memory of Jack's warm body was still at the front of Donna's thoughts, overshadowing everything before her.

***

CHAPTER 27

... Death was near. It hovered ominously, in wait for her. Or maybe she was merely extracting lifelike fears from the memories, from the loss of her mother. And Jen. Their faces swam before Donna, contrasted only by shades of black. She could feel herself floating, untouchable except for that sharp sensation in her hand a while ago, whenever "a while ago" was.

Deep inside, she knew she was thirty, but her mother's face was so clear and aroused such intense emotions, that chronological order seemed irrelevant. With no discernable past or present, elements of her life had blended—preteen incidents were on level with things years later—and this made sense far into her soul. Until now, the countless stored pictures were simple delineations of experiences, lacking in strength or even meaning. Seeing them in the darkness gave them back their original proportions and Donna was struck by their force. Her mind had been turned inside out, every experience inflated to its original size, emotions filling her heart all over again.

Death was, by far, the hardest to face. These people who had left her life had also taken with them their most defining moments. Never before was the loss so egregious, not even during the most acute period of mourning. There was no break from the feelings assaulting her, no time to step back and negotiate for peace of mind, not even while ...

***

Jen slept heavily for most of the afternoon, one of the few blessings granted to terminal patients. Even babies never slept so soundly. Before

Mr. and Mrs. Brammon returned, Billy walked in and set a plastic bag on the foot of the bed.

"What's that?" Donna asked.

He awkwardly pulled out a sweater. "I think this one was her favorite."

"Your whole closet was her favorite."

"Yeah, well, if I brought everything and let her choose, that would take the fun out of it."

"Don't worry. We'll tell her that in her delirium, she bullied me into stealing it for her."

He chuckled, "OK. She'd never want it if she thought I'd let her have it."

"How are the others taking it?"

"Well, Jeffrey's on top of it, but he always seems like that so who knows? Carl's weird. I think he's going through some kind of guilt about it. I don't know what he's got to feel guilty about."

"How about the time he locked her out of the house in her underwear? Or when he told her the laxatives were chewable calcium? Or when—"

"Yeah OK, he should rot in hell."

"Along with you! Carl just did your bidding."

He snorted, "Yeah, she never did figure that out."

"Well, no point in blowing your cover now. So, how are you?"

He glanced up at her, and then batted his hand down as if striking the lid shut on a box. On a slighter frame, the gesture would have appeared effeminate.

"Oh, I'm just me. I don't have much to say."

Donna was tempted to coax some elaboration, but Billy's mood had clearly shifted. His eyes reminded her of the Ric incident. In them swam a contentious element of high-handed justice, the quiet yet impassioned satisfaction of righting a wrong. He had stepped in, erasing Donna's problem with aggressive efficiency, but Jen was another matter. Forced to stand by and watch it grow until it abruptly removed itself from view, he wasn't used to problems existing without some control over their outcome.

"How long do you think she has?" he asked hesitantly, as though afraid the question was improper.

She glanced at Jen.

(Any first-year resident knows not to talk about patients within earshot. Oh, what would it matter?)

"Days, maybe a week, but knowing her she'd probably hang on longer just to prove me wrong."

"Well, if heredity has anything to do with it, she'll be back. ... Didn't she ever tell you about that? When our grandparents died, me and Mom kept getting these feelings like they were in the room.

"That's kinda creepy."

"It didn't seem bad. Normal really. The last time was about a year after they were gone."

"Do you think it was just a sign that you felt strongly about their leaving?"

"Maybe if it happened at different times, but we'd be sitting in the kitchen and just look at each other 'cause it felt like someone was there. Jen said I was picking up Mom's thoughts 'cause I was tangled up in her apron strings or something asinine like that. And Carl would stand up and yell, 'Grandpa!' to the ceiling to piss us off."

Donna smirked.

"Haven't you come across that in any of your patients?" he asked.

The smirk dropped a notch. All those times she felt mother watching over her.

"To tell you the truth, yes, but I've always thought it was just part of the bereavement process. The people who told me these stories were always the ones who were most broken up about their loss. You don't think that was it?"

"No," he answered firmly, "It's one thing to have a passing thought about them or really miss them, but it's different when you think they're right beside you. I can't explain it. It's just different. You don't question it, 'cause it's so real. Mom and I were closer to her parents than the others. Maybe that's why we were the only ones who sensed them. Dad thought we were nuts, but we know what we felt. I think some spirits are stronger or more 'out there' than others. And I think some people pick up on that stuff more than others."

"Well, if anyone on this earth is 'out there', it's Jen."

Billy snickered lightly and let the statement remain unanswered. Content with the silence, he calmly stared at the bed and appeared to be dissecting the problem before him, as though Jen were a series of equations to be memorized for the next exam. Death provoked such varied reactions from people. Equally stubborn and sweet, if Billy couldn't stop her death, he put stock in a resurrection of sorts.

Though Donna found it hard to believe in ghosts, what about all those odd moments? She remembered when her father announced that her mother was finally gone. Donna had asked for an ice cream cone. It was all she could focus on. Analyzing the chocolate swirls endlessly, she searched for patterns and connections in the lines until most of it melted. Steadily dripping on the kitchen floor, the pool created an abstract maze of lines.

They made ever-changing pictures only visible to a child, some of her mother, and the realism was as if God himself had commanded the pictures into place. Her father threw out the cone and cleaned up the floor, wiping away the memories etched into the swirls. Then, she collapsed in tears in his arms.

She felt like that now, trying to make sense of the senseless. Apparently, Jen's family was having the same difficulty. The only person who knew how to act was Jen. With those typically piercing observations, had Donna closed her eyes, she could have sworn the same buoyant girl was sitting there instead of this weakened body with Jen's voice.

At 4:30, Donna left Billy to watch over her. Passing the emergency entrance, she stopped to allow an ambulance the right of way, and the night of her own ride in one came rushing back. It had been easy to feel sorry for herself until she saw Jen's injuries. A pneumothorax. Funny how people could recover from a rib stabbing their lung, but die from an invisible little virus.

Then, her thoughts followed their automatic route back to Jack, much like her car seemed to instinctively know the way home.

***

"Mr. Morin, can you hear me? ... Albert?"

The patient opened his eyes slowly. "Whaa?"

He blinked and squinted at the stark light. There was no place in this room to escape the brightness. Filling every corner, it even bounced off the stranger's white coat and directly into his eyes.

"Mr. Morin? I'm Dr. Sheffield. You're in the hospital. You were brought in at 4:30 this afternoon after collapsing in a store. You had a seizure."

"How ... how'd-I-ged-ere?"

The words were awkward to pronounce through a stiff and swollen mouth, and he was tired. He never felt so tired in all his life. His limbs weighed a ton.

"Witnesses called an ambulance."

Al groaned, "Feel-lak-'ell."

"The seizure lasted two minutes. The people there were not able to prevent you from biting your tongue, and you have fractured your collarbone, probably from the initial fall."

The doctor paused to allow Al to digest this news. Then, he bluntly asked, "Are you an alcoholic?"

A tiny nod was the weary reply. Dr. Sheffield didn't seem surprised.

"Wha-dime-izi?"

"It's 6:40. Albert, your fluids are now stabilized but you were severely dehydrated when you came in. Your blood work also showed a marked deficiency in vitamin B-12. We're giving you a general shot of B vitamins along with the fluids."

For emphasis, Dr. Sheffield tapped a transparent hanging cord with his pen. Al followed the line of plastic downward and saw that it attached to a needle in his wrist. He sighed, closing his eyes briefly, and turned his head up again. The doctor looked carefully into Al's eyes.

"Your liver is badly impaired."

"Ushalee-iz." He tried to smile, but the corners of his lips wouldn't move.

"When was the last time you had a drink?"

Not that again ... It was the question people constantly asked, as if this one aspect of his personality blotted out everything else that could define him. The question, "How are you?" always meant, "Are you drinking? Did you drink yesterday? Are you thinking of drinking? Well, are you???" He got so tired of it, along with the well-intentioned people in his life.

He often theorized about his life's path had just one element veered along the way: taken different courses in university, moved across the country, married a different woman ...

Sometimes the face of one girl he dated long ago came drifting through his mind, usually during the deep solitude of sleep. Long brown hair, steel blue eyes, and a mind to match. They were eyes that spoke volumes without any words. He would see himself reflected in them, his entire soul summed up in those blue circles. She knew what he was, how unhappy his life had become, but she also knew the good side of him struggling to reappear. When he looked into those eyes, not only did he see a balance of his good and bad traits, he also saw an unquestioning acceptance. They held no demands, no judgments, just an honest display of reality, serving neither to sever nor soothe. It was the kind of reality that maybe he could swallow on a regular basis.

During those nights, his dreams were colored with an elusive quality of sad miscalculation, of things slipping through his fingers like water. In the morning he would awake remembering little, except ... no matter how he tried, he couldn't hold whatever it was he was supposed to have in the cup of his hand. And he would sigh at the certainty of another day like all the rest, a day in which all he could hold was a bottle.

Today, he had been standing in a line-up to buy a hockey stick for his son, when the same feeling suddenly surrounded him. He was supposed to be somewhere else, doing something else, with someone else, and that was the last thing he remembered ... until this doctor asked him the same old question he got asked, day in and day out. When was the last time he had a drink?

(Forever ...)

"Day-b'for-estaday."

"OK, I'm not going to make this pretty. You have to stop drinking. Completely. If you don't, you'll die. ... Do you have family?"

"Divorced. Kidz-er-wid-er."

The doctor nodded briefly. Al saw compassion in his eyes, despite his austere approach.

"All right, get some more rest and we'll see about discharging you in a while. I assume you won't be driving home?"

Al shook his head slowly, not because he was unsure, but because of the pain in his mouth. The following week, he received an ambulance bill for two-hundred and forty dollars.

***

Jack arrived at dinnertime to find Jen alone, asleep. For a minute he stood and openly stared, relieved that she missed the look of shock on his face. Then, he sat in the quiet room and thought about high school and the days since. The three of them had been a real team. Now it was all screwed up. Jen was dying ... and this thing with him and Donna. It shouldn't have happened.

There was too much to think about. The passion from last night kept sneaking in, little scenes of her body under his, and he could hardly deal with it. Just shut the door. Deal with what's right here, right now—this small person who could have conquered the world, lying near death with tubes to feed her body.

Occasionally, the muted pitch of conversation and soft-soled footsteps were heard outside the room, but for the most part, it was quiet. The dim light over Jen's bed gave off an electrical hum.

Jack never took note of things like that, but the tiniest sounds were inflated. He could hear his own breathing, an even relaxed pace, unlike the hurried passion of last night, and those green eyes swam before him again, chased by the feel of her hands across his chest and later down his spine. Timid fingers, enticing, tormenting ...

He looked down at the hands before him. They were the only part of Jen that remained unchanged, except for a prominent patch of dark skin on her right wrist. Jack reached out and cradled her hand. She didn't move. He sighed and sat motionless as if his touch would sustain her life. Thirty minutes passed. He almost started dozing off, when he felt her fingers jerk.

229

Turning a sleepy face toward him, Jen whispered, "Hey there."

"Hi." He leaned forward attentively.

"When d'you get here?"

"Just now."

"Liar ... Sorry, Jack."

"Oh I've been called worse, mostly by you."

"I'm not sorry for that you dough-head! You *are* a liar. I wouldn't mind if you weren't such a shitty one. ... I'm just sorry I didn't tell you about this sooner."

He tilted his head and dropped his eyes. When Donna had announced Jen's condition, it seemed he was the last one to find out he was going to lose this friend, but he'd channeled those negative thoughts into something more constructive, through prayer. He knew praying for any sort of recovery was a fool's game. Instead, he prayed for her to look death in the face and steal its thunder with sarcastic fortitude. If he could feel that, then maybe he'd be able to accept it.

"Well, I guess you handled it the way you needed to. That's not something to be sorry about."

"Gracious, but allow me the apology. I make so few of them. I knew about this for a couple of years now, and I waited a long time before I told Don. When I did tell her, it was by forcing her to be my doctor. I just didn't know how else to do it. I was afraid you guys would ... stay away."

All those months of knowing she would develop symptoms that terrified everyone. It must have been hell.

He said, "Of course we wouldn't have. Don't underestimate your friends Jen, and don't waste your time being sorry for things you had to do. You got nothing to feel bad about."

She acknowledged his advice with a nod, her eyes settled with the offer and acceptance of the confession.

"What's going on with you guys?"

He looked at her carefully and then chuckled. "I thought you would have dragged that out of her in about two seconds."

"I did."

"Oh, good. I was afraid you were losing your touch."

They smiled awkwardly. Things normally funny had a weird edge now.

"What did she say?"

Jen gave him a wry look and beckoned with bending fingers. "You know better than that. You were crazy about her. What happened?"

Jack described the woman he had met and lost. Though Jen coughed wretchedly through it, her analytical eyes were sharp on him. She watched his face as he depicted a woman who must have been an angel. Jen could have taken any conversation from seven years ago and seen the same look of adoration on his face, but at that time, it would have been for Donna. Secretly, she wondered at the way both friends had confessed their most intense regrets at her bedside, their pain underscored with the same haunting tones.

Closing her eyes, Jen gathered her energies. "Jack, you stupid fuck."

He startled, tucking his chin in and raising both eyebrows sharply. Then he made a face.

"I love you too. You can die now."

Jen laughed sharply and then paid with a fit of coughs. "Listen, I'm going to be blunt—"

"And that would *so* unusual," he muttered, glancing to the ceiling. No one on this earth could ever make him enjoy behaving so badly. And that was the worst part, knowing that all this would go with her.

"Shut up already. This may be the last bit of unsolicited advice I have for you." Steeling her gaze on him, she explained, "You're a total idiot if you think you should maintain allegiance to some flame, when there are people, *someone* who loves you now."

"Come on, Jen. That was over for me a long time ago."

"Because of this other woman?"

"Yeah, it changed everything. My whole life."

"*You* are the only thing that changed. And I bet the person you're ignoring is exactly who you saw in this other woman." She stopped to study his face and saw that he had taken her words literally. "I don't just mean appearance. You were nuts about Donna back then, and you probably spent all your time with your ex thinking she was just another version of her. And now, you're doing the same thing to Donna. We never see who people really are, only what we want them to be, but in your case it's even more tragic, 'cause you did it twice. That's why you're so unhappy. People are never happy when they deny reality. Trust me, I've been there."

His expression unaffected, she almost repeated herself, but didn't have the energy to clarify it, not twice in one day and not to people whose line of vision stopped at their own hearts.

She turned her hand palm up and Jack covered it with his own, careful to avoid her intravenous line. Had they been sitting at a table, they would have been in a perfect position to arm wrestle. In a way, they were wrestling.

This visit was not supposed to be about him, but should he have expected anything else? Jen had a way of peeling the layers off people one by one, until they were either resentful or redeemed. Right now, resentment took the lead and he chastised himself for wanting to argue with her. Never was there a less appropriate time.

Her words sat in front of his mind like a dead weight. He was vaguely aware of some deeper meaning than he was grasping, or maybe it seemed like that because of the circumstances. Maybe he just wanted their words to carry some cosmic significance, a climactic conclusion to cap off their years and justify his investment in the friendship. In any case, she was right—she wouldn't be her if she didn't speak her mind.

Her speech was still sitting there, challenging him to respond. He couldn't move it out of the way or step around it. It demanded an answer.

Promising, "I'll talk to her about it," his tone was gentle, but his face declared the topic now closed.

Jen gave the tiniest of nods, heavy-lidded. She coughed more, thick painful sounds from deep in her chest. A nurse came in, took her blood pressure, and asked whether she wanted anything. Just more water. The urge to do something, anything, was enormous. Jack would have run to Brazil for water if need be, and suddenly he understood the pain her parents felt. How do you sit by and just watch someone hurt like this?

"Are you worried about dying?" he asked softly, trying to present the question with an appropriate mix of candor and tact.

"Yes and no. I mean yes I'd rather live, but not with this kind of pain. ... Believe me, I've thought about getting this over with quicker. At least that way, I'd have some control over it."

He looked up sharply. For a moment, her eyes were as hard as nails.

"How would you have done it?" he asked tentatively, envisioning her sneaking a handful of pills one night.

She probably still could. No, she couldn't even get out of bed by herself. Someone would have to help her do it. He experienced a swift insight into assisted suicide. The appeal of the thought scared him and he shoved it away abruptly. What the hell was he thinking?

He didn't know how to deal with this. The only experience he had with death was on the job, the officer coming to deliver bad news to people like himself. He wasn't wholly removed from those situations, but they paled compared to discussing suicide options while staring Jen in the face.

"Oh, drive my car over a bridge or something else equally dramatic," she answered, "Nothing tame for me ... and you forget I've been there before so it's not that scary."

Jack was momentarily perplexed before he remembered the image of Jen's body angling up sharply in the ambulance. "What was it like?" He had no frame of reference for a near-death experience.

Jen's face softened. The tension left her eyes.

"I was never cold. Surrounded by warmth ... and people. I wasn't alone at all. Hard to explain. I just knew I'd never be cold or lonely or tired. I felt cushioned, like there was something wrapped around me, connected to … well, I don't know what but it was something here. Whatever it was, I wasn't supposed to leave it yet. There's nothing like looking death right up the ass to put your life in perspective. Ironically, I think that was the point when I really started living. You know, you spend your first eighteen years with people you probably wouldn't associate with if they didn't share your DNA, and then you finally figure out how to be your own person. Well, my time came when I was dead, because there was total acceptance. It doesn't matter what we do, just that we're doing stuff."

He responded, "I don't know. You make it sound like people can just do whatever they want. What if you hurt them? Isn't that why you're in this bed right now?"

He felt an immediate stab of guilt at voicing such a blunt assertion, but her eyes glowed with the spirit of debate.

"Maybe … or maybe I'm sick because of a choice I made all by myself. Who knows? Who cares? The point is—those are questions for the land of the living. When I go, they're not going with me. That's what I remember most about that night … except … you know Jack, there was something I never told you guys."

"What?"

"You remember how Donna thought there was a woman at the accident?"

"Yeah?"

"Well, there was. It's not like I opened my eyes and saw anyone. I think I felt that someone was there. It was the only moment I felt sad. That's not right either. *I* didn't feel sad," she clarified, "I felt *her* being sad. And then when Donna described this woman crying beside me, I was so freaked out. I even remember hearing someone cry, but maybe I just invented that after the fact. It was pretty bizarre. Anyway, I didn't say anything. I thought you guys would think I was out of my tree. I wondered if some woman had died there on that spot and I was sensing a ghost. I also remember thinking she had dark hair and she wasn't dressed for winter, like Donna said. Stood out to me."

"How? You said you didn't actually see her."

"No, but somehow I knew these things about her. She was really hurting bad. I didn't know why. At the time, I was more worried about her than me. … Jack, you know when the three of us went out for dinner last year?"

"At Fioritti's?"

"Yeah."

He nodded.

"Remember how we talked about comas?"

"Sort of," he smirked sarcastically, "I usually tune you out after a couple of sentences, but if I remember correctly, you figured they could run around and talk to people in some kind of time warp, or in their heads or something."

"Wow, you *were* listening. I'm impressed. Now do it some more—Donna and I sensed that woman right down to details of her appearance, and at the time, we both had head injuries. Remember? Donna never said anything about this, but I always thought the woman was someone who wasn't supposed to be there. At least, she wasn't supposed to be there yet."

"What, you mean like she was a premonition?"

"Kind of ... like some ghost, but not a ghost from the past, more like someone who was going to be a ghost. All these years, I've been expecting her to pop out of the woodwork—someone I would see on the street or in one of my classes. There was a time years ago, when I'm sure she was close and I just missed her. It bugged me for the longest time. If I ever had the chance again, I'd know exactly what to say to get rid of her pain."

"What?" Jack asked, wondering how she could possibly know what to say, when she couldn't even identify the woman's problem. Then, his thoughts retreated further as he wondered why his mind accepted the existence of an apparition just because Jen believed it. Strength emanated from her face. He had seen people with that look before, the more fanatical ones in his church. There wasn't even a grain of doubt. It reminded him of his old girlfriend and the discussions that stole his heart, sparked from the simple purity of her belief.

Jen said, "I'd tell her not to look back. Live as completely as you can and have faith things will work out exactly the way they're supposed to."

Noting his ashen face, she tilted her head toward him enquiringly, and after a moment he shook his own head slightly.

"Somebody ... somebody told me those exact words a long time ago."

They sat in silence for a while for very different reasons. For Jen, the mysterious woman and her tears were a calming memory; however odd the scenario, it had served to prepare her for her final days. But Jack found it disturbing. During much of the evening, it pestered him tenaciously and he didn't know why, like the key to something important sitting just out of view; an elusive word on the tip of his tongue; the answer to an irrelevant question, which at one time was all-encompassing.

At least, he was given an answer of sorts to his prayer; Jen's final days were credited with the same fortitude she'd shown in life and with her own brand of dignity.

***

234

CHAPTER 28

Better hurry or she would be late. She parked the car quickly, leaving the rear wheels a little too far from the curb, and hopped out. The theater doors were heavy. No staff? Not a soul to be seen, but she could hear what sounded like a television behind one of the doors. When she tugged it open, the noises amplified, finding their way out at last.

Donna looked around carefully. The movie had already started. Scenes sped by too fast to follow, but she sensed that it was a romance. Ignoring the screen, she moved slowly along an aisle.

(Who? Who am I looking for?)

Maybe he was hiding behind one of the chairs, waiting to jump out playfully. No, the place was empty. Rows of seats sat politely facing forward. Frustrated by the pervasive feeling of having missed something crucial, she searched for clues in the movie, but the speed made it impossible to follow.

Reaching the front row, she noticed a large table centered before the screen. Long and smooth, its surface polished to a deep shine, a lacy tablecloth lay draped over one half of the table and solid metal handles peeked out from underneath the lace. Suddenly, Donna realized this table was really a coffin and there was someone in it.

It was Jen. But … she was alive and healthy, looking like a page straight out of high school, young and bright-eyed, dressed in a huge T-shirt and jeans. She was lying on her side, propped up on one elbow, embedded in plush white satin and peeling an orange.

"You're late." She made a face as she tapped her watch and Donna's eyes followed the tiny noise. What an elegant piece of jewelry. Didn't suit her at all.

"Want some?"

Jen casually spoke as if nothing had changed in her life, as if lying in this coffin and sharing an orange were the most natural things in the world. Donna lifted the offering to her mouth. It burst with tangy flavor. For a moment, she stopped listening because the fruit was so captivating, a refreshing combination of sour sweetness.

"These are great," Jen was saying, "They shock your taste buds into waking up. They demand you pay attention and experience every second they're in your mouth. Best after you've tried something bland, but you know, when you bite into just the right one, it's like you've never had food 'til now. Where's yours? Well, don't just stand there. Get looking. It's totally worth it. ..."

As Donna listened to her friend, she sensed a deep correctness in the words, and drawn by them, anticipated some perfect enlightenment. Suddenly a bird sang from overhead, distracting her. She wanted to concentrate on Jen, but the bird chirped again, this time more insistently. It swooped down to land lightly on the back of a seat, a few feet to Donna's left.

(Not now. I need to understand. It'll change everything.)

Donna turned sideways as though the sound of the bird pulled her with a taut rope. She reached out when it loudly chirped again, but eluding her, it gleefully hopped from seat to seat. This time, she stretched purposefully. There, grabbing the noisy creature, she brought it to her ear. ...

"Hello?"

"Oh, hi Donna. I thought I would get your machine. You're not at work today?"

"No," she replied groggily, "I'm taking some time off this week." Rubbing her eyes, she squinted at the wall of her bedroom.

(Did the movie end?)

"What's up?"

"Well, your dad and I were wondering if you could come for supper Wednesday, around six."

Paula heard an uncomfortable pause through the silence.

Then, Donna finally answered, "No, I can't ..." and almost as an afterthought, "but thanks."

Paula didn't expect to hear any shining warmth flowing through the phone, but she was surprised at the utter lack of interest from Donna. Her voice sounded dull and distracted, as though a second conversation overlapped in the background.

"Is everything all right?"

Another pause, more pronounced this time and then Donna bluntly stated, "No, Jen died yesterday. I'm going to the funeral Wednesday. So, I can't come for supper."

"Oh, I'm sorry Donna. We didn't know. Are you all right?"

"Yeah, fine. No worries. Listen I'd better get going here, but thanks for the invitation. Bye."

"OK, well, call if you need—"

Click!

Donna laid back and studied the ceiling. She had been having a dream about Jen and a theater and other things … but their specifics were already melting away. In the dream, Jen was alive and full of spirited observations, exactly the way she would always be remembered. She was in a coffin trying to explain something. It was important to the point that Donna's happiness depended on it, something from long ago, but as much as she concentrated, the dream had completely recessed into the mist of sleep.

***

Jen's funeral was entirely too conservative for someone of her character.

Donna arrived a few minutes early and found Jack kneeling alone before a pew. His head was bent over with his arm along the bench in front of him, his forehead lightly resting against the back of his wrist. When he finished his prayer and sat back on the bench, he saw her and slid sideways, giving her room to sit. As often happens during momentous occasions, conversation fell strangely short of the amount needed. Instead, they listened to the gentle music floating from the speakers and waved discreetly to a few familiar people.

Her mind barely there, Donna took in her surroundings with a distracted sadness. It was the first time she had seen Jack since their passionate night, and here he was, sitting beside her in a suit. She remembered the other time she saw him in a suit and her thoughts wandered to various memories of those days. An enormous difference separated the boy, who wanted to be on every sports team, from the man sitting beside her today.

Several hymns and formal prayers started the service. Donna couldn't identify with the cheery songs, such a contrast to the serious overtones of prayer. Stand … kneel … bow your head … She followed the cues of the crowd, but concentrating was hard with Jack's hands merely inches away. Stand again … sing …

As he grasped the book of hymns reverently, she envisioned her breasts cupped there instead. Donna was vaguely aware that having sexual thoughts during her closest friend's funeral wasn't normal, but they were doubly intrusive in his presence. She had thought about their night a lot in the last week. It was an escape to carry her through the hospital visits and subsequent announcement of Jen's passing. Otherwise, the old ache of abandonment would creep into her head, reminding her of the other death long ago.

As a twelve-year-old, she'd withdrawn from the world until the Brammons had coaxed her back. At that time, Donna emerged from the experience with a strong self-reliance. Now, she was responding in a different direction by reaching out to Jack. A fleeting insight suggested she was trying to replace Jen with Jack. And not just Jen, but Jen's whole family. Though she understood the futility of this and knew Jack could never fill all those shoes—would never want to either—his face stayed in the front of her mind, firmly blocking out her mother and the Brammons. They could have gained Donna's attention, but she simply enlarged Jack's image to make room for no one else.

One glance told her how upset Jack was. With shoulders hunched and that careful expressionless face he'd mastered since Red Deer, she grasped his sorrow as if he were shouting it to the sky. Placing her hand over his, she turned his palm up and entwined their fingers to form a tight grasp. Donna stared at their hands and willed the service to continue as long as possible.

The pastor gave a short speech. She only caught snippets—"God", "everlasting peace", "what Christ means to those who pass on". Jack seemed to be listening attentively, but a small feeling of resentment surfaced in Donna. Anyone who knew Jen would immediately recognize the unsuitability of this speech. A Christian pep talk in disguise. This wasn't what Jen was all about. Nothing in this room characterized someone who had argued against formal religion, and here they were collectively bidding her farewell in a church-like setting. Once, Donna had jokingly remarked that Jen wouldn't be allowed in the door of any church. She wanted to relay the irony to Jack, but it was the type of statement that could only be appreciated by Jen. Donna's isolation acute, she clutched Jack's hand tighter.

The pastor invited Jeffrey to deliver a eulogy. Jen had specifically asked him, partly because of their closeness and partly because she knew he wouldn't exaggerate her life. Rising to the occasion as expected, he had organized the funeral himself, his parents unable to face those details. Though he projected a calm countenance, a white pallor betrayed his pain. After a deep breath, he spoke.

"I was nine when my parents told me I was going to have another brother or sister. If I remember correctly, my response was, 'Just don't have a girl. Girls are no fun,' but a few months later, this little baby girl came home. I thought girls were boring. They colored inside the lines and never got dirty, but as Jenny grew up, she played baseball and soccer with us. Little Jenny, surrounded by these three big brothers."

Jeffrey smiled a little at the memory and an array of faces smiled back.

"She would get mad if she thought we were being easy on her. And when it was time to pack up and come in for supper, she would be the one saying, 'Just five more minutes.' Jenny laughed a lot, often at herself. And she made you laugh at yourself, whether you wanted to or not. She didn't pretend to be perfect, and she wasn't one to hide behind her faults. I admired that in her.

"A young life leaving us is tragic. It isn't right. She wasn't ready to go. I'll always wonder what she would have accomplished, if she had lived to an old age. Jenny didn't believe in coloring inside the lines. And she spent her whole life coloring. Like many of you, I have pictures right up here in my head—"

His index finger touched the side of his forehead lightly and bounced off, as though hot.

"—that she created out of her words or the expressions on her face or the things she did. I see them in these big colors. They won't fade or get lost and they are absolutely irreplaceable. If that counts for something, then I think she accomplished more than a lot of us have.

"I've never known anyone with the kind of life she has," he stopped to correct himself, "had inside her. And I'm sure I never will. I can't begin to describe how much I'll miss her ... our family will miss her. It is a great compliment to her memory that all of you are here today. On behalf of my family, thank you for coming."

A final prayer finished Jen's funeral. Jack kneeled in the pew and whispered another quick silent prayer. The funeral home staff invited everyone into an adjacent reception room. Tables and chairs were set out near a long table of food. Centered among the snacks was an arrangement of flowers and pictures of Jen in her childhood.

Donna summed it up with a tiny smile emanating from her eyes. "You know, Jen would think this is really stupid. She would have wanted us to throw a beach party or something."

Jack gave a small nod and a smirk pulled his lips up, but it abruptly disappeared when they suddenly found themselves face to face with Jen's parents.

Mrs. Brammon said, "Thank you both for coming."

The statement was spoken as though they were two people who had never sat at the Brammon's kitchen table playing Rummoli and eating potato chips. Donna stiffened at the formality in this woman's voice, and for a moment, she was at a loss to find a response. She could reach out and hug Jen's parents. She should. It would be the right thing to do, but something in their eyes stopped her.

Then Jack answered, "Thanks for letting us know. We'll miss her."

His simplistic words were accepted with two courteous nods, and Jack guided Donna away with a hand lightly pressed against her back.

They found two chairs and sat alone with small paper plates of food. A few minutes later, Jeffrey approached them, the family delegate. Standing before them, he handed Donna a small wrapped package.

"She asked me to give this to you."

Donna carefully peeled back the paper. A Barry Manilow CD. A flood of emotions passed through her mind. Until now, this funeral had been painted in formal overtones—the hymns, prayers, perfectly placed wreaths—and none of it was Jen. But this ... this simple gift was something substantial and befitting the occasion.

She could imagine Jen grinning wryly while tossing the little square package at her. "Here, now your geek potential is complete!" A slow smile spread across Donna's face, just enough to show a seed of contentment. Had Jack's expression not contained an equal thread of pain, the two of them would have resembled parents overwhelmed by the awe of a newborn.

Jeffrey peered at the gift in her hand. He scanned their faces quizzically, but neither could offer an explanation to adequately cover so many years.

***

CHAPTER 29

Only a short walk from the bus stop, this music store housed a perfect view of the community center. Al pretended to browse the CDs, occasionally picking one up to glance at the title, but mostly he kept his eyes on a trail of kids leaving a building.

Cars driven by patient parents lined the front. Soon, he spotted Tracy pulling up in her blue Ford. It was a marital asset Tracy had demanded in their divorce settlement, and Al didn't argue. He wasn't allowed to get behind the wheel anyway. His third impaired charge prohibited him from driving for another three years. A hefty fine was paid, but at least he wouldn't go to jail, not this time anyway.

He remembered the night he got caught: getting cocky, risking driving here and there for groceries, work-related errands, booze. ... He had driven no further than a block, when flashing lights came out of nowhere. Handling him with poorly contained annoyance, a cop made him sit in the backseat of the cruiser like a criminal. He wasn't even very drunk at the time. What a dick. Come to think of it, they were all dicks, just big meaty guys who toured in their white cars, nabbing people like Al, when there were real criminals running around out there. Murderers, rapists, child molesters. What the hell were they doing with him?

Tracy's car sat idling. She was leaning forward, looking toward the front of the building. Once she sat back, another profile was suddenly visible in the passenger side. A man. So, Tracy had a boyfriend.

(Well, good for her ... Bitch.)

Then, Al lit up at the sight of his kids when they ran excitedly toward the car. They were so big. It must have been months—Kevin's hair was shorter now, but Ashley's brown curls were long and wavy. She was beautiful. She would be beautiful in a few years too, long-limbed, graceful like a colt, and he felt a sudden stab of resentment at the inevitable attraction of teenage boys.

He could imagine her a fully grown woman, her strong face framed by long brown hair. The image sparked a faint thought, veiled by layers of years, and he couldn't pinpoint its origin, but it sent an additional obscure feeling of loss through him. Something indefinable and out of reach.

His kids struggled with the door handle, the one that always stuck. Tracy didn't get that fixed yet? Al wanted to go to them, but the man in the passenger seat stepped out. He was a big guy, tall with looming shoulders. He opened the door with ease and the kids scampered inside. Then, when he turned to get back in, Al startled.

The cop! The one who arrested him. He was dressed like any other guy, but it was the same face. You don't forget the face of the man who puts handcuffs on you and makes you sit in a cop car for all to see. Al thought back to the night of his arrest and realized just how conveniently situated that fuck had been to catch him so fast.

Now, Constable Fuck was in the Ford with Al's kids while he had to take a bus, just to catch ten seconds worth of fatherhood. As the car disappeared down the street, the illusion of another happy family, his eyes filled with angry tears.

***

... Warmth pressed in from above. And this was strange—such absolute blackness was never associated with burning heat of the sun. Still, an image of color and texture knitted itself together in her mind. As hindsight added its emotional slant, Donna's dread grew. She knew the memory was necessary, pivotal even. It had been one of those turning points, just one of many, but one which placed her that much closer to this dark existence. And she really didn't want to relive all those tears again.

She tried to turn away, but without the brilliance of the external world to fill her eyes, these images were the only ones of substance. She could hear the hymns, see those people filling the pews, and then that long belt of grass as ...

***

They walked out into a very sunny afternoon, Jack's suit jacket slung over his shoulder. This bright day represented Jen's countenance more than any part of the funeral, and when Donna commented on it, Jack agreed at

242

once. They wandered down the street and into a little corner store. With sodas in hand, they searched for a seat outside.

"Let's go over there," Jack suggested.

He pointed to a park across the street. Towering trees surrounded a building and its adjacent playground. Kids were pouring out of the building and into various cars lining the curb. They looked like a colorful array of scattering ants.

Choosing a shaded park bench, they sat down. Jack hung his jacket over the back of it. Donna wanted to lean against him, feel some remnant of his solid frame, his melting caresses. And in the next moment, her wish was granted when he took her hand.

"How are you?"

She made a face and bent an ear toward her shoulder. Let him assume she was upset about Jen. She was, of course, but those feelings were eclipsed by her miserable need of him. A disquieting layer of guilt reminded her that Jack would likely think less of her if he knew her innermost thoughts. They were supposed to be focused on Jen today, but she hadn't thought about anything except him for a full week.

Jack remarked, "They told me you were at the hospital a lot. I went a few times. Once I'd just missed you."

"I tried to go when I thought other people wouldn't. I just wanted to sit with her, even if she was drugged up."

"I hadn't seen her for a long time, over a year, so it was a pretty big shock. Do people know it wasn't just cancer?"

"I think so. The chronic pneumonia, skin spots, never quite recovering. It's easy to connect those symptoms."

(Or it should have been …)

She shrugged. It was depressing and she didn't want to encourage the topic.

"You know," Donna smiled contritely, as she fiddled with the CD in her free hand, "I really do like Barry Manilow. A lot."

Grinning and shaking his head, Jack muttered, "Thirty coffees …"

"What?"

"If you'd admitted that ten years ago, I would have won a month's worth of coffee."

"You guys bet on me?"

"Oh, like you never did? And I'm not talkin' some crappy fifty-cent cup of sludge. She was gonna have to splurge on the expensive stuff and hand deliver it every day, even weekends."

"So you lost? What did you have to do?"

"Slave for a day."

"Not a month?"

243

Jack leveled a look at Donna. "Are you kidding? Trust me—that was a *long* day."

Until now, his eyes had been everywhere except on hers. Now, here they were along with a smile and a laugh, her hand still woven in his. They were at some place beyond their starting point in high school, but past the cushioned confidence of friendship, despite their relaxed efforts. Smiles and words were not enough, not anymore.

Donna was through with living in a cushioned world. Jen's death had slapped her awake to look at her own life differently. There was only one life, a single chance to pull another person into her soul. Jack was that person, but he would never take the lead, never broach the subject. It was up to her to show him what they could have together.

"Jack, have you been avoiding me?"

He glanced out at the street and let go of her hand. After an interminable time, he answered, "Don, I don't know. ... I mean no, not really. I just didn't know if I should call or what."

She smiled sadly and he read her expression correctly.

"I know I should have talked to you about it sooner."

"We're not going to happen, are we?"

Seven years ago, he could have been the one to ask that question. "I've thought about this a lot." He added quickly, "I'm sorry about that night. It shouldn't have happened—"

(Yes, it should have. It should have happened a long time ago. You're actually ashamed of what we did, almost did. It was incredible. How can you think anything less of it?)

"—you needed someone to stay with you and I should have left at the first sign of trouble. You needed a friend and I just wasn't one."

Jack leaned forward and cradled his chin in his hands. He took a deep breath, eyes downcast.

"Don, my choice to accept Jesus Christ wasn't a breeze. Sex has always been a problem. I mean, it's easy for me to get affected by a pretty face. I needed religion to get me on track. I never really explained why I became a Christian. It happened when I left."

His expression was strange; those distant eyes again. She resented that entire sections of his life excluded her, but she also knew how selective he was in his choice of confidantes. Cravings to feel close to him battled against her resentment and won.

"You were with Ric then. That really got to me."

Donna interrupted him with a stricken look. "You never told me!"

"I didn't think it would change anything. Would I have stood a chance then?"

She thought for a moment, then dropped her eyes, shaking her head slightly. "Not at first, but you would have near the end ... definitely *at* the end."

"What do you mean?"

"He hit me."

"What!" Jack exclaimed.

"I didn't tell anyone, just Jen and Billy. It happened around the time you left town. One night he was drinking—well, he was always drinking—and we were arguing. ..."

***

As she shut the door behind him, he leaned close for a kiss, the same as usual, which momentarily disarmed her. Ric strolled through the living room. She heard the refrigerator open and the sharp fizzle of a beer cap being popped off. When he reappeared, he lifted the bottle to his mouth and took a long drink, then strode right into the bathroom.

The suspense was enormous. What would he say about the toilet seat, about stealing her money and breaking into her apartment? Maybe he'd flat out deny it.

Bracing herself for a nasty argument, the bathroom door finally opened and Ric emerged. He held a cool expression and avoided her eyes as he lounged against the balcony door. His posture was strangely defiant, putting his masculinity in the forefront.

Reaching behind, he flipped the balcony lock, slid the glass door open, and stepped through. A sudden spike of anxiety overtook her, but she followed him outside.

"Ric, we have to talk."

He practically snorted. "Here it comes."

"Were you on campus this morning?"

Staring at her knowingly, his dark eyes took on a disconcerting gleam. "Yeah, I came to have *coffee* with you." Another long drink from his bottle. The beer was half gone and the remaining liquid swirled inside the bottle recklessly.

Her eyes narrowed. "But you went away with more than just coffee didn't you?"

"You might say that."

(He did take the money! And my key!)

"That does it! You stay away from me. I'm changing my locks and I never want to see you again!"

Swiftly turning away, Donna felt his fingers digging into her arm and heard him growl, "Why? You expecting someone? Gonna fuck *another* guy right under my nose?"

She pulled against him, at first in anger, and then in horror felt herself being shuffled toward the railing.

(Oh my God, what's he doing?)

"Ric! Ric!" Powerless, Donna struggled until a desperate maneuver occurred to her. Instead of pulling away, she threw all her weight directly against his body. Finding himself bent partway over the railing, his grip loosened, and twisting free, she leaped through the balcony door.

Out of the corner of her eye, she registered the bottle flying. It hit the kitchen counter and shattered, leaving a foamy wet pattern to slowly weave its way down the cupboards.

He tackled her face down on the sofa. A child would have thought it a game. There was even the fleeting memory of her father tossing her similarly and her childish laughter ringing out.

Ric angled over her and she felt his hands anchoring her head into a pillow. Choking, a terror-stricken thought punctuated in her head.

(He's going to kill me! Kill me! Kill—)

One hand was pinned under her chest and she couldn't get it out. The other clawed the air behind her. Kicking a leg futilely on the floor, scratching, scraping to shift her head off the pillow, she couldn't dislodge his grip as white spots danced across her eyelids. The obscene sound of his heavy breathing taunted the denial of air.

Donna focused on the pinned arm. Digging her fingers between her chin and the pillow, she created a tiny air pocket. The other hand pretended to claw his forearm uselessly while she inhaled slowly. ... Relaxing completely, she let her hand fall away from his forearm to glide limply down over the sofa edge. Fingers grazed the carpet as her strength gradually returned, fueled by adrenaline.

(Breathe ... one—one-thousand, two—one-thousand, breathe ...)

His weight lifted off her. The air hole widened a bit. Air, precious air. She stayed limp and concentrated.

(... five—one-thousand, six—one-thousand, breathe ...)

He was still there right beside the couch, but at least he wasn't touching her. If he touched her, she'd scream.

(... don't tense ... ready ... now!)

Suddenly, she sprang up and shoved him hard. He fell over the arm of the couch and onto the floor. Donna spun in the opposite direction. The front door was only a few feet away, but the couch stood in her way. No time to go around. One foot on the cushions, she vaulted over the back end, and in two more steps she was there.

Seizing the deadbolt latch with one hand as the other turned the doorknob, she managed to open it a few inches when his arm shot out to slam the door closed.

"Where you goin'?" he hissed.

Cornered, she tried to dart past his heavy body and into the bathroom. She'd lock the door and scream until someone heard her. She took no more than one step when he anticipated her, blocking her path solidly with his other arm.

Donna stood frozen under his malicious gaze. An eternity passed while she stared into those eyes. And then, he swiftly drew his right hand back and slammed his palm flat onto the wall, inches from her face. She thought she screamed, throwing her arms up automatically to protect herself, but the only sound in the apartment came from right beside her ear. The *whap!* of his hand was louder than anything she had ever heard in her life. Everything was magnified: his snarling voice, his breath on her face, the echo of the wall, his black eyes.

Pinned against the wall, the doorknob to safety peeked out from under his arm as he brought his hand back. *Wham!* Again he hit a spot beside her. And again. And again ... Then, he stopped. Her eyes had been closed, but now she opened them, letting her shaking hands come down to cover her mouth.

A pained look crossed his face straight at Donna, as if she were responsible for his hand hurting.

In a flash, she saw two things: the look in his eyes changed to a coarse expression of delight and his arm pulled back again. Caught by his eyes, she couldn't react and this time, his fist landed across her left cheek. The force of it knocked her sideways, striking her head on the wall. Her knees buckled and she fell to the floor senseless. The room moved on its own, those white spots dancing again. Then, it slowed down to right itself.

She screamed something, the only thing she could think of. "NO!—NO!—NO! ..."

Over and over, it looped itself in her head and kept coming out of her mouth, but the sound was too hoarse to carry. He looked huge standing over her. Next the kicks would start, into her ribs, her stomach, her head, and that's where they would find her, in a pool of her own blood two feet from the door.

Her arms flailed around, frantic hands, sharp sobs, anything to put between them. But surprisingly, Ric stepped back instead, black eyes concentrated.

It took her a few seconds to realize that there was space between them, but not enough and she shrunk against the wall. He wasn't kicking her. He wasn't hitting her or choking her. He had stopped. ...

Hands hid her face as frightened cries overlapped to become the steady sound of weeping. He would never stop.

Finally, he spoke. "I'm going out for a smoke."

The front door closed behind him. She couldn't believe the click of the latch was real, that there was a solid barrier between them. He just ... went out to smoke? Like this was a coffee break? It didn't seem possible. None of this did. His footsteps faded down the stairway.

(He's gone! Go!)

Snatching her keys, she raced down the hall, down a different flight of stairs to the back entrance. Her car was blandly waiting for her outside. Take her to the police or to the nearest 7-Eleven—made no difference to a Toyota—but first she had to cross the parking lot, fit the key in the car door, scoot inside, and start the motor. Those four little tasks routinely committed in everyday life were now paramount.

Shaking, she fumbled with the back door of the building. The knob would turn, but something in the latch was stuck. It was supposed to open outward. She pushed harder, and then threw the side of her body against it. *Bang—rattle!* It didn't budge. The jarring movement brought a sharp pain across her face. Hot tears sprang from her eyes and she pushed on the door with her back, again and again. Finally, her head bent down into her hands as she recklessly sobbed. No way out.

Donna shut her eyes tightly and then sped up the stairs. She banged on the other doors, but none opened to her pounding and pleading. Precious asylum denied by two inches of wood.

The echoing sounds of footsteps from the front entrance narrowed her racing thoughts. If it were Ric, he shouldn't find her trying to escape. She should be in her apartment. If it weren't him, she would hear the person go past her door, and she could intercept him then.

But it was Ric. He heard the toilet flush and saw her standing at the bathroom sink, setting down a towel he didn't know concealed a kitchen knife and cell phone. The regular phones had no dial tone.

Looking resigned and ready to talk, she steeled herself to smile and say all the right things. He sat her down next to him, one arm thrown around her shoulders. Her skin crawled at his touch. Her heart raced again.

(Oh God, what if he stays? What if he ...)

She should have hid a knife under her pillow, but there wasn't time.

Give up your cash. Threat isn't consent. Don't resist. It's not worth your life. ... Later, she would hear those strategies characterized as "smart survival techniques" by experts who had never clawed at someone while being suffocated. Particularly galling was the phrase, "No means no." Yeah, he'd listen to that.

"The back door's busted," Ric bluntly announced. Then he shrugged. "Look, you fell and hit your face on the table. You've been clumsy lately. Everybody's seen you buggin' out and nobody will believe I had anything to do with it. You're not ending this. Deal with it."

Donna nodded meekly. Then she quietly suggested, "I should rinse my face."

Ric smiled at the timid question in her voice asking his permission, but his dark stare quickly returned. It was too late to fix this. Her fate was sealed. He just needed it to be a little darker out. Sweeping one hand dismissively toward the bathroom, he leaned back comfortably into the couch.

Knowing she'd never outrun him, it took everything Donna had not to sprint out the front door. Instead, she calmly stepped into the bathroom and slid the cell phone out from the folds of the towel. She carefully punched in Jen's number through blurry tears, gripped the knife, and wondered if she were capable of killing a man.

***

CHAPTER 30

Jack stared in horror. As she spoke, one hand grazed her cheek.

"I was scared shitless he was going to come after me, you know, stalk me. In fact, all these years, I thought it would happen. I'd see him somewhere totally unexpected. It's creepy but I've never been able to shake it. Anyway, I moved to a different apartment and so far so good."

Donna shook her head at the awful memory. She leaned back on the park bench, weary. A further thought ran alongside those memories. She recalled it was roughly the time when Jack disappeared from Calgary. Needing his protective presence, she had left messages with his mom, all unanswered, and two years passed before he returned. There was always a seed of resentment over this, which she had avoided admitting to herself, but now it chafed her mind. Why wasn't he there for her when she really needed him?

Staring sadly out at the street, she summed up quietly, "So you see, you would have stood a chance. You would have been someone safe."

She sighed and picked up her soda. It tasted cool and spicy in the summer sun. Lately, little things escaped her notice, like the taste of food or the wind through her hair, but today everything seemed accentuated. She realized she had only been paying attention to details that related to their steamy night. Everything else was viewed through glasses with a unique filtering agent.

After a respectful pause, Jack finally responded, "I'm sorry. I never knew. I wish I'd been there."

"Me too. He didn't like you much. You were also the target of some of his accusations. He probably sensed something that was right for once. It just wasn't right at that time. Well, I'm not the only woman in the world with that story. At least I got out of it."

"Did you report it?"

"No. I know that sounds stupid. He was so obviously sick. I told people I got beaned playing racquetball or something." She shrugged her shoulders. "He was my first lover, so I didn't really know what to think of it all. Too weird. Even after it, I just couldn't believe there was this other side to him ... but I'll never forget the look in his eyes when he was wailing on the wall. He would have killed me. I've treated several women I suspect are victims. They have that same look I saw in the mirror. I do my best to stay unemotional and lay out their options, but I can understand why some of them choose to stay. Either way, it's scary."

It was good to tell someone about her frightening night with Ric. Now that Jen was gone, Jack was the next best ear, though Donna knew she was using up words in an effort to prolong his attention. She could sit on this bench with him forever. Maybe these confessions would somehow spark a need for her in his life, but deep down, she knew he'd remain unconvinced. Shifting on the bench, Donna steered the discussion back to its original path.

"Well, that's the story of Ric and me. Sorry, I kind of high-jacked the conversation there. You were explaining about becoming a Christian?"

"Right ... Where was I?"

"When you left." She had a morbid curiosity about this private element of Jack's past.

"Oh, yeah ... Well, Jen thought you'd break up, but I figured if he left, you'd end up with somebody else anyway. She told me I should just find a girl who looked like you and get you out of my system."

"She knew how you felt? She never told me!"

"I asked her not to."

A nasty feeling of betrayal swept through her. Respect for Jen's loyalty competed with anger at her silence. She could have changed Donna's past for the better. It made her sick inside, partly because bitterness also created guilt. The dead must be applauded, especially dead friends. It was ironic how the three of them remained such good friends that their secrets were honored, even from each other.

"Anyway, after that, I got together with this other woman. You gotta remember—this was a time when I just didn't know what the heck I wanted to do with my life. And she set me straight." He stopped to study her face. "She reminded me a lot of you."

(When you were with me, you closed your eyes and fantasized about her? I knew you were thinking about someone else when you had your body on mine! At least leave me the memories of that night—don't make them about her. Don't tell me any more. I can't hear this.)

"So, what happened?"

"It didn't last long. She went back to some guy she was seeing before me. At least I think she did. I tried to find her. That was part of why I became a cop—so I'd have the resources to do the search—but by the time I became one, I'd pretty much given up. I did find one match on her name, but the person died ten years before we even met. Besides that dead end, I've never come close to another lead. It's like she disappeared into thin air. ..."

Donna studied the bitter lines around his mouth and eyes, especially his eyes, and wondered what that woman had done to this poor man.

"We had this connection, almost spiritual. She was a pretty strong Christian—I mean her beliefs were solid in her. She really knew what she thought. I'd never met anyone with that ability to ... It was a kind of centeredness. She was someone who got things done and I needed that.

"When she left, I searched everywhere, places I thought she could be, restaurants, churches. I must have hit every church in that city two or three times looking for her. Then, I hooked up with the pastor who did the counseling for me. Got re-baptized and been a Christian ever since. I'm finally getting to the point where I can go through a whole day without wondering where she is and what she's doing."

Donna remembered her university graduation and how surprised she was by the change in his values. So, that's what happened—the talk about his church, becoming a cop, finding his father. Now it made sense and it was all because of this one woman. Donna felt comparatively insignificant.

He laid one arm across the back of the bench. "It's wrong to get caught up in physical things." His other arm sliced downward, emphasizing the exact division between right and wrong. "It's something I agreed on when I took Jesus into my life, and that's why I couldn't do any more than I did with you. I'm sorry Don. I got carried away and I let you get carried away. I've offended my relationship with God and my relationship with you. ... What else can I say?"

Donna's heart sank. The flattery of his candor appealed to sincerity, but it sounded a little too clean, too prepared. He had forgotten he wasn't the only one trained to dig for the truth. A part of her still hoped he would finish his speech with, "Donna, I want you," but even her most idealistic expectations wouldn't entertain the possibility for long. This was it, the end of his speech, and with it went the last of her hopes.

Jack picked up his drink again. She watched his fingers fold around the can of pop, and remembered them circling her breast. They were connected to the hands that had caressed her skin and the arms around her body, and she felt confused all over again. He was telling her that being in bed with her was wrong, but how could such endearing passion be wrong?

(He must have been envisioning her the entire time. Jack, how could you tell me this? Jen, I need you. Why did you die? ...)

Donna's thoughts ran around in circles, begging and blaming her friends. Jack had used her and Jen had lied to her. She kept Donna out of her illness until the very last moment, and he kept her separated from everything that mattered to him. Donna would have attended church with him if it meant they'd be closer, but after openly resisting the offer, all his talk of friendship suddenly dissolved. If Jack wouldn't share the one aspect of his life underlying every decision and philosophy that he held, her value to him couldn't be high. He'd admitted as much by saying he should have left her alone that night at the first sign of trouble. Trouble? She'd asked him to stay to enhance their connection. He stayed because their connection was long gone.

All this time, she'd clung to a two-dimensional portrait of this man suspended in her mind, his touch guiding the brush strokes, her fantasies forming the frame. Desires placed the finished creation at a height no other could reach, but by giving her this kindly wrapped bundle of words, Jack was clawing his way through the canvas, ripping long tears across her precious painting, and her heart sank at seeing him as he really was: vulnerable, selfish, flawed. Every good thing she knew him to be disappeared. Jack the Lover was heading out the door hand in hand with Jack the Friend.

And Jen was gone in a real sense. These two people who had meant so much to her over the years. The double loss was debilitating ... all because of God and some woman out there. This God was a barrier to him, the ex-girlfriend a thief. Jack was meant for Donna long before he was ever aware of their existences. How dare he attribute the most intense night of her life to them?

Shaking, she turned to him, her face hardened.

"You think you're the only one who gets affected by sex? Everyone has that problem, including me. Hell, you saw me. You saw me in a way no one else has. Yes, you got me to respond—because I was with you—not because I was with some Ric clone and couldn't resist. I knew who I was in bed with. You think I could have asked anyone else to stay with me that night? I wanted to be in your arms and feel close to you for once."

Jack's eyes went wide. His mouth opened to answer, but she cut him off with a low voice as though others were within earshot.

"You're saying that while you were with me, you were actually with God and your ex-girlfriend? They weren't the ones in bed with you—*I* was. Do you know how many nights I laid awake, wishing you were doing exactly what you almost did that night? And since then, I've ached to feel like that again. And now you're telling me it was a mistake? Fuck your religious confession!"

253

He had expected her to be upset, but he had badly underestimated the depth of her feelings. Jen tried to tell him in the hospital and he'd chosen to skip around the issue.

Donna's glare was ruthless. This wasn't the astute self-contained girl from high school. This was someone looking for a way out, blaming him for her pain. Well, he had dealt with his own frustrations enough over the years, until they had practically torn him apart. He couldn't be responsible for hers too.

Unable to distinguish between anger provoked by grief and anger due him, Jack reacted with equal force. He jumped up, and for a few seconds, she thought he was leaving. Her mind wildly pleaded *(No! Say anything you want, just don't walk away!),* but instead, he paced before the bench like a caged animal searching for an escape.

"Haven't you heard anything I said? Being a Christian means everything to me. It's how I live. I can't ignore that. You want me to abandon it and just be what you want, but it's not gonna happen."

He stopped pacing and abruptly faced her.

"Don't lay this on me Donna. I feel guilty enough about that night, but what about you? I thought you were upset about Jen. Now you say it was all crap, you *wanted* it to happen? Did you even consider what that would do to me?"

He suddenly towered over her, his face inches away, teeth clenched.

"You lied to me, said you thought we wouldn't make a good couple. You weren't even thinking about Jen. Just what were all those tears about anyway?"

Donna shrank back against the bench. She was all eyes. Jack walking away would have been infinitely better than hearing him accuse her of steely manipulation.

She raised one hand to cover her quivering chin. His breath was warm on her fingers. His face swam through the tears in her eyes.

Two weeks ago, he had kissed her with overwhelming strength and softness, but these menacing lips would not. The trustworthy congenial friend of so many years vanished before her eyes, to be replaced by someone harsh with brutal words of honesty. Taking hold of the exact lie shielding her, he'd thrust it roughly into the open. He was right. Jen hadn't entered her mind that night, not when his intoxicating body was there to block her out. Jen's death was a convenient camouflage ... but it was more complicated than that.

When Donna said they wouldn't make a good couple, that lie contained a confusing element of inner truth. In bed, she'd delivered the words with light conviction, conscious of her deception. Still, an intuitive awareness gave permission for it. The next day to Jen, Donna confessed the true incongruity by observing that Jack was right and wrong for her at the same time.

If she had lied to him, it was a lie that was also true, like a two-headed coin. Opposite sides of the same issue; no matter what side he looked at, there was a face staring up at him. Donna knew her face was etched onto one side of the coin Jack held, but it was the other side he saw; the woman he'd lost.

Leaning close and staring straight into her, he opened his mouth with more accusations. She flinched as her hands instinctively covered her face, and his eyes went wide with amazement.

(She thinks I'm going to hit her!)

Sobbing openly, she babbled almost incoherently between gulping breaths, "I didn't lie to you! I didn't! I don't think we'd make a good couple, but I can't help wanting you. I've never felt like that. I couldn't think about Jen. I couldn't think about anything. I still can't. I'm sorry—I'm sorry. ..."

She cried helplessly, her head bowed, and Jack's tense posture slowly softened. It wasn't her flood of tears or the strained anguish in her voice that caused his anger to seep away. It wasn't even the humbling realization that she held a hidden fear of men, and that for a second, she had lumped him in a category with violent ones like Ric. It was simply the chord of truthfulness in her words. The authenticity about their confusing suitability for each other struck him right in the center of his soul, and for a moment, he was reminded exactly how he'd felt about his ex-girlfriend. The bad timing identically detailing their situations renewed his compassion.

Jack lowered his body back onto the bench and enfolded Donna in his arms. Still crying, she laid her head against his neck.

"I'm sorry too," he said wearily.

When she was calm, she raised her head. Her eyes were misery itself.

"Don, I can't do this. I can't take responsibility for it. I'm hurting too."

What did he mean? Was he hurting about Jen ... or his ex-girlfriend? She hoped her own words weren't the cause, but part of her didn't care. It was time he experienced a small fraction of what she'd gone through because of him.

He stood up and they gazed at each other unhappily. Then, her earlier fear materialized; he picked up his suit jacket and walked away. Turning her back on his footsteps, Donna stared at the bench. The Barry Manilow CD smiled up at her and she concentrated on it, as fallen tears blurred the plastic picture.

***

CHAPTER 31

... Things were speeding up. It was hard to distinguish reality from wishful thinking, but either way, Jack was near.

Donna could hear his footsteps fading away, hollow lifeless percussions waning with the ebb of a tide, but in what direction? This place gave no glimmer of escape, not so much as a thread of light to follow him.

The only trail she could sense was through the memories of her professional life, all settled invitingly before her. Despite their lack of threat, Donna still balked at their pull and searched desperately for Jack, but his voice had faded to an echo, and resignedly ...

***

Donna followed Gene into his office. He closed the door behind her as she sat in the seat before his desk, and he took the opposite chair. This was where she had sat during her interview. It was funny how a chair is only as comfortable as the reason for being in it. To deflect attention from her lack of experience, she had gone on the offensive, questioning Gene about his business solvency. The chair became increasingly comfortable as the hour went on.

Right now, Gene was shifting as though someone had tossed gravel onto his seat. And that was really unusual.

He was such a gentle man, a widower with a son who had gone his own way in the world. No following in his father's footsteps. Donna suspected she filled some gap for Gene by fulfilling the path he had hoped his son would follow. Both relatively alone, the two doctors were surrounded by people living their own lives. She enjoyed this part of their relationship, since it was something missing with her own father. Raymond deserved his own life independent of fatherly love, but she continued to feel a thin barrier between them, as if cautiously treading among eggshells. No odd feelings intruded with Gene, just soft-spoken words of encouragement.

The alliance bolstered security in her career. Many of his patients had transferred over to her, which allowed Gene to ease into his retirement, and also gave her the confidence to envision the business as her own. Professionally, things were as good as could be.

He asked, "How are you doing?"

The words were delivered with a casual conversational air, but his eyes were sharp. She realized he was studying her, much like she would study one of her own patients.

As her brow puckered, he continued, "Your work here is fine. You don't have a lot of free spaces in the log and Anne says the patients speak highly of you, but you don't leave yourself a lot of time for breaks. You're not making mistakes yet, but I have to admit, I am concerned. Are you sure we shouldn't put you on a tricyclic?"

Donna shook her head. "We've been here before, Gene. Antidepressants won't change anything. My mood's not endogenous. Besides, I don't need a lot of breaks," she lied, and then remembering who she was talking to, added, "Well, I find it's easier to get involved in other people's problems."

He observed Donna gracefully cross her legs and fold her hands in her lap. And wasn't buying it. Though thoroughly professional on the job, she'd gone through a trying time after the death of her friend. They must have been close. Since then, Donna's grief manifested itself in various ways and she seemed no closer to resolving it than a year ago. People didn't usually take this long to reach the acceptance stage. Couldn't be sleeping well either by that tired gaze she carried. And when was the last time he'd heard her laugh? Not just polite chuckles, but ear to ear grinning laughter. A year? More?

"Look, I'm not saying this as your boss. I'm telling you as a doctor and a friend that I think you need help."

She stared at him with big eyes. If she opened them wide enough, they would hold in all the tears threatening to escape. They escaped daily, but only in the confines of her apartment. Now, in front of this kind man, she let them come.

Gene thought her problems centered on Jen. He had no idea that Jen was never in the center. Swimming around the periphery of Donna's thoughts, she only came into view occasionally, and when she did, Donna remembered her with a sad sense of neglect. Today was especially strange, since Gene had chosen to open the subject on the anniversary of Jen's funeral. Donna was aware of this day in the back of her mind, but she primarily thought of it as "The Day Jack Walked Away From Me". She knew the deceased were owed a greater show of sorrow, but Jack took up so much more room in Donna's heart.

How could she explain that? The only person capable of understanding was Jen, who would have thrown some pointed statements at Donna and pulled her out of it in no time, but there was no one to do that now. And the situation with Jack was simply too personal. She didn't understand it herself, let alone try to acquaint another person with it. Words couldn't describe the empty void he'd created by turning his back on her. So, just as she let Jack misunderstand her tears, she now did the same with Gene.

He handed her a tissue and waited until she became more composed. Finally, Donna raised her head, pushing the thought of Jack aside, and looked at Gene squarely, almost defiantly while he started with the standard diagnostic questions.

Was she crying a lot? Yes.

Was she still sleeping poorly? Yes.

How was her appetite? Same, not very good. She had lost a lot of weight in the past year.

Did she have a support system at home? Spent time with family or friends? A boyfriend? No, No, and No. A fresh set of tears almost escaped after the last question.

And then the cruncher: Did she have thoughts of hurting herself or anyone else? Though unsure, she refrained from confessing this. The thoughts that plagued her were disturbing, but vague, and until they became more specific, she would keep quiet. Self-harm was a concept that formed only in the general thought, "If I were dead, I wouldn't feel so bad all the time." Hurting others was something that had never occurred to her.

She smiled a little at the image of her busting into work one day, all bugged out waving a gun around—she didn't even know where to get one—and quipped, "Don't worry, you're safe. Anne hid the scalpels."

His lips curled up as he quietly retorted, "It's you I'm worried about. You're a good doctor, but right now you're obviously down and I don't see it getting better. Do you need some time off? Say, a couple of weeks. Get away and relax."

Donna collected herself, straightened up, and took another deep breath. "Just let me handle this on my own, OK?"

"Well, all right, but think about what I said and let me know how you're doing."

"Yes ... of course." Handing him an envelope, she raised her smile to a professional level. "It's all in order. We just have to sign and set a date."

"Smooth changing the subject," Gene remarked and then he glanced at the title. "Mountain View Medical Clinic. Catchy, but not as catchy as

'Dr. Shonberg and Associates.' Why don't you just change the name to yours?"

"Think about it. *Carlin* sounds like someone who plants potatoes. I want relaxing, but I don't want to put my patients into a coma. 'Mountain View' sounds uplifting and healing."

"True. Are you sure you're ready to take over the whole operation?"

"Well, it's either that or find those scalpels. I got to get rid of you somehow. ..." As he chuckled, she smiled kindly and lowered her tone. "Gene, I'm not the only one in this room who has no life. This would be good for both of us and you know it."

"Oh no, you don't get to make this conversation about me. You—"

"Sure I do," Donna interrupted, "When's the last time *you* went on a date? We're not all that different, only I'm prepared to move forward."

Anne poked her head in and Gene waved an acknowledgment. "Well for now, move forward into exam room one. They're lined up solid this afternoon."

As Donna stepped out with her doctor-face firmly on, he had to admit, she was good.

(No one takes a position as convincingly as her, even when she's the only one being convinced.)

***

If Donna had been honest with Gene and with herself for that matter, she would have recognized how badly depressed she was, but work was important to her. It was the one thing that wouldn't die like Jen or refuse her calls like Jack. She had given up phoning him, resigned to the end of a wonderful and terrible friendship. The last time they spoke was several months ago. It was awful and she was left feeling that what was once a bad situation was now quite hopeless.

She had survived their dramatic exchange on the park bench crushed, but within days, longing for him gradually replaced her anger and resentment. Soon after, even that dissolved into the simple need for a friend.

Her apologetic call only roused responses distant and cautious. Unsatisfied, she kept calling, trying to present herself as the old buddy he was used to but the damage was done. He didn't return her messages, and when she did manage to catch him at home, he made excuses to get off the phone. He wouldn't even agree to meet at The Bean—neutral territory if ever there were any—muttering, "Coffee is never just coffee. No more, Donna."

She was amazed Jack thought her capable of that kind of duplicity after all the truths that had come to light. She certainly wasn't stupid enough to continue pushing his affections, especially if they were only sexual. With a growing despondency, she faced the possibility of never seeing him again.

It wasn't until months later when she realized his meaning. Afraid of being faced with the same opportunity, he would succumb to the temptations of the sin. He had clearly stated celibacy was a challenge for him. Was any woman a danger or chiefly her? Insecurity begged an answer and caused Donna to second-guess herself at every turn.

She must have been wrong about him for a long time. In high school, she thought they would continue to be close, and the assumption had stuck like a bad habit, through his early crush and then hers returned, but the reality was that they were never as close as they should have been. He'd buried his feelings when she was seeing Ric, and he practically fell off the face of the earth when his ex-girlfriend left him.

The most important events of their lives were shared only after time saw fit to distort them. Reduced to manageable little memories stored in small corners of their minds, they were easy to take out and examine and display, their real qualities shrunken to nothing. Jack never saw the bruise Ric left, nor heard her trembling voice describe the terror he'd caused. And Donna had been engrossed in her studies when Jack was healing himself in Red Deer. Only introduced to these facts well after they ceased to be relevant, how close are two people who don't share their deepest secrets until clutching each other in heated passion?

Everywhere, she saw him. Not just in strange men walking along the street, but in ads and products and phrases. "Jumping jacks, Carjacking, Jack of clubs, Jackpot, Jack-o'-lantern, Jack Frost …" There was a Jack for every season and Donna saw him in everyone, her heart leaping into her throat each time a muscular man passed by.

Who had he seen when he was with her?

Having three people in bed can't be explained away in ten or ten-thousand words. It would always stay between them, as long as they knew each other. So, Jack had taken the simplest approach and just cut her out of the equation.

Filling her spare time with anything to distract her from Jack's absence, the gym became her second home. Every night after work, she put in two hard hours, too focused to chat with prospective dates. At home, books and TV filled the evening's edges. Not exciting, but it kept the tears at bay. Singularly insulated.

Today would be no different. At 5:30, Donna was ready to change into her fitness gear. She held the biking shorts in her hand, but reminded of

Gene's concern, her perspective suddenly took a different light. His gentle worries alerted her that she should give herself a much needed break. Working ten hours a day and probably over-exercising on top of that was considered red-flag behavior in diagnosing her own patients.

Abruptly, she twisted around and tossed the shorts into her gym bag. Collecting her purse from the desk drawer, Donna locked the office to run an important errand, one long overdue.

***

The paper cup warmed her fingers as she walked purposefully across the grounds. She didn't really want the coffee, but after all of their meetings at The Bean, it seemed appropriate to have one in hand. This was a pretty area, one swelling grassy rise after another. Headstones and flat plaques created solid rows, which would stop for a while and then suddenly continue a little further on. In between, sections of poplar trees stretched toward the sky. The scenery boasted its resiliency, green leaves bursting from every tree, branches swaying with the strong westerly wind. Donna was glad it was windy; Calgary could be so hot in July without the breezes that often swept down from the mountains.

She found the modest plaque in a small central section of the grounds.

Jennifer Robin Brammon
October 20, 1968–July 24, 1998
Never Forgotten

Donna stared at the simple wording etched into the stone. It just didn't convey the real person behind it. Kneeling down, she tucked one leg under her and set the cup down on the ground.

(Jen, it's been a whole year and it's still not real to me—you going. I didn't pay attention during the funeral. And I still catch myself talking to you, like you're a phone call away. ... I don't know how to go on from here. I thought I was always independent, but I was never really alone until now. You and Jack were always around to fill in the gaps, keep me guessing, keep me sane. I still hurt over him too, ache for him, even if we could just go back to being friends. ...)

Fresh tears welled up in her eyes. God, was she ever going to get past this stuff? She bent her head into one hand and quietly cried.

At the height of her tears, a sudden conspicuous sensation passed over her. She straightened up, not wanting a stranger to witness her emotional moments ... but no one was there. Confusion rose as the feeling continued. Then, she relaxed and let it slide over her, through her. An image accompanied it, just out of focus.

(Someone propped up on an elbow, eating something.)

Donna tried to make the picture clearer, but it stayed a bit fuzzy as if visible only through her peripheral vision. Glancing to her right and gazing steadily at the patch of grass, she imagined more than what was concretely there. Calmness stole over her and absorbed all her heartfelt emotions. She was left with an intellectual perception of Jen. Devoid of those earlier tears, it lacked sorrow and guilt and shame. No room for dramatic enhancements. She sensed its position in her mind on such a base level, it seemed to exist all on its own, the simplest of concepts leaving no space for sad questions, much like Jen.

Time passed as it slowly diffused. She imagined the wind carrying it lightly upward, over the bending branches of the trees and away into the evening. She wasn't sorry to see it go. In its place, Donna was filled with a glimpse of her former strong self. It wasn't much, but from it she derived a tiny spark of optimism. This was the way she felt years ago without consciously being aware. She hadn't realized the strength existing inside until it peeked around the corner to wave at her again.

Now, without harsh glare, Jen's absence was cushioned in calm reflection. There was a spark of her left behind in this grass, in the cloudless sky, even in the steam of the coffee. Blending with affectionate memories in Donna's mind, it created a distinction she could almost taste ... like peanut butter smoothly mixed into a bagel.

Donna sat quietly beside the stone for a while, and then went home with a small measure of balance returned to her heart. As she walked away, the untouched cup sat squarely on the ground, a peace offering for her neglected friend.

***

CHAPTER 32

"I'm going to go now if it's all right with you."

Glancing at the clock, Donna exclaimed, "Oh, I'm sorry. I didn't mean for you to stay so late. I'm totally behind."

Anne handed her a steaming mug of tea and Donna perched it on a stack of files strewn across the desk.

"Thanks. Yikes, that's hot!"

"Sorry. Normally it's not a problem. It's just that I have to be somewhere shortly."

There was a bright tone to Anne's voice.

Donna smiled slyly and asked, "And does somewhere involve someone?"

"Well ... yes. I met a guy a while ago and he's finally asked me out. We're going to a really nice restaurant. I haven't known him long, but I think it has a lot of potential. I hope it does anyway. He's picking me up at six."

"Where are you going?"

"Can't remember the name. Something Italian."

"Italian's good. Italian's *romantic*, definitely a good start."

Blushing, Anne's eyes dropped down to the desk. She had the kind of face that displayed every thought and feeling, and lately it was full of uplifting smiles. At least someone was happy.

"Stop looking at me like that! It's just dinner."

"Dinner's foreplay. It's what happens later that I'll want a report on."

"Donna!" Anne laughed, "Trust me. There'll be nothing to hear about."

"Well, just don't do anything drastic. You know, tattoos, piercings, head shaving ... not that you have a lot to shave right now."

"I think I'll be pretty safe. This guy is Mr. Conservative. Anyway," Anne pinched a lock of her hair, "this is as short as it gets. You should try it. It's less work."

"No changing the subject. Be gone with you, oh cryptic one. Go be with Mr. Conservative." Donna dismissed her assistant with a flick of her pen.

"See you tomorrow."

"Good night."

It took Donna another half-hour to finish her work. She went straight to the gym, but felt distracted by Anne and her active love life.

Anne was a free spirit, the kind who was happy wherever she ended up. The combination of this buoyant charm and the experience at the cemetery gave Donna an objective insight into how morose she'd been, how necessary it was to snap out of her useless depression.

In the locker room, she studied her hair in the mirror and imagined it cropped. Some people could wear short hair really well, but she never considered herself in that category.

After brushing it back and holding it out of sight, she turned to profile the downward slope of her chin. It was a versatile face, not too square, not too round. Her cheekbones appeared more prominent. Her neck seemed longer and slimmer and the details of her face stood out.

(Yes, I could use a change and maybe this would be a good place to start.)

She made an appointment with her regular hairstylist for the following week.

"The usual trim?"

Donna's expression was determined. "No, Allie. Surprise me. Just make it short."

"Really?"

"Really."

"You're sure?"

"Positive."

To underscore the point, Donna relaxed with a magazine and refused to watch the process. Blonde locks fell in small piles on the floor. Finally, Allie announced she was finished.

Donna looked up and burst out laughing.

(Damn it Jen, I'm a doctor, not an engineer!)

She hadn't worn short hair since grade twelve, when her friends compared her appearance to Nurse Chapel. And they were right—this person in the mirror belonged on the Star Ship Enterprise. She remembered Jen convincing them of Chapel's ability to take over command and run things. With amusement, she envisioned traveling through space and time to save the universe.

As her laughter slowed down, she saw Allie's mortified expression and Donna was immediately ashamed.

"I'm sorry. It looks great. I really like it. It just reminded me of something." Then, studying herself again, she made a sudden decision. "Listen, do you have time to dye my hair? I don't think blonde suits me anymore."

They chose a dark brown shade. Donna also had her eyebrows and eyelashes dyed to match. When she left the salon, she looked like a different person. On her way out, she tipped Allie well, still conscious of her earlier blunder.

The change was refreshing and long overdue. She decided to set up a series of facials and manicures. They made her feel pampered in an elegant way. Finally, she bought some outfits to emphasize her fit body.

People, who previously worried about her, now commented on her radiant style. The first time Paula saw the new Donna, she was especially supportive, but Raymond's reaction was different.

Donna had always resembled her mother and now she was the spitting image. Her entrance into their kitchen with a bag of bagels, sporting her new look, threw him back to his days with Patricia. Raymond looked at her and saw the woman who transformed him into a single parent so long ago. Patricia had often worn this exact shade of red, a rust color that set off her brown hair and made her complexion glow. His eyes went wide. Then he stammered, trying to think of something nice to say.

Paula saved him by gushing over her. "How wonderful. I always wanted to do something like that with my hair. It really suits you. You know, when people shorten their hair, it usually makes them look older, but you look at least five years younger."

Paula's words were kind, but Donna couldn't mistake the utter separation between her father and herself. He'd looked at her just now as though she'd broken into his house. With sadness, she concluded that they'd likely never regain the closeness they shared during her youth. At least Paula's enthusiasm served to relinquish the blame Donna constantly attributed to her. Maybe this woman had created the distance between father and daughter, but Raymond clearly needed no prompting to continue it.

He stayed in the kitchen, trying to reestablish a jovial mood over tea, but no matter how light the conversation was, Donna's voice kept coming out of Patricia's mouth. Finally, he thought the best way to compliment her would be to take her picture. Excusing himself, he hid around the corner with the camera.

Donna shook her head, whispering. "You know, if he didn't hoof around like a damned elephant, he might actually get a natural shot of someone."

Paula nodded. There were no truly candid photos of her either.

"Just hide it," Donna suggested, "That's what I used to do."

"I do. He keeps finding it. I think he put a homing device on it or something."

Donna was sitting perched on the chair in her usual way: one leg tucked under, one knee up, an elbow resting on her raised knee. And just then, an old memory came to mind.

(Where'd you learn to be a pretzel? Where'd you learn to inhale food?)

Donna could see the Rummoli board as clear as day. It was a good memory to pass through her head at that moment. As Raymond stepped into the kitchen, his camera poised, she turned sideways toward him and smiled broadly with her chin resting in the palm of her hand.

Click!

Raymond thought this picture would turn out beautifully. Her blouse was an excellent contrast in this bright kitchen lighting, and that dark hair made her green eyes stand out. She showed such a deep smile. It was so deep, he felt forgiven for treating her strangely earlier.

The evening was considerably more pleasant than it had started, but not due to Raymond's efforts. The lovely memory of Jack and Jen, that simple moment demonstrated to Donna how much of her life had been meaningful. In the past, good things seemed to fall into her lap, but from now on, she would have to work to create them. She resolved to concentrate on what she could have, rather than what she was missing.

At work, Donna seemed like a new woman. She was even livelier in spirit. The short hair enhanced her face, drawing attention to her light skin and soft smile, and the new clothes presented an attractive air of sophistication. It had been so long since she felt appealing without the fantasy of Jack's hands tracing the image. A beautiful woman with an open future.

Her professional practice was thriving, so much that Gene accepted her offer to take over the business. With the first legible signature she'd penned in years, Donna became the sole owner of the newly formed "Mountain View Medical Clinic" ... and Gene's boss. She chose against listing their names as part of the title to allow for future adjustments in staff, including Gene's imminent retirement. The place would be all hers.

For the first time in years, she felt good things were right around the corner.

***

A vague feeling of rejuvenation gripped the heels of August. September seemed a month of renewal, always signifying changes in Donna's life: the start of a fresh school year, moving out on her own, the escape from Ric, even employment with Gene ... as though September were some pivotal point when time would fold in on itself and start over again. The changes were always challenging ones, forcing her to take on a little more of the world, and sometimes she wondered how much of herself she unwittingly relinquished in the process.

The first week of the month was steady as far as her clientele was concerned, no more nor less busy than most times of the year, but she had taken Gene's advice to heart by strategically scheduling in breaks, which eliminated that extra paperwork into the dinner hour.

Then there were the constant interruptions: patients needing a prescription phoned into the pharmacy, or worried they were dying of some obscure disease, the symptoms being invariably minor. And of course, it was imperative they speak with Dr. Carlin *right now.*

Anne was superb at handling the persistent ones. She would talk in such a soothingly persuasive way, that by the end of the conversation, they were happy to make an appointment and forget about their troubles until then. So on September seventh, it was with genuine regret that Donna received Anne's news.

"I have to give you two things. First this."

She placed a small box on top of Donna's stack of files. Donna pulled off the bright ribbon and lifted the lid.

"Anne! It's not my birthday."

"I remembered you whining about all your boy jewelry. I figured this would go with your new look. Is silver OK?"

"I prefer silver ... but Anne, this face is exquisite! I've been so used to the sporty digital stuff, I've forgotten what girl watches look like. *Obviously* overpaying you ... Thank you so much. It's gorgeous, but why?"

"Well, I'm buttering you up for this other thing I have to give you."

What?" Donna asked, clipping the watch around her wrist. Too tight. There, just right. The time was already set correctly. Only Anne would be so considerate.

"My resignation. I'm moving to Halifax."

Donna gaped. "OK, take the watch back. I'll keep you."

Anne smiled uncomfortably.

"Why are you moving?"

"My boyfriend is going and he's asked me to live with him."

With honest sincerity, Donna congratulated Anne. "When will you need to leave work?"

"What's today? The seventh? We're going to move at the end of the month, so I can work until then."

"We'll be sorry to see you go. You've done an excellent job. I don't know how I'm going to replace you. Is your boyfriend taking a job there? I'm sorry—I don't even know his name."

"It's Jack. Jack Petrasyk. No, he doesn't have a job lined up. It's odder than that. He's been looking for his biological father for a few years. A couple of months ago, he found him in Halifax. They've never met. They wrote some letters and now his dad wants to meet him. It's quite exciting. I thought Jack would want to see him on his own, but he really wants me to be with him. In fact, we plan to open a business of our own out there. Are you OK? You look a little pale."

Numb inside, Donna's ears heard that magic name and her mind ground to a screeching halt in the middle of the conversation. Jack. *Her* Jack was moving across the country with another woman. What had happened to his Christian principles that he could meet one young lady and suddenly decide to live in sin? The injustice of his moral defection was utterly painful after he had clearly used it as the means of dividing himself from Donna, even from her friendship.

(It can't be the same person. It has to be another Jack!)

As the thought dripped with denial, her knees bent unsteadily. She groped for the chair behind her and practically fell onto it. In that split-second between standing and sitting, Donna was encased in vertigo, a sickening feeling of falling through space, waiting for the jolt of injury versus the cushion of safety. When her arms landed on the arms of the chair, Jack raced through her mind. His face, his hair, his body, and especially his arms. *He* should be catching her.

"I'm fine. I … didn't eat much today."

"You want an orange? I have one here."

"Oh, no thanks. Ah, what kind of business will you be opening?"

"A sort of healthy fast food outlet. I know that sounds corny, but it's an idea he's had for a while."

"What does Jack do for a living now?"

"He's a cop. He's done that for about six years, but he's ready for a change."

"How so?"

"I guess a friend of his died last year and he doesn't have any other ties here—I mean except for his mom, but apparently they're not very close—so it's an easy choice for him. I hope this is enough notice. I'll give you a formal resignation tomorrow. You know, you really don't look very good. I'll get you that orange. Doug Skeet is in exam room one, but I have to take his BP still. Here ..."

Anne reached into a paper bag and extended the offering to Donna. The orange held her transfixed, cueing something on the edge of her mind. Jack was supposed to be hers, and she was being offered a watch and this round object instead.

Finally, she said, "No, Anne. It's yours," as she carried Mr. Skeet's file into exam room one.

***

"Jack, I can't get this thing to print!"

Anne glared at the machine. Maybe one of his pictures had fallen into it or something. He was a decorating moron, one of those guys who taped photos onto walls and mirrors instead of buying decent picture frames. They were always falling down and then he'd just retape them. Or they were packed into envelopes and stuffed into drawers. It was a guy thing. Pictures deserved presentation, proper albums and frames. She would change that in their new place.

Wandering in, he leaned over the desk and stated, "You're in the wrong screen. What are you trying to print?"

"My resignation."

"It'll cost ya."

"I'll make you some cookies."

"Not what I was thinkin', but hey, cookies work too."

Jack hit the right buttons in the right sequence and the printer sprang to life. A minute later, when he was handing her a copy, one line caught his eye.

"To: Dr. Donna Carlin"

He looked closely at the paper and asked, "Is this a second job?"

"No, Donna—Dr. Carlin owns the clinic. She bought it from Dr. Shonberg, but I mostly work under her anyway, so now it's just official. She's the one who actually hired me. I'll miss her. She's a good boss." Anne saw Jack's odd expression and quickly added, "But you know I'm excited about going with you. She listened to me babble about you—I hope that's OK. I know it's personal, but I feel really close to her."

For a long moment, Jack was totally speechless as his thoughts funneled into one focused line. Never had he expected this part of his life to cross into Anne's. And here they were working side by side the whole time he'd known her.

Respecting confidentiality, Anne never discussed the details of her job. Co-workers and patients were equally deserving in her mind. They stayed at work and that's the way it should be. Anne had specified that he was to call her on her cell phone, to leave her work line open for patients. During lunch though, he called the clinic anyway and heard, "Good afternoon, Mountain View Medical." The last he knew, Donna worked for someone named Shonberg. How could he have known? He should speak now. Any subsequent confession would seem planned, falsified.

(Do it. Do it now!)

Jack blinked a few times and then smiled. "Oh, sure, that's fine."

What else could he say? No, that's not fine. She was someone I got tangled up in for years before *she* got tangled up in *me*? It was done with.

He would have taken Anne's hand, but his were suddenly clammy. Instead, he gave her waist a squeeze and walked back to the living room.

Everything seemed to lead back to Donna. Would he suddenly run into her in Halifax? Wasn't any part of his life off-limits?

"Are you working tonight?" Anne called from the bedroom.

"Uh-huh," he answered distractedly, then raising his voice, "I have to leave right away."

His shift wasn't scheduled for a couple of hours, but he needed some time to think alone, and minutes later, shock finally gave way to racing thoughts as he clutched a steaming coffee at The Bean. It was disturbing to discover a close connection between the only two people he hoped would never meet. At least, Donna hadn't said anything about him. Of that, he was certain. She was simply too honorable ... and she was probably over him anyway.

***

Donna stood alone in the doorway of her office. She had seen patients, written prescriptions, and taken notes until the last person left. Hardly aware of anything, she functioned by closing her mind and diagnosing the people in front of her. After gingerly shutting her office door, she leaned back against it. The stack of files in her arms fell one by one, slowly at first, then cascading madly around her feet. Her body immediately followed in a haphazard slide all the way to the floor, and she sat there numbly.

Slowly, she became conscious of her heart beating. It felt almost ... loud. The sound filled her chest until there was no room to breathe. Her lungs cried out for air, as if her brain had forgotten how to coordinate that function. Breathing became panting, shallow and fast, and then the dizziness started.

(Panic attack. Just a panic attack. So this is what it feels like, your chest and throat being crushed. Oh God, I never want to die of suffocation. I can't breathe!)

She'd treated numerous cases of panic attacks, but despite recognizing the symptoms in herself, the surreal sensations still floored her.

Minutes rolled by while she held her head in her hands, wanting to cry, wanting to scream, wanting something. The dizziness finally dissipated and her breathing steadied its pace, but that mental tornado kept rolling around inside her with nowhere to go. Powerless to pull her out of this, it was as if her body had reached its limit and refused to feel anything more. If she could feel, then it would be real ... and that just couldn't be.

***

CHAPTER 33

Gliding smoothly through sable streets, the cruiser's white exterior reflected the passing glare of streetlamps to defiantly toss each light aside, the way a shark cuts cleanly through its habitat, searching for anything out of the ordinary. An urban predator.

Night shifts tended to be all or nothing. They were called to emergencies, which were either completely out of hand or completely false. Jack was the senior officer tonight. His partner had only put in a few months and it really showed. He reminded Jack of himself in his rookie days: eager, attentive, and peppering his superiors with questions. It was privately reassuring that Jack knew most of the answers.

After six years on the job, he'd seen a lot of bizarre situations. Calgarians possessed no real awareness of the subcultures existing there. Comprised of a hundred different kinds of people, all groups thought they were the dominant factor. *They* made up Calgary, not the others. *They* had this specific situation for the police to straighten out. *Their* needs counted far above anyone else. Jack knew every person he encountered on the job held this perception. He used to derive a bit of humor from this, but it was getting harder to look at things from a light standpoint.

The time had come to leave and meet his father, and Anne was a logical person to include. Jack had always seemed surrounded by sharp-witted and strong-willed women, but Anne's ways were naturally gentle. She made him feel capable while dissolving his stresses.

It was her idea to send Frank Petrasyk a letter to introduce himself; a phone call out of the blue would have been too tense for both of them. Watching the envelope fall into the mailbox, Jack's heart swung nervously between his hopes and fears, until four weeks later he received a letter back with a phone number. The area code was 902, Halifax. Over and over, Jack stared at the numbers and the polite invitation to use them soon.

Finally, soon became now. That first call was stilted as the two men struggled with their words.

His father confessed, "I almost didn't send the reply."

"I understand. It took me a long time to send my letter. But I'm glad I did and I'm glad you answered it." Jack's cautious empathy seemed to make the difference and they waded less warily through the conversation.

"I had a ring I think was yours."

"Had?"

"Yeah, it's gone. If I knew where it was, I'd give it back to you."

A studied pause. "What does it look like?"

"Small, steel, little marks all over it. It fit my small finger."

He heard his father exhale briefly on the other end. "Oh, I thought I'd lost that thing. She must have taken it. Well, it doesn't matter," he answered softly.

"I was wondering ... What did you wear it for? I mean, was it special?"

"It's an engineering ring. I got it after I finished my degree." Frank chuckled, adding, "That was about a million years ago. I used to work in chemical engineering, but I haven't been in that field for a long time. It's been at least ... I'd say twenty-five years or more."

The satisfaction of long-awaited answers was quietly overshadowed by a sheen of guilt; his father's property would never be returned, even if it magically appeared right this minute. The ring had created a connection with Frank long before the phone did, and with so many years invested in that one object, it represented something consistent in a sad boy's life. Solid and unending in its circularity, it meant too much, especially since it went missing. Garnering hope for lost items was a baleful endeavor. He'd sure learned that.

"I can't speak for Mark, but I'd like to meet you."

"Who's Mark?"

"My brother ... your other son."

"Not mine. I never had any other kids."

"Um, maybe we left before you knew about him."

"Still can't take credit for him. I got snipped right after you were born. Look, don't feel bad about this, but the truth is I never planned to have any kids."

It made perfect sense. There had always been something about his brother, *half* brother that didn't mesh. When Jack said "day", Mark said "night", the animosities subtle only as long as they didn't stumble too far into each other's space. This made Jack Frank's only offspring, even if unintended, and for the first time in his life, he felt securely rooted. He now had a family tree and he was the only branch.

Even so, it was a shock to hear the man state so matter-of-factly that Jack's birth was an accident. The thought of being unwanted right from the start had never crossed his mind. Having always assumed both parents valued his existence, at least in the beginning, it threw him for a loop, but he took heart in the possibility that what was missing with Mark and his mother might finally be filled in by this man on the phone. He paced his questions, trying to hide his eagerness to learn all the details that made up his father.

Their similarities were startling. Frank was an athletic man with a stocky build. After spending three years in the military, he left to take up engineering and finally a trade in welding. With skills he pulled together over the years, he gradually built his own business into a decent living.

They stayed away from talking about Frank's early life with Jack's mother. There would be enough time for that topic face to face. Only one clue was offered as to the marital breakup—Frank made an obscure reference to some past problems with alcohol.

***

Al's keys wouldn't fit. After a minute, he realized why. He was swaying too much. But this was important—the store wasn't within walking distance. A six-pack would get him through the night nicely, a case even better.

He peered at the car door, eyes concentrated into slits, and willed all his available steadiness into his hand. Finally, the key slid into the lock and a desperate relief stole through him.

He had lost weight again. His pants hung loosely around his hips as he fell onto the front seat of the vehicle. Glancing shakily at the interior, pieces of the past came to life: his daughter in her booster seat, his son in the baby seat, Tracy beside him.

(Well, maybe not the best memory, but two out of three ain't bad!)

He snickered at the jovial way he handled the thought of her. He would have to tell that one to the sponsor, if he ever got around to phoning the guy. Al was just under such stress these days. Nobody understood what he was up against. Work was a nightmare. After losing two positions with oil and gas firms, he took on contracts when he controlled the bottle and turned them down in the reverse.

A good chunk of cash went to Tracy every month. Al agreed to supervised visits, disappointed he wouldn't be allowed to see his kids alone, but there was a further condition in the fine print of the divorce settlement; Tracy was required to authorize the supervisor. He hadn't foreseen the powerful hand she could play, because apparently, she thought *no one* was good enough to watch her ex-husband and their kids together.

At first, he threw himself into numerous contracts, biding his time until she would give in, but then an accident occurred on a job. A co-worker was killed in an explosion and Al realized how easily it could have been him. He drank badly after that and was afraid to commit to more jobs. Several child support payments were missed, twelve-thousand dollars' worth. And now, she was threatening to sue, like she didn't have anything better to do with her time.

"Sue? For what?" he shouted into the phone.

"For money to support your kids!" she had shouted back.

"What kids? Oh, the ones I never see ...?"

She was even screwing a cop now. Asshole got to see Al's kids more than he did.

Yeah, he could really use a six-pack, maybe a case. He started the car and maneuvered down the street. There was a liquor store near the university. Better get there quick before they closed.

Unfortunately, it was almost three in the morning. The liquor store closed at midnight.

***

Donna was surprised to look down at her new watch; two hours had passed. The files were sitting neatly on the floor in front of her. When did she do that? She picked herself up and placed the pile on her desk, but instead of finishing them, wandered out of the office with only a set of car keys in hand.

She drove aimlessly that evening, weaving through streets as though lost. At some timeless point, the evening blended into night. White lines divided the dark pavement and flew by uninterrupted, hypnotically creating a straight pattern out of simple painted rectangles. Each one came up fast and then disappeared behind the car. They were like the patients she saw day in and day out, one after another. She treated them and then they disappeared into their own lives, as if they'd never been there in the first place ... like Jack.

Every altered relationship danced before her. She saw her mother there one minute and gone the next. Her father had walked down the aisle with Paula and never looked back. Donna needed Jen's strength, right when Jen needed hers the most. She was cut off from the Brammons in a way that allowed no real time to adjust to Jen's death. And then Jack followed on their heels.

Everyone had walked away in one form or another, but Jack's departure was the worst. He left willingly. At least her father still tried to include her in his life, but Jack had made a clean break.

"Jack. Jack Petrasyk," Anne said, blissfully unaware that those five syllables jammed a knife into Donna's back.

Turning onto Crowchild Trail, she drove south along the empty freeway. Little white lines everywhere. Even missing one, the pattern would continue with barely a glitch. In the wink of an eye, she could skip two or three of them and hardly care. What was the importance of any one line? They were as easily overlooked as most things in life: ragged clothes, faded pictures, their usefulness brief and unacknowledged. She was just like one of those lines, sitting on the road stubbornly, while the people she knew left her behind. They were all miles ahead. Jack had moved so far out of reach, she could barely see him.

As her car picked up speed, so did her anger. And her pain. The speed limit was eighty kilometers, but with so few traffic lights, she easily surpassed it. Faster and faster, trying to outrun betrayal and despair. She had gone up against God and Jack's ex-girlfriend and couldn't cut it, but her chipper little assistant could change his convictions in an instant.

There were no cars to steer around. Headlights of a single vehicle were briefly visible in the north-bound lane. It passed by in the other direction slowly, but Donna barely registered the weaving car.

She saw the university ahead ... and the solid concrete wall just off the road. If she hit it straight on, she would feel nothing. Her fingers flicked open the seatbelt lock to allow the nylon fabric to snake across her chest toward the door. Donna's eyes opened wide at the concrete block looming larger as she gripped the steering wheel tightly. Closer and closer it came, and still she kept her focus.

But at the very last second, a sudden sense of familiarity overwhelmed her.

(I've seen this before!)

Stepping outside of herself with intense clarity, it was as if someone grabbed the wheel and yanked it hard. The car spun sharply, narrowly missing the wall. Rolling from the momentum and propelling Donna with it, she was thrown around the interior like a pinball. Up and over and over again. Three times it flipped on the university grass, and almost a fourth, edging out of its speed. Poised on two side tires rearing the undercarriage up, it slammed back down to become no more than a steaming heap.

***

Jack motioned for the rookie to turn into the parking lot ahead. When Constable Dellasandro stopped the car, he took one look at the building and said, "You're not serious."

"I'll have one with chocolate icing and see if they have those little sprinkles too. Oh, and a large coffee, black."

"I'm not going in there."

"Yes, you are."

"No, I'm not."

"Who's senior here?"

"Pull rank all you want. You're getting your own fucking doughnut ... Sir."

Jack's smiling response was interrupted as static broke in. "10-1, serious traffic accident, Crowchild Trail and Brisebois Drive Northwest, single vehicle, EMS dispatched, requested Delta Response."

Jack lifted the transmitter to his mouth, "We copy, on our way." He turned to the rookie. "We'll pick this up later."

Dellasandro switched on the flashing lights and sped down the street.

"Let me know everything you're doing as you're doing it, and if you're unsure about anything, you ask. Clear?"

"Clear. What if the ambulance is there first?"

"Let's hope they are. They're the ones who can deal with that stuff best. Just hope the reporters don't beat them to it."

A minute later, they were first on the scene. It looked pretty bad. They followed two skid marks on Crowchild Trail, swerving through a patch of grass where a car had struck a lamppost. There appeared to be one occupant in the front driver's side. Jack could hear an ambulance siren approaching from the south.

The two officers ran swiftly to the vehicle. Safety first. Jack stepped around the front of the car and squatted to look underneath. Electrical cords, sparks, gas? No obvious dangers.

The hood was folded around the base of the lamppost. Its light was flickering and the post angled away as if trying to escape the vehicle.

Jack pointed his flashlight at the windshield. There was a star-shaped design where the driver's head had struck it, and corresponding patches of dark red creating the image of stained-glass, the kind in Jack's church. It obscured his sight of the victim, who was wrestling with the door. Battered and scraped in the crash, it resisted. The driver's side window was gone, except for a serrated line of pieces pointing up from the door. A tiny row of transparent mountains.

Dellasandro yanked on the door several times and finally jerked it open. He leaned in to tell the driver not to move, but the person didn't seem to hear him. One bloody hand grabbed at the doorframe. The other reached out toward Dellasandro. The officer automatically put his own arm out and Jack wished he'd instructed the rookie to put on gloves.

The victim swung his legs to the ground, almost losing his balance, and lifted himself to stand. Damp grass shifted under his runners; one leg slid sideways, but he caught himself with a wide predatory stance. Lines of blood were flowing down his face from a gash on his forehead. Drops fell onto the grass from his chin. His chest looked sunken in and he was struggling to breathe. One little gasp after another.

It was painful to watch. With the steering wheel bent and pushed into the dashboard, the impact must have driven his sternum right into his lungs. Of all the injuries people could get in a car, chest compression was the worst. Something as natural as breathing would cause unbearable pain. Regardless of injuries, panic alone could send them into shock.

(My God, how can this guy move?)

A split-second later, the officers realized why; he was loaded. Probably had seventeen broken bones and felt nothing.

Dellasandro steadied him. At first, the man let him. Then he peered at the officer, his face changing expression from stunned confusion to malice. Sneering, he reached behind him.

Dellasandro said, "Hey, just relax." Glancing at Jack, he exclaimed, "This guy's gonna bleed all over his ID."

"Don't touch him. Go get gloves," Jack barked impatiently as he stepped forward to intercede.

(Note to self—put in request for smarter rookies!)

Then Jack saw what the man was grasping behind his back. He heard him say, 'Yeah, I got sumpin fer you buddy,' as a shiny metallic object was brought around front and shoved up against Dellasandro's neck. The rookie froze in place.

"You thing you cin take ma kidz too?"

Jack grabbed his own gun and whipped it around to point straight at the man's ribcage. Dellasandro was facing Jack, his eyes wide. Jack would have a good shot through the empty driver's side window, and he adjusted his stance so the assailant's neck, shoulders, and chest were exposed.

"Police! Don't move! Put it down NOW!"

The drunk half turned toward the new voice with a small staggering movement, and it was enough to make him lower his gun arm to keep his balance. The metal piece dipped ungracefully away from Dellasandro's neck, sweeping down and across his chest in a jerking motion. The rookie jumped backward and pulled out his forty-cal.

Snapping out of his frozen state, he started yelling along with Jack, who barely heard him over his own bellowing voice, "DROP YOUR WEAPON!"

The man swiveled, having forgotten the first cop, and turned to set his sights on the other one.

(Was she screwing all of them?)

He tried to aim the gun, but at best, merely waved it in Jack's direction. Lunging haphazardly, the gun searched for a target in Jack for a full second, the longest second of his life. His eyes hypnotically followed it, swinging here … swinging there … a jagged pendulum slowing down to center on its midpoint. Back and forth, side to side …

Then a powerful shot rang out, piercing the air in a deadly race toward Jack.

***

PART III

MEETING JACK

CHAPTER 34

She was dizzy from rolling so much. The toboggan skidded down the hill and they were falling over each other. Donna was thrown sideways as Jen bounced off the car. She wondered when the hard curb would shoot pain along the side of her body and up into her head. Then, the cops would keep asking her stupid questions when she just wanted to sleep.

A million compressed memories played out their tale in mere seconds—school, work, pain, laughter, fear, desires, his face so clear and unreachable, her heart torn—as she spun over and over and over.

(No!)

As soon as the word entered her head, she stopped to lie still on the soft ground. For a minute, the world kept spinning. Though desperately trying to catch her breath, she couldn't shake the sickening feeling of having the wind knocked out of her. Why did they go tobogganing? A movie would have been safer. Where was she? But as she stretched her mind toward the answer, it slid elusively into the pool of darkness, almost taking her with it.

She struggled to grasp her surroundings. They were so black, except the glow of a light shining near. A streetlamp? Lying just outside of its circle, its luminescence only swelled far enough to leave her partly in the dark. Still on her back, she blinked and peered around, then shifted her head to a silhouette of towering trees against a clouded sky. Something was wrong here. They didn't look right. ...

There was no snow on them! How could they be tobogganing with no snow? Where was Jack? Where was Jen? Oh, right, she had been too sick to come, but where was the snow? This was so weird.

The shapes around her gradually faded as she slipped back into the darkness.

***

The call came at 5:30. Abruptly, Raymond dropped the phone back to its cradle, as if an obscene caller had ruined his sleep. Springing out of bed, he grabbed a shirt hanging over a chair.

At the feel of his weight lifting off the bed, Paula stirred. Though a heavy sleeper, she was still sensitive to her husband's restlessness. She turned on her bedside lamp and squinted with one hand shielding her eyes.

"Ray?"

"Where are my jeans? Where!"

Paula sat up on one elbow. "What's going on?" she asked weakly.

At first he ignored her, intent on finding the missing pants. She watched him lift pieces off a pile of folded laundry and throw them aside in a futile search, creating disarray in his path.

Alarm quickly replaced sleepiness.

"Ray, what happened?"

He stopped, frozen. Then, his shoulders slumped and a big breath escaped his chest. It felt as though a huge weight sat dead center, which barely allowed the words out.

"Donna's been in an accident."

"How serious?"

"Serious."

Raymond spotted his jeans peeking out from under the bed and pulled them on. As he slid the shirt over his head, Paula realized that if she wasted another moment, he would leave without her. She got out of bed and started dressing.

He wanted to tell her not to bother coming—that Donna was his responsibility—but he didn't argue the point. They rushed out of the house and into the car, where Paula maneuvered herself obstinately into the driver's side.

"Forget it. You're not driving."

For a moment, he stared at her and then quickly moved around to the passenger side.

Powerlessness smothered him all the way to the hospital as white road lines flickered by endlessly. Staring at them helped numb his mind to the severity of the situation. Just how serious was it? Not knowing was the worst part. She could be dead before they got there.

"Go faster," he growled at Paula.

She let him out at the emergency entrance and went to park the car. Within seconds, he disappeared into the building, the way a bird narrowly escapes the hood of an oncoming vehicle.

Every minute he spent in the waiting area was like a week. Finally, a doctor led him to the ICU and explained exactly what was happening, and it was worse than he could have imagined. Raymond clung to the only crumb of hope—the preliminary pain tests on Donna's hands. Pulling one back was supposed to be a good sign.

"Know that I love you, Sweetheart. ... Know that I love you."

***

The sounds of morning gently called for her attention.

Donna opened her eyes to see a hazy, but clearer version of the earlier scene. The sky had taken on a light gray tone. In contrast, streetlamps were dimming, their job done for another night. The trees seemed friendlier with dawn to lessen their towering image. Birds were calling out to each other, organizing themselves for the coming day. Other sounds overlapped their chirps. Cars. Not many, but the distinct putter of an engine flowed past every so often.

Donna lay shivering. She rolled onto her side, leaned on one elbow, and rubbed her face. Trying to stand, she awkwardly fell back half expecting Jack to catch her, but no one was there. Her shirt clung to her back from the damp grass and she hardly noticed, too exhausted to care. What was she doing here in this park?

Then, recognition hit her. The university! She was lying on the university grounds and there was Crowchild Trail thirty feet in front of her. Sitting up again, she stupidly stared as another car drove by. The driver stared back. It must look pretty strange to be sitting here at ...

A glance down revealed that her watch had stopped just after 3:00. It was brand new, so what had she been doing at 3:00 to wreck her watch? Then, sluggishly weaving a path through her confusion, the specific concept of time finally jarred those blurred thoughts into place.

She remembered driving late at night, upset about something ... about what exactly?

About Jack. He was moving to Halifax. And Anne was going with him. Donna had driven her car for hours, thinking and not thinking at the same time. And then ... racing toward the wall so fast it seemed to stretch in all directions, an enormous concrete hammer ready to slam her to pieces.

The accident was not a dream. Of that, she was certain. And she was equally certain she was not fabricating this scene. Even the most vivid dream could not compare with the cold sensations of time ticking away with utter constancy. Yes, time was passing deep inside her. No surrealism to exaggerate its depth, no swift currents to selectively alter its pace. She knew this grass and these trees were real. And so was she.

These determinations chased away the alarm of waking up without her car, when her car should have been here. Could she have been thrown from the vehicle and landed unscathed? No, as soon as the idea entered her head, she dismissed it. There was no vehicle here. It *had* been here, rolling across the grass with her in it, and then just as unfailingly, it was gone.

Despite the placid scenery, fuzzy static hung in the air as if a radio dial were off a notch or two. Where was all that noise coming from?

A sharp pain dug into her index finger and she almost jumped back in surprise.

Someone was standing close, not just one person, but several. Invisible people. They were talking in crisp sentences, not in a regular kind of conversation, just blurting things out at each other. She couldn't hear the exact words. Too much static.

Frowning at her sore finger, one more trigger brought it all home. The ever-present noise dwindled and another voice joined the hum to slowly become distinct in its presence. Her hand warmed all on its own. She strained to hear the syllables almost out of reach.

(Know that I love you. ...)

It echoed in her mind with empty sadness, the image of her father.

Then the moments preceding the crash came flooding back, the way dreams sometimes do after hiding their dimensions in one's mind.

Donna saw the hard wall rushing at her and suddenly, it turned into a huge viewing screen with sections of her life displayed in no chronological order, just random scenes speeding past. She was able to register each one perfectly; more than that, she could feel, taste every element. Evolved from when she actually lived them, they were stripped of their coverings, allowing Donna to witness the absolute naked truth of each one.

Here was the ice cream cone dripping on the kitchen floor, but this time, the chocolate swirls showed an outline of her mother smiling with love. Raymond was holding her to transfer the strength he could cultivate only for her sake. In a flash, the swirls changed shape into Ric above her in bed, possessiveness alive in his eyes. The picture swiveled to erase the lovers and replace them with her dying friend. Jen gazed calmly off to the side and beckoned toward something pleasant. Donna's peace of mind for her friend reversed itself as the hospital bed was transformed into an icy street. A younger Jen lay unconscious while the stranger covered her with a blanket. Jack was helping Donna into the car as she simultaneously kneeled next to her friend on the street. Donna could feel her pain despite Jen's unconscious state, and she cried openly for her. Her blonde self seemed to stare right at her from that car. Then, her tears became tears of frustration as Jack kept the comfort of his arms just out of reach. When they did reach her, he wore a suit and she a pastel green dress to dance at their graduation. His feelings for her were obvious and she thought, "I was such a fool. I didn't see it."

She heard echoes of sentences overlapping through time: "... another cookie Mom's gone congratulations Dr. Carlin where you goin' Donna you're gonna be late for school we'd make a lousy couple time of death ten-forty-two I've offended my relationship with God didn't you warn him about me doesn't have to be tonight do an AIDS test Pattycake it's time to go to the funeral marry me what a good girl you are Jack what are we doing he's pretty insecure Raymond here's your coffee Jen wouldn't care if the grad blew up I'm Dr. Carlin has had a number of episodes of pneumonia Daddy my tummy hurts I can't move I can't breathe Jack ..."

As the scenes flew past her eyes, they sorted themselves into two piles. Once viewed, most of them were discarded as one by one they fell into a gaping hole that ripped open like the seam of an earthquake beneath the concrete wall. Representing the finished aspects of her life, she need not worry about these anymore. They were in the True Past and the True Past was filled with balance, but other scenes were fixed to the pillar, refusing to be tossed into the hole. They called her, taunted her with their persistence.

Impossible to ignore, she saw each one with perfect clarity. Racing before her mind, as though it were a movie she had seen years ago and forgotten, every scene provoked an analysis boiling them down into a neat and tidy summation of its individual effect on her life, on the kind of person she became. Two scenes grew larger than the rest. Expanding like balloons, they blocked out the other unresolved scenes and battled each other for space.

One picture showed a time from years ago, when she had ended it with Ric. She was walking away from him, and off in the corner, Jack was preparing to walk away from her. His body was turned sideways, was *turning* sideways. The picture slowed down as if someone were operating an old film projector, the kind that would stick on a frame or two. *Click!* They jerked along, showing crisp movement chopped into one frame at a time. Jack and Donna were instantly reduced into a robotic parody of their natural motions.

Jack grew within the picture, becoming the central figure. Donna was swept sideways to take a place at the lower right corner. Ric was an even smaller figure, poised to fall down into the gaping hole of the True Past, but still visible at the far edge of the picture. Jack was looking back at Donna, at *memories of Donna*. She could tell that at this point, he was resigned to them. Though his face turned toward her longingly, his body was squared opposite with one leg raised to take its first step away. Her own body faced him directly, seeing the worth of the man, but her legs stayed put. It was here that the picture finally froze in place.

The second picture mirrored the scene she was now living, the moment of her self-destruction. She saw herself within the vehicle, ready to collide head-on with that concrete wall. Raymond stood as a distant figure. Watching her sadly, his mouth opened to utter the first syllable of "goodbye" but couldn't bring himself to say it. Again, the image was reduced into sharp little frames, crisply moving the car closer and closer to the concrete wall. An overpowering slide show. Finally, it too froze in place, her car only meters from the wall. Terror sprung from her eyes.

Those last two scenes were the climactic finish. Until now, they had played out their separate stories without interfering with each other, but the straight edges of their borders seemed to bend, as though a pool of water poured over them. Their boundaries dissolved away to allow a complete overlap. As they melded into one, she could still see their distinct qualities. The antithesis of each other.

Jack and Donna's image embodied possibilities in life, turning to discover the opportunities that lay near and seizing them with both hands. The car, only meters from the concrete wall, epitomized hopelessness, despair, and death. Despite the two pictures becoming joined, their properties remained separate. They presented a choice to her. One could be taken and embraced, and in doing so, the power of the other would abate.

In the space of one quick moment, Donna had experienced a powerful summary of her existence, finishing with a terrible lack of completion. There was more to do. There was more to undo. She realized how she would hurt her father by leaving this way, how she was just as responsible for her despair as Jack was, how she had neglected to passionately embrace life. She saw herself as the talented, intelligent, tender person she was, and finally understood the importance of living those traits.

Looking at the united images, she saw which one she wanted to embrace, and once her heart had determined its choice, the impending doom of the car scene faded into the background. Automatically, the other came alive with color and depth. The realism was blinding, but the scene of destruction was still there quietly waiting for her. No, it wouldn't take her. It couldn't.

With a shriek of despair, she turned the steering wheel, and in doing so, felt herself being split in two. One half remained with the scene of destruction. The car interior became Ric's fists, striking her viciously, tossing her back and forth as the car rolled, while her other half embraced the image of Jack and Donna completely. This strong side was hurled out of the accident before it could happen and straight into the picture with paralyzing speed, but she felt no fear. Much like being thrown into a pool of water, all shock and trauma were absorbed as it wrapped itself around her. Spinning softly through the waves, toward the image of life, toward Jack. Into the drywall and through the waves at the same time. She wasn't sure when the water transformed into grass, but she was rolling on it ... over and over and over.

It wasn't until her mind screamed for it to stop that she finally lay still, trying to piece together this strange arrival.

***

As two paramedics lifted the stretcher, it slid into the back of the ambulance in one frictionless movement. A fireman closed the back doors and hurried to the front. Reporters tried to snap a picture of the victim through the ambulance windshield. It was the only untinted window, but the space inside was tight with equipment and one of the paramedics blocked his view. Not a useable shot. Then, a police officer ordered them to retreat.

Inside, paramedics could work in peace while police and firemen coordinated the path of the ambulance. One good thing about a Delta Response—always lots of help around. Firemen were a real God-send. They would do anything they were asked, lift patients, carry equipment, follow the paramedics anywhere, even drive the ambulance. It was great. Unfortunately, this team knew their efforts would be futile; the patient was really struggling. Any minute now, they would probably need to shock him. Chances were that he would die, even with the drugs and defibrillation, if not that day, then the next.

The paramedics took their cues from each other. Performing a carefully orchestrated dance, the two were so rhythmically tied, it was hard to distinguish the leader.

An intravenous needle was inserted into the patient's arm. One electrode was placed above the entry wound, the other below the left ribs, metal side down. Appearing harmless, like two pieces of tin foil with a slippery gel side against the skin, they were easier to use than the paddles. Covered wires connected electrodes to the lifepak machine, which made a constant piercing beep. In all, the tasks took less than thirty seconds.

"IV's wide open."

The senior paramedic ordered, "Pressure infuse. This guy's gonna crash."

His partner squeezed a bag of liquid, forcing it into the intravenous line. The beeping sounds were becoming more erratic. The man had lost a lot of blood, but his bleeding was not the primary concern. It was the location of the entry wound: lower right quadrant of his chest, safe from his heart, but lodged well into the lung tissue. His breathing was labored, short and shallow. The strain showed on every inch of his face. His heart fought for oxygen, and he lashed out at the paramedics, futile sweeps of his arms through the air. Better sedate this guy fast.

"Draw up 2.5 milligrams of versed."

The drug was pushed through the intravenous port, and moments later, the patient went limp. An endotracheal tube was slid down his throat.

"Intubated."

The screen suddenly went haywire, jumping spastically.

"V-tach!"

"Pulse?"

"Yes."

"Get ready to cardiovert this guy to normal sinus rhythm. Charge to one hundred joules."

The first shock was delivered. The patient seemed to come alive. His body stiffened like the straight edge of a table, and as the current left his system, it relaxed completely, his head lolling with the movements of the ambulance. Instantly, the smell of burnt skin permeated the tight space around them.

"No change, still v-tach."

"Shock at 200."

"Lost the rhythm. He's in asystole."

"Try to pace him. Charge up to 200 milliamps."

"Nothing. No capture."

"Get the epi and atropine."

The junior paramedic injected one milligram of epinephrine into the IV and adjusted a knob on the machine.

"No change."

"Atropine, one milligram IV push."

"Nothing."

The epinephrine and atropine combination were injected two more times.

"Starting CPR."

Their efforts continued until they reached the hospital, but the screen remained blank. It was as lifeless as the patient. There was no struggling for breath, no fight left in him. It was the face of absolute calm.

He was pronounced dead on arrival.

***

CHAPTER 35

(What a beautiful morning.)

Sitting calmly on the sloped grass of the university grounds, Donna's composure increased with the height of the sun. A steady stream of cars trundled past toward the downtown core; their sounds filled the space that had surrounded her just hours earlier. There was a crispness to Calgary she'd never noticed before.

Still feeling a little disoriented, bits of sentences floated about, but the voices they belonged to were fading in and out. In their place, a seed of quiet strength took root.

How long had she sat here? Why was she here? She thought about the scenes of her life, about grasping the image of Jack and Donna, and felt surrounded by it now as though she were positioned ... right inside of it ... but her logical side pushed the perception away.

(Maybe this is just some bizarre realistic dream—had plenty of those before.)

Seconds ticked by with each car that passed, exactly the way they would in any waking state. The sun rose with a subtle steadiness never apparent in the chaotic constructions of her dreams. If this were an altered state of consciousness, why did time elapse in such a real way? Seemingly in answer to those questions, something pestered her.

(Something to resolve, unfinished business, something ...)

An undeniable concept with old roots, Donna couldn't shove it aside. For years, those acute episodes of déjà vu never revealed the essence of their familiarity; things were actually being viewed a second time through.

The first time was at the accident in high school, with Jack leading her into the backseat of that man's car. And then the movie clips started. Some door from her future must have opened to show a quick glimpse of

291

her life, but unable to recall any details, she was left holding a disgruntled feeling in the back of her mind, as if something needed attention and she just couldn't remember what. She had that same feeling now. Something needed completing here ... even if this were a mere dream.

Picking herself up, Donna slowly walked toward the Biological Sciences building. Her clothes were almost dry. They were the gray form-fitting dress pants and rust blouse she wore to work. No rips or stains indicated any car accident. Though dressed a little better, for all intents and purposes she looked like any other student walking to school, except that she wasn't carrying anything. Her purse was still at the office and her keys were nowhere to be found.

(Must still be in the car.)

Back in those endless school days, she had practically lived in the Bio Sciences building. Distracted by her surroundings, she wandered aimlessly. This place looked exactly like it did eight years ago, but now, immaterial background details drew together nostalgically: fluorescent lights reflecting off the tile floors, dull yellow lockers lining the walls, graduation pictures posted at the end of the hallway. The building even smelled the same. Countless faces in the picture frames glided past. Each one listed a graduation year, 1988, 1989, 1990. She'd been past them a hundred times with no more than a glance.

Mixed memories flitted through her mind: constantly pushed with exams, Ric pressing for more of her time, Jen laughing at life's moments, Jack waiting in the wings. She knew this was what he had done. Donna had watched the film clips of her life with eye-opening surprise at his adoration. Staying silent in the face of her relationship with Ric, Jack effectively deferred his own desires. Over the years, he'd offered a million signs of his love and she hadn't seen them at all. If she could only do one thing, it would be to find him and apologize.

A hall clock showed 9:15. She walked through the Social Sciences building as though being pulled by a string, searching for something, but what? There was nothing out of place here ... except The Pit. It had been converted back into a lounge area. To adhere to health by-laws, management had turned it into a study area after smokers started congregating there. That was years ago. And now they were back like mosquitoes in summer heat.

Plop! A young man unloaded a stack of campus newspapers on the floor beside her, clipping her foot, and she stepped sideways and sat down to get out of his way. Smoke drifted from across the room.

(Ric?)

Her eyes followed the scent to see a student butt out one cigarette and mechanically light up another. A willowy cloud escaped upward to obscure a "No Smoking" sign.

Her restlessness persisted. Was she supposed to be somewhere else? Or right here? One hand rested on the newspapers, but she barely noticed the dry sensation on her fingertips. Then she saw the date: September 8, 1991.

"An old issue," she reasoned, but the reasoning felt weak. The texture of the paper was brand new and she had watched the man delivering them. Lifting a copy, she noted its perfect fold. No edges sticking out jaggedly, no smudges of hands having separated the pages, no faded print or torn corners.

Her hand turned the first page to reveal an identical date on the second. And another and another, checking for the real date, the one that should end in the number nine. None of them did. This wasn't right. She couldn't focus her thoughts. Slowly, Donna admitted she didn't want to focus them. A feeling deep down told her that yes, she was in 1991 and not 1999 anymore. Well, part of her was still in the future—a battered and weakened part—but most of her was here. Right here.

Reluctantly raising her head, Donna studied her surroundings again, this time with such an alert perspective, it were as if a strong pair of glasses dropped over her eyes. She could see what she had carelessly overlooked just a minute ago. Peering at the people around her, she now viewed them as intangible figures of a scene long gone. Were they ghosts? Maybe she was the ghost wandering through her own memories.

This newspaper was like herself, full of stories about her life, each one different depending on what page she turned to. The cover alone didn't tell the whole story. Flipping through another section showed a separate part of her life. Here was Donna the doctor maintaining a thriving practice, and then *flip!*—here she was in the middle of her past.

Her thoughts still resisted what couldn't logically be, what shouldn't be … except for the certainty in her soul of this situation. Someone had simply turned a few pages back.

What would be the purpose of throwing her into this time frame? What or who could be capable of such feats? Just a while ago, she had been reflecting on regrets and making amends.

Jack …

She leaned forward with her chin on her hands and catalogued the past.

(OK, separate everything, one at a time.)

September eighth was the day she broke up with Ric. After spying on her having coffee with Dennis Fontaine, he'd gone nuts that night. Jack was employed in a research job in this building. Jen was taking classes here. ... She was *alive.*

Donna realized with faint excitement that both were probably on campus right now. She could warn Jen, stop her from getting infected. She could see Jack and apologize. Right—face him as her thirty-year-old dark-haired self from the future. At best, he would undoubtedly believe himself to be the butt of some cruel joke.

She couldn't do that to Jack. Even Jen couldn't. She would talk about it, right down to the tiniest detail, but in the end she was equally protective of Jack. Now, Donna understood the real need to protect him. Through the years he had always seemed to be his own strong person, especially later on when he spent so much energy denying himself, but here and now, there was a totally different character to this air being pulled in and out of her lungs. It was the air of her struggling youth, when she was struggling far less than Jack.

Even Jen was having a tough time of things here. Donna could almost feel her friend's ache beneath all the layers of bravado. Jen had carefully maintained a shield against an unfulfilled heart. How strange that Donna could suddenly sense the extent of it, as though Jen and her desires were sweeping through The Pit at this very moment. She could see her stepping purposefully by. Down the stairs, pivoting away from Donna, down the next set of stairs, a brown knapsack hanging off one shoulder.

(Oh, hi Jen ...)

Donna's mouth dropped open as the ghostly image disappeared from sight. Was that Jen or just Donna's mind playing tricks on her? It was a Jen she had dreamt about, alive and well and full of spirited advice, a Jen ignorant of her early death. She was no dream. Dreams didn't sustain this kind of detail, like the color of her knapsack and the way her long hair bounced from side to side with every step. She was very real, an integrated part of the air around them.

Shooting to her feet, Donna dropped the newspaper in a crumpled pile. The smoker scowled at the mess she left as she trailed Jen to the lower level hallway. Donna matched her quickening pace. The hallway curved around to the left. Jen was practically running now and she slipped out of view around the corner.

Donna picked up speed, checking to see if she had turned into one of the classrooms. Not there. Right, left, nope. A small group of people were suddenly in her way and they seemed to take up the whole hallway. With no space to dart around them, Donna realized in horror that Jen was one of those people only a few feet away. The knapsack enlarged grotesquely until it was all Donna could see. Then—*Crash!*

Down went Jen and her knapsack with a heavy thud.

The instant Donna touched her she knew Jen was in the True Past. Running into her, connecting with her physically brought Jen's soul up to the surface, which appeared even clearer than during the flash-backs. With utter certainty, her death was unalterable. Even at this point in time, it was too late and all Donna could absorb was the truth of Jen's fortitude.

Their bond was unique. It lacked the continual battles of self-image and blame Donna had experienced with Jack. She knew, really knew that despite Jen's inevitable demise, this person was the strongest soul Donna would ever encounter ... and this soul would be at peace in the future. One touch allowed the strength at the cemetery to course through her, and with it, years of satisfied balance.

For a split-second, Donna was ready to help her friend up, and then she realized how incongruous her appearance would be. Jen's back was still turned away, but she was shifting her weight onto her feet. One of her classmates held out an arm and she grabbed it firmly. Her head started to turn. Donna spun around quickly and ran past before Jen could get a clear look at her face.

"Hey, what the hell are you doing?" Jen yelled at the fleeing culprit, "I know what you look like! You'll be seeing me again!"

"You got that right," Donna thought as she sped down the hall, around the corner, and up the stairs. Flattening herself against a wall, she tried to calm her racing heart, her chest heaving with frightened breaths. What could she possibly say to her?

(Hi Jen, it's me. I know I look a little different, but time travel can do that to you. By the way, thanks for being such a good part of my life. ...)

Even if Jen believed in time travel, no sentences could summarize Donna's feelings. How do you put that kind of history into words and have it make sense? And to what purpose? Jen was in the True Past, as good a summary as there could be.

The hallway suddenly filled with bodies as several classes ended at once. Students moved in all directions and instantly, the foyer became crowded.

She stood conspicuously, as though people would take one look at her and automatically know she didn't belong here. ... Actually, people *were* looking at her, quick scrutinizing glances and double glances. It was unnerving.

Then her intimidation reversed itself, pivoting gracefully in the opposite direction. A calm sensation drifted through her: the undisturbed haven of a millpond, its beauty equally vulnerable and underestimated.

There were knapsacks everywhere, harmless canvas bags containing books and more books. White noise. Some students carried coffee cups.

Others used refillable mugs, strapped to their belongings. This was the culture every year. So predictable, so consistent ... like Brian.

There he goes, same hair, blue plaid shirt. She had talked him out of wearing that thing. Donna followed like a delirious sleepwalker. He was moving through the main foyer and she stopped at the entrance, knowing exactly what she would see.

At one of the tables along the wall, there sat Dennis and a blonde woman. The woman's back was to Donna but her clothes looked familiar. A beige sweater, the one she had worn on her lunch date with Ric. Eight years from now, it would still be hanging in her closet.

"Turn around!" she mentally commanded the blonde. Then the woman seemed to register the order; she twisted her head when Dennis pointed out Brian across the foyer.

The face of the woman was herself! Herself!

An eerie feeling of stolen duplication crept across her spine, as if someone had snapped her picture without permission. This was unbelievable ... but this whole thing—this mix of sight and sound—was more real than anything in her life.

Past Donna was fiddling with something on the table. The fake sugar. Jack once said she'd grow horns from that stuff. Donna used to pour it in every coffee.

As quickly as the foyer filled with students, it emptied while they disappeared into other classrooms. She watched Brian go down a set of stairs ... and then her eyes opened wide. There, by the stairs. Ric was peering at the table from around the corner. He bore an angry expression when Past Donna smiled at Dennis. As they strolled toward the Biological Sciences corridor together, Ric followed at a discreet distance.

An old fear came racing back, the one that made her see the dark side of people, the side that could terrorize, destroy one's faith in the world. She wanted to grab her blonde self and shield her, keep her from discovering this. Ric wouldn't hurt her until tonight, but the mere sight of him provoked such helplessness.

Could she change it? Try to warn herself somehow?

There was too much to sort out here. Overpowered, she felt herself losing control. Her breathing sped up with little gasps and the square floor tiles blurred. Donna backed away, barely aware of the cold metal of a locker brushing her shoulders. Dizzy, she started sliding down toward the floor, down to something horrible: black eyes and a tightened fist striking her senseless.

Her shaking knees locked. No, she wouldn't falter. She would face this. He was dangerous, but she had one advantage; he didn't know she was here. Believing Donna to be the target, he would never suspect he was also hers.

Ric was almost out of sight down the hall. She hurried to catch up to him. After all these years, terrified at the possibility of seeing him again, she was actually placing herself in close proximity. As the gap closed to ten feet, she spotted his hands swinging by his sides: the ones that had undressed her for the first time, ran over her body passionately, flipped her around to try a new position ... shoved her face into a pillow and nearly suffocated her to death. Her pace slowed to create more distance.

Past Donna was going to her locker. And Ric knew the combination. He hovered at the end of the hallway while her blonde self left her things in the locker. Then she and Dennis hurried to class.

Donna pretended to wrestle with a lock down the hallway. He wouldn't notice someone who wasn't blonde. Ric crouched before her locker and opened it easily. Reaching into his pocket, he slid her bank card into her wallet and then replaced it in her knapsack. She spied him sliding her apartment key back on the ring, and with a sinking heart, she realized he must have already copied the key and stolen the money. But then, her eyebrows puckered further when she saw him handling her aspartame jar. Lifting the lid, he tipped the contents of another container into it.

What the hell was he doing? Putting everything back, he closed the locker and stood, gripping something metallic. Her cell phone. Donna froze at the thought that he might walk toward her, but he turned to the opposite exit. Fear of being violated stood against her anger and she forced herself to stop and think as he disappeared through the door.

OK, he now had access to her apartment. There was no changing that, but she could follow him. If he went to her apartment, she should also have the key to get in. Standing before her old locker, Donna thought hard to remember the combination. It was years since she'd needed those numbers. With concentration, the memory so diligently trained in its recall capabilities kicked in.

(Visualize turning right, stop, left, stop, right again, stop.)

She tried one set of numbers, but they didn't feel correct in her head. It didn't open. The first and second numbers were right, which correlated with her age and address.

(22–41–3?)

This time it opened.

Her old knapsack sat invitingly on the floor of the locker. Dragging it forward, she unzipped the front pouch. There was the key to her old apartment. She worked it around in circles until it fell away by itself, and then put the rest of the keys back in the pouch.

Searching for the aspartame jar, she reached into the knapsack and her fingers brushed a couple of pebbles. She pulled out two pills. Antipsychotic meds. She'd prescribed these for reducing manic episodes in bipolar patients. But a healthy person would easily develop delusional side effects, anxiety, even hyperactivity, everything she remembered experiencing in the weeks leading up to her breakup with Ric.

She grabbed the jar and poured some of the powder into her palm. It should have had a thin yellow crystallized look. This stuff was whiter and denser. He had been spiking her jar with meds and after she was found dead under her balcony, they would find these pills in her knapsack. Of course it would be assumed she was experimenting with drugs she had access to through her studies. Suicide, case closed.

She quickly locked everything and ran down the hallway. Could she still catch up to Ric? Tossing the jar and pills into a garbage can, she flew down the stairs of the exit and burst through the outside door. Her head scanned quickly. There—he was walking through the parking lot at a good speed. Cutting through rows of cars, she tried to stay behind the taller vehicles.

At a far row, Ric stopped and looked around. Donna darted behind a truck. He was standing at Jen's car. The Valiant. Seeing its perfect passenger window was another bizarre piece of evidence that she was squarely in the past.

He took something from inside his jacket and pressed his body close to the door. Then it just seemed to magically open. Swiftly he leaned in and was out just as quickly, shutting the door after snapping the lock latch down.

Donna watched him stroll away. When he was out of sight, she approached the Valiant and peered into the window. Shading the reflection of the sun, she could see something peeking out from under the seat. Money. A big wad of it. He had stolen the money and hid it there, knowing that Jen would drive Donna home and have to explain why the exact amount missing from Donna's bank account had materialized in Jen's car. Her honest inability to explain would be proof of her guilt. And she in turn would accuse Donna of leaving it there herself. The fight would lend credence to Donna's instability while eliminating her biggest support.

Her eyes shifted with her racing thoughts. Protecting Jen would be the same as protecting herself since Jen would be her escape from Ric. Past Donna and Jen had to be on good terms tonight. Two things would guarantee her safety: fix whatever was making this car crap out all the time and get the money out of there.

Ric must have had one of those tools locksmiths use. Christ, the man could get in anywhere. Well, she had her own skills.

She lifted the hood. There wasn't much room, because Jen had parked the front end really close to a retaining wall. A quick look was all Donna needed to ascertain the problem, which was the same as before—a loose wire on the ignition coil. She unhooked it and, finding a small rock, crimped the loose connector tighter by pressing it between some level pavement and the rock, then reattached it to the alternator cap and ignition coil. It wouldn't come off again, at least not soon. Perusing the engine, she tried to spot other problems, but as far as she could tell there weren't any.

She sighed, hoping this simple fix would do the trick. Completing one automotives course back in high school could only boast the most rudimentary skill level. And so much depended on this.

As she studied the engine, her eyes narrowed. The feeling of potential threat dissipated. Yes, the ignition coil was the only problem. This car would start. The intuitive air of this time frame told her so, as a calm layer of relief fell on her like soft snow. She was almost safe.

She lowered the hood with a solid *bang!* Leaning against the car, Donna scanned the area for something heavy. A big tree branch or a hefty rock. There was nothing in sight. No, wait ... the retaining wall. It consisted of stacked stones, but they all looked pretty solid. She ran her hands along the top edge, pushing on each cap stone until she found one that jiggled slightly. With a new level of focus, she worked it back and forth. Finally, the cap loosened and she lifted it into her hands.

Voices turned her attention. Students a couple of rows over, walking leisurely. Donna waited until they were out of sight and then checked the parking lot for any other witnesses. With a big breath, she swung the stone, but to her dismay it didn't instantly shatter the window, merely cracked it. It had sounded so loud. She didn't want to risk more noise, but swinging again, this time a decent hole was made in the glass. She dropped the stone, kicked the glass enough to widen the hole, and stood surveying the damage. This was exactly the way it had looked for years. Jen never fixed it, just slapped tape on to cover the hole.

(Mine ... It was me.)

How many of her actions were already set? Was she creating this awful day for her past self? No, Ric had made this happen, not her. Her actions would save her life. How could that even be up for debate?

(Deal with it later.)

She was now able to reach in without cutting herself and lift the lock. Careful to avoid the glass shards, she scooped up the money. Bending to check under the seat, a rectangular silver object sat among old candy wrappers. Donna reached in and pulled out her cell phone. Staring quizzically, she realized how close she had been to missing this.

Ric had called her that day, when she was in Jen's car and she hadn't bothered to answer it. If this phone had rung under the seat, Past Donna would have discovered it and the money and accused Jen for sure. She needed to get this thing back into the knapsack.

She shut the door and ran to a group of trees on the green space. There was exactly one thousand dollars in her hands. God, it felt as if she were racing through a minefield, guessing at each step along the way. What *was* the next step?

Ric must be on his way to her apartment. She'd better deal with that too.

***

CHAPTER 36

Donna's footsteps blended one into another with a smooth rhythm, and before she knew it, she was standing at the side of her old apartment.

Was he in there? Should she spy on her apartment door or wait for him to exit the building? Deciding it was safer to wait, she leaned against the brick wall. Minutes passed. In the time it had taken for the smash and grab at Jen's car, Ric could have done his business here and been long gone.

(Wait a minute—he would have taken his car here.)

Donna peered down the street, but it wasn't in sight. Her head swiveled suddenly and she ran to the rear of the building. Peaking around the corner, her heart sank again.

Ric was working on the back door ... closed it, yanked on the handle. The door stuck. Satisfied, he walked quickly to his car in the back alley. She could see his confidence bursting with every stride.

At least he was gone. He wouldn't come back here until tonight. Inside the building, Donna checked the hallway for witnesses. How strange to enter her old dwelling like a burglar!

(At least, the fingerprints I leave behind will be my own. ...)

The apartment was just as she remembered it—cluttered. Nothing like Jen's place, but still reflecting the lifestyle of someone who prioritized studying above cleaning: books and class notes scattered all over the kitchen table, a cereal bowl and spoon perched like a paperweight on top, evidence of a quick breakfast before rushing out the door, instant coffee and mug on the counter.

The familiarity of the rooms contrasted sharply with her memory, which naturally sought to place this scene into an irretrievable past. It was as though a two-dimensional picture suddenly took on a new depth. She could pluck out pieces of the picture and enjoy their lifelike features, when only hours earlier she had to be content with running her mind's eye over the flat surface of the memory.

She strode into the bedroom. A pile of colorful laundry sat on the floor near the closet. The owner had taken the time to clean it, but not to fold anything neatly or hang things up. The bed was unmade, the covers carelessly thrown toward two pillows, which were lying at angles against the headboard.

She imagined Ric in this bed so many years ago, caressing her skin with a skill that belied his true nature. The many indications of his controlling personality filled her forebodingly with sadness for Past Donna. She almost bent over at the realistic nausea, which weighed her down with a pressure in the pit of her stomach.

She was conscious of vibrations from this apartment: danger, hard work, being pulled in too many directions, other things more subtle and hazy. Some of the impressions extended beyond her own past; a few were from previous tenants, although their vibrations were much fainter. Sensing those ones were like watching news clips instead of witnessing some horrible incident right in front of her. They lacked the graphic realism only perceived from direct experience. They were safe, easy to separate and dismiss.

The phone by her bed didn't work. He'd already messed with it. The other one was in the kitchen. No dial tone from it either. Even taking them apart, she'd have no clue how to fix them. Her repair skills stopped at cars and people. The only option was to make sure Past Donna had her cell phone.

Stepping close to the kitchen table, to her seat during the last Rummoli game, the chair to her right was suffocating, Ric's chair. Physically turning away, she concentrated on the chair to her left and felt Jack's frustration and loneliness—even more—his lengthy devotion to her. It existed within him and without him at the same time, a separate entity yet deeply ingrained.

She understood it with utter clarity, because it also existed in her. It was old, much older than their years, seemingly resilient and endless, but Jack was tired from carrying the effort so long. She now recognized the slow turning of the tide that had caused her to take over the effort. ... If only she had done it sooner.

Next, the opposite chair. The feeling at the cemetery breezed through her: new horizons, perseverance, the best of life both settled and excited. The wind had lightly carried the sensation up and away, but now it returned to infuse a quiet strength. The chairs to her right and left could make demands all they wanted. It was the chair straight across that would get her through this.

(Get to work. You'll need things.)

Donna grabbed a plastic bag under the kitchen sink and moved around, swiftly filling it with small items: an extra toothbrush, hairbrush, underwear, things that wouldn't be missed. She stood in front of her old closet with one hand on her favorite pair of jeans. These were worn the first day she met Jack, back in high school when the fabric was brand new. There was a measure of comfort from the faded material. The denim, soft and pliable from years of wear, had gradually molded to her shape. She was tempted to take this, but its absence would certainly be noticed. Then she remembered that with her current weight, the jeans would probably fall off her, but she stood gripping the material as if it were an old friend.

Suddenly a sound erupted from the other room. Jerking around, she was startled to hear her own voice, speaking in a chipper paced delivery. "Hi, I'm buried under a mountain of books right now, but if you have the means to clear my student loan, I'll call you back. ..." Her answering machine. She always forgot to lower the volume. Of course it would still work. The phone line went directly into it, so it could still record messages even if she couldn't call out.

She rushed back into the living room, stood beside Ric's chair, and was hit with a sickening certainty. It was him. He emanated from the machine, just as he did from the chair. Fresh nausea returned in waves, peaking with a heart-wrenching fear up her spine.

Something awful hung in the air: the possibility that Billy might fail. It was not just a simple case of getting Donna away from Ric that night. Billy would have to beat the obsession out of Ric so another night was never an option for him. And Donna had no control over that whatsoever.

The outgoing message was done. In a moment, she would hear a beep and the recording would start. She lunged at the power button. Hearing his voice would have made her throw up. Despite cutting him off, the apartment seemed alive with an awareness of her. Ric was everywhere. And it made her sick.

(Oh my God, I am!)

Dropping the bag, Donna dove into the bathroom, yanked the toilet seat up, and hung her head as her stomach heaved uselessly. There was nothing to vomit. The curve of the seat smiled blandly as she willed herself not to hyperventilate.

After a minute, she rose shakily and wandered back to the living room. This place was absolutely frightening. It made her feel like the intruder she believed Ric to be ... that she was herself. She should not be here. This was a place of danger.

Clutching the bag of necessities, Donna took one last look before locking the door behind her. Years of heavy thoughts were in there. Completely fatigued, she was reminded of the long rotations during her residency and staggered outside. She stood leaning against a tree as though its hard frame would protect her.

The bright sunlight washed her mind free of claustrophobic terror, cleansing a layer of fear and that drunken unsteadiness. Closing her eyes and inhaling deeply, a strong release let the breath go. As it carried away the pain of Ric's fist across her face, Donna realized that it erased even more.

A deep-seated fear had lived in the back of her mind—a fear that men held the power to harm her. After that awful night, she had never looked at another man without wondering if and when it could happen again. Most of the time the thought wasn't even conscious, just simmering beneath her awareness. Now, it floated away like a steamy breath in winter. She knew this kind of fear would never own her again.

Ric was far away. And Jack was near. At the thought of him, she visibly relaxed. Now she could walk with graceful fortitude back to campus.

***

Jack glanced at his watch. Good thing his breaks were flexible; he was starving. As a research assistant, no one had to mind the store when he took lunch, but he decided to get the next batch of data sheets done first.

Tossing a finished set on a table, he retrieved a fresh file folder from the upright cabinet and shut the door with his foot a little too hard, as his thoughts stole once again to the Rummoli game on the weekend. He could have decked Ric about fifty times that night, especially after pulling his wallet out. Might as well have been his dick, the way he'd orchestrated that pissing contest right in front of Jen and Donna.

It was fortunate this job allowed Jack a measure of seclusion in his monotonous duties: prepare data sheets, distribute data sheets, collect data sheets, input data sheets. ... Today it was an absolute blessing.

Jack welcomed the isolation as he faithfully went about his tasks, but recognized the limitations. Research was only something short-term, not a career. There was no change in it. He wasn't someone who could look at a pile of data and automatically know what it meant. You had to search for the correlations and causations in order to paint the resultant picture, and even then, someone would come along to refute your conclusions anyway. There was a certain artistic license in analyzing statistics that made Jack uncomfortable. He wanted to know exactly what he was dealing with and match a solution to the problem at hand.

Like the problem of Ric and Donna ... Jen might be confident in their demise, but could he stand around and wait forever? Should he? It felt like he had waited that long already. While a part of him believed it was the right thing to do, another imagined being with another woman, someone like Michelle who would look at him and see the man as well as the friend. The problem was that every time he thought of her, she automatically took on Donna's features. There was no matchable solution to this problem.

He heard the office door creak and turned to face Jen.

"Hi Bud."

"What are you doing here?"

All her classes were in the Fine Arts building. She never came to Social or Bio, except to use Donna's locker.

"I just met with my group. You know, the one I'm doing that production with."

Clueless, he nodded anyway.

Stepping around his desk, she unceremoniously dropped her knapsack on the floor, its second beating of the day. Then she pushed aside a stack of papers on the table, jumped up, and leaned back swinging her legs. One heel rhythmically bounced against a table leg in a dull clunking sound.

"Well, just make yourself at home, Princess," he said agreeably, "Can I get you anything?"

"Got any body armor? I was the victim of some psycho hit and run student and that's been the highlight of my day so far. You know, I think this is one of those days that should have been erased, 'cause nothing good's gonna come of it. I can just feel it. Where's your boss?"

"He comes by once a day to pick up the summaries. I don't see him much."

"Now that's a job I could like. Think about it. Who in their right mind likes their boss? You're not supposed to. It's some Rule." She sliced her hand straight down, demonstrating the absolutism of the Rule. "Be glad he's not here."

"Oh, it could be worse. He could be you."

Jen gave him a big smile and a rock solid punch on the arm. He hid his grimace by turning away.

"That's the spirit, J.P! You must be feeling better. Come on—let's go for a coffee, my treat."

He frowned. His bicep was throbbing. "I should get this stuff done before lunch. Will you be around in an hour?"

"Got a class. One is expected to periodically attend these things. Wow, that's totally something Donna would say!"

"Yeah, but it lacks something without the pretzeling."

She hopped off the table, picked up her knapsack, and swung it onto her back in one spry movement.

"Do you want me to get you one anyway?"

He considered pointing out her niceness—better than any insult by far—but merely replied, "No. What I really need is some food."

"Well, don't count on me for that. There isn't enough cash in Canada to cover your appetite!"

And with that, she headed out the door. He chuckled and lifted his hand in response, letting her have the last word as usual.

On her way out, she decided to keep quiet about seeing Donna having coffee with some guy. She would mention it to Donna later ... but Jack didn't need to hear about it. He was bummed out enough about Ric.

***

During the twenty-minute walk back to campus, a strong sun presided over Donna's pace with a guiding pull. Turning her face upwards, she welcomed the bright warmth. It covered her like a soft blanket, fresh out of the dryer. It was funny that in this time frame, the concept of a blanket—once tied only to the saddest of memories—could now denote nothing but wonderful comfort, easing her frantic heart. In fact, she almost felt ... elated.

There was perfection to the day. Every concrete seam in the sidewalk was equidistant to the next one. They reminded her of a television screen with a broken vertical hold; a scene flickered repeatedly, each square edging the final product a little closer to its completed version, like the flash-backs. She was doing the same by revisiting her own old haunts, but this time they held a beauty she had overlooked eight years ago. Donna was stepping straight into a movie set as the principle character, discovering a new glamour to the props and makeup. She knew exactly how each scene should be played out and perfect them in one take. ...

(Well, two takes!)

It was wonderfully buoyant. She was starting to think that this was a day where nothing could go wrong. She could just feel it. If only that unfinished feeling wasn't still plaguing her.

The plastic bag swung rhythmically as Donna entered Bio Sciences. Stopping against a row of lockers, she shut her eyes. She could still see the flash-back of Jack walking away from her, while Ric stayed stubbornly in the corner of the picture. There was also her father in the other picture, unwilling to let her go. Although Ric was a central danger, though now sufficiently diffused, Jack was still some kind of problem in this time frame ... and so was her dad. They were not in the True Past like Jen and they would have to be dealt with somehow.

Concentrate. Faces lined up and she prioritized them into separate levels. Closing her mind to Jen, she put Raymond on hold and centered her thoughts on Jack. He was definitely the pivotal point. Assuming his future feelings were unalterable, maybe it would help to convey an apology, even if he didn't know it was from Donna.

How could she arrange this?

Leaving a note for him now would make no sense to him. She could have one delivered at a specific date in the future, but this date in the past would still be traceable as its point of origin. Definitely need more thought on this.

Her body relaxed against the lockers, molding her back to them with straightened posture, but she still felt weak. Donna's stomach rumbled. When was the last time she ate? Maybe that was making her light-headed as well. So wrapped up in those hours before the accident, and then dealing with Ric, she hadn't eaten for almost twenty-four hours. Her mind glibly corrected itself.

(Eight years and twenty-four hours!)

It wouldn't be such an issue if that feeling of temporary time still hung over her, but as the morning progressed, so did her sense of destiny. She would be here for some time yet. Whatever divine force had deposited her was in no hurry to yank her away.

Then she smiled. She had money. All the way from the apartment, she had been brainstorming ways of returning the cash, but this was actually kind of convenient. She'd get something to eat and then go to the bank and deposit the rest. Maybe the difference would be chalked up to some bank error. So Past Donna wouldn't get the whole amount back. Tough.

The priority was to return the key and cell phone to the knapsack, but she had lots of time and the Food Court wasn't far. Donna pushed herself away from the lockers and strode quickly across campus.

***

Dr. Wendy Moyer entered the hospital room and scanned the chart of the patient. Donna Patricia Carlin, age thirty, severe head trauma, EDH, ICP relieved by emergency burr hole, asymmetrical limited response to pain stimuli ...

A catalogue of test results followed. She'd written the notes hours ago, before snagging two straight hours of sleep in the staff lounge. That and a decent meal compliments of Dr. Capri had done wonders. She almost felt human again.

The patient's father was reclined in an adjustable chair, dozing restlessly, and Wendy took care not to wake him. As she gingerly lifted a page on the chart and folded it over, a frown flitted across her lips.

"Donna Carlin."

The words were barely audible under her breath. Did she know this person? The name sounded familiar, but then again, after a few of these shifts she might answer to it herself. During the transitional phase of shift work, her internal clock got so turned around. Once, after a long rotation, she woke up the evening before work and raced to the hospital, panicking all the way, only to discover she was owed twelve more hours of sleep.

Carlin. Wasn't there a blonde doctor by that name a year or two ahead of her at school? This couldn't be the same one. The hair was different. Then again, the age was right. Earlier, Wendy had been so tired, that the patient had simply been another case. Now this lifeless woman possessed an existence as real as her own.

(I'll have to ask this guy when he wakes up.)

She glanced at her watch. Dr. Capri expected to meet after her rounds. Back to work.

The woman's pupils showed no change. Wendy uncovered the left foot of the patient and pressed into the sole with her pen. No response. She pressed it into the right foot, which jerked back slightly. Her findings were jotted down on the patient's chart, along with the time—11:15—and she glanced at the sleeping man again.

Before leaving, she retrieved a blanket from a supply cart and gently covered him.

***

Being utterly famished, the smells of the Food Court were overpowering. Donna stepped into a line-up, impatient to get some food into her stomach, and another consideration came to mind. Where would she stay tonight?

In addition to the fact that a large bank withdrawal, followed by a large deposit, would make her blonde self feel even crazier than she had that week, tomorrow Past Donna would start carrying her valuables on her. This would be the only opportunity to take the much needed funds. Right now, Past Donna was in class, straight through until 1:00. Neurology, a tough subject. She never skipped classes. There was time to deal with everything, especially without the bank errand.

Donna felt a sudden presence near. At first, panic struck, remembering the sickly feeling of Ric in the apartment, but after a minute she let herself absorb the sensations. They had nothing to do with Ric. A quick glance to each side ... No one was near.

It wasn't the boy ahead of her and as someone stepped into line behind her, she knew it wasn't that person either. Donna didn't even have to look at him; it wasn't anyone in this time frame. There was a different feel to this presence, far away in physical dimensions but very close in its essence.

Donna closed her eyes and concentrated. Her left foot tingled so slightly, she thought she imagined it. Then, a sharp sensation hit her right foot. The knife-like pain completely throwing her off-guard, her knee buckled, she cried out, and collapsed backwards.

Two solid arms came from behind and caught her before she hit the floor. They kindly steadied her to stand again as a voice said, "Whoops ... Hey you all right?"

She stayed hunched over momentarily, but the sharp pain disappeared as quickly as it came. For some reason, she'd expected the pain to last.

As Donna rose, the man's hand held her forearm securely and guided her upright, not letting go until she stood squarely again. It took a few seconds to catch her bearings and realize that someone had prevented her from becoming injured.

Embarrassed, she turned to thank him and found herself looking straight into Jack's face.

***

CHAPTER 37

He was young, fresh-faced, muscular, and standing no more than twelve inches away.

His whole look was altered, relaxed, enhanced by longer hair the way it was in high school. Donna was so accustomed to the military crew cut; combined with his youth, he appeared a casual version of his older self.

For a long moment, Donna held her breath.

He seemed to be doing the same while his eyes raced over her. Despite subtle differences, the resemblance was striking; this woman was older, same eye color, but her hair was darker and shorter and her face thinner. She seemed tall, but he was holding his head at the same level as he did when facing Donna.

(They must even be the same height!)

This woman was slimmer and there was something about her eyes missing in the other pair he knew so well. He didn't know what, but definitely something. Put a wig on her and add a few pounds and this could be Donna. Bizarre.

Her shimmering rust-colored blouse contrasted with gray pants, the cut of which seemed out of style with other women around campus, but they molded to her hips alluringly. The short-sleeved blouse showed a slight rounding of her biceps curving gently into smooth forearms. He automatically checked for the scar from their high school accident. It wasn't there. Her skin was perfect—arms, neck, face—and this was strange. No scars or discolorations. Not even a freckle. She wore no jewelry. It would have taken away from the rest of her. This woman needed no dressing up to pull a man's eyes.

Jack shook his head suddenly, realizing he had been openly staring. He muttered, "Sorry, I ah ... You look like someone I know. I mean, I know that sounds like a line, but you ... really do."

He was so flustered he didn't notice the shock on her face. He hoped she wasn't offended by his hands on her. It was just instinct. She had practically dropped into his arms. Jack started to stumble around another apology, but as she smiled, a beautiful smile, he couldn't help staring again.

She offered, "I get that a lot."

(I bet you do.)

"Um, sorry. I must have stepped on my foot wrong or something. Sorry I crashed into you like that."

"Don't worry about it. You OK now?"

"Yeah, fine ... thanks."

They faced each other awkwardly, both trying not to stare and neither succeeding. The line moved forward to create a gap. They stepped ahead until she was next to place her order.

Donna, seeing the opportunity almost out of range, impulsively extended her hand and announced, "I'm Patty ... Slobodian. Nice to crash into you."

He shook her hand firmly. "I'm Jack Petrasyk. Nice to catch you."

The cashier behind the counter jumped in impatiently, "And I'm Craig. Nice to take your order," but they barely noticed him.

"Can I buy you a burger, Jack? You know, to keep up that strength?"

"Well, since you're the one passing out in public, why don't I buy *you* one?"

They smiled, two people flirting confidently, every nuance accepted and returned in concert. Craig rolled his eyes.

Jack paid for their meals and carried the tray of food to an empty table. The Food Court was humming with people either between classes or on a break from work. Despite being surrounded, Donna felt uniquely secluded with him, as though nestled in the romantic ambiance of Fioritti's ... or being wrapped up in bed.

He was so young and energetic. She hadn't seen him look this content in a long time. Jack had lost something in his smile years ago and here it was, brighter than ever, and for *her*, though instinctively Donna knew that his ex-girlfriend was still an issue. Whoever she was, she hadn't taken the chance to hurt him yet, but the threat existed.

Seeing his youthfulness was the same as watching Jen in the flashbacks when she was at peace with her illness. It was the only time Donna had really said goodbye to her. She couldn't concentrate on it at the funeral. Even at the cemetery a year later, Jack was there in the back of her mind. Only during her brush with death could she comprehend Jen's inner peace with such clarity, and seeing Jack now was similar. In all her fantasies, she never conceived of him looking so light-hearted.

As a cop, he was careful with people, even a bit jaded. The religion was a vehicle to reach his personal goals, but it never filled the space left by his distrust in people. She traced it back to whatever his ex had done to him. It could have arisen from a number of events in his life, but on that park bench, Donna had heard him describe things about that woman with a bittersweet melancholy. Nothing in his life had provoked such emotion, not even wanting to find his father.

"So, what are you taking, Patty?"

"Oh, I'm not in school." She cast around for some explanation of her presence on campus and decided on the truth. "I just arrived in town this morning. I ... came here for a meeting."

"Business?" he asked hopefully.

"Well, no. He was a friend."

"Was?"

She stammered, not knowing how to explain it without sounding insane, but he read her discomfort incorrectly.

"It's none of my business."

One hand rubbed the air as if erasing his question. The steel ring waved back and forth. She'd forgotten about that thing. It was so much a part of him and then he just didn't wear it anymore. She never did ask why, just assumed he'd outgrown the ring along with his ideals.

Jack raised the burger to his mouth and took another bite. "You don't have to tell me."

But she did. Badly. Here was the perfect opportunity to convey an apology directly and indirectly at the same time. She hoped it would be enough to soothe her soul. It would have to be.

Struggling to appear casual, Donna chose her words carefully.

"No, it's not a problem. I can talk about it. You see, I was good friends with a fellow I knew for a long time and then we had a falling out. I wanted to let him know I was wrong about some things. He cared more than I knew and I kind of ruined it. So, I wanted to say I'm sorry."

Watching her face as she spoke, Jack noted her unnerving way of talking right to him, *into* him. She was speaking about some other guy, but he felt displaced as if he were involved. Right in the middle of it. It was her eyes. They centered on his as though they could see through him, almost mesmerizing.

The other guy must have been more than a friend. After all, she came from out of town to deal with it. This dude had really screwed up if he'd tossed her to the wind. Or had he?

"Did you get to see him?"

She paused, smiling gently at him. "Yes. We're on speaking terms again, so I'm glad."

He studied her a moment longer before asking, "Are you staying with friends?"

"No, I plan to get a hotel."

Jack suggested a chain of motels all grouped in one complex. There were some restaurants and bars mixed in too. "It's just off campus, down Crowchild Trail across from the stadium. Do you know where Crowchild Trail is?" he asked solicitously.

She nodded.

(Yes, it runs past the university and somewhere beside it, my car is lying crushed on the grass ... or will be.)

"Well, it's only a stone's throw. It's called Motel Village, but I call it 'Motel-Hell.'"

Donna chuckled, not so much at the joke as how he took credit for one that was originally hers.

"Thanks," she said, "I'll go there and check in somewhere this afternoon."

They talked long after their burgers were finished. Tables around them started to empty as the afternoon began. Jack described his research job and Donna listened, content to hear the lilt of his voice wash over her. Beneath his words, there was a subtle energy twenty-two-year-olds haven't learned to hide yet: brewing interest, being on his best behavior.

"Holy cow," he exclaimed, peering at his watch, "I've got to get back. I've taken a really long lunch. Uh, which way are you headed?"

"To Bio Sciences." She still needed to return to the locker before Past Donna got out of neurology.

"I can walk with you. My office is on the way."

He liked being able to say "my office", as if it were really his and not some borrowed workspace. Once there, he casually leaned one shoulder against the doorframe.

"Well, this is where I disappear for the afternoon. ... Listen, this is gonna sound weird, but—"

He shifted his feet and scanned the wall as though inspecting it for defects. Donna watched him warily.

"—do you like Barry Manilow?"

A huge grin spread across her face. "Love him. Can't get enough of the guy."

(There, that's thirty coffees Jen!)

"Really?" The intrigue in his tone resembled more of a statement than a question, but he still searched her eyes, which met his squarely.

"Really."

He was staring again.

(Take the plunge.)

"Well that's stiff competition, but assuming he doesn't show up at five, do you want to do something? I'm done work then. We could have dinner somewhere."

Years fell away and they stood in Café-Abe. Donna saw the same brown eyes asking her to their high school graduation, and she realized just how important that date had been to him. At the time, she wasn't astute enough to define it as a date, not until years later when nostalgia mixed with desire.

She knew she shouldn't prolong her time with him. Having delivered the apology that would make the difference, Jack should be in the True Past … but he wasn't. She still felt that invisible blanket of destiny lying softly over them, a niggling lack of closure. Strangely, it gave her strength because it implied a safe recklessness. She could extend herself to him with confidence and there would be no danger of being hurt, not in this time frame and not by him.

Donna engaged his stare and answered, "I'd love to, Jack."

***

(I'll need a hotel.)

Michelle opened her suitcase on the bed and filled it with enough clothes for a few days. She smiled to herself, imagining how little she would use them. Jack had no idea she was coming. She would drive to Calgary today and find a decent hotel near the campus. Imagine his surprise to see her in his office! And he worked alone.

It would be perfect. Stroll in with her best Scarlet O'Hara face and win him over. Start by suggesting dinner at that lovely hotel dining room in Motel Village. He'd mentioned the place once when referring to his high school grad, and Michelle sensed that the sentimentality would assist in her seduction. Men were so predictable. She'd have him upstairs and naked before his steak hit the grill.

Michelle wasn't naturally impulsive. That was more Colin's style, whose face now passed before her, crestfallen at the realization of losing her. It must have cut him in two after having committed to her so whole-heartedly. A quiet guilt encroached but she quickly corrected her thinking. He was the one who had abandoned her first. And with someone else. Could he really expect her to jump back into his arms as if nothing had happened? Before dating Jack, she was crying almost every day over Colin, burying herself in classes and in the Bible, trying to fill her mind with other things, anything to blot out the pain.

Then she'd stumbled into the poker group. Though Michelle wasn't big on poker, it was a fun atmosphere. They were just students like her, diverting stresses with their weekly games. One guy almost asked her out, but effectively eluding the topic, she gently closed that door. It was less harsh than giving a point-blank refusal.

Jack was different, intriguing. Michelle could smell a conversation designed to investigate her availability, or rather, her lay-ability. Speaking with a combination of freedom and caution, Jack was just plain friendly, as though he lacked any sort of dishonorable motives.

After turning the tables and asking him out, she was surprised he agreed, even more surprised that he became her boyfriend. How wonderful it would be to capture that feeling again, to reach out and step into his arms. There would be no period of prudence this time. They had done all that before, learning each other's physical boundaries, well, *her* physical boundaries. Now the gate would be lifted and they could meet on common ground.

As she locked the suitcase in the trunk of her car, her smile carried a warm glow. She was going to meet Jack.

***

CHAPTER 38

As Paula pushed a button, coffee poured automatically from the spout. A little too much. She carefully placed the overflowing cup on the tray and pressed a lid on top, the muffled *snap!* of plastic on cardboard. A thin line of liquid dribbled down one side. Another *snap!* when a second cup joined the first. She reached for two creamers, two sugar packets, and a stir stick. That was for her. Raymond drank his black.

She remembered her first night at Raymond's house, back in her smoking days. They weren't married yet. Donna was still in high school. Paula came downstairs in the morning to find her making coffee, and Donna didn't seem surprised at her entrance: just handed her a cup and asked what she took in it. Paula was grateful to be spared an uncomfortable scene.

Raymond worried that premarital sex would set a bad example for Donna, but Paula pointed out that if his daughter was still a virgin, what they did wouldn't influence it much. What they needed to influence was her breakfast skills! Eventually, Paula took over the coffee prep, partly to have a decent cup, but also just to help. The first moment she met Raymond, she knew how serious they could become. Making coffee was one of many overtures designed to charm Donna, who proved a tough nut to crack.

Shopping for the grad dress was pleasant, but those earrings topped off the day beautifully. A gift from a motherly figure to a motherless daughter was somehow more than just a gesture to compliment a dress. It was the moment marking a true connection ... or at least the attempt at one.

This seemed to escape Raymond, who privately commented that the ensemble made Donna look too old and sophisticated for her age. The real adjective he couldn't bring himself to voice was "sexy". The night before, he'd presented Paula with a red negligee, which he then stripped off her with his teeth. She marveled at the hypocrisy.

She shook her head at him and said, "Ray, she's your daughter and she'll always be that, but she's also a woman. You have to let her be that too."

His soured reaction was equally amusing and sad.

For a high school student, Donna was so old. And private. Instead of running around like other kids programmed to grab any scrap of attention they could get, she was just another adult around the house. It must have been strange for Donna to adjust to Raymond's second marriage. The father and daughter had been a team for so long; the house was really only his in name. Paula was afraid Donna would accuse her of trying to replace her mother, but she sensed a deeper understanding from the teenager that this simply couldn't be done anyway.

Though Donna stayed pretty much to herself, her new stepmother was secretly relieved when she moved out. At the time, Paula's priority was to make this marriage last. Donna had a way of making her feel intrusive without any words at all; there was just something lacking in that girl's smile. It never quite reached her eyes and she often showed a tight line around her mouth, as though her teeth were barring the release of sharp-edged words.

For the first year or two of their marriage, Paula walked on eggshells, inadvertently coming between the father and daughter. They'd shared so much history: the bagels, hiding those blankets all over the place, the candid camera.

Raymond was clear that he valued his wife and would support Paula completely. Wasn't she the one who told him to let his daughter be a woman too? To underline the point, he stated, "Look at it this way—she's in a competitive field and she hasn't had a mother for a long time. She's not going to turn around and start needing one now. Donna's always carried her own life."

At the time, Paula didn't know how to explain that it had nothing to do with Donna's career. Carrying her life and becoming isolated in that life were two different things. In later years, Paula grew to feel ashamed of her initial territoriality. She should have spent more time with Donna.

Carefully balancing the tray, she stepped out of the elevator. Raymond was still dozing by her bedside. When Paula approached, a young professional-looking woman came out of the room. A stethoscope held the lapels of her lab coat in place. A pager was fixed onto the belt of her pants. All the signs of importance present and accounted for.

"Are you a doctor?"

"Dr. Moyer. I'm the neurology resident on call today."

"Is there any change?"

She shook her head.

"My husband's hoping for a recovery," but after catching the doctor's expression, Paula added, "I guess we shouldn't be."

Dr. Moyer swallowed uncomfortably. "I've just tested Donna for brain activity. It appears to have deteriorated since her arrival, but we'll keep testing her."

Paula's brow furrowed. They must see this kind of thing all the time, but here was this professional woman looking just as troubled over Donna's condition as family.

Then the doctor collected herself and stated, "It's unlikely your daughter will recover sufficient brain activity to sustain her life without the use of a ventilator. I'm sorry to have to tell you that, but you'll need to be prepared."

She let Paula digest this and then tactfully asked, "I was wondering ... What does your daughter do for a living?" She was careful to use the present tense. There was no consent to remove the ventilator yet.

Paula smiled sadly. "She's my stepdaughter. Her mother died—" She motioned with her head as if Patricia stood behind them, "—a long time ago." And then remembering the question put to her, "Donna is a family doctor."

Dr. Moyer exhaled audibly and they exchanged a sad look of respectful contemplation before she excused herself to continue her rounds.

Crossing the room, Paula set the tray down on a table. She stared at the figure on the bed, seeing the high school student. It wasn't until Raymond stirred at the smell of coffee that she noticed the blanket covering him. And a chill crept across her shoulders.

***

Donna strolled along the corridor toward Bio Sciences. This day was turning out quite well. Falling into his arms was the turning point. She could feel it in the air all through lunch, as though a gear had shifted down into its proper place, the engine never quite running properly until that very moment.

Calm at the sight of his hands and lips, the feeling of friendly communication eliminated the nerves she used to have in his presence. He wasn't in control of the situation anymore and neither was she. Some other force was.

His features were at the point that they exuded a solid masculinity as well as a lovely energy. It was what she'd rediscovered in herself during the

318

flash-backs. Jack and Donna flowed along a perfectly coordinated point in their personal histories, and she wanted it to continue as long as possible.

Her thoughts were all-consuming until a familiar voice behind her complained, "Well, that guy went to auctioneer's school. Why do profs talk so fast? Did you get everything?"

Two questions in a row. It was her voice. And this time, it wasn't an answering machine.

(It's her—me! What do I do? Don't look around. Just keep walking. Oh God, she's heading back to her locker! Wait, what are they saying?)

"Not everything. We should trade notes. Do you want to meet tonight and go over it?"

It was years since she'd heard Dennis's voice, but there was no mistake.

"I can't. I got something I can't get out of."

(The breakup with Ric. Slow down, listen to them. Where are they going? Where?)

"Why don't you dump that loser and let me hook you up with Brian? ... OK, OK, I'll lay off. Well, do you want to go over this stuff now instead of tonight?"

"No, let's meet tomorrow. I have errands."

(Oh, no—the locker!)

Donna walked steadily until she turned the corner to the stairwell. Then she sprinted as fast as possible, taking the stairs two at a time. She'd never run so fast in her life. The adrenaline kicked in to speed her along, and finally all those months in the gym had a purpose. Everything else suspended, only this one goal remained.

Feet pounding away, she wiggled her fingers into her pocket and coaxed the cell phone out. The key was too awkward to reach. She almost lost her balance and had to slow down for a moment. Then gripping the phone like a relay baton, she sped up again.

Down the hall, she reached the lockers and grabbed at the combination lock madly. The plastic bag of borrowed items dropped to her feet. Brushed roughly aside, its contents scattered across the tiled floor. The candy red toothbrush lay with its bristles quietly pointing toward the exit sign down the hall.

A young woman stood about ten feet away, and with curious amusement, watched Donna spinning the dial furiously. Then she left, off to some class. Donna hardly noticed her.

The lock wouldn't open. Damn it! She tried again more carefully this time. It half opened, but stuck, one of its cogs not quite in place. She yanked on it, again, two, three times. *Click—click—click!* Open. Pulling the stubborn lock off the door too hard, it flew out of her sweaty hand and rebounded against the opposite set of lockers with a loud *crash!* Donna ignored it and swung the door open.

The knapsack was sitting angled where she had left it. She tore at the side pouch, and in a flash, the phone was back where it was supposed to be. Digging down into her pants pocket, she turned it inside out to get at the apartment key. No time to maneuver it back onto the key ring. Donna tossed it at the front pouch recklessly.

And missed.

It bounced over the knapsack to land somewhere on the floor of the locker. The staccato sound of metal hitting metal punctuated the silent hallway, and she answered the sound with her own small cry of frustration as her fingers dove in after it. This time, it landed in the pouch. Two points! Knapsack away, door closed.

(Where is the lock? Where did it go?)

Her head whipped around frantically and she finally spotted it across the hall. There it is. Lunge, grab ... *Bang—bang—click!*

The transfer complete, she almost forgot about the plastic bag. The items were still strewn about. She scooped them into her arms and stood up, throwing her head to each side. The locker was exactly halfway between the stairs at both ends of the hallway, too far. With her mental clock ticking away, Past Donna's arrival would be any second now.

Her bag in hand, she ran a few steps until a class entrance provided an indentation in the wall to hide her, and she flattened her back against the side wall. The monotone voice of a lecturer drifted out from close by, but her racing heart confused her directional senses and her ears were filtering out any sound that was not her other self. She strained to hear footsteps. Her eyes darted to the next set of stairs.

She had just decided to make a run for it when her other voice floated over from down the hall, back the way she'd come. Past Donna and Dennis leisurely walking to her locker. Donna heard the same lock that so annoyingly stuck for her comply easily for her blonde self ... followed by the sound of nylon sliding over the metal locker floor ... the front pouch zipping up ... the door shutting. *Bang—bang—click!*

(OK, go the other way.)

They were still talking. Donna stayed sandwiched against the wall, the classroom door brushing against one shoulder.

"Hey, then you can set me up with that friend of yours."

"Oh, is that what this is all about?"

"OK, I've been scopin' her out," Dennis confessed, "She seems, ah—"

"Ready to chew you up and spit you out like old gum? That would be Jen."

"Just my kind of gal."

"Trust me. If you didn't already get the Welcome Signal, the door's locked."

"I'll use my master key."

"You're a pig, but that's beside the point 'cause she might actually like that. ... Look it's a combination lock and she's the only one with the numbers. That party's by invitation only."

"So get me an invite. Trade favors."

(Thank God I never got them together. He'd be dead too.)

"With our luck, Brian would end up with Jen and then I'd be stuck with you."

"Yeah, the person who got you through immunology, 'cause you were too busy swapping germs with the Linguini Lover. You could do worse, Carlin."

"Funny how you got me through it and I scored four points higher. *You* could do worse."

Their voices were getting louder.

(Shit! They're coming this way. I can't let her see me. I can't let her see me.)

All her frantic thoughts had a way of doubling themselves up in her mind. She didn't know why she felt barred from coming face to face with her counterpart, but it had something to do with the flash-backs. They catalogued what had happened in her life and this confrontation did not exist in them, not even at some remote level of possibility.

But escape was possible. Escape was crucial. Her impulses were automatic, just like the night she had eluded Ric—faking a blackout until he took his guard down. Tonight, Past Donna would be doing exactly that.

Panicking, she heard their footsteps coming closer and closer. Clutching the plastic bag to her chest, her free hand reached out and tested the doorknob. It rotated easily. The room was unlocked. Donna turned the doorknob and pivoted abruptly around the open door, swinging herself quickly into the classroom. The momentum of the door brought it closed behind her.

Thump!

She froze. Forty young faces stared at her from desks, their pens perched above their writing pads attentively. Some of them jumped in their seats at her sudden intrusion. A young lab instructor was standing a few feet away with a felt pen connected to an overhead projector. He startled and then summoned his sternest look. It wasn't very effective and Donna almost laughed. He had such a baby face; his expression more closely resembled the pout of a spoiled brat. An illegible scrawl of biological terms floated against the screen at the front of the room. A breeze from the door caused the screen to lift away from the chalkboard behind it. Gently swinging back and forth, the writing swayed distortedly.

Her spinning entrance caused the bright red toothbrush to fly out of her grasp. It slid several feet along the floor to land under someone's desk. The fellow gaped at her. Here was this wild-eyed woman, clasping a shopping bag to her chest as though it were all she possessed in the world. This was an absurd change from the usual dull lectures.

Dennis and Past Donna strolled by the door, engrossed in their conversation. Without a viable escape, she was trapped in front of these intrigued faces whose expressions demanded an explanation. Turning to the instructor, she presented her most innocent face.

"Is this Chem 201?"

Laughter coursed through the room. The instructor glared and replied that it was not.

"Oh …" She needed a few more seconds of hiding. "Well, do you know where it is?"

He stated curtly that he did not.

"Oh. Well, thanks anyway."

The gaping student handed Donna her toothbrush. He announced just loud enough to amuse the whole class, "Here, you dropped this. You might need it for chem."

More laughter. She smiled agreeably at the young man. He hesitated, returning her smile with his own candid one, and then seemed embarrassed as if caught peeking into her bedroom window. He sheepishly returned to his seat but continued to stare.

Her hand resting on the doorknob, she addressed the instructor one last time.

"You, ah, spelled hologynic wrong. It has one L."

He peered at the screen behind him and glared at her again.

Back in the hallway, Past Donna was gone. Bent over, she giggled until she was filled with uncontained laughter. The look on the lab instructor's face when she corrected his spelling! And racing around to hide from her own damned self! She never would have had the nerve to pull that off before today. It was exciting. It was fun. Alive and unconcerned about the normal things that used to constrain her, she straightened up, tall and purposeful, and headed down the hall.

***

Now what? She had money and a few scant necessities, but there was still the question of clothes and a place to stay. Distance was no problem;

Donna could walk fifty miles if need be. As the day went on, her body felt as though it had never known pain, only the plushest pampering, especially after securing Past Donna's safety. She was Patty, Conqueror-of-the-Time-Warp. Jen would have loved that.

The nearest mall sported some essentials, a shirt and a pair of jeans on sale. A glance at a store clock made her hasten her purchases, but Donna took the time to choose a makeup compact. Though debating spending the money, in the end, she decided Jack deserved some effort on their only real date.

It seemed that everywhere she went, people were staring at her. Were her clothes that out of style? Even the cashier was stealing looks. A little spooked now, Donna hurried out of the mall.

Reaching the chain of hotels in Motel Village required doubling back an extra mile, but Donna hardly felt the effort it took. The air of this time frame was energizing, her senses alive, akin to the very first bite of a juicy ripe orange, not just at the end of a meal but after a long hunger. And it was the right orange too, not some cast off, specially prepared for her to enjoy at this precise moment.

Impulsively, Donna chose the best hotel on the block. It seemed fitting, since this was exactly where they'd gone for their high school graduation. What better way to rectify an incomplete evening.

After checking in, she tossed her key on the nightstand and sat on the bed. Her money would run out within a week, so she resolved to be frugal with her thousand-dollar stash. Pay for the hotel daily and spend as little as possible on food.

What time was it? The bedside clock blinked 3:50 in stiff red lines. She should call Jack and let him know what hotel she was at. He had given her his office phone number, before she left to go tearing all over the Bio Sciences building. She punched the buttons and he answered on the second ring.

"Hi, I'm looking for Barry Manilow?"

A chuckle. "Speaking."

"How's your afternoon going?"

"Great, but I can't make it. I'm sending my assistant instead. Can't sing a note, but much better looking."

"Not that Jack creep."

"Oh, give the guy a chance. He has no life."

"Fine, I haven't been on a pity-date for a while. When are you done there?"

"Another hour. Have you thought about where you'd like to go for dinner?"

"There are a couple of restaurants in the hotel, if you don't mind coming here."

"Sure. Where are you?"

As she relayed the name, she resisted adding, "You know, the one we were at in 1987, when our pride was bigger than our crushes? ..."

"Oh yeah, that's a decent place. OK, why don't I meet you in the lobby at 5:15?"

"All right, see you then."

As Donna hung up the phone, she frowned. Another worry suddenly came into the edge of her awareness. It resembled footsteps creeping up from behind, knowing a person is approaching without actually seeing anyone yet. The ex-girlfriend ... Donna could sense her drawing near. Yes, it was definitely her. She hadn't intercepted Jack yet, but she was on her way.

(No, don't think about this. It's not like the Ric worry.)

These thoughts were materializing from nowhere, turning her concerns on and off like a faucet. It was strange how natural they felt, like they were working entirely in her favor ... or were they?

(I need to chill out, take a shower or something. Yeah, that might help.)

She stepped into the spotless bathroom and something in the mirror caught her eye. Staring, her hands grasped the top button of her blouse.

This woman in the mirror ... This woman was her *mother*, or at least a close approximation. Donna's general features remained the same—short dark hair and a fit body—but her skin glowed. All the little worry lines that had crept up on her were gone. Skimming her face, porcelain smoothness glazed her fingertips.

She looked quickly at her hands. They too were smooth and soft to the touch. The familiar scar on her forearm was missing, simply erased. So were all the other childhood marks. Her hair shimmered. In one of the few instances unprovoked by nervousness, she ran her fingers through it, and it felt thick and healthy in a way it never did before the accident.

But the biggest change was her eyes. Something in the green circles jumped out at her instantly, a longing and a fulfillment at the same time. They were never so deep with color. She realized how unnecessary the makeup purchase had been and understood the open compliment in the eyes of the student, the one who retrieved her toothbrush. No wonder people stared. She was stunning.

All her wonderful thoughts and feelings in the day were somehow demonstrating themselves through her face. This was the glimmer Donna had momentarily witnessed the morning after her night with Jack, but it had blossomed, shaping her face with a softened radiance and giving her a beauty beyond what she had ever felt. She gazed at herself in awe.

Who was she now? Where did this elegant face come from? It was still her, but ... better, as if someone had painted her picture and yielded more glamour than really existed.

Why didn't she see this earlier? Oh, yes. There was no time to look at herself in the apartment and the change rooms in the store lacked mirrors. The jeans just seemed to fit, so she bought them without checking their appearance.

Donna was hit with a sudden understanding. There was a particular sensation in seeing this image of her mother, a knowledge she could actually taste, so thorough that her mind couldn't wave it away. It was the same during her episodes of déjà vu. All those times in her life, her mother wasn't watching over her—*she* was—an inadvertent witness through the flash-backs, through that portal which had allowed Past Donna to spot herself kneeling over Jen. Each time, Past Donna had intuitively made the connection but mistaken the source. The realization brought unanswered elements of her life to a full circle. Little pieces of a jigsaw puzzle now floated down to gently land in their rightful places, the picture complete.

She took her time in the shower, enjoying the hot stream flowing down her skin. Trails of water covered her body like a quilt. One of the flash-backs had made her feel like this. Which one? There were hundreds, all flying by at an insane speed. ... Jack on the couch with her. He had surrounded her with his arms, dusting trails along the side of her body in the darkness. That evening, his hands were more sensuous than anything she had ever felt.

When her hair was dry, she dressed in her new clothes, all the while imagining his skin replacing the fabric. One more glance in the mirror— the perfect picture of serene confidence—and she carelessly tossed the makeup in the waste basket.

She was going to meet Jack.

***

Michelle arrived in Calgary after a three-hour drive. Crowchild Trail would take her straight to the university and right to Jack. She impatiently fought rush hour traffic, conscious that he would leave work at five, but to her relief she pulled into the campus grounds and found a parking spot with fifteen minutes to spare.

Though she spotted the Social Sciences building easily, Jack's office was a little trickier. There were some funny curved hallways confusing her sense of direction. Then, the sight of the main foyer triggered a memory of Jack saying that his office was just around the corner … and there it was.

With a deep breath, she reached out to turn the knob.

***

CHAPTER 39

On entering the lobby, the mere sight of Jack eagerly waiting brought immediate warmth from head to toe. Donna now understood his constant gaze and returned it with her own shining one.

"Have you been waiting long?"

"Just got here."

(Liar.)

With a pleasant expression, he pointed across the lobby to a formal dining room. "Why don't we go there?"

She took his hand, and with a beguiling smile, led the way.

As they exited the lobby, another young hopeful entered and walked straight up to the front desk. Though disappointed at missing Jack at work, Michelle was by no means deterred.

Faced with his locked office door, her heart had sunk, all the way to this gorgeous hotel lobby. Then anticipation returned. Hotels had phones and so did Jack, but to her surprise a woman answered, and for a moment Michelle was tongue-tied. She'd forgotten that he didn't live alone.

"May I please speak with Jack?"

"No, he's not home," the voice stated irritably, "I don't know where he is. Would you like to leave a message?"

(Sure, tell your son to call some girl at a hotel and then don't expect him home all night. … Yeah, that's the first impression I want to leave on Jack's mother!)

"No. I'll call later. Thanks."

Leaning back against the pillows, Michelle reconsidered. She'd call again in a while and if he wasn't home, well, it might be better to surprise him in person anyway. Hit his office first thing. She absent-mindedly surfed channels while imagining the next day.

They could have dinner in that fancy dining room. Might as well check it out. Her steps were light along the carpeted hallway. The elevator was empty, except for the shaded mirrors reflecting tender optimism as her thoughts wandered with open-ended plans.

Four floors down and past the lobby, a waiter whisked away two empty dinner plates. Coffee and desserts were set down as Donna listened to Jack describe his family, his school experiences, his thoughts on the future. They were bright words, full of ambition and faith in things to come. It was so long since she'd heard him speak with such a young frame of mind. Again, she let his words wash over her.

She asked him question after question to avoid any about herself. It was a history he was already familiar with, and it would be too strange for him to hear about her father and her upbringing. The similarities to "Donna" might scare him and she just didn't want to lie. They had spent too many years lying to each other. Safer to keep the conversation on a carefully worded path through neutral topics.

"How old are you, if you don't mind me asking?"

Pausing thoughtfully, she replied, "Well, I'm either thirty or twenty-two. I haven't decided, but today I feel twenty-two."

He laughed, "Me too. All week I felt at least fifty. Shitty week."

Then he smiled to show how much the week had improved. He thought thirty seemed logical. She looked closer to his own age, but the way she carried herself gave it away. No eyes his age possessed such worldly knowledge, though set within a much younger-looking face. It was that perfect skin, all the way down to her fingertips. As his eyes skimmed the length of her arm, her watch was the only interruption in the flow.

He observed, "Your watch has stopped."

"It must need a new battery."

Leaning across the table, he pulled her wrist lightly toward him.

At that exact moment, Michelle stepped through the dining room entrance, glanced at the tables before her, and saw pure elegance. A small candle was centered on every table. Drooping leaves strategically divided each area for a sensual air of privacy. The staff moved gracefully, almost like dancers, as they disappeared and reappeared around the plants. This was a place where lovers met, lovers and those who were well on their way. After a slow sweep of her head, she was satisfied this would be perfect for a romantic evening.

Seated at one of the smaller tables, a beautiful brunette stood out among the people. The face of her dinner partner was hidden behind some leaves, but Michelle could see a manly hand extending across the shiny wood surface to touch the woman's arm. Whoever he was, the brunette was certainly in love with him. She imagined herself in the woman's place and Jack behind the leaves.

(Tomorrow, that's exactly how I'll look, like everything I ever wanted was mine for the taking.)

Michelle was so caught by the lovely woman, she failed to recognize the glint of steel on the man's pinkie finger.

Jack could feel the smooth softness of Donna's skin, and he stifled the urge to run his fingers all the way up her arm. "3:07 … Do you ever wonder why things happen at that exact time? I mean, why didn't your watch stop at 3:02 or 3:09? Why 3:07?"

He wondered if he sounded like a babbling idiot, but this lovely woman kept peering at him as though everything he said was full of impressive depth.

Jack colored at the realization that his fingers were still resting on her wrist while he stared. He was about to remove them when she said, "I think everything happens for a reason. Sometimes the things that seem the least important are really the most."

Her other hand moved to touch his watch with her index finger.

"Take this for instance. Inside it's a maze of electronic systems. Delivers an amazing function—the ability to relay the exact time at any given moment—"

His hand stayed on her left wrist. He forgot about it as her finger traced a line away from his watch and down his hand. The ticklish sensation was lightly erotic. In an abrupt deviation off topic, a thought raced through his mind, an image of her soft smooth hands on his body flowing like warm water. His pulse quickened, but he arranged his face to show just the right amount of conscientious interest. The path she traced stopped at the ring on his smallest finger. The distance from his wrist was only a few inches, but in his mind, she'd already covered most of his body in one breathtaking sweep.

"—the watch may have all the use in the world, but who's to say it holds more value than this little piece of metal. It doesn't do anything. Just sits there. Certainly a thief would be interested in the watch, but maybe this ring means more to you than the watch ever could." She raised her eyes to meet his across the table. "And maybe 3:07 means something special too."

(It was the moment I saw my life. It was the moment that became eight years. And it was the moment I came back to find you again …)

He listened intently to her words, sensing something else mixed into them, but he couldn't pinpoint what that might be. She was fascinating. What was in her voice to magnify her words so charismatically? He glanced down at their oddly connected hands. Hers sandwiched his left hand with a touch, both slight and compelling, like the warm whisper of a secret in his ear. Reluctantly releasing her hands, he sat back in his seat ... and in full view of Michelle.

As Michelle continued to stare at the striking woman, the host suddenly materialized, blocking her view of the restaurant. Standing before her, he simultaneously concealed Jack and preserved her romantic plans.

"Would you care for a table, miss?"

With a European accent she could not place, every word sounded as if tempting her with a decadent dessert.

"No thank you, not tonight."

"Very well, tomorrow then," he responded as though she had promised to return only to see him, and Michelle felt her cheeks turning red. Could he see the fantasy in her eyes?

Embarrassed, she left the dining room and the host returned to his duties.

Back in her room, she put the phone down. Though unable to reach Jack a second time, Michelle maintained her master plan. Just adapt the details.

(Tomorrow Jack, tomorrow ...)

Carried away with fantasies she'd never allowed herself before, it almost felt like he was there anyway. Before drifting off to sleep in the king-size bed, her thoughts were content in the assumption that desire equals outcome.

"Man," Jack remarked to Donna, "I've been talking your ears off. Listen, there's a country bar down the block. It would be a chance to listen to something else instead of me. Do you feel like doing some two-stepping?"

Donna remembered his rhythmic sway guiding her around the dance floor. He'd worn a suit for the occasion and picked her up in his mother's car. They thought they were grown-ups back then. This was the real thing, maybe because of his voice. She had the strange feeling he'd just asked her to be his lover, not go two-stepping down the block. It was an invitation she had longed for in another life and those feelings renewed themselves in his deep brown eyes.

She smiled with pleasure and answered, "Yes. ..."

Staring, he had the strange feeling she'd just agreed to be his lover. Her eyes were looking through him again. He knew what it was—she looked at him as though they had already been lovers, not working up to it. Incredibly erotic, but still subtle enough to keep him on his toes.

He thought she was following his lead, but she was tuned in to a different wavelength. It was that other photograph, the faint one she could only sense. There was a pervasive feeling that whatever they did tonight had already happened on some other plane. In the past without even existing yet. It buoyed her confidence immediately with the light lift of a balloon. With every passing minute, Donna moved closer to Jack and further from her worries, as if securing him would forever place him between herself and harm. Guarded by serene strength, she felt ... safe.

***

Inside the apartment, Billy stood quietly beside the door. His posture was deceptively relaxed, ready to spring into action. When the sound of steps echoed from the stairs, his body tensed all the way down to two menacing fists.

Ric quietly inserted the key and turned the knob. Slowly opening the door, he tip-toed into the darkened apartment.

(Good, she's in bed. Need something heavy.)

Silently, he started toward the bookcase, moving softly along the carpet. Billy glided behind careful to stay out of his peripheral vision. Hefting one large book, Ric slid it back in place and chose another instead.

Suddenly, a fist slammed into Ric's face. The book toppled to the floor and landed open. An uppercut was enough to stun him but not quite knock him off his feet, so using that precious second, Billy slid sideways behind his opponent. As he did, he braced his hands on Ric's shoulder blades. Before Ric could even catch his breath, Billy stepped around to the side and brought his knee up hard into Ric's stomach. Then, shoving his bleeding face down into the carpet, he yanked Ric's arm behind his back. A horrid needle-like pain shot through it.

"Newsflash. This is how she felt, Asswipe."

Ric fought to turn over, to get his arm out from behind his back, but he was firmly pinned by an angled wrist. It was pathetic the miniscule effort it took to level this piece of shit: just a matter of sequence, timing, and pressure points.

He could imagine the police going over his clothes and finding splotches of DNA. Assault charges and court dates would follow. Was anyone worth that? She was, but done right, this pissant wouldn't even be able to identify his attacker.

Ric was pushing against the carpet with his free hand. He managed to lift his body up a few inches until Billy stomped on his fingers. When Ric screamed into the carpet, Billy knew he'd broken at least one of them.

"Listen, you fuck! If you ever come near her again, she'll be the last thing you ever see."

He shoved his knee roughly into Ric's side and yanked his wrist around harder. A sudden sharp *pop!* came from the twisted shoulder. He didn't know what sounded worse, the joint dislocating or Ric's cry of agony.

"Shut up! Anything happens to her, you won't be in jail 'cause I'll fucking kill you. And I can do it."

Ric swallowed the pain by taking in quick shallow breaths, while Billy explained exactly how he would do it, pausing here and there to press his knee further into Ric's kidney.

"They'll never even find you."

When Billy dragged him up to his feet, he maintained a tight grip on the injured arm. It hung at an odd angle, the dislocation making his shoulder seem sunken and sloped. The sudden movement caused Ric to whimper sharply.

Even in the dark, a pool of blood could be seen on Donna's living room carpet, some tiny spots nearby. It would mix in with the beige tone to produce a rust color.

Ric's nose sat at a crooked angle, still dripping blood, and Billy was careful to stay behind him. He would have to get this sniveling asshole out of here without being seen.

Spinning Ric around toward the front door, he growled close to his ear, "Gonna stay away? Say yes. Say it!"

When he tugged on the shoulder again, Ric almost screamed, "Yes— yes! *Fuck!*" and dropped to one knee.

"Atta boy ..." Billy hoisted him back up. "Now you're going to drive yourself to the hospital. Your clumsy ass fell down a shit-load of stairs, right?"

Ric nodded and a searing pain spiked into his forehead. More blood washed down his chin. A stale coppery taste filled his mouth.

Steering him toward the door, Billy instructed, "Get the fuck outta here. If you tell anyone about this, you'll wish you only had broken bones."

Billy gripped the back of Ric's neck while ushering him out. From a distance, the gesture cut a picture of two drinking buddies on a Friday night, but the pinch of sensitive muscles kept Ric rigidly contained as he passed through the door.

It was impossible to stay calm with his screaming shoulder. The slightest movement was like gritty sandpaper rubbing through to the bone. He could barely grip the steering wheel, but somehow he arrived at the hospital and delivered Billy's explanation to many discerning eyes, carefully avoiding them with his own.

***

332

The hospital room overlooked an expansive view of the city. It was like Christmas out there. Sparkling streetlights decorated the blackness while other tiny lights drifted across the horizon. Raymond could see the intermittent red signal of the odd airplane too. An element of mystery cloaked this scene, of things existing under the cover of darkness. They were real, but hidden ... like his memories.

It was hard to look at her, to be faced with such a traumatized image of his daughter. This wasn't her. She was the three-year-old playing Pat-a-cake. She was the doctor reaching for her university diploma. She was the eighteen-year-old he had danced with at her high school graduation. At that point in her life, he could still see the little girl part of her, the energetic innocence that fades with age.

City lights swirled around them, bouncing off the smooth hardwood floor. The band played as they slowly pivoted, and the swimming lights created their own rhythm racing through the room. Cigarette smoke chased the dancing couples with a pervasive haze. He was reminded of Mexican music, the kind that was popular now. Guitars strumming to a sexy beat.

(Why would this style of music come to mind? There was none of it at her high school graduation.)

Imagining her in that light green dress, he tried to overlook her grown-up appearance and the way Jack's eyes followed her every move. He liked Jack, but there was a feeling of interference hanging in the air, as though the young man were cutting in. This was supposed to be Raymond's dance with his daughter.

He closed his eyes and focused on the space around them, shutting out the reality of her accident—another pivot, sway, step, step sway—but as much as he concentrated, he couldn't keep the musical memory centered in his head.

Opening his eyes, he watched the spinning lights come to a sudden stop across the city landscape. They were only streetlights after all. The hospital room was silent. And Donna's condition was still critical. She would never dance again.

But ... he could smell cigarettes. Was Paula smoking in the bathroom? No, he must have imagined it.

He strained his senses, listening for ... what? Strange—for one enchanting second, he could almost hear guitars.

***

Smoky excitement filled the bar, people looking for people. On a high stage, the band was positioned before an enormous screen where country music videos played during their breaks.

Jack and Donna danced comfortably in each other's arms. In between songs, he held her hand, entwining his fingers in hers. Even sounds were more distinct now. She couldn't chalk it up to the reverberations of a live band. Everything was just accentuated, displayed with an extra shot of brilliance. Never had Donna felt so alive.

After several fast songs, the lead singer announced, "Now we're going to take this south of the border, way south!"

A slow Latin rhythm surrounded them and Jack pulled her close. The bittersweet chords, strummed with a sad and soulful passion, swept them up in the air of the evening.

Every now and then, the smooth skin of her forearm brushed against his. Before today, his romantic inexperience kindled annoying little self-doubts that always got in the way. To orchestrate a full seduction entailed an elusive confidence. Now, composure and courage were single-handedly settling into place.

Donna thought about their episode in bed, the one now years away. She remembered begging Jack to kiss her, a desperate and futile feel to her needs, wanting his lips so badly. She stared at them as they swayed together.

Her free hand slid up along his shoulder. Slipping through his wavy hair, her fingers stroked the back of his neck. Their eyes locked just as they did all those years ago and she said, "Please kiss me."

For Jack, the entire room vanished. No one there but her. One arm circled her waist, pulling her closer as his grip tightened on her hand. Her breath caught. His lips were soft, testing the waters. She let the sensation exist without exaggerating its depth, but it still rattled her inside. They were the same lips she had craved so desperately, and for the first time Jack was kissing her willingly, without tension or guilt.

As soon as it happened, Donna felt another shift in the time frame. The motor transferred another gear down and the engine was running fine. Any fatigue from her long day disappeared, carried off in the energy waves of this era.

She was on a strange journey with tired pieces of herself blowing off little by little as she flew down the highway. Until now, they had been tragically mismatched, but as eight years dissolved, their desires synchronized into a perfect rhythm. If such things as soulmates existed, she knew he was hers.

Now, both arms were around her, pressing her against him. Jack kept kissing her in the middle of the dance floor, oblivious to the smirks all around. Finally, she leaned back breathless and weak. If he didn't stop, she would melt right into him, right here and now.

She stood inside herself, precariously perched on the edge of the cliff, but this time, Jack was ready to fall with her. Donna could feel them both tipping toward the crashing waves below; she was never meant to fall alone. The heart-stopping seconds before they landed in the water were stretched out while she swam in the depths of his eyes. Her hand touched his cheek. ...

And they both knew that he wouldn't be going home tonight.

***

CHAPTER 40

Calgary woke to another crisp morning. People showered, dressed, ate breakfast, and drove their cars along Crowchild Trail, unaware a tragic accident had occurred there only yesterday. Raymond and Paula would blend in with the rush hour traffic, before turning off to the hospital. They slept at home, at least as well as they could, after Paula convinced him of the futility of remaining by Donna's bedside.

She saw how terrible he felt, tired and downcast. A distinct look of disbelief clung to him, as though he thought by just sticking to the morning routines, his daughter would walk in with a bag of bagels.

Standing in the bathroom, staring at her reflection, little questions suddenly took on major proportions as Paula held a tube of lipstick indecisively. Would Raymond see her makeup and accuse her of approaching this day like any other? If she wore none, would he consider it a sign of disrespect, that she hadn't thought enough of the day to look presentable? Focusing with avid intensity, the issue volleyed back and forth until she gazed into the mirror and saw the real distress in her eyes.

It wasn't the makeup. She had summed it up to Dr. Moyer yesterday; Donna was not her daughter. No matter what she did to ease her husband's pain, she would never share it with him to the same extent. He was truly alone in this and the realization made her feel inadequate, as though she could not hold her proper place in his life if she suffered less.

The frustration lacked a release of tears to subdue its ache. It just sat there fueling her anxiety. Finally, she put the lipstick down and accompanied him to the car.

***

Rippling sheets along the bed molded the folds into a cocoon. Jack could feel her body against him, but not enough, and he pressed in closer. Just a few more minutes. No, he had to have a shower and get going. Though tempting to phone in sick, behavior like that could cost him an extension on the research job.

Sleeping soundly, she looked like an angel. No classic puffy face. He didn't think she was wearing any makeup and yet she still looked perfect. Just a few more minutes ...

The shower helped him wake up. Reluctantly he dressed and bent over to kiss her again. She stirred with a drowsy smile that spread across her face seductively, eyelids half-closed. The sheets were tucked under one arm and draped across her lower back, hips barely covered.

(Man, I want to tear my clothes off and get back in this bed!)

Jack whispered, "I'm off to work. Sleep some more and call me later."

She turned from her side onto her back, and pulled his head close with one hand. He kissed her lips, her cheek, her lips again, and he almost stayed.

He drove against the downtown traffic, glad that he worked alone. No one would notice the same outfit two days in a row. Yesterday, these clothes were just pieces of cloth hanging off his body, but last night, they became obstacles. Patty slowly peeled away the layers, inching their way in degrees to a smooth nakedness. While her fingers moved along each button, she murmured to him: what she wanted to feel, where she wanted his hands. It was almost as erotic as feeling his pants slide down with her palms on his thighs. Then it was his hands taking over, holding her face, crushing her body against his, their clothes abandoned on the carpet, a shirt draped over the edge of the bed, another over the phone ... which rang just as he arrived at 9:00.

He punched the speaker button eagerly, but this female voice was older and angry.

"How could you stay out all night and not call? I was worried. You didn't come home for supper and then you didn't come home at all. I didn't sleep all night. ..."

Making a face, he patiently waited to cut in.

"Sorry Mom, I thought I told you. I'm helping some guys move office stuff this week. It's taking a long time, so I just stayed at their place last night. I have to do some more tonight, so I won't be home again ... except I should pick up a change of clothes for tomorrow. But I won't be home for supper, so don't make anything for me."

The story worked. It carried just the right mix of sketchy detail to sound plausible. He added one more apology at the end and that did the trick. She soon deviated to other topics, relieved her son was not a complete jerk.

"Oh, you got some phone calls last night. One was your friend Jen. She sounded urgent about something."

"Yeah, what's new? I'll call her later. Who were the others?"

"I don't know. They didn't say. Well, I just wanted to make sure you're all right."

"I know, Mom. Bye."

Michelle didn't even cross his mind. A silly smile stayed on his face as he cheerfully photocopied fresh data sheets. He thought about how he'd finally achieved his promise to himself that someday he would stay in that posh hotel. The smell of Patty enveloped him, keeping his mind on little else. In the process, he completely forgot to return Jen's call.

***

Dr. Moyer entered the hospital room to find Mr. Carlin talking to his daughter, trying to reach some part of her long gone.

The patient looked even worse. The facial bruises and swelling were more prominent. Another CT scan showed that no more fluid had accumulated along the temporal lobe or in any other areas of Donna's brain. Dr. Moyer did another pain test, pressing a sharp instrument into Donna's hands, but at best, the asymmetrical response was sluggish. Neurologically this patient should be capable of recovery. Physically she showed no signs of improvement.

Mr. Carlin had questions: Why wasn't she getting better if they'd gotten the pressure off her brain? What was the procedure? Should they do it again? Couldn't they do anything else?

It was hard trying to explain the situation to this man. He so obviously would give anything to deny his daughter's fate. So often when people wanted medical details, it was a desperate way to feel like they were doing something themselves; question the treatment plan, the effort put into the patient, even the qualifications of the staff.

Taking a seat beside Raymond and Paula, Dr. Moyer answered each question in turn. She tried to soften her explanation of the burr hole procedure, but how could he not be horrified at the thought of someone drilling into his daughter's skull to drain blood out? She had to emphasize that this one procedure saved lives, possibly Donna's.

Handling family members was part of the job. They had life and death questions, questions which sometimes had answers and sometimes not. Usually she didn't allow herself to delve too personally, but this particular patient was someone just like her, same age, both female physicians.

338

She wondered about Donna's private life, whether she was married or would have been at some point. Their profession had a way of delaying that kind of thing indefinitely, but what if this woman did have someone special, someone to lose her head about and make her feel lost inside her own skin?

Then she realized that they'd actually met, several years ago when she was just Wendy Moyer applying for med school. Her friend Dennis had talked about his lab partner, a girl who was going out with some asshole. Wendy hadn't paid particular attention to the topic, but her awareness of Donna Carlin arose on the day he introduced them. She was a handsome blonde ... except for the shiner.

The woman in this bed was a brunette, though Wendy was sure it was the same person. She should be able to fix Donna's injuries. The brain was a remarkable organ, capable of regeneration, of learning and relearning amazing things most people took for granted.

She struggled with the hope, but at best it was fleeting. People didn't recover once brain activity slowed down this much and that was what Mr. Carlin really needed to understand.

"Donna's condition is worsening. She's not responding as much as she did earlier. I'm sorry, but I need to prepare you to make a decision soon."

"How the hell do you prepare for your daughter's death?" Raymond reacted right in front of her. And then his face filled with guilt at his outburst. She was probably the one who put the blanket on him. She couldn't have known that piling on blankets was Donna's job, another quirk in their relationship untouched by outsiders.

He stammered an apology, but she waved his effort away with compassionate eyes. Wendy had heard worse.

***

Michelle walked across the university grounds toward the Social Sciences building. With the sun already hot at 9:30, it would be a beautiful day, just the kind to accommodate her plans with Jack. She looked forward to feeling his arms around her waist and his lips kissing hers. She looked forward to everything that would happen today. The timing felt right somehow, as if fate itself had painted this canvas well in advance.

She opened the office door gingerly and saw Jack sitting across the room in front of a computer, his back to her. Engrossed in his work, he obviously didn't hear the door creak. It had sure sounded loud to her.

Picking up a pen, he made some marks on a sheet of paper. Michelle carefully closed the door behind her, wanting to surprise him with her eager smile, but when she was about to speak, the phone rang to his right. He pressed the speaker button and a woman's velvety voice filled the room.

"Good morning."

He reclined his chair, dropped the pen on the desk, and placed his hands behind his head. His voice was equally engaging. "Good morning! Are you up and about?"

"I will be shortly. How is your day going?"

"Not as good as my night. I got to tell you I haven't stopped thinking about you for the last hour. I'm having a hard time getting anything done around here and I mean that in every sense of the word. It's good I work alone."

The woman gave a low laugh of pleasure. Even from behind, Michelle could tell he would leap across Canada to get to that voice.

"I can't wait to see you again, Jack. Can I meet you for lunch?"

"I have a better idea. I'll meet *you* for lunch. Stay right where you are. Don't even get out of bed. Be there in a couple of hours."

A flirtatious giggle. "OK, I'll keep the bed warm for you."

Michelle's face crumpled. It was that Donna person. It had to be. She wanted to slam her hand down on the phone, cutting off their flirtations. She wanted to slap him for lying to her all those months, but her feet were glued to the spot. Couldn't move at all.

She remembered Colin's offer to wait in that deli. If true to his word, he would be sitting there right now swallowing another corned beef sandwich. He hated corned beef. Colin had come to her openly, confessing his sins, and she had turned him down in favor of someone with even worse morals. What a fool she was. Twice.

(Get out, just get out and get away from here!)

She snapped out of her frozen state. Turning as quietly as possible, Michelle held her breath lest he hear the tiniest sound. As she closed the door behind her, a glimpse of Jack's profile—smug and happy with the world—was the last she ever saw of him.

***

CHAPTER 41

Donna put the phone down, laid her arms above her head, and breathed in the musky smell clinging to the pillows. Last night had been lovely ... erotic. ... One word couldn't adequately describe how he had covered her with his lips and then his body.

For one night, he had been completely hers; no stolen moments mistakenly treasured as real and poignant, no overlay of another's face pulling his desires to a separate time. No separation at all. The ex-girlfriend was gone. Donna could feel her absence acutely, as much as she could feel the slippery polyester quilt draped across her own body.

Donna had changed history, altered her past, or had she? It didn't feel altered. This time frame only felt correct once she bumped into Jack. *Fell* into Jack.

A conversation with Jen wandered through her mind, words from long ago debating the possibilities of time travel. Even if you could only change what was already correct, Jen had argued the possibility of two time periods of equal importance. Was this how Donna kept sensing the other time frame, the one in the future? Were these events correct or corrected?

She theorized that the future minutes were running on level with this one. The pain she felt in her foot had probably occurred at exactly the same clock time as it did here. There was no concrete evidence, only an awareness of the late morning sunshine in both time periods. On her arrival, she had been questioning every perception, but now a certainty had solidified, a trust within herself.

An hour later, Donna was still deep in thought when something intruded on her senses. At first she ignored it, believing it to be a realistic part of her imagination, but slowly she distinguished her inner thoughts from the whisper-thin sensations around her.

It was the other time frame. What was happening there? Closing her eyes, she concentrated hard.

A purely intellectual thought reached her mind: someone touching her left hand. There was no physical sensation and no corresponding emotion either, but regardless, she was somehow certain this had occurred. It was the same sort of knowledge she naturally overlooked, like the awareness of her head rotating on its vertebral axis to look behind. It just occurred and she pretty much took it for granted. Without question, someone had just touched her hand, but it drew her attention in a way the automatic workings of her body never did.

She stared at her palms, wondering if the visual aid would prompt a clearer understanding. The heart line on her left hand caught her eye and the predictions of Paula's palm reading now made sense. The loop in her heart line was supposed to represent a repeated love. Circles are continuous with no discernible starting or ending points. She had simply looped back in time to continue the path.

Now someone was touching her right hand. Suddenly, a painful signal traveled from the nerve in her hand straight up to her brain. *Ouch!* She curled her fingers into a fist and jerked her hand back into her body. What the hell?

For a moment, a faint energy from the intruder's touch lingered on her hands. It wasn't her father, although he was definitely close by, which evoked a measure of calm. It wasn't anyone she knew well. She could sense vague familiarity in the energy traces, as well as an obscure associated similarity to Donna. It was a woman, a tired young woman with a peculiar mix of sympathetic and routine responses. She was someone undertaking a necessary task and not feeling good about it, but at the same time, the task was entirely natural.

Donna was reminded of a time during her residency. At a point when she'd been on duty for about twenty hours, a man came into the hospital complaining of chest pains. Before they could even ask his name, he fell to the floor. No writhing in pain or clutching his chest with important last words to convey, just standing one minute and dead the next.

After attempting to revive him, Donna was instructed to pronounce his time of death. It was the seventh person she'd legally declared dead, but despite the unpleasantness of the task, she carried it out devoid of emotion. It just had to be done, and for whatever reason, this tired young woman was doing the same by delivering a stinging sensation to her hand just now. Then it was gone, dissolved into the future.

Now the most prominent presence was her father who was trying to communicate something. So faint. Yesterday she had picked out one sentence clearly, but today she was only conscious of him near. He was scared, though why was a mystery, just that it involved her somehow.

(I'm fine, Dad, more than fine.)

But his worries stubbornly hung on, the way the smell of smoke lingers after a fire, even one several miles away, permeating everything within reach. Slowly, her father faded as his time frame drifted in and out.

Jack would arrive soon with an appetite in tow. Donna phoned room service and ordered two sandwiches, then changed it to three. The Godzilla Gut. She would have to be careful not to use their old jokes around him— which was hard to avoid—but she could just imagine the weird reaction she'd get by coming out with one of those now.

Donna also called the front desk to reserve the room another night. Could they please cancel housekeeping? She would be sleeping. The sandwiches arrived minutes before Jack. Tastefully presented on shiny white dishes, they were almost too perfect to disturb.

At 11:30, a knock sounded on the door and she opened it with a big smile, cloaked in a bed sheet. Her hands loosely clutched the fabric behind her back. Her eyes shone with a seductive invitation. Circling Donna in his arms and edging her toward the bed, he maneuvered the sheet out of her grasp.

She said, "I ordered some food. I thought you might be hungry."

Without so much as a glance at the tray, he answered, "Yeah, it looks great. I'm starved," as he bent down to kiss her.

She giggled and they flopped down on the bed.

"Here, let me have a bite of that," he murmured, nibbling her neck. "Ummm, that's good. Let's try this. ..."

She relaxed in his arms and enjoyed it all over again. An hour later, the sandwiches still sat untouched.

***

Donna lay in bed long after Jack rushed back to work. He had frantically dressed between kisses and finally dashed out the door, clutching two sandwiches. Even after he was gone, she could feel his body covering her with intimate strength and she continued to embrace the sensations.

When she left the hotel room, it was after 2:00. A plan formed in the back of her mind, whispering its intentions like a playful child. This morning, her father's presence had jarred loose another flash-back, one she needed to face. It was the moment of irritation Donna had experienced the first time he delivered a bag of bagels to her. The irritation felt wrong somehow, that she could replace it with balance by replacing the source. And the source was Paula.

She rode on the subway to the downtown core. Skyscrapers of concrete and glass towered over her, but somehow they were not as menacing as the gloomy trees from yesterday morning. Was it only yesterday she had arrived, ready to right the wrongs of her life? It seemed an eternity, that she and Jack had been together much longer. Years could not compare with the centuries their two souls had been entwined, an insight reaffirmed with every minute of this time frame.

She walked steadily along the endless pavement until she found what she was looking for—the bagel bakery—across the street from her father's office building. Warm smells drifted out as she stood in front of the bakery and gazed up at his building. Seventh floor. He was probably in there right now. He would work until 4:00 and then cross over to the parkade, like clockwork.

(Yes, this should be fun.)

She entered the bakery and confidently strode up to the counter, where a man in his forties was counting a handful of change.

Donna recognized him from the numerous special orders she had placed in the last eight years ... or would place. She hoped her request would take him by surprise, that Paula had not beaten her to the punch.

The baker straightened up at the sight of her. This guy was a bit creepy. A certain level of friendliness edges beyond customer service and it was a line he just seemed to cross in some unidentifiable way. But she met his gaze squarely.

Unveiling a winning smile, she declared, "I'd like you to make a dozen peanut butter flavored bagels to go."

He pushed his eyebrows together and pursed his lips. "Uh, we don't have that flavor. Why don't you just buy plain bagels and put peanut butter on them?"

She'd forgotten how soft his voice was and angled closer to the counter. He almost grinned. The tactic usually forced them to lean nicely, and with the right shirt, he got a decent view. This one he could imagine on all fours.

Suddenly her limited resources were insignificant in light of this important mission. She slapped a twenty-dollar bill on the counter and heightened her smile.

"No, I really want peanut butter mixed into the batter. Will that cover the cost? I need them before 4:00."

At 3:45, her order was ready. Though the baker muttered at her absurd request, he delivered the bagels on time, hot and steaming. And he didn't even charge her much. Maybe she had misjudged him.

She offered a parting remark, "You should consider adding this to your regular menu. I'm sure you'll have people asking for it."

(Just you lady. You'd be asking for it and wouldn't I fucking give it to you.)

She caught his eyes skimming her blouse. No misjudging this one. He was just plain creepy through and through. But at least she got the bagels.

Darting over to the parkade, Donna started a silent countdown, and as 4:00 approached, her childlike excitement increased. Stationed next to Raymond's car on the third floor, she carefully watched the front entrance of his office building. Her second stake-out.

She ran her fingers lightly over the surface of the hard parkade railing. Cool to the touch, dull in color and impervious to the elements of nature, it would endure wind, rain, and snow to remain strong in its function. In and of itself, the solid lifeless consistency lacked poignant meaning, but never again would Donna look at a smooth line of concrete without seeing the replay of her life.

Leaning against it, she considered how fragile it really was compared to the invisible forces that shaped her time here. In one easy step, she had glided into a complete attitude change. Now Jen's perspective on the flexibility of time made perfect sense. Often transparent, it could move with unadulterated speed, gone before a person could even register its presence. Then, other moments could stretch their length like rubber. The elasticity of a person's perceptions was both laughable and frightening. If she were to prevent the creation of this solid structure, it would simply disappear from her future. No more parking spots. The thought was humbling. How easily could that same force transplant her to wherever it saw fit?

At 4:05, Raymond passed through the entrance doors and out onto the sidewalk. He was one of many crisp suits with a briefcase in hand. Her eyes followed his path until he was out of sight, entering the parkade two floors below. Then she placed the warm bag on the hood of his car and positioned herself a safe distance away. Crouched down, she had a perfect view through the windows of the car concealing her.

A minute later, there he was, stepping off the elevator. His mind must have been elsewhere, because he didn't notice the bag right away. One hand was in his pocket, fishing for keys. When he reached the driver's side, he stopped abruptly and stared with annoyance at the object perched on the hood, the way people do when they believe someone has tampered with their vehicle.

Then, he leaned over to take a look. Donna smiled to see his face gradually change from annoyance, to curiosity, and finally to pleasant surprise. He reached into the bag, and smiling at the indisputable scent, pulled out a steaming bagel.

Raymond scanned the area for his daughter. The bagels were so warm, she must have timed this gift and snuck out minutes earlier. Donna ducked her head below the level of the windows and tried not to giggle. She stayed securely hidden until she heard his car moving away.

Mission accomplished. She had put in motion years of special bagel orders, which would serve to unite father and daughter. Paula may have been the original culprit, but Donna had now taken over. She could see her father in her mind's eye, connecting the bagels with his daughter the way he should have from the very start. She leaned over the railing to watch him drive down the street. He would start another breezy fall evening with his wife. It was all right now that he had a wife. Donna had secured her own place in his past.

Again, light waves from this time frame deftly moved through her. Shifting the past, they resettled the order of events like a splash of water levels sand on the shore. She sensed that this act created a layer of polish to her life, a supple leather interior to compliment the engine. It wasn't crucial to get from Point A to Point B, but the ride was lovely.

***

Raymond stayed by her bedside all afternoon, except to go to the cafeteria. What did she call her high school cafeteria? Something, but it escaped him. Other odd tidbits came to mind as well: breakfast, just the two of them, her medical graduation, candid photos ... the bagels.

During the afternoon, he felt a sudden urge for one of them. He had the strange feeling that should he leave Donna's bedside for the bakery, she would still be there with him somehow. He envisioned driving to the parkade and walking down the block. He could smell the warm scent floating up from the paper bag—the one that mysteriously appeared as a gift eight years ago—as though it sat under his nose right now.

"Ray ... Honey, we have to talk about it."

Instantly the past disappeared and he was faced with Paula, studying his frightened eyes.

"Not in front of her. She told me you don't talk in front of patients. *(Probably didn't think she'd be one ...)*

"Let's go outside, OK?" She held out her hand. The glint of her wedding band reflected a concentrated beam of light onto the wall, right above Donna's bed.

He nodded and followed Paula to the elevator. They sat on a bench outside the front entrance where smokers were milling around. Whiffs of their cigarettes encircled them. Paula had quit years ago, but she could feel her mouth around a filtered tip, inhaling the uplifting sensation of nicotine to race through her bloodstream and relax her. She saw that Raymond was oblivious to the tainted air breezing past, and chastised herself for her preoccupied thoughts.

"Ray, I know this is awful to face, but you have to let them turn it off."

"How can I do that? What if she really is OK? People stay in comas for years and then wake up. How can I end her life before she's even had a chance to fight?"

"She's already losing the fight. They've seen lots of these cases before. They're telling you not to hope, because they know there is no hope. I hate saying that to you, Honey."

She stopped, tears forming in her eyes. She was afraid everything she said sounded belittling. Hooking her arm in his, Paula leaned against his shoulder.

Raymond was staring blankly at the hospital entrance.

"You know how many hours she spent here doing her residency? I told her to move home, but she wouldn't. We could have made things easier for her, meals and laundry. I thought she and Brian were working up to an engagement. I thought that's why she wanted to stay on her own, but she just walked in the house one day and said, 'Well, I have news. I don't have a boyfriend anymore, but I got a job so things are even.' She wouldn't talk about her and Brian. ... You know, she won't have any more opportunities like that and she could have had anybody. How am I supposed to believe that bruised person in there is her?"

Paula sighed. Their relationship had never been tested beyond the usual marital irritations, and she had no idea what to do. Finally she said, "Let's face it tomorrow. Just enjoy having her here another day."

***

347

CHAPTER 42

By 4:00, Jack could feel the effects of living on love. His late arrival back to work was no problem—nobody really kept track of him anyway—but his boss required a lot of data summaries that afternoon. In the hope of returning to Patty by 5:00, his fingers sped over the keyboard, just as they had sped over her three hours earlier.

He would have to go home first and pick up a change of clothes, his razor as well. Plus that stereo. His mom wouldn't care if he borrowed it. He checked twice to make sure the tape was cued. Boy he was tired, but even that disappeared at the sight of her again.

"Hey, what are you doing with all those clothes on? I left you specific instructions to be naked when I got back."

He stepped forward and set the stereo down on the nightstand. An overnight bag hung off one shoulder as the hotel door shut behind him, and Donna jumped out of his reach.

"Hypocrite," she retorted, "You seem pretty well-clothed yourself."

A delightful pause while they stared each other down, gunslingers poised to draw.

"Hey, I can strip faster than you can call room service," he boasted.

"Care to bet on that?"

"What if I win?"

Keeping a sedate expression, she slipped over to his side and whispered in his ear.

His eyes went wide. "Hmmm ... anywhere?"

"Yeah. And if I win ..." Her lips whispered in his other ear and he broke out in a huge grin. The overnight bag thumped to the floor.

Her chin rose challengingly. "Do you agree to the terms of the wager?"

"Agree? Hell, I might throw the contest just to try that second option. First one done and on the bed wins."

"Deal."

Donna extended her hand professionally. When Jack cordially grasped it, she suddenly yanked his hand down hard, and with him off-balance, grabbed her own shirt and whipped it over her head. It flew behind her as she snaked out of her jeans.

Jack fell to the floor. "No cheating!"

Staying on his back, his fingers wrestled with the button on his pants. She was already out of her jeans, but the bra was slowing her down. Forget the hooks. She wiggled it over her head and tossed it toward her shirt, which was lying in a tiny heap in the bathroom doorway. Jack had managed to slide his pants and underwear off together. He was catching up fast. He pulled his shirt over his head, popping a button off while Donna jumped out of her panties, and with a giant leap, Jack dove onto the bed.

He punched one hand straight up. "I win!"

"You still have socks on," Donna pouted, crawling up beside him, "That's worth another five seconds. Take your penalty like a big boy and concede defeat."

"In the penalty box?"

She laughed as Jack leaned on all fours toward the nightstand. He flicked a button on the stereo and instantly, the drumbeat of "Copacabana" filled the room.

"Barry, my love!" Donna cried as Jack pulled her hips under him. Her arms flailed in surrender. "Take me, Barry!"

Bending over her, he instructed, "Yeah, just pretend I'm him and we'll get along fine. ..."

***

Jack never knew that sex was so good. He didn't want to tell her he was new at it, but if he read those all-knowing eyes correctly, she already suspected. Regardless, she seemed to be having a good time. And he was learning quickly. When he did this, she said "Jack ..." letting the word hang lightly in the air. When he did that, she said, "*Jack* ..." caressing it with a low moan. The mere sound pulled him closer than he ever thought possible. She'd say his name like that and he would become lost in her eyes, in her smell, lost in every part of her. It was amazing how this woman could surround him so completely.

Later, they ordered room service and ate on the balcony as the evening fell into its own rhythm. There was something methodically peaceful about traffic pacing endlessly past the hotel. At this gentle time of day with pastel shades flowing across the skyline, the thought *(Jen would like this sunset)* occurred to both of them, but of course neither voiced it.

"So, how long are you staying?"

"I'm not sure. I have a decent budget for this trip, but if we keep ordering room service, that'll dry up pretty fast."

He was quick to answer, "Well, don't worry about that. I can cover the cost. Where are you from anyway?"

"I grew up here. ... I'm at a strange point in my life. I'm kind of in between jobs. I'm not sure what I'm supposed to be doing now."

"Well, what do you want to do?" he asked, wondering how he could work himself into that equation.

(What would you do if you couldn't be a doctor anymore?)

A couple of Christmases ago they had already had this conversation. She remembered tobogganing and hot chocolate on her couch, while they discussed their respective careers. Her attitude had been so limited then.

(It would take a pretty serious situation to make me consider anything else.)

Well, this pretty much qualified as a serious situation—going back in time and recreating major elements of her life. Practicing medicine seemed comparatively inconsequential. What did she want to do? Nothing could possibly satisfy her more than these moments with Jack.

"I haven't decided yet. Recently, I've felt like there's something in store for me. I just don't know what it is right now. A while ago, I went through a strange time. I didn't like the way I was living. There were questions without answers and old pains that needed clearing up."

"You mean that guy you came to see?"

Her eyes went through him again. "Yes, I was in love with him and never told him. I thought he'd hate me for it."

"For not telling him?"

"For loving him. He knew anyway, but at the time, he didn't want anything more than friendship. There was someone else on his mind."

"Then he was an idiot," Jack stated with a firm dismissive air.

"It was just bad timing. He was a strong Christian with a beautiful heart. I loved him for how his beliefs shaped him. They gave him an inner strength I admired, but at the time, I didn't possess it to the same degree. We weren't matched. Eventually, he abandoned those beliefs and I was really hurt by that. ..."

During her explanation, she seemed far away with an embracing unhappiness. When her eyes found him again, he was taken aback at how troubled he felt. It was as though he himself were responsible for her pain.

"It sounds like this guy really meant something to you."

Her eyes contradicted the serenity in her voice. "He meant everything to me. I just put too many things first ... and then it was too late." Changing her face abruptly, she pulled a composed appearance to the surface again. "Anyway, that's all done with."

(No, it isn't. It's written all over you. Whoever he is, he's still under your skin.)

He felt a sharp note of jealousy at how her eyes encapsulated another man. His heart contracted painfully at the thought of her being possessed by someone else, her beauty, her spirit. A few months ago, there was a similar look in Michelle's eyes when she confessed her relationship with Colin. Jack wondered at the way women could hang on to their old loves, as if each man would carve out a piece of her and garner it forever. Then he realized the hypocrisy of his assumption; women weren't the only ones who cling to the past. He'd spent five years doing exactly the same thing, and with not so much as a kiss between them, his wasn't even a real past.

Patty was so honest, inside and out. She was free in a way he only dreamed about. Suddenly, it was so obvious. He needed to let go to move on. For years he'd maintained a deceptive exterior, only confessing the truth when circumstances demanded, and it was time to admit just how exhausting that was.

Last week, Jen had dug her gritty little paws into his secrets, but afterward a light relief had followed the confession. He was tired of keeping secrets. What was their purpose? They didn't age gracefully like expensive wine. They were akin to an awkwardly healed fracture, forever out of sync with the other limbs. Face to face with Patty, he reached down and finally set himself free.

"There's someone that I cared about too. It's been going on for years, actually since the first day we met, at least for me, but we've never gone past being friends. I suppose she could turn around tomorrow and suddenly see me different, but as you say, that's all done with too."

Donna almost gaped at his profile. In the future she came from, that situation was the root of her despair, but it was also the reason she was here now. On top of it all, there was a heavy curiosity about his ex-girlfriend.

Donna probed, "Were there any others?"

"Yeah, I was seeing a girl at school this year. I was taking the summer to think about things with her, but I think she's meant for someone else. Weird thing is—I think I knew it all along. Sounds like we've both had some bad luck, you and I."

He summed it up with a simplicity only easy to those who can repudiate transgressions of the past. Whether he realized it or not, he was the one who could always walk away and start over, only this time he was taking her by the hand. But it was still unsettling.

351

(No Jack, don't push aside what's happened to you. Don't forget how you felt for me before. It's why you have me now.)

Finally, she responded, "It wasn't bad luck. You and I were just too scared to take chances, but things have a way of coming back to you."

Had this been spoken by anyone else, Jack would have glossed over the message, but with her face so concentrated, the phrase "you and I" sounded like it referred to the two of them together, not separate situations described similarly. Why was he interpreting everything she said in an intimate light? It was just conversation, personal conversation, but still just words strung together. Why did it seem so indefinably meaningful?

He suspected her words were unleashed from somewhere intensely guarded. As she stared out at the horizon, he saw an absolute certainty in them. She was someone who knew where she had been and where she was going. He wanted to reach right into her and take that strength for himself. How did she possibly develop that?

Guessing it cut across her spiritual side, he asked, "Do you believe in God?"

Those painful seconds before her accident, when she witnessed every meaningful event from her old life … Something had arranged for her to avoid that wall, just as it had deposited her right in the middle of 1991, transferring everything positive from her former existence and displaying the beauty of living to her fullest. If that wasn't God, what was?

Leveling an odd look, she answered, "Yes," as if to exclaim, "Doesn't everybody?"

"What do you believe exactly?"

Her head tilted back against the chair on the balcony, eyes deep with understanding. There was a knowledge in them that he couldn't pinpoint until now. It suddenly occurred to him that everything about her was tied up in the faith she held, and he envied this calm balance.

She spoke slowly and carefully, trying to express what she knew to be true. "Have you ever looked at yourself by accident? I mean, like in a store window, somewhere you didn't expect to see yourself, so you didn't have time to prep your face or the look in your eyes? Well, I got to see myself. I *really* did and it was hard. I saw pictures of me that changed everything. I used to think snapshots were just a limited moment in time, but catching the right moment can change it all—how you see yourself, your beliefs about what's possible, your choices. You realize you have the power to fix things. That's why I came here, to clear things up … but the negative stuff is only part of it. There's also stuff that's good if you're calm enough to take it in. You can't get at it if you're caught up trying to be things you're not. That kind of realization is a gift from somewhere else, somewhere big. For me, it's a faith that if you live fully, then things will work out exactly the way they're supposed to. ... What do you believe?"

"I like to think there's a God and He takes care of us and all, but I've never felt connected enough. I mean, how do you attain that peace of mind? Do you go to church, do good deeds, what? I think I'm a good person, but we're all so flawed. It's an impossible hurdle."

"But you're assuming you have to be perfect to be close to God. That's not what I'm saying. I'm saying you need to bring whatever force is out there into you, not the other way around."

"I just don't think you can do that, unless you cultivate the moral side of yourself. There have to be some lines of distinction between what would make you a better person and what would drag you down."

"Do you think what we've done for the last twenty-four hours is wrong?"

Jack shifted in his seat uncomfortably.

"Well, if I was a die-hard Christian, I guess I would, but it's hard to think that way when it feels so right. Do you think it's wrong?"

He finished his sentence staring at her with puckered brows.

Donna smiled softly and placed her hand in his. "Loving someone is never wrong. ..." Peaceful warmth radiated from her face.

"What's happening to me?" he wondered. Yesterday he was frustrated as hell with his heart, and today he was all caught up with someone he barely knew ... but it sure felt like he knew her. She even debated like Donna.

(All that's missing is Jen and a pile of coffee!)

Despite their bizarre similarities, there was a key difference between the person he had fantasized about for five years and the one beside him. This woman appeared out of nowhere to completely divert him from his disappointments. He'd never seen such an enticing manner. Her sense of self-worth and value toward life came off her in waves, and it was captivating, something he badly wanted for himself. He didn't understand just how much he was searching for those elements in his own life, until now.

Michelle possessed something similar. Maybe Michelle was the initial spark to set this fire, the fire in which he now found himself engulfed. Her religious stance was admirable, even alluring, but Patty eclipsed those sparks with her own brilliant flames. She had changed his life. Well, no, that wasn't quite right, but her presence had changed something. ... It was in the air at lunch yesterday, anticipation unrelated to the possibility of sex. From that moment, whatever his problems were, they were gone and all he had to do was pay attention to her, just follow the sense of destiny surrounding them. If anything would bring him closer to having faith, she was it. Almost as though she'd been sent to take care of him.

The feeling was so strong, he didn't register her words right away. Then, he realized that she had basically said she loved him. Some part of him already knew, of course, but to hear it spoken with such certainty was disarming. No fear of rejection or offense, just an easy truthfulness compelling the same in return. Any barriers that remained were discarded and it was a huge weight lifting off him.

He answered, "I love you too."

***

She was late again. The movie was almost over before she got there. It was at the drive-in, but instead of playing on a tall white screen, the scenes were near a broken lamppost, and this time they depicted someone else's life. It was an action film, suspenseful and uncontrollably scary.

She watched a cop stiffen up with sudden fright as a bleeding man pointed a gun at his neck, and then the bleeding man turned. In a second, there would be loud exploding noises, chased by cries of agony.

(No!)

With her arm outstretched, lunging around the cop seemed to take forever. She couldn't move fast enough. Her fingers grazed the man's arm like a careless caress. A bullet fired from the gun, splicing the air in slow motion, and she could see it sliding in a straight line toward Jack.

In desperation she fell forward, tumbling down to the ground ... and then she was lying beside him. Where was he hit? There was no blood. She was a doctor. Maybe he had a chance if she could find the entry wound. Then her mind backtracked. There was no blood because there was no entry wound. Not only that—he was breathing fine, looking relaxed and youthful in a way only sleep allows.

Propped up on her elbows, her head swiveled around the room and checked for grass and trees. The clock on the nightstand showed 3:07, the numbers frozen at that one moment. It felt as if time stood still and she held her breath endlessly, staring at the clock until it abruptly changed one digit into 3:08.

Collapsing back onto her side, her breath escaped over Jack's pillow and she scanned the length of his body, still except for the steady rise and fall of his chest. Despite his healthy appearance, the realism of the dream overshadowed this calm image before her, and though details were already fading, resting her hand on his chest made them crystal-clear.

She could see into his alternative destiny, the one she had changed. The fog in her mind lifted, not her conscious daily mind that saw the world with a selective perception, but her soul's mind—the one that knew only truth, the one that could sense realities over a multitude of time and distance barriers. With mounting alarm, she saw the bullet fly toward him and felt his jumbled thoughts of terror.

(He's shooting! I'm going to die! No, not before I get to see his face! My whole life I've always wondered if I look like him and now I'll never know. His hair, his nose and chin, his eyes, his eyes are a black hole, a little black hole—)

In that split-second, Donna knew a thousand frantic thoughts about his life. So many included her. They lined up and flew by as quickly as shuffling a deck of cards. He wouldn't even remember most of them, but they added up to a moment which would inevitably destroy him.

The future Jack she had grown to desire could die in that future. It felt horribly real. Her heart beat with a frightened panic at the idea of losing him in any time frame. She needed to focus on this time, on this bed, where Jack was alive and breathing with a vital strength. It was not real. It would not become real. If he were destined to die, surely she would sense it, feel it smothering her as much as him.

She forced her thoughts back to their evening together: her breathy whispers, his exquisite touch. His body had moved over her with deft strength, bringing her to heights of passion, and then letting her glide down on long heavy sighs. He used his entire body, always keeping her aware of the whole man surrounding her. She felt controlled in a way that wasn't suffocating like Ric. Instead, it was riveting to feel their souls held up against each other.

In one intense moment, everything from her former life—all the hard work—the desperate longings—were silhouetted against the beauty of this time frame. She was under him and she recklessly pleaded, "Jack, Jack, come away with me. Go somewhere, just us. Leave everything here."

His lips on hers, he agreed, "Yes ... yes."

He knew this was an amazing decision to make, but it had practically been made for him. Something surreal had enveloped them in its grasp to push them along this course of action.

They had fallen asleep in tranquil warmth, and now she concentrated on that. Though tentacles of fear still clung tenaciously to her heart, the glare of the dream faded along with that unrelenting pull to correct it. The image of the bullet would not fade as easily, but gained distance; a layer of this time frame graciously inserted itself between them and that scary possibility.

Resting her head against Jack's shoulder, she covered his chest with the same arm which had stretched out to protect him only minutes earlier, and slowly the false future became diffused by the here and now. Her breathing soon matched his slow rhythm, content as sleep ensued.

***

CHAPTER 43

For many Canadians, September tenth represented another monotonous part of the work week, a prescribed set of hours and decisions steadily edging one toward Friday. For Raymond Carlin, it was the day he would authorize his daughter's death. This was even worse than watching Patricia go. There had been no decisions to speed up that process.

Rich flavors from the coffee maker encircled him. Raymond saw Donna's hand adding too many scoops into the filter and flip the switch. She would pour him a cup with a teenage smile to start his day. Realizing just how worthwhile it had been to drink that mud as long as it was her handing it to him, he saw her arm outstretched, her lips curled up in a younger version of Patricia's morning smile, and he took the cup gratefully. A sudden memory of peanut butter breakfasts followed the scent.

(My Pattycake has a date. …)

As he raised the coffee to his lips, he kept his mind's eye on Donna. The hot liquid tasted great, just the right number of scoops. … In an instant, his daughter disappeared and he was left holding a savory cup of Paula's coffee. Clutching the mug, he stared at the empty space beside him, his face pinched and tight.

As Paula walked into the kitchen, he muttered, "This is good." When she left the room, he abruptly tipped it over, spilling the dark brown liquid into the sink.

***

This morning, Donna stirred first. The terror-filled moments of last night's dream faded like rain on a hot day, evaporating with barely a trace, and confidence swelled as she inhaled the air around her. She felt even better than yesterday. With peacefulness to her soul, she knew this was the correct version, even if it was corrected.

Exhausted from their two nights, Jack woke up to her smiling face; her infectious energy kept him alert and connected. The research job was irrelevant. No longer caring if it was extended, he would go anywhere with Patty. The more time they spent together, the more Jack was convinced he'd been waiting for her his whole life. What an enormous statement. How many people came and went through the years, contributing to his growth, his ambition, all the good things? Ready to dismiss them, instead of recognizing commonality, one woman was set apart from the others. Any traits overlapping hers were disregarded as minor. She was everything.

Last night, he had committed his heart. The second those words of love were out of his mouth, a persistent sense of fate shifted within him as if all the preceding days were just one big prelude. There was something similar in their first meeting two days ago, but this was richer, fuller. He could live forever in the serenity of this feeling.

Donna also felt the shift of fate, a very finalistic maneuver. The time frame had punched out one last kink in its exterior and now ran with sleek precision. At this point, it was all that existed for her. Except for the weird flash into Jack's threat of death, the other era hadn't pushed itself into her senses since yesterday. And as the morning minutes ticked away, Donna believed with added strength that she had succeeded in changing her past, and would stay in the new past to live the way she hadn't bothered to the first time.

Jack would not die. He wouldn't face the dark barrel of a loaded gun and see his life race by as fast as the bullet. He wouldn't be distant or remove himself from her life. No ex-girlfriend would harm his outlook. Donna had taken her place and kept him safe.

She existed completely in this time frame now. No pieces were left hanging in that other era, except for her most perishable and debilitated scraps. And she was glad to be rid of them. Everything strong and proportioned and beautiful was here inside her, infused into her face and mind with a gentle shine.

People and objects which at one time had meaning for her were elsewhere. Donna wasn't concerned for her father anymore. The bagels had created a fantastic balance. In any case, he was in a future that wouldn't exist. She was a hundred percent here in the past with Jack and this was all that mattered from now on.

A layer of sheer curtains covered the balcony windows. A thicker layer framed them like a delicate picture. Left ajar last night, the moonlight had painted their room in sultry shades of gray. Now, the sun broke through the glass. As a wide beam of light stretched across the room and over their bed, Donna slid her leg over his and rolled into the side of his body. Jack pulled her close, enjoying her smell and wisps of hair brushing against his shoulder. There was no need to rush out of bed. Still time before work.

His hand slid over the swell of her hips and he adjusted his head to kiss her. She slipped one hand around his shoulders. The other traced a line down his stomach. He groaned when she suddenly gripped him and his kisses intensified.

Jack's hands were everywhere, exploring, revealing, coaxing. And Donna felt herself lured into another overpowering surrender. He was in her body, in her heart, inside every part of her, until there was no line of division between the two.

With carefully measured thrusts, he was learning to control the depth and soon she seemed to take over, arching her back, lifting her hips hard against him. She clutched his waist, pressed him in deeper, and cried out, the release unbearably intoxicating. Losing control in the center of passion. Losing herself.

Gradually, the tension dissipated as their bodies relaxed. For a time, neither spoke, just lying close with arms and legs tightly entwined until finally, he rolled onto his back and drew her close.

"I got to go to work soon."

"Too soon."

"Yeah."

"So, I suppose you plan to come here at lunchtime and maul me again?"

"Let's see. Fast food at the Food Court, or fantastic sex at Patty's hotel. Hmmm ... a burger *would* be good," he remarked offhandedly and quickly slid under the covers to escape a slap, which landed where his shoulder had been a moment earlier.

"Coward," she taunted, but he refused to resurface. "Fine, well let's say you make it a very *small* burger. What time can I expect you?"

Jack sat up again and Donna promptly slapped him anyway. "Ow! ... About noon." Catching her hands, he felt her relax in his grasp. She fingered the steel ring carelessly and he let her wiggle it off. Turning it over, she remarked, "I always liked this—these kinds of rings. All these little marks. It doesn't pretend to be perfect, but it is."

She spoke so abstractedly, but in some weird way, he knew exactly what she meant and nodded. She slipped it on her own pinkie finger and swiveled it around loosely. Jack held her hand as he slid it off easily.

"Doesn't fit me. Guess I'm not a boy," she smiled.

"Naw, it's just on the wrong one." He moved it onto her ring finger, where it seemed to fit. He kissed her gently and she sighed.

(I'll keep it safe for you. You can stay just like you are now, unscathed and marked only with character, just like this ring. That's my real commitment to you. ...)

Something in the depths of her eyes glowed, something real and unquestioning.

He gauged her eyes carefully. "You really meant what you said last night about taking off together? I mean, if I just picked a place—and you agreed to stop hitting me—that would be it?"

Despite the jest, the question carried a note of caution. Morning is typically a time of truth. Promises of the night explore fantasy until the light of day extinguishes all but stark reality ... but in this case, Donna's eyes transcended those doubts. She stared longingly at him.

"Absolutely."

One look into her green eyes was all it took. "OK," he said, "I'd like to get out of Calgary, but I don't want to move too far away. What do you think of Red Deer? Not too big, not too small. We could always go somewhere else if that doesn't pan out."

"Red Deer it is."

It was unbelievable, but of course he would choose that city. It seemed to be the only choice to make, and this time she would be with him. That's what would solidify his safety, and suddenly, she needed it to happen as soon as possible.

Impulsively, she suggested, "Let's go today. We'll have to get an apartment and jobs. What exactly do you want to do?"

"There are only a couple of things I've thought of doing—becoming a cop or starting a business of some kind—"

The sharp image of the racing bullet jerked her thoughts, and for a moment, the wrong future seemed near again. For an anxious aching moment ...

"—what do you want to do?"

Donna remembered his comment about opening a fast food place, which was unexpectedly appealing. It would be the icing on the cake, the ultimate coup to trade her sad future for Anne's. She felt no inequity with this decision. Anne was a naturally happy person. Donna, on the other hand, would have to create her happiness ... with Jack. She could see them working side by side. They would be putting in long hours, but long hours with this man would be no punishment.

"Well, I can't see me becoming a cop, so if we're going to do something together, I guess we'll have to start a business." She remarked to herself, "Maybe a restaurant ... but it would have to be a healthy one." Her voice dissolved with the memory of Jack on her couch sadly quoting that same

360

sentence. Then recovering, she added, "Speaking of which, we should order breakfast. I'm really craving some coffee."

Sitting up, she stretched her arms toward the ceiling. Donna's back straightened elegantly, chest lifting with a slight arch. Jack watched the bend of her neck slope down into the heavy curves of her breasts. Head tilted back, her hair brushed bare shoulders. She turned to call room service, but suddenly, his lips grazed her shoulders. Jack's arms circled from behind, cradling Donna with his body, and she inhaled sharply. One hand rose up to become tangled in his hair. Sliding his tongue along her neck, he murmured, "Still want that coffee?"

The phone fell to the carpeted floor as she guided Jack's hands across her thighs.

***

At the hospital, Dr. Moyer and her supervisor met with Raymond and Paula. They attempted several pain tests, but there was no reaction, none at all. She didn't pull her hands away. There wasn't even a delay. It just didn't exist. They explained that Donna was brain-dead, and the only thing keeping her body alive was the ventilator. Its exact rhythmic pace gave one the false impression of hope. Raymond had to understand and accept that without this machine, Donna's body would cease to function altogether.

Two more people joined in the conference. A nurse had been assigned to carry out the practical duties, and a social worker was present to discuss organ donation. When his turn arrived, he showed Raymond a donor card Donna had filled out during medical school. It requested her preference to leave her body to medical research. The social worker was careful to state that in the end, Mr. Carlin had the right to override his daughter's written wishes. If his family practiced religious beliefs that went against it, he could decide on burial or cremation instead. It was another awful decision for him to make. The donor card was a surprise, though it made sense, being exactly the kind of choice which defined her.

Raymond took a deep breath and stated, "We will respect her decision."

"Do you need some time to discuss things with your wife?"

"No, we know that … We know it has to be done." Then, he turned to the two doctors. "Am I supposed to sign something?"

"A verbal decision is all that's required."

Raymond answered, "You can turn off the ventilator, but I want a few minutes with her first." His tone was clipped, resentful. He couldn't help it, but they didn't seem to take it personally.

"Of course, take all the time you need."

He knew they were trying to be sensitive to his pain, but their professionalism only served to remind Raymond of his relative inexperience. How often did a person have to sentence someone to death? Apparently they did it all the time.

Several minutes passed while he sat with her, trying to envision the bright part of her that used to be. He apologized over and over and explained how much she would be missed, how he didn't want to see her die.

Thoughts of Donna at different ages flew through his mind. She was a premature baby, a doctor, a teenager, a little girl. She was so many things. He had known her longer than his first wife. It scared him how Patricia's face sometimes got sketchy. Would he forget Donna's features and have to refresh his memories through photographs?

Finally, he stood over the face that didn't look like her at all, and gripping her hand, kissed her cheeks as tears fell down his own. Conscious that this would be their last touch, his hands sandwiched hers. An odd ring encircled her fourth finger. No stone.

(That wasn't there before. ... It wasn't. Was it?)

She couldn't have gotten engaged without him knowing. It was too ugly to be an engagement ring anyway. Must just be part of her new style. His thoughts bantered hollowly along a conversational vein, more delaying tactics. Can't say goodbye. Just can't.

Finally, he forced himself to leave the room.

As he nodded to the people in the hallway, his head felt enormously heavy. Raymond didn't want to see everyone go in there, but when the latch clicked shut behind them, he abruptly pivoted and his eyes were nailed to that door. He wasn't ready for this. Paula put one hand on his arm to stop him and they spun around each other, trading places in an unintentional dance.

"Ray, no."

He started to pull away. "No, I ... I can't. She ..."

Her distressed gaze locked onto his, which stared back desperately. Paula shook her head and pulled him in close. For a moment, he resisted and then clung to her, trying to ease the sick feeling in the center of his chest. Paula closed her eyes and held him and wondered if they would ever be able to erase this terrible day.

***

CHAPTER 44

Their breakfast arrived from room service long before Jack left for work. Standing with their plates, they leaned against the balcony railing and against each other. The sky from last night stretched out, an exact reverse of the sunset. It was beautiful. Just up the road, her car lay smoldering after flipping over three times. She could see the area in the distance, but it had not really happened, would not happen in their new future.

The coffee sat heated in a smooth white flask. As she poured them each another cup, a slight breeze blew past, lifting the steam away at angles. There was calmness to the morning, as though the responsibility of decisions would never again weigh heavily on them. It was a perfectly relaxed sense of freedom. Though steam could be whisked away, the cups remained in their grasp, a solid reminder that the last two days were real and not just some incredible dream.

She wouldn't be snatched away from this precious time with Jack. No struggling for coherent thoughts to make sense of her surroundings. No swimming up to the surface of her mind to discover the deceptive reality where dreams are disguised. Though everything here existed under a veil of transparency, its origin was as tangible as the steam and the coffee it came from. Donna could stand here on this balcony all day, sipping this cup and basking in the moment.

He kissed her at the door slowly, something to linger on her soft lips during his time at work. With a reverent caress, he held her chin in the palm of his hand. Her fingers rested on his wrist, the steel ring directly between them on her finger.

Jack whispered, "See you at noon. ... I love you."

Back in the other time frame, she'd wanted to say those words, but impossible to hold accountable private thoughts, Donna resisted in the hope of keeping his friendship. By remaining silent, he couldn't use it against her, tender accolades so easily transforming into a weapon's edge, turning in an instant on its speaker. That period in her life seemed ancient and pointless. It was as unreal as her father's pain. This was real, Jack holding her chin and smiling sweetly at her. The past two days had yielded a lifetime's worth of love.

Suddenly, those three words were not enough, could never be enough to describe the life inside her, the one she'd discovered because of him, but his ears deserved to hear the emotions circling her shining eyes. He deserved every part of her to hold and enjoy. Wasn't that what love was? The intimate moments given freely, the stares that caressed, the syllables whispered with simple earnest. No, those three words could never be enough ... but they were everything she was from this day forward.

She stroked his forearm lightly and replied, "I love you."

***

A nurse removed the ventilator while doctors monitored Donna's heart rate. It remained strong for a minute, and then became irregular. The staff waited patiently for her heart to stop. And at 9:55, the real struggle began.

***

Leaning against the balcony railing, Donna surveyed the horizon. Her fingers absorbed gentle warmth from the coffee. There was something comforting about the heat radiating through the mug. Everything was comforting now: this view, the climbing temperature, even the smooth concrete under her bare feet. Everything was as it should be. For once in her life, nothing needed attention, but still, she had to consider what was to come.

What about all the years she had put into her career? Could it really be abandoned? Maybe it wouldn't have to be. Fake some ID, enough to design a past, complete with university transcripts, and apply to med school all over again. It would be a breeze the second time around. The possibility of an open future based on elements from her own past was intriguing, like Christmas morning when presents were about to be opened. There was a sneaky sort of glitter in the certainty of a happy outcome.

There was a lot to consider, but this morning was too bright and chipper to ignore just yet. A choppy line of mountains cut into the sky. Scanning their rough edges, the briefest thought raced past almost as fast as a flash-back. For a quick moment, she imagined seeing right through

364

the mountains as though they were made of glass, and for some reason this odd picture tugged her heart painfully.

She blinked and transferred her gaze to the sky instead. This was the kind of morning that made her think of Jen: bold, totally in charge and alive with color, the way Jeffrey described in his eulogy. The sun was strong for being so early. Well, it wasn't so early anymore, close to ten. Better get rolling.

She turned but abruptly halted as the image of her father passed through her mind, and with it, memories of breakfast conversations long gone. Strange disjointed thoughts followed closely on their heels: pain, guilt, protective love, resignation, fragile pieces of ... someone? Her intellectual side covered that last piece of intuition like a heavy sweater.

(Everything is fragile at some point.)

Even the coffee cup in her hand. Envisioning it falling from the balcony, it would spin midair on some unseen edge, indifferent to gravity's pull, before the delicate porcelain would shatter on the pavement below. She saw the scattered pieces in her mind and frowned. What had made her associate her father with such a destructive thought? He was supposed to be in the True Past.

She narrowed her focus, reaching a strong mental hand to the other time frame. He was there. She could feel his energy and his sadness. Though directly connected to her, there was a separate measure of culpability. Whatever was happening there was his problem and his alone. Her debt had been rectified by creating the bagel exchange. That one act established a balance, a clean slate between her and Raymond ... but the distressing feeling persisted.

Donna tried to close the window to the future. She wasn't a part of it anymore, not a mental part and certainly not a physical part. Her body was definitely shutting down in that other time frame, probably to the point of being in a coma. Was she even alive? Must be if she could sense people like her dad nearby.

(Everything is fragile at some point ... and that point always comes.)

A debate flourished in her head. Is someone in a coma state actually alive? Could this extreme state of relaxation smooth over all the stresses that take their toll on a body, erase the worry lines on her forehead, inject her muscles with unending energy, or give her such expansion of thought to sense her father's distress from eight years away?

At an unconscious level, her father could sense her needs too; a key document buried under an avalanche of papers. Some part of his mind felt it there, prolonging his struggle. She needed to shut the door to that other world, give him reason to move on without her. A corner of the paper peeked out, but his focus was on the top of the pile, magnifying the hard facts of his own world—the thirty-year-old woman in the hospital bed.

The more she deteriorated in the future, the more strength of body and spirit she accumulated in this past. It was as if her thoughts had acquired some wonderful kind of texture her mind could savor ... one tangy orange segment after another.

Maybe the answer was death. If Donna were dead in that future, she could completely embed her soul here with Jack. As long as her future self continued to breathe in the air of 1999, some part of her awareness would be linked with an unhappy life. Perhaps the only way she could escape was to die on the other side of that door. Could that already have happened, having rewritten a place in her own past? Either way, she concluded, no more ill feelings should be finding her through the time waves.

(... that point always comes ...)

Donna shook off the dense sensations, and went back inside the hotel room. She collected their breakfast dishes, stacking them neatly on the tray, and placed it out in the hallway. Her money was tucked in the front pocket of her pants.

Twenty—forty—sixty—eighty—*one,* twenty—forty—sixty— eighty—*two,* twenty—forty ... Over seven hundred left, but she and Jack would need to scrape together a lot for their move. It may take them a while to get jobs.

Donna peered again at the bills in her hand. They looked odd, as if their straight edges were bending right before her eyes. A sudden weight pressed itself onto her chest and she struggled to take a breath. It began like chest constriction from a simple adrenaline rush and then suddenly erupted.

Oh, this hurt!

It was sharper than anything she'd ever experienced: nails driving right through her, Ric's knuckles pounding into her flesh, squeezing her from all directions—and there was no escape.

One desperate look into the dresser mirror revealed an eerie sight. Wind was circling her body, compressing her forcefully, and her eyes filled with fear. Cloudy swirls of the other time frame wrapped tightly around her.

(No—you're not supposed to exist anymore! I changed you!)

This time, it wasn't a mere panic attack. She was suffocating. She remembered discussing suicide with Jack and Jen, how she had lumped asphyxiation in with other "fast" methods. Jack was right; there was nothing fast about this. It went on and on, stretching each moment of stabbing chest pain with unbearable elasticity. How long would it take to kill her, to collapse her lungs in spastic exhaustion?

The money fell as she clawed at the fresh air just out of reach. Twenty-dollar bills floated down, heavy bits of snow to gently decorate the carpet around her feet in a circular patch. Her heart beat madly, trying to transport the oxygen that was shut out. Her lungs ached, everything ached. The pain was excruciating, but when her brain screamed for her legs to move, they wouldn't respond. They were blocks of stone.

In a flash, she understood exactly what was happening. The other time frame wanted her. It *demanded* her ... and it would rip her apart as surely as she could rip one of those twenty-dollar bills on the floor.

With horror, Donna realized how blind she had been. She was the original bagel culprit. Paula had never instigated the joke. Raymond's mischievous grin alluding to a mystery donor was accurately aimed at her all along. Now when Past Donna would place her first order, thinking Paula had beaten her to the punch, the baker would willingly comply having seen the same smile before.

Blindly embracing the wonderful gift of second chances, it was ruined all over again. Had she refused the grand temptation of playing God with her past, her future self could have recognized Jack's love. Had she not captured his attention that first night, he would have received Jen's phone call ... and saved Past Donna from Ric. That turning point, that one act would have unveiled their hesitant desires to incite a deeper understanding.

If only Patty hadn't brought Jack to the hotel. If only Patty hadn't claimed him for her own. A thousand "if only's" laughing cruelly at the twists of fate.

He would never love Past Donna again. She saw him coming back at noon to discover Patty gone. He would search for her all the way to Red Deer, and finally come back beaten and jaded.

Even his resources as a cop would produce no leads; Patricia Slobodian died of breast cancer back in 1981. When she married Raymond, she never took his name. Jack would never make the connection.

He would adopt Christian beliefs, trying to be the person he thought Patty left him for, and then use those beliefs to build a barrier against Donna. She was the ex-girlfriend all along, the one he held in his heart while Donna struggled to be noticed. Constantly aching for the one person she'd always had.

(... always comes ...)

The irony of it exploded in her mind as the swirling space tightened its grip. A horrible pressure crushed her body. Her eyes grabbed at the objects in the hotel room, pleading with them to bind her here forever. The dresser, the bed, the clock on the nightstand. 9:55 blinked at her in bright red lines.

The numbers were her enemy dressed in deceptive camouflage. Now the layers were stripped away to uncover the only true time frame.

The future hadn't disappeared. Pulsating quietly, it aligned itself with an unchangeable past as she borrowed more tender qualities from her former self. They were only borrowed. They were not hers for the keeping. The only consistency was the pernicious ability of the past to be correct regardless of her efforts. It beat its way through her mind in a rhythmic chant.

(... correct and corrected, correct and corrected, correct and corrected ...)

Once again, the flash-backs flew across her line of vision. They circled her, blocking out the hotel room. Surrounding her body, they moved as one solid object with no start or finish, scene after scene connected to each other until they became a tightly woven filmstrip. The speed was astounding, the sensations deafening, a tornado of sight and sound spinning over and over, a lifetime of images assaulting her mind into madness, and when the last ounce of oxygen escaped her body, she couldn't hold on to the past any longer.

(Oh God, please don't take me away now. I need to stay. Jack! Ja—)

Time folded in on itself. She vanished from the hotel room, leaving the money lying innocently before the dresser. In a split-second, she was thrown violently to the future as her shrieks echoed behind in a silent vacuum. Her soul tore through eight years with a horrific speed ... only to stop as sharply as it started.

There was no reverse of inertia to signal any change. No sick feeling of being flipped upside down and suddenly righted. There were no sensations at all anymore, just a singular buoyancy, every inch of her supported by invisible waves, watery currents rising and falling around her, without causing movement of any kind. Perfectly balanced existence. And then she heard the voice ...

***

Raymond was still clutching his wife when the door finally opened and two of the team emerged. At most, it was supposed to take a few minutes, but they had been in there much longer.

He didn't even want to look at the doctor and nurse. They would say, "She's gone." That would really be the end. And the thought actually made Raymond back up a step or two before the doctor spoke.

"Mr. Carlin, something's occurred that we didn't expect. Your daughter's breathing on her own. She's struggling and we don't know if it will last, but for now she's still alive."

Not only could he look at them, he stepped closer, right where he had been standing a moment ago, waiting to hear a completely different announcement. His mouth opened to speak, but nothing came out. Darting around them and through the door, Raymond pushed past the staff still hovering around Donna's bed. Now his words might really reach her, make a difference, but just like two days ago, only one phrase came to mind.

***

"Know that I love you, Sweetheart. ..."

She knew this voice. This was his pain, what she was sensing from him across all those years. Donna wanted to tell him she was sorry, that she didn't want him to hurt. Suddenly, it took on more importance than her loss of Jack, but powerless to act, the same force which had shaped her decisions of the last two days now encased her.

The weight of the time periods was gone. Donna knew what was close, a place of timelessness, where qualities of existence are never measured and souls can wait for each other without impatient strain.

If she embraced it, a piece of her would still linger behind, like the feeling of Jen at the cemetery, or a soft hand on a lover's cheek, a gentle reminder of how the skin under that hand was cherished. Her touch would be as light as a dream, but would extend across any time and space to reach its lover. It was a connection established on the thinnest of strings, allowing two souls to exist in separate realities, yet stay imperceptibly tied to one another, a string that would stretch far and wide and never break.

It was the True Past.

***

369

CHAPTER 45

The bullet raced toward Jack. In the blink of an eye, it ricocheted off the lamppost beside him, making a sharp pinging sound, and punctured the hood of the car to become embedded somewhere in the engine. A few inches to the left and it would have hit him. Just one little swing of the pendulum.

Jack's decision was absolute.

He pulled the trigger and saw the drunk disappear behind the open door. The soft sound of metal hitting the ground reverberated through his ears and the heavier thud of the man's body followed it. Jack came around to the side of the vehicle, his arm still outstretched, his gun now on its own search mission. The drunk was lying on his back, gasping from a wound below his right shoulder.

Dellasandro snatched up the fallen weapon and both of them tried to calm their racing hearts. Their adrenaline was still high when the firetruck and ambulance pulled up. It was one of the paramedics who gently pushed Jack's arm down to point the gun elsewhere.

They moved in quickly to assess the injured man. One of them glanced up at Jack and commented, "Unbelievable night—there's another accident up the road that's even worse than this."

Collecting himself, Jack put his gun away and called in the situation. "Shots fired, suspect has been hit, ambulance has arrived." Suspect? The word was strange, as though they were unsure if the right man had been shot.

He turned to Dellasandro. "You OK?"

"Yeah ... he stuck a piece on me," Dellasandro muttered, one hand protectively holding his throat, "and I didn't see it coming." Then he remembered who the suspect had actually fired at. "Hey, thanks man. Are you OK?"

"Sure," Jack answered shortly.

(Just peachy. Hey, maybe I'll rent a video on the way home … after I watch this guy bleed out another pint.)

They leaned against the hood of their car and waited. Jack felt as though he had wandered into the middle of a stage play instead of being an integral part of this commotion. Did they just say something to each other? His mind was peculiarly distracted by little things.

Like his left shoelace hanging untied. The two ends pointed loosely down to the ground. A stone sat nearby and he tapped it with the solid toe of his shoe. It flew a few feet, rolling to a new resting place near the curb. The laces swung in reaction to the movement and then hung limply again, a puppet with no one to control the strings.

A second squad car arrived to take over the policing. One officer took Jack and Dellasandro aside and the other went to the front of the ambulance. Blocking the view of the interior, he interrupted two reporters who reluctantly backed off, then immediately switched to Plan B: scan the area for useful shots. There weren't many.

"Good thing they didn't get here earlier," Dellasandro remarked.

Jack barely heard him. A fireman jumped into the front seat of the ambulance. Red lights spun around on top of the vehicle, shrinking as it sped away. With a strange sense of relief, Jack watched the bulky vehicle disappear. Despite the drunk being disarmed, Jack's feeling of dire threat had hovered ominously until the suspect was removed.

The duty sergeant arrived, followed by two homicide officers. The sergeant extended his hand and Jack almost reached to shake it with automatic politeness when he noticed the man's index finger pointing to Jack's waist.

"We'll need your forty. Got to do ballistics."

He would have to give up his gun? There was nothing more humiliating. A cop was naked without a weapon. Dellasandro had even coined a phrase for such unfortunates, "Streakers". Without a gun, you were just a big naked moving target.

Obediently, Jack reached to unclip the safety strap.

"Not now. Do it in the unloading bay."

He nodded and forced his hands to relax by his sides. Then, one of the homicide officers stepped up frowning.

"Listen, this is policy. I got to run through this." He read from a small card in the palm of his hand. "You have the right to retain and instruct counsel without delay. You can call any lawyer you wish or get free advice from duty counsel immediately. If you wish to contact any lawyer, we will provide you with a telephone and telephone book. If you wish to contact duty counsel, we will provide you with a telephone and a list and ..."

Jack stared at the officer.

(Am I being ... arrested?)

Just as his senses had risen to the task in the face of the suspect, they now shut off completely, leaving him numb. He heard the words and his mind tried to convince himself they were being spoken to someone else, someone bad.

(A phone book? What?)

Wait a minute—this couldn't be happening to him. He was the guy who couldn't shoot anyone. This was insane.

He could run. A casual step sideways, followed by a mad sprint to ... somewhere, anywhere but here. And the rush of panicked freedom he would feel for the minute or two before they caught him. He could taste that first step in his mind's eye, even thought he angled his foot slightly in response, but it was just an illusion. Even if the choice had been determined, his legs were frozen.

"Do you understand these rights as I have read them?"

(Run! Now!)

"I need you to say 'yes' or 'no'."

"Yes."

"Do you wish to speak with counsel?"

"No."

"We can get someone to the station right away."

"No."

The officer placed a hand on Jack's arm. "OK, we need your statements. We'll try to get through this as soon as we can."

And suddenly, Jack's legs would move again as he was guided away.

***

It was an interesting movie full of twists and turns, much like his own life. There was even a brief section where the lead character was happy in his marriage before the disease took him over. Then, the story line became more and more depressing and Al wanted to watch something else, but the remote control was nowhere to be found. He couldn't tear his eyes away from the screen anyway, especially during that last scene, the one where the drunk pulled a gun on the cops. There was a distinct feel to the pictures as if he could trail his fingertips over their texture. Furiously speeding around, they placed him in the center and forced him to experience it all over again.

The metal object felt cold in his hand, lifeless. Aiming it at the second cop was like staring into a mirror. An identical weapon was pointing right back at him, beneath an identical pair of eyes. That was the worst part—facing those eyes. They looked too much like his own. Only one way to erase them.

He pulled the trigger and the gun went off, but when it did, Al felt something as soft as a breeze nudging his elbow and his arm abruptly wove. There was a flash of an image—as quick as the bullet leaving its chamber—of a desperate lovely woman ... but he could have sworn no one was within reach. No, it must have been the alcohol, always the alcohol coloring his mind.

Then a terrible pain ripped through his chest and he was shoved backward to fall and keep falling while the world spun madly, until the movie suddenly stopped. There were no grand credits rolling past, no music to complete the mood of the viewer, and he was left with a dull feeling that the entire exercise had been pointless.

Al kept expecting the lights to turn on since there were people nearby, invisible people. He knew they were talking about him, discussing something of importance, but as the minutes passed, he lost interest in the whole thing. A comfortable feeling of relaxation crawled through him; a bath cradled his cold tired body, fueling him with calm energy.

Gravity was gradually suspended and he slid sideways. It reminded him of the momentary vertigo he sometimes experienced at the brink of sleep, as though escaping out of something, being released from confined spaces and breathing open air for the first time.

As he felt himself slipping away, his first thought bordered on terror.

(Don't—don't—don't let it be dark. ...)

But the gentle sensations were amazing. They washed through him with a cleansing sweep and away went a lifetime of stresses. Gone as if never there. None of the old regrets clung to him as they had for so long, swirling around in endless circles in his subconsciousness. They melted away, giving him a new knowledge of life without self-destructive desires, the ability to be in perfect balance between drunkenness and raw sobriety. He had never felt such unclouded awareness. There were no barriers here, no boundaries to differentiate himself from his surroundings.

In recent years the dark had unnerved him, but now it held a comfortable warmth. It lifted him gently upward, a summer wind letting a child's kite glide to new heights.

She was there. It was her pulling him along. He felt no resistance. If the sensations could be translated into visual dimensions, she would be leading him by the hand. Gazing into a still pond, he could see her translucent reflection, steadfast in her devotion. They were the same blue eyes, the same but opposite, a mirror image of himself reversed in the soul he now knew was a perfect match to his own. She had been waiting for him all this time. Time? Their lost years became meaningless.

Thoughts that used to have hard angles were tipping off the edge of his mind. Everything that was lovely and secure filled him with ease.

How did he get here? He couldn't remember, but no matter. She was here, this other soul to draw him in to the beauty above. He willingly followed her, and finally, there was peace.

***

"Doctor?"

"Go away, Julie."

"Just one more thing, OK?"

"This is my last chart and then I'm eating and sleeping, in that order. ... That means 'no'."

Wendy scrawled an illegible signature on the bottom of the page. Sliding it neatly into a file folder, she rose and almost ran into the nurse who was wearing one of her stubborn expressions, the kind where Wendy would be roped into a pile of extra work.

"It's the GSW, the one that cop shot? He needs to be pronounced."

"I thought Dr. Fong did that."

"Homicides require two signatures."

"Oh, find one of Capri's minions."

She stepped sideways to skirt around the nurse, but Julie moved with her.

Blocking Wendy's exit, she crisply stated, "The order is from Dr. Capri. Then I promise I'll fake your death to get you some sleep."

Wendy closed her eyes and sighed. "Lead the way, but I want more than a faked death for this. I'm starved."

"Hey, every death—faked or not—deserves a last supper. Do I have a present for you!" Julie waved a small plastic rectangle in front of Wendy's face, where a slow grin broke out.

"His cafeteria card? How did you get that?"

"What do you care? Just get yourself some food so you stop being such a bag. But hurry, Capri's treated three nurses and a porter to the Special already and he's bound to notice it gone sooner or later. But first, go pronounce that gunshot guy."

With a smirk, Julie stepped gracefully aside and held the card up between two fingers. Wendy snatched it out of her hand, stuffed it into the pocket of her lab coat, and accompanied her out the door.

"Did you say a cop shot him?"

"Yeah, but from what I understand, he tried to shoot the cop first."
"Hmmm ... Then maybe Capri should buy him a meal too."

***

It took hours to sort out, so long that the questioning officers ordered food for Jack and his partner. There was a twenty-four-hour Chinese food place they recommended. Jack didn't bother explaining that he'd eaten there before. In fact, this meal was almost an exact duplicate of the one he'd shared with Donna for their birthdays. But this one tasted like cardboard.

Though the officers handled Jack with patient regard, he still felt pinned to the wall. They let him know that he could go back on duty within the next week or he could take time off. Stress leave.

He spoke wearily, "I was leaving the force in two weeks anyway. Moving to Halifax. Great way to end a job."

"Well, you'll have to delay that for a few weeks. You can't leave until our investigation is finished."

Did they think he wanted to spend another minute in this city? Jack all but glared at them, but his resentment was quickly tempered by their genuine sympathy.

"Hey," they calmly stated, "better to be tried by twelve, than carried by six. We may have more questions. For now, try to put it out of your mind. We'll get in touch with you."

They considered him a good officer caught in the procedural requirements of the job, which diluted some of his antagonism, but that didn't soften those questions spiraling along a perpetual path in his mind. Yes, he was trained to deal with self-defense situations. And yes, discharging his weapon was a brutal choice, the only choice ... but that split-second of commitment was pure ease compared to the lifelong weight of silent allocution now awaiting him.

***

CHAPTER 46

By the time Jack finished sorting out the preliminary details of the shooting, it was 8:30 in the morning. With Anne already gone to work, the apartment was both blessedly quiet and frighteningly morose.

Before leaving duty, his sergeant informed him that the suspect didn't make it. Those were his words. "Didn't make it." Make what? A cake, a deadline, a snowman? Ridiculous semantics taunted him amid endless questions and paperwork. The guy wasn't even a *suspect* anymore. He was someone with a name and a life—Albert Morin.

Jack Petrasyk did exactly what he believed himself incapable of doing. He'd killed a man and he'd done it with no thought at all. It scared him to remember what passed through his mind right then. The other gun sent a bullet in Jack's direction and instantly, the man was reduced to a mere target like the ones hanging at the firing range. Albert's face dissolved in favor of a clear outline of his head, shoulders, and chest. They were a border pointing to all the vital organs Jack could hit, was *supposed* to hit according to his rookie training. Shoot to stop, not to kill. Straight out of the training manual … but how do you hit vital organs without killing anyone? The contradiction never appeared with such clarity until the aftermath of that insane moment.

All the impersonal elements Jack had ascribed to Albert Morin's existence reversed themselves with the early morning light. The sun rose to cast a growing glare over the dark target and it became transformed into a bright picture of the man, full of color and shaded folds and history. Now Jack sat in his living room, seeing the man's face over and over, painted on the walls, on the carpet, over every face on the television screen, lifelike accusations jumping out from his stunned eyes as the bullet tore into him.

Jack remembered watching that swerving gun trying to find him. He envisioned the little black hole of the barrel, which would show its perfect roundness when settled on center. Had Jack not frozen when his opponent pulled the trigger, he would have fired first. Easily.

The sight of Albert's gun was burned into his brain, but Albert's eyes even more so. How could he have taken note of the man's face while focused on the weapon? However he'd done it, there was a recognizable difference between the two. The barrel was empty and black, but those eyes ... They didn't hold the capacity to understand his actions and make a solid choice. They were the eyes of confusion, not intent. Only this latent insight brought the truth to light. Albert was no killer.

But Jack was ...

He wondered about the next of kin, people who would scrutinize Jack militantly for what he'd done. He imagined the frustrated anger and pain they would feel, and the faceless target would coldly swivel to become him.

Despite the continuous banter from the television, this apartment seemed deadly quiet. Aiming the remote control, he clicked the off button. The simple movement was dull and heavy as though his thumb alone weighed twenty pounds. With teary strain etched all over his face, he laid his head along the back of the couch and closed his eyes.

Grateful for Anne's absence, Jack didn't know how to deal with the stress of looking down the barrel of a gun and choosing his own life above that of another man. He didn't want to be talking it out. He didn't want to be sleeping. He didn't want to *be*.

***

"Let's go gang! The Mom Bus is leaving!"

Ashley and Kevin ran down the stairs to the front door. Tracy was holding two lunch bags in one hand, a slim leather briefcase in the other. The matching navy pants and vest were purchased a few days ago in preparation for her interview. It was a slick professional look, especially with her hair tied back.

She bit her lip, which turned frost white before disappearing back to pale red. It was so long since she held a permanent full-time job. In the past two years, she'd secured two temporary positions in oil and gas firms. Though only short-term, they got her foot in the door of the energy industry. Men rarely took time off for things like paternity leave, so opportunities were scarce. Added to that was the problem of family. Try to get a job that minimized travel and maximized regular hours. Flexible hours would be even better. Someone from her last temporary position phoned to tell her of an opening. It sounded like a good job, everything she needed to get on her feet and start moving forward. Her and her kids. "The Three Musketeers," Ashley called them.

Despite the strength of her legal position, counting on Al was impractical and her boyfriend wasn't panning out. The feeling he brought of "protective custody" was a welcome contrast to her married years, but Terry wasn't keen on inheriting an entire family. Since Tracy and her kids were a package deal, the limitations of their relationship were clear.

"Come on, hustle guys. I can't be late and neither can you. Ten seconds—ten, nine, eight, seven ..." While Ashley and Kevin scrambled into their coats and shoes, she turned with one hand on the doorknob.

Ding Dong!

"Oh, what now? I don't have time for this."

But she opened the door to face a police officer. Her first reaction was one of slight confusion *(That's not Terry)* as she couldn't rectify the image of the uniform without her boyfriend in it.

"Are you Tracy Morin?"

Fear raced across her heart. It was never good news when a cop came to your door with that question. They never came just to say, "Hey, I wanted to stop by and let you know we're patrolling the area and everything looks great out here."

Her next thought jumped to Al's last arrest. She had told Terry about her ex-husband's alcoholism, purely to vent some frustration. Then, about a week later, he matter-of-factly stated that Al had been arrested on another drunk-driving charge. Of course, she already knew; Al had called Tracy with accusations right after it happened. He seemed to believe she'd arranged it somehow. When she asked Terry, "How did you know about that?" his answer was, "Because I arrested him."

"How could you do that? If he goes to jail, how is he supposed to get to his jobs? Don't you realize, if he doesn't work, we don't eat? Are *you* gonna feed us?" A terrible fight followed, but in the end, Terry admitted that the arrest was more for his own satisfaction than hers.

"Yes. What can I do for you?" she warily asked this officer.

"Is your husband Albert Morin?"

"Ex-husband. What's he done now?"

"Just some routine business," he announced with a false smile. "Is there some place we could talk?"

She turned to her kids with a face that said, "Everything's fine, in fact, more than fine. It's just fantastic." The officer joined her in a smile verifying just how fantastic everything was, but the kids didn't seem to care one way or the other. They were used to seeing Terry around in his uniform. What's another cop?

Tracy handed Ashley the car keys. "OK gang, you two head to the car. I'll be there before you can count down from a hundred."

They took off out the front door yelling, "100, 99, 98! ..."

She apprehensively faced the cop again and he began his speech.

More lip biting. She asked a few questions about the details, odd ones, not the usual "Where did it happen?" or "How did he die?" She wanted to know who was on duty at the time, what district the officers worked in. The questions made him nervous and he stumbled around them until she bluntly asked, "Was it an officer named Terry Halliday?"

"No, no one by that name was involved."

His answer seemed to settle her. Then, she politely thanked him for informing her and explained that she had to get her kids to school.

A tenacious feeling of guilt followed her to the car. Why had she assumed Terry's involvement in this?

Quickly wrestling with herself, she decided not to tell Ashley and Kevin until after her interview. She would give them until noon to pretend it was just business as usual, dropping kids off, finding work, making lunch. Then she would tell them, but for now, they deserved a normal morning with school and recess and a world with a father in it.

***

While Jack sat like a stone on the couch, Anne arrived at work to find the front doors of the clinic unlocked. Donna's purse was on her desk, along with a stack of patient files from yesterday. That was strange; Donna always finished her notes before leaving. Maybe she came in early this morning to do it, but she was nowhere to be found.

(Must have run out to that coffee place she talks about. The Coffee Bean? Something like that.)

Anne left her letter of resignation on Donna's desk and prepared the morning files. When the phone rang, it was awkward to answer with so many folders in her arms.

"Good morning, Mountain View Medical ... Oh, hello Mrs. Carlin. Donna's not here. I think she just stepped out. What? ... Who's in critical? ... Oh, my God ... No, oh no ... When? ..."

To Anne, the conversation was a blur of words, and she sat down heavily on the reception chair until the phone was finally returned to its cradle. Mortified, she put her feelings on hold and quickly cancelled the morning appointments.

When Gene walked in, she let him know and excused herself to be alone. Donna was a private professional and Anne respected that, but she also made the job enjoyable. It was tragic. Was she the victim of a drunk driver? Sure, she'd been depressed for much of this year. No one had told Anne—she could see it for herself—but Donna seemed to snap out of it, especially last month, when she walked in with a drastic make over and started wearing smart outfits. Practically reeked of New Man.

She phoned Jack for emotional support, shock making her sluggish. For a few seconds, he was silent and she wondered if he hadn't heard her. Then, there was a heavy breath on the other end of the phone.

He quietly asked, "When did it happen?"

He was sounding badly strained, genuinely upset for her, and Anne marveled at her luck in finding this wonderfully empathetic man.

"Last night, around three in the morning."

Three in the morning. There was something specific about that time, but as much as he searched his mind, it remained buried. It was something from long ago and something from yesterday all at the same time, as if two eras could overlap and produce a distinct reality on their own.

Pushing the feeling away, Jack was glad Anne couldn't see his face. It was a terrible thing to be told on top of the night he just had. At this point, he couldn't confess his actual connection with Donna, that she'd been more than a friend and less than a lover, something in between. He'd dismissed his chance last night. And what would Anne think anyway? Probably that she was the reason Donna had rolled her car to pieces. Instead, he listened to her narrate the tragedy of her boss's accident and refrained from snapping, "She was more to me than she ever was to you!" He had given up the privilege in order to keep that part of his past silent.

Anne didn't learn about his trauma from the night before until she arrived home from work. As the details unfolded, he was disturbed to discover the identical timing of the two accidents. Both occurred at virtually the same moment and less than a mile apart. He could easily have been called to Donna's accident instead. In a weird way, the shooting had been the easier of the two situations to face.

Of course, Anne asked him to accompany her to the hospital. The last thing Jack needed was for Raymond Carlin to shake his hand and remark on how much Donna valued knowing him all those years.

"I have to report in for questioning about the gun incident."

The lie was so plausible, it earned him a sympathetic smile and a reassuring shoulder nuzzle, which did nothing to assuage his guilt. He just hoped Anne didn't casually bring up his name in conversation. It was bad enough she wouldn't shut up about Donna and all he could do was simmer in deception.

Instead, Jack went for a long walk remembering scenes from their friendship years. Then, he sat at their old table at The Bean and looked sadly out the window, hearing the voices of his two friends bat around an amusing point long gone.

(I'm much more trouble than some orange vegetable. …)

***

Michelle turned her face away from the blast of heat when she lowered the oven door. Where were the toothpicks? Colin never put things away in the same place twice. She hoped he would be home on time; he pulled so much overtime. Her job was much more consistent. Could set a clock by her.

Sales and Distributions wasn't what she'd predicted of her career, but it was OK for now. Having learned to stop worrying about what life would bring, God had taken care of her so far and she was confident that He would continue to do so.

After graduating with his commerce degree, Colin investigated entry level accounting positions, but they didn't interest him much. Instead, he applied at an insurance brokerage and started training in the field. Particularly adept at marketing the business to attract volume investors, he soon became indispensable. Sometimes an interesting claim would be submitted.

Like today—he received a client call just before he was ready to leave for the day. After checking his files, he verified that yes, her children were the stated beneficiaries of her ex-husband's policy. Unfortunately, the claim was deemed null and void because the policy holder had died in the commission of a crime. An automatic exclusion.

"Hi, I'm home!" he called, closing the front door behind him. He could hear her moving around in the kitchen. The thick smell of chocolate swept past his nose and he inhaled deeply. "Is that what I think it is?" He stepped into the kitchen eagerly.

Michelle closed the oven door and tossed two thick mitts onto the counter. A rectangular pan sat on a metal cooling rack, and steam wafted up toward the open kitchen window. She was still in her work clothes, the mauve skirt. He liked that one. From the back, you couldn't even tell she was pregnant.

"You bet," she answered and slapped his hand crisply, "Hey, you know the rules. No tasting 'til it's cool."

"Uh-uh! The only way to eat chocolate cake is when it's so hot, your tongue gets third-degree burns."

A prominent pout formed across his lower lip and his chin stuck out defiantly. It was funny how this one food could turn him into a child. He pretended to lunge for the pan, but she stopped him by throwing her arms around his waist. Her rounded stomach pressed into him, and in reaction, the baby gave a sudden kick. Colin smiled, fascinated with the tiny movement as his hand stroked her belly.

"Hey, settle down in there. I'm fighting for cake-rights."

They swayed together contently in the middle of the kitchen.

"Happy anniversary," she said softly.

"Happy anniversary yourself."

She tilted her face up to reach his lips and her hair hung down her back, tickling his hands. When they were single, he'd convinced her to grow it long. Well, he may have been one influence, but the truth was she didn't want to look into the mirror and be reminded of sadder days. The only time in her life when she had short hair was during her relationship with Jack.

Michelle broke the kiss suddenly. "What's that smell?"

"Wow, talk about pregnancy-brain. You're the one baking."

"No, on you." She leaned toward his collar.

"Oh, right. OK, gift time," he announced, placing a palm-sized box in her hand. "I got some on me and spent the afternoon fighting off the entire sales team. Do you like it?"

"You tell me." She dabbed a tiny amount along her neck and giggled when his lips followed the scent. Pricey stuff, but worth it.

With the gratitude of a scarred heart, Michelle said a private prayer, thanking God for this man. He really had turned out to be the right man after all.

Staring wistfully into his eyes, she said, "I know it's technically five, but to me it's more like eight. Seems like a lot of years, but it's sure gone by fast."

"Like that."

He snapped his fingers and the sound was sharp. It punctuated the air and disappeared into the walls.

"Good thing you showed up."

"Good thing you waited."

"Had the whole left side of the menu."

"Yeah, that pretty much swung it for me. A man willing to eat variations of corned beef for two days is worth coming back to. Trustworthy indeed."

Colin's smile was genuine. Life was pretty good. Decent starter home, family on the way, solid career, Emma … and if they wore the same perfume, Michelle would never suspect.

***

CHAPTER 47

During the investigation, Jack chose against going back on duty. In addition to stress leave, he took some overdue holiday time. Restlessly wading through each day, his life edged closer to the verdict.

The Verdict.

Now, he understood the investigator's advice. At the time, an immediate return to duty sounded absurd, but the lack of distractions was a quiet torture shadowing his tired eyes daily.

Anne carefully watched him distance himself from everything, including her. It was hard to see him hurting so much, impossible to imagine shooting someone, but she could certainly understand the anxiety to follow. She figured talking about Donna would serve to alleviate her sadness and maybe distract him from his. Make him see the brighter side. At least, he wasn't hanging on to life by a thread.

Swimming in a coma but breathing on her own, Donna was neither here nor there. After four weeks the bruises and facial swelling were gone, but hard bulky casts encased her. Only one arm had escaped harm. Immediately following each visit, Anne reported the physical details to Jack, along with a hopeful prediction of Donna's prognosis.

Jack wondered, "What happens to a body trapped in a coma day after day?" He remembered having an intense discussion with Donna and Jen about that very topic. Limbo-Land, that's what he'd called it. She could wake up tomorrow or never, an outcome riddled with uncertainty.

Jack met with a staff therapist a few times. By examining the issues surrounding the shooting, he became resigned to the fact that emotional acceptance would forever elude him; however, the sessions brought home the psychological similarity between shooting that man and destroying a part of himself in the process. Jack suspected Donna was the one person who would understand this—not only understand, but grieve alongside him for losing the part of him she loved most.

There had been a weird moment as he stared down the barrel of Albert Morin's gun: He imagined Donna's hand reaching out protectively to save him. In retrospect, it was too fast to decipher, but his mind insisted she was throwing herself between him and the bullet.

The therapist attributed the image to Jack's guilt at terminating their friendship.

"When faced with a life or death situation, many people have images of those they've wronged. It happens so fast, they often forget the details later, but it's probably best described as 'seeing your life flash before your eyes'. It's very common. Some people only have a single picture that stands out, whatever is the most significant aspect of their life, and later, that's the only memory they have of the near-death experience."

Jack nodded at the tidy analysis, but he couldn't shake the feeling he was alive simply because Donna had willed it.

Perplexing emotions about her also persisted. She represented someone with a gentle balance of strength and sadness, much like him. In a way, she was a mirror image, different yet the same underneath. An intricate part of his life until he locked her out of it, the prospect of her death now proffered a sick feeling of finality. It was like losing an arm or a leg, something conspicuous only by its absence. Strangely, compared to fatally shooting a man, coming to terms with her accident would prove a more difficult task.

Of all the people who knew Donna, Jack and Gene alone suspected self-harm. Gene considered it best to let those theories sleep with her. No point in hurting her family with answers that only provoked more questions. From Jack's perspective, the thought was horrible that he could cause someone to go that far.

Jack never really understood the depth to which Donna existed inside him. Though able to discard the person he thought he was before pulling the trigger, she was another matter. Donna held a place swimming in the currents of his soul, a match of sorts fitting into his life with an unparalleled persistence.

And the concept of suicide ripped that to shreds.

A deep part of Jack's truthful self realized that the same forces shaping his life were also tied up in Donna. Entirely associated with everything since high school—even when she wasn't in the picture at all—there was just something keeping her in the back of his mind, guiding his decisions, making him question himself, and still loving him despite the turmoil they caused each other … but that part of him was very deep. He avoided facing it like he avoided her calls.

She was even the reason he adopted his religious beliefs. Well, no, that was just someone who looked like her, but Donna was the reason he walked away from them. Left his carefully constructed beliefs sitting on that park bench after she threw them in his face. Seeing right through Jack, how much he was using God as an excuse to pretend he was a different person, she highlighted a despicable side of him, and his resentment swelled instantaneous and unforgiving.

For a few Sundays, he still attended church services, but it didn't feel the same. Whatever spiritual force he possessed remained firmly glued to that park bench. Stubbornly refusing to see her, he was determined to retrieve it himself, but after a lot of soul-searching, he just stopped trying. With Donna's friendship went the final threads of beliefs he'd fabricated in the last eight years, leaving a basic internal sense of right and wrong, a simple skeleton of his former moral strength. Firing his gun had almost destroyed that too.

No one in his life had affected such influence. Well, there was one other person. ...

He remembered Patty's lovely presence. How could he not? This beauty—so obviously relaxed right down to her very soul—claimed a peacefulness even the pastor didn't possess. Jack knew as soon as he saw her that she should be his first lover, first, last, and everyone in between, craving whatever it was she exuded ... but that was a long time ago.

When she disappeared, he tried to find her. And then he tried to forget her, convincing himself that she was just some vivid elusive dream invading his daytime as well as his nights. Especially his nights.

Finally, he concluded that she must have returned to the man she came to see in Calgary, the one she'd loved before. Jack's bitter confession to the pastor depicted a man who fell madly in love with a woman on the rebound—so badly on the rebound, she'd give a false name to leave no trail when the dust cleared. As much as he'd fallen for her, she must have fallen for someone else harder. Jack would never forget the haunted look in her eyes while she described that guy. If everything else about their brief time together faded, this one image would certainly stay; an exquisite woman bound heart and soul to another man. There followed several years subconsciously molding his inner beliefs to match the man Patty displayed in her sad eyes.

In a way, Anne reminded him of his fling years ago. She wasn't razor sharp like Patty, and she didn't have those intense green eyes that floored him the moment he saw her, but she showed a spark of that same deep contentment. He'd only known Anne a short time, but it was comfortable with her. No history within a history. Just a pleasant bright young woman.

Unfortunately, his remorse would never let him appreciate her to the proper degree. He just didn't have anything left to give.

If Anne was similar to Patty, then Donna was doubly so. It was uncanny. They even talked the same, but Patty's eyes contained an irresistible energy which grabbed him more than Donna's ever did. Thereafter, the heart-wrenching resemblance of one became a painful reminder of another's inexplicable absence.

He moved from that part of his life straight into a church. Though denying that his religious convictions were as flexible as they were, after arguing with Donna it was a necessary truth to face. The reality was that if anyone outside him could plant the seed of his beliefs, then anyone could also strip them away, leaving his spirit uprooted and vandalized. One woman had created the foundation for a lifelong strength of character, and the other tore it down while her unhappy tears fell on the bench. That was the day he walked away from both of them, Patty and Donna. ...

At least, he thought he had.

For some reason, Patty kept creeping into his mind lately. The dreams of her took on an unnervingly vivid quality since Donna's accident. He would drift off only to find himself back on that dance floor, holding her securely to a slow beat. The other dancers in the country bar melted away one by one, until they were alone. The band also melted away as the stage ballooned into an inviting bed. She placed one hand lightly against his cheek while slowly undressing him with the other. His clothes seemed to dissolve at her touch. Her entire face smiled at him. Those eyes ...

He moved forward drawn by her lips, and awoke, sitting up disoriented, swearing he could still feel her soft palm on his face. The sensation abruptly disappeared at the sight of his bedroom furniture, but that was not what startled him.

It was seeing Anne's short dark hair in bed next to him.

***

"Would you like a coffee, officer?"

Jack leaned forward in the upholstered chair. For once, the thought of the drink turned his stomach and he shook his head at the receptionist. He wasn't here to ask about the guy's wife and kids. If he needed anything, bourbon would probably do the trick. Losing an unwanted career was manageable. It was the possibility of criminal charges that ate him up inside. And it would all come to a head in mere minutes.

Finally, the sergeant called him into his office.

"Well, Constable Petrasyk, the incident on September eighth was wrapped up earlier this week, and I'm happy to inform you that the investigating officers concluded that you were involved in a good shoot. Your record will remain unaffected, and your salary and benefits will continue at their present level."

He expected to feel relieved ... but *a good shoot?* Hearing such ironic wording solidified the decision on the spot that Jack would never carry a gun again.

A polite, "Thank you sir," was all he said before walking straight out the door.

Fumbling with his apartment key, even delayed calm eluded him. A release of some kind would be natural with any verdict, especially one entirely in his favor, but instead he just felt jumpy and drained. Gripping the key, his hands quivered as he guided it into the deadbolt. The lock was loose and the key had to fit into the slot perfectly or it wouldn't turn. Rattle, rattle. Give it a little twist. That usually worked.

Finally, the door swung open. Anne's back was to him, seated at the kitchen table, and he wondered why she hadn't just unlocked the door for him. She must have heard him fumbling with it. Her head bent low, she seemed focused on something in her hands.

Forcing a measure of cheerfulness, he said, "Hey, I got officially cleared. We can go any time."

Anne didn't turn around, not even to glance his way. There was a heavy pause before she answered, "She never gave you away, not once." A machine could not have delivered a more monotone sentence.

Jack stiffened, his mind racing. After a moment, he quietly shut the door and sat in the chair next to her. She was holding an envelope, by all appearances nothing extraordinary, but he sensed that it could only contain bad news.

"Donna's father gave me a picture of her—"

Jack glanced at the four by six square face down in front of her.

"—my albums were all packed, so I went to put it with yours and found these." She reached into the envelope, pulled out a stack of pictures, and handed it to him.

There was the shot of Jack and Donna dressed up for their high school graduation, standing in her father's living room. He had outgrown that suit long ago. Donna and Jen sitting in front of the Valiant. Tools were scattered around their feet. Donna was holding a rag and there was a big grease stain on her cheek, elongating her smile on one side. Judging from her hair length and Jen's healthy appearance, they must have been about twenty-five. There were others depicting various times in her life, but he put them down before he finished looking through them.

"Donna's out of her coma. Woke up Friday. So far, they can't detect any brain damage, but seeing as she's crying more than talking, it's hard to tell. That one looks like it's from high school. You don't go to grad with just anyone. So, how long were you two screwing after you met me?"

Jack took a deep breath. "It wasn't like that. I didn't want to tell you—"

"Why? Because of the flack you'd face from cheating on me? Or because of the way we drove her to suicide?"

"I didn't know you worked for her. It was over long before you and I met."

"Bullshit! If you'd seen her—she was struggling with something, but I was so happy with you, I couldn't see past us. Now I know why her face turned white when I told her your name. And then she goes out and tries to kill herself that night. Jesus Jack! You must have known and you didn't even tell me!"

He raised his voice. "Tell you what? That we'd *almost* had an affair and she didn't happen to get over it? How do you think I felt when I saw your letter? What good would it have done? You'd just be thinking what you're thinking now and it's not even true."

"You don't get it. It doesn't matter if it's true or not. The fact is you lied to me and it was a biggie. I've known something wasn't right since that night, but I thought it was the shooting. Here I was giving you the space to come to me with it or not—I thought I was being considerate by letting you handle it your own way—but you've been getting more and more distant. It wasn't the shooting at all."

They stared uncomfortably at each other. The wooden chair felt as hard as a rock.

Jack faced her squarely and said, "You … will never know what it feels like to kill someone, to look them right in the eye and watch them die."

Her gaze narrowed sharply. Tears swam in her eyelids but refused to fall. "Well, thanks to you, I almost did."

Rising abruptly, Anne walked toward the door. He suddenly noticed her suitcases lined up neatly along the wall.

"These won't be going to Halifax. It seems my job prospects here have been renewed. I'll get the rest of my stuff tomorrow."

Jack silently watched her pick up her bags and step out the door. There was finality to her fading footsteps, despite the hollow echo lingering behind in the hallway. He wasn't sure what he felt. Bad for her, bad for them, but underneath it all a glimmer of relief shone that the truth was finally out. He couldn't have kept waking up next to her, sweating, wanting to turn her into someone else. …

He glanced down at the pictures again. He'd look through these once and never again. They would stay hidden in some box from the move, with other items whose only value is sentimental. Just remnants of his past, kept separate from the here and now but never truly discarded. He could let Anne go, but he couldn't bring himself to part with these shiny scraps of paper. Somehow, they were achingly special, more special than he could put into words.

Stuff them into a box along with that broken watch. He'd left the money he found strewn all over the carpet—hundreds of dollars in fact—but that one piece of jewelry, frozen at some special moment, was significant. Even now, some small part of him still hoped he could find her, hand it to her along with some succinct statement to summarize his need, the pain he'd carried for so long. Until then, that watch was his only memento of their precious time together, a sorry substitute for never getting her picture. By stretching his thinking, these ones of Donna could almost suffice.

The one Raymond had given Anne was still face down. Jack flipped it up and then stared in confusion. A woman in her late twenties with short dark hair and a slender figure, rust-colored blouse and gray pants. At first his mind catalogued the characteristics automatically, the way he memorized features on a suspect's photo array. Then everything in his mind just slammed shut.

(Oh God, it's—)

The same hair, the same clothes as when he first met her. Was she a relative of the Carlin's? The back of the picture was dated "August 1999", just before Donna's accident. Then he looked closely at the face and realized that it was Donna after all. Her expression was not as captivating as he remembered on Patty, but the resemblance was haunting.

Smiling broadly, her face angled sideways toward the camera. Her chin rested in the palm of her hand. Jack remembered the last time he saw Patty, smiling at him as he held her chin in the palm of his hand.

Donna's left leg was crossed under her, the other knee pulled up against her chest. Her elbow sat perched on the raised knee. The dark hair made her green eyes stand out, playfully drawing in his gaze. As he wondered what she was thinking at that moment, he was reminded of a time from years ago. Rummoli. Jen's kitchen table.

(Where'd you learn to be a pretzel? Where'd you learn to inhale food?)

If he hadn't seen Donna sit all scrunched up like that before, he would have thought it was posed. He could imagine Mr. Carlin sneaking up to catch a candid profile shot. She always knew he was coming.

Jack traced one finger around her face. A blur of tears filled his eyes. They distorted the picture, bending the edges as though viewing it through a pool of water. An illusion of depth followed; the flat surface came alive and for a split-second, Jack felt the eerie sensation that if he really wanted to, he could actually step inside this picture. Pull her into his arms. If time could hold open a doorway, he would walk through, even if only for a day or two. ...

Memories flew through his mind and he struggled to sort out the possibilities. There were none. It wasn't possible. He shook off his bewilderment, but just like eight years ago, found himself staring as a single tear traced a jagged path down his face.

***

... All she could see were pictures, spinning endlessly around her, over and over. She might catch one, should they ever falter in their race. So many, so fast. All individual snapshots in time, taunting her to reach out and capture just one. She knew which to embrace if she could—cherish it like gold forever.

Remembering his touch, its warmth, the grip of his fingers encircling every inch of her, she could almost feel him now. And she covered his hand with her own. He did the same, sandwiching hers securely the way they had in the restaurant. The lights had been dim and sultry, but now they glowed brightly as ...

***

Afternoon sunshine filled the room with caressing warmth. Donna blinked and sighed. The nurse must have opened the curtains again. It got too hot if they did that after lunch.

Closing her bleary eyes, she realized the only heat was a soothing sensation surrounding her left hand. No, must be the casts again. The cloistered immobility played havoc with her senses. Yesterday, she'd even woken up thinking she was standing, and in her confusion, tried to walk to the bathroom. If not for the guardrails, she would have done a face plant.

(Feel like a damned toddler.)

No, the temperature really was OK ... except for that hand in the cast. Take another week to lose that thing, a month for the legs.

"You're lucky," they'd said, "There doesn't appear to be any long-term brain injury." And later, she'd overheard them commenting, "Unbelievable. She should be dead." They thought she was sleeping at the time. A big faux pas in the medical world: any first-year resident knows not to talk about patients within earshot, even if they're out like a light.

For weeks, she'd been out like a light. The dark held no perception of time, and lying there, it seemed a lifetime's worth of memories had paced methodically through her mind. Starting with that first moment of meeting Jack, every scene had been catalogued and presented as though fresh and new, drawing her into the center of each one along the way. Exhilarating. Exhausting.

Ironically, upon escaping the coma Donna slept as much as possible, which temporarily shelved the pain. And the tears. So many tears ... of worry, loss, and horrendous regret ... but worst of all were the confined senses; her empowering intuition had stayed in the past with their love affair. Except through her dreams, she couldn't feel his presence at all.

Was he dead? In a coma like she had been? Jaunting around Halifax with Anne on his arm? She would gladly release him if it meant keeping him safe ... somewhere in this world. God, she loved him.

Determined to coax another blessed slumber, her thoughts tried to skirt around those persistent sensations from only moments ago and she strained to focus on that last dream. Warmth, from him, from his touch, the lovely feeling of his skin against hers ... just like the illusion created by this cast on her left hand.

Wait a minute—it wasn't on the left.

Opening her eyes to the cheery afternoon windows, Donna slowly swiveled her head on the pillows. Her gaze traveled across the cast solidly gripping her entire right arm, then the bulkier pair surrounding her legs, and finally found her left hand. Someone was holding it protectively. A warm hand underneath and another over top. Masculine hands ... younger than her father's.

A sharp breath caught in her throat as her eyes darted up the length of his body. And then they opened wide at the sight of his military hair. He penetratingly scanned her features like he saw a ghost. There was the ring, exactly where he'd last left it, along with his heart and softly spoken declarations.

(Maybe this ring means more to you than the watch ever could. And maybe 3:07 means something special too.)

This was *real*. He was here and here was now, not back then and not some dream to carry away his soothing image the second the sun's rays infiltrated her windows.

He was clasping her hand, as though fearing she could fall over the edge of a cliff at any moment with him as her only lifeline to safety. Then, one hand reached into his jacket pocket. A silver watch was placed carefully on the bed, her new broken watch from Anne.

"You left this," he stated quietly.

Matching his haunted look, Donna gripped his wrist. The last time she'd seen him, this was exactly where her fingers had caressed him, along his forearm as he held her chin in the palm of his hand, only a few weeks or a few years separating them.

"You're OK. ... Oh God, you're OK," she cried hoarsely.

Fresh tears sprang from her eyes, the green ones that held an unequaled depth all these years.

His face crumpling, Jack leaned over, buried his head in her chest, and wrapped her in his arms.

"I will be," he said, "*we* will be."

Their tears released, something undefined shifted within their souls. A final encompassing realignment immersed the time frames into one with countless layers of emotions to quell the True Past, which now lingered a world away, safe in some unknown future.

***